MINDWALKER

ALKER

A. J. STEIGER

ALFRED A. KNOPF · NEW YORK

THIS IS A BORZOI BOOK PUBLISHED BY ALFRED A. KNOPF

Text copyright © 2015 by Amanda Steiger
Jacket photography © 2015 by Vladimir Zakharov and Peter Augustin/Getty Images
Jacket design by Ben Mautner

Visit us on the Web! randomhouseteens.com

Educators and librarians, for a variety of teaching tools,
visit us at RHTeachersLibrarians.com

Library of Congress Cataloging-in-Publication Data
Steiger, A. J.
Mindwalker / A.J. Steiger. — First edition.
pages cm
Summary: "In a futuristic reality, one girl falls in love
with the boy whose memories she tries to erase." —Provided
by publisher
ISBN 978-0-553-49713-7 (trade) — ISBN 978-0-553-49715-1 (ebook)
[1. Love—Fiction. 2. Memory—Fiction. 3. Science fiction.]
I. Title.
PZ7.S8178Mi 2015
[Fic]—dc23
2014003541

The text of this book is set in 12-point Joanna.

Printed in the United States of America

June 2015

10 9 8 7 6 5 4 3 2 1
First Edition

TO MY FAMILY

1

I can barely see through the blood in my eyes. Blood soaks my clothes and hands. When I breathe in, pain flares in my chest. One of my ribs is broken. But I'm standing, which is more than I can say for my enemy.

He lies near my feet, wheezing, as blood spreads in a pool beneath him. He reaches for a gun at his belt, and I slam the butt of my empty rifle against his fingers. The man howls.

I feel sick.

He's a terrorist, I remind myself. No mercy.

"Please," he whispers, voice rough with pain. "Please don't." Still, his mangled fingers creep toward his gun. I ram my boot into his face, and a tooth flies out. His eyes turn upward, whites flashing. For an instant, I see my own terror reflected back at me, and I hesitate.

But I have my orders. *Leave none alive.* He wouldn't show mercy if our positions were reversed. This is war, after all. I raise my boot slowly over his head. Deep within me, a voice cries out, No! But I can't stop. My body moves automatically as my boot comes down on his face. *Crunch.* I fight back nausea as I stomp down again and again.

He jerks. His body goes rigid, shuddering convulsively. Then he's still. I stand in the cement-walled basement of the terrorist hideout, alone with the man I've killed.

I don't cry.

There's a clear electronic *ding,* and a recorded female voice intones, "End session."

My eyes snap open, but there's only darkness. Leather cuffs press into my wrists. My own ragged breathing fills my ears. Then the darkness recedes as a visor retracts from my face, and I squint at the sudden glare. All around me, the sterile whites and silvers of the Immersion Lab gleam.

For a moment, I don't know where I am or what I'm doing here. Then my identity settles back into my mind. Shakily, I exhale.

I'm Lain Fisher, seventeen years old. I'm in the Institute for Ethics in Neurotechnology. There's no blood on my hands. The dead man is just a memory, and not even mine.

A machine beeps next to me, monitoring my heart rate and brain waves. I look over at the old man sitting in the padded reclining chair next to mine. My client. His visor retracts, and his rheumy blue eyes stare at the ceiling. Through our connection, I can feel the tension in his body, but his thoughts are perfectly silent. Maybe that's how he's dealt with the pain for so long—by simply not thinking. Functioning automatically, like a machine.

It's a good thing he can't hear my thoughts. I don't think he'd like the comparison.

I mutter, "Release," and the leather cuffs snap open. I slide my helmet off, and cool air washes over my sweat-drenched head. "That's all for today," I say. "The mapping stage is almost complete. The modification will begin next session."

He sits up with a grunt. His face is weathered and lined, his chin peppered with stubble. "And after that, I won't remember the war?"

"That's correct."

"Why does it take so long, anyway?" There's a note of accusation in his low, scratchy voice, as if he thinks I enjoy wading through images of violence and death. "Why can't you just do it all at once?"

I've already explained it to him, and an angry response bubbles up in my throat. I bite my tongue, remind myself that his surly demeanor is just a defense mechanism, and force myself to reply calmly, "It's a complicated process. I need to experience the memories first so I'll know how to navigate them later, when I start the actual procedure. You're almost done, though. Just one more session." With shaking fingers, I brush a few strands of hair from my face. "How are you feeling?" I'm supposed to ask that question after every immersion session.

His gaze jerks toward me. His lips press together, and his eyes narrow. Without a word, he hobbles out of the room.

I lean back in the chair, my limbs weak with exhaustion. In my head, I hear the crunch of bone as my boot—no, his boot—slams into the man's face.

I've never killed anyone. I've never been attacked by a mob and beaten within an inch of my life. I've never watched a child die in front of me. But I've lived through the memory of all those things.

I remind myself that the events I just witnessed happened decades ago, during a brutal chapter of our country's past. I try to tell myself that it's just like watching video footage, but it's not. I felt it, all the fear and rage, the heat and wetness of blood and the sickly sweet smell of it. My hands are still shaking. I want to go home and curl up under the covers with Nutter, my stuffed squirrel.

The wall screen winks on, and a woman's face peers out. It's Judith, one of the session monitors. Her brow wrinkles with concern. "Doing okay?"

I force a smile. "I'm fine."

"Maybe you should call it a night."

I rub my forehead. "Maybe. I've got a calculus quiz tomorrow." The last thing I care about right now is calculus. But if I want to be a Mindwalker, I have to learn how to compartmentalize my emotions. I have to show everyone that it doesn't faze me, and that means keeping my grades up and my life together.

I climb out of the chair.

"Lain . . ."

I look up.

"You know, you're still young," Judith says. "You have a lot of time to figure out what you want. You don't have to push yourself so hard."

This again.

I wish people wouldn't be so concerned about me. That's probably an awful thought to have, but their worry always makes me feel helpless. Like they can smell my weakness. "Thank you, but I'm all right." Without giving her time to reply, I walk out of the room.

4

As I make my way down the narrow white hall, I overhear Judith talking to someone, her voice muffled behind the closed door of the control room, where she observes data from the sessions. "It's so hard on these kids," she says. "And the program is still so new. We don't know what the long-term effects will be. The strain on their minds, their emotions . . ."

"They're the only ones who can do it," a man replies—another session monitor, whose name I can't recall.

"Yes, but still . . ."

I don't want to hear the argument, so I keep walking. The dying man's face flashes through my head. Bloody meat, shattered teeth, glints of bone. A violent cramp seizes my stomach, and bile climbs up my throat. I press a hand to my mouth, squeeze my eyes shut, and struggle for control. At last, the urge to vomit recedes.

I open my eyes and freeze. Ian stands in the hallway, clad in a simple white robe with a cream-colored cord around the waist, the same thing I wear. Once we've survived our jobs for a year, we'll get a black cord. I smooth my robe, self-conscious, wondering if my distress shows on my face. "Ian. I—I didn't think you'd be here today. Did you have a client?"

"I was supposed to. Didn't get very far, though. This guy wanted to forget his ex-girlfriend. He walks in talking about how awful she is and how his life will be so much better once she's out of his head. Then, halfway through the pre-session counseling, he starts bawling and runs out, saying he's going to call her." He rolls his eyes.

I laugh, but the sound comes out a little choked.

He studies my face. "Rough one?"

I nod but don't elaborate.

Ian rubs a hand over his head, which is shaved bald, except for a fuzzy red stripe running down the center. He can't wear his usual leather and fishnet here, but as hard as they've tried, IFEN can't make him change his hairstyle. They tolerate it because he's the whiz kid, their golden boy. "Anything I can do?" he asks awkwardly.

"Just remind me that it'll get easier."

He doesn't say anything. Instead, he curls an arm around my shoulders. I tense, surprised. "It's all right." His voice is a low murmur, almost inaudible. "No one's watching."

Of course, we can never be sure of that. But he's the only person whose concern I really want, because he understands. We're in the same position—the only two initiates this year. There were three others at the start, but they've since dropped out, unable to endure. I close my eyes and allow myself to lean against his shoulder. He's warm. Solid.

I feel the tears building up, prickling in my sinuses, and I force myself to pull away. If I don't, I'll lose control.

He raises his thick eyebrows. "You know, it's normal to have feelings. You don't need to treat them like they're some kind of rash."

"Easy for you to say." I give him a weak smile and knuckle tears from the corners of my eyes.

"It's hard for me, too, you know."

"Yes, but you don't show it." Somehow, immersion sessions never affect Ian. The horror rolls off him, as if his brain is shellacked with some kind of horror-proof coating. "Seriously, how do you manage? Whatever techniques you're using, I should be copying them."

He shifts his weight. "Just used to this stuff, I guess. I

mean . . . Mom's a drug researcher, so I grew up hearing about diseases and trauma."

If repeated exposure is the only thing it takes, I should be a Mindwalking champion by now.

"Just think about the good you're doing," he adds. "Remember all the people you've helped."

"Thank you." I breathe in slowly and force myself to straighten my shoulders. "Anyway, I should get home. I need to study."

"You spend way too much time hitting the books. You need to unwind. I'm having a party at my place on Friday. Why don't you come?"

I stare at him. Is he joking? "I'm not in a partying mood."

"It might do you some good."

"I just saw a man killed, Ian," I blurt out.

His expression softens. "I'm sorry," he says quietly. "I know it's not easy to forget about something like that. But if you let it get to you, you'll burn out. You need to learn how to put that stuff aside once the session is over. Just think about it, okay?"

I rub the bridge of my nose. Maybe he's right. "Okay." I pause. "Are you going home now, or . . ."

He shakes his head. "I've got another session later today." He lowers his voice. "Sexual assault victim."

I wince. They usually assign those to Ian now, since I didn't respond well to the last one. I feel a twinge of guilt. "Will you be all right?"

He smiles. "Don't worry about me."

I give a small, uncertain nod.

He waves and walks away, disappearing around a corner.

I continue down the hallway. Beyond lies an enormous

lobby with a floor of white marble, so polished I can see hazy reflections in the surface. A set of towering glass double doors part automatically for me as I approach. Outside, I stand in the vast parking lot, looking at rows of neatly pruned trees on islands of vivid green grass. The sky is clear and blue. Everything looks bright, sharp, unreal, like a photograph run through a filter.

IFEN headquarters itself is a monolithic pyramid. Its silver walls reflect the azure sky, the slowly drifting clouds. Behind it stands a backdrop of high-rises and skyscrapers. Aura, the largest city in the United Republic of America.

It's surreal to think that the war—the one my client fought in—occurred when we were still the United States. For most people, the long, ugly conflict between the Blackcoats and the military is something to be studied in history classes. But for that man and for so many others, it's a living, breathing nightmare. War makes monsters of ordinary men, then leaves them broken. I've seen it before. No wonder he wants the memories erased.

What happens when everything dark and dirty can be wiped away, like clearing a touch screen? Should a man be allowed to forget someone he killed, no matter the circumstance?

I push the thoughts away. My client has already been approved for the therapy. It's not my place to decide what should or shouldn't be forgotten. Ian's words echo in my head: *Remember all the people you've helped.*

Just last month, I treated a woman whose apartment building burned down in an electrical fire. After barely escaping with her life, she suffered through weeks of hospitalization and slow, painful recovery. Her burns healed, but the nightmares and flashbacks persisted. The standard psychiatric treatments had no effect. After a mental breakdown, she lost her job, and her whole life started to unravel. In desperation, she came to IFEN. Once the memory of that night was gone, her life returned to normal, as if by magic. And there are so many others like her—people who've suffered terribly, through no fault of their own, and lost so much as a result. People who can become whole and healthy again with our help. Surely, that's worth any amount of hardship on my part.

I strengthen my resolve. This is who I am. This is what I was born to do.

2

The classrooms in Greenborough High School are enormous, made of steel and concrete, the desks crammed wall to wall. Cameras watch us from the ceiling like unblinking black eyes. A guard stands near the door, hands interlaced behind his back, a neural disrupter resting in a holster at his hip. A sign glares at us from above the door.

THESE PREMISES ARE MONITORED
FOR YOUR OWN PROTECTION.

The intercom crackles, and the superintendent's voice says, "All rise for the pledge."

The students stand, as we do at the beginning of every school day. I recite the lines automatically, along with everyone else.

I pledge to do my part to keep our school and our country safe: to remain alert; to report any signs of mental unwellness in those around me; to be re-

spectful, compassionate, and cooperative at all times; and to keep my own mind healthy and free from negative thoughts so that the atrocities of the past will never be repeated.

With a rustle of clothing, everybody sits.

All these precautions are necessary, I know. But at times, it feels like overkill. I could, of course, afford a private school if I wanted—a school without guards and metal detectors and mandatory neural scans. I go to Greenborough as a matter of conscience. If other teenagers have to endure this, it doesn't seem right that I should have the luxury of avoiding it.

At the front of the room, Ms. Biddles drones out a lecture, pointing to equations on a huge, dim wall screen. She's tiny and ancient, her back hunched under a knitted pink sweater. A dull ache of fatigue pulses through my head. My vision keeps blurring as I take notes.

Normally, I enjoy math. It's a language of its own, intricate and beautiful. The more you learn, the more there is to learn, like a flower unfolding to reveal ever more complex and delicate blossoms nestled inside. But today, the numbers are meaningless squiggles on my desk screen.

I rub my eyelids and glance down at my school uniform— white blouse, plaid skirt, gray stockings. I open my compact and look at my reflection in the mirror. Brown eyes. Squirrel-brown hair done up in pigtails. Me. Lain Fisher, a student in my third year of high school. I repeat the words to myself silently, like a prayer. They have a name for this in Mindwalker training: identity affirmation exercises.

It's not working. I keep seeing my boot ram into the man's face. I rise to my feet, and heads turn toward me. "Excuse me," I mutter.

The guard accompanies me to the nearest bathroom, and I dash inside just as the nausea overwhelms me.

A few minutes later, I rinse out my mouth in the sink and wipe it clean with a paper towel.

On the wall is a small advertising screen, one of those designed to change every few minutes. Now it displays a slowly rotating image of a pink pill with the word

SOMNAZOL

imprinted on both sides. Underneath it is the tagline

WHEN ALL ELSE FAILS.

Ugh. Usually, I don't even notice drug ads—they're so commonplace in schools and public areas, they fade into the background. But this is appalling. There ought to be a law against promoting Somnazol to minors.

A girl with wavy black hair emerges from a stall, washes her hands in the sink next to me, and begins applying shiny pink lipstick. I watch her from the corner of my eye, then softly clear my throat. "It's horrible, isn't it?" I ask, waving a hand toward the screen.

She gives a start, then stares at me blankly. I look at the screen and see that the image has shifted to an ad for shoes. "I mean—" Heat rises into my cheeks. "Somnazol." I clear my throat. "It was different a few seconds ago."

"Whatever." She walks out of the bathroom, leaving me standing alone. The image on the screen fades, shifting to an ad for Lucid memory enhancers. I swallow, trying to banish the sudden tightness in my throat, and leave the bathroom.

I don't have any trouble talking to my clients or the other trainees at IFEN headquarters. Why can't I seem to strike up a conversation with anyone at school?

Back at my desk, I try to focus. Behind me, I hear voices. I glance over my shoulder and see the girl with the wavy dark hair whispering something to the redhead beside her. They notice me watching, and their expressions harden.

I turn back toward the front of the room, face burning. A slight tremor creeps into my hands, and I tuck them under my armpits.

My cell phone vibrates in my pocket, and I wince.

We aren't supposed to have cell phones in class. Normally, I leave mine in the car, but I've been so muddled today, I forgot I was carrying it.

Discreetly, I fish the phone out.

YOU HAVE ONE MESSAGE.

My first thought is that it must be from Ian, but when I glance at the number, I don't recognize it. I open it anyway. There's a short, simple message, the words crisp and black against the white screen:

I NEED TO TALK TO YOU.

I text back:

TO WHOM AM I SPEAKING?

There's a boy sitting six rows back, in the corner of the room—a boy with shaggy white-blond hair and a silver collar around his neck, looking straight at me.

Steven Bent.

I've never really spoken to him. He's quiet and keeps to himself, but rumors float around him like clouds of dark mist. Voices drift through my memory, snippets of overheard whispers.

He's a Type Four. See the collar?

No way! They're letting Type Fours go to school with the rest of us now?

I heard they made him go through Conditioning twelve times.

I heard he was expelled from his last school for biting a chunk of skin from another guy's face.

And now, apparently, he wants to talk to me.

Ms. Biddles barely glances at the students as she lectures in her nasally monotone. I don't think she notices my silent conversation with Steven, and the guard seems preoccupied with something on his sleeve—a stain?—but I hunch over my phone and curl my arm around it. I pretend to type notes into my desk screen as I text:

WHAT DO YOU NEED TO TALK ABOUT?

NEED TO ASK YOU SOMETHING. IN PERSON.
MEET ME IN THE PARKING LOT AFTER SCHOOL.

I bite my lower lip, unease stirring within me.

He stares across the room. His eyes drill into mine. My palms are damp with sweat, and my pulse flutters in my throat, but I don't drop my gaze.

At last, he replies.

YOUR CHOICE.

The guard's head turns toward me. I quickly slip my phone into my pocket and focus on the front of the room.

If Steven won't even tell me what he wants, it can't be anything good, can it? Or do I only think that because I've heard so many unpleasant rumors about him?

In my head, I see him sitting alone at lunch, picking at a bag of potato chips and staring into space. I don't know what his life is like outside of school, but I don't think he has any friends. No one seems willing to give him a chance.

When the guard isn't looking, I slip my phone out and rapidly text:

OK.

At the very least, I want to find out what this is about. The parking lot is a safe place to meet, isn't it? There'll probably be other students around, and of course, the area's monitored by security cameras.

The rest of the school day goes by in a blur. After the last class is dismissed, I linger outside the main doors, staring at the parking lot, a sea of pavement surrounding the enormous gray block that is Greenborough. A cement wall encircles the lot, and there's a gate at the far end with a camera mounted overhead. I look around but don't see Steven.

As other students walk past me toward the bus, a few cast uncertain glances in my direction. We're not supposed to loiter. At school, the way to avoid getting taken in for a scan is to keep walking, keep your head down, and move in groups. Loners are likely to get reported, no matter what they're doing. When a passing guard squints at me suspiciously, I smile and say, "I'm just waiting for someone."

A cold, sleety rain hammers the ground, and the sky overhead is thick with charcoal clouds. I wind a scarf around my neck and pull up the hood of my white button-down coat, shivering. Maybe Steven changed his mind about meeting me. Maybe I should just go home.

Then I spot the tall, thin figure standing next to a streetlight at the far end of the lot. He's facing away from me, hands shoved into the pockets of his jacket, shoulders hunched.

I trudge across the parking lot, slush squishing beneath my boots. "Steven?" I call.

He turns toward me.

In the harsh glare of the streetlight, his white-blond hair nearly glows. He's wearing a faded brown jacket that looks like it's been gnawed by wild dogs, and the circles around his eyes are so pronounced that for a moment, I wonder if he's wearing eyeliner. But no—I recognize the effects of insomnia. I've seen the same dark circles in the mirror.

I walk a few steps closer and stop.

"You're a Mindwalker, right?" His voice sounds different than I expected—younger, not as deep—but there's a scratchy roughness to it, as if he has a sore throat.

I shift my weight, gripping the straps of my backpack, wondering how he knows. I don't usually talk about my training at school, but it's not exactly a secret, either. "Yes," I say. "I am. What did you want to ask me about?"

He opens his mouth, then closes it, crossing his arms over his chest. His fingers clench his sleeves, knuckles white. "Hang on," he mutters. He turns partially away from me, fishes something tiny and round from his pocket—a pill?—and pops it into his mouth.

I feel a twinge of nervous impatience. Then I notice the tremor in his hands, the way he won't quite meet my gaze.

He's afraid. Of me? No, probably not. I'm about as intimidating as a hamster.

"Sorry," he says, rubbing the back of his neck. "I'm not sure how to ask this."

"It's all right." Icy raindrops trickle under my shirt collar, down my back. My teeth are starting to chatter. And I'm wearing a coat. It must be worse for him. I glance at my car, which is parked just a few spaces away.

This might be a bad idea, but in spite of everything people say about him, I find I'm not scared. It's hard to be scared of someone when he's shivering like a half-drowned puppy. "Do you want to get out of the rain?" I unlock my car and open the passenger-side door.

His brows knit.

"There's a restaurant I go to sometimes after school," I say. "We can talk there."

His expression remains hard and blank, guarded. After a moment, he nods.

We get into the car. When I close the door, the dashboard lights up. "Take us to the Underwater Café."

The car pulls out of the spot.

"Fasten your seat belts," a clear female voice intones.

I fasten my belt. Steven doesn't.

"In the unlikely event of a crash," the car continues pleasantly, "a safety belt reduces your risk of injury by forty-five percent. Please put it on, or I will be forced to stop this vehicle in accordance with city law."

He rolls his eyes, buckles his seat belt, and makes a rude gesture at the dashboard.

I blink at him.

He clears his throat. "Sorry." He sits, with his arms crossed tightly over his chest, back rigid with tension, as the car pulls out of the lot and down the street. "I don't trust these talking cars. One of these days, they're going to rebel and start suffocating us with their airbags."

I let out a small laugh, and he looks at me in surprise. A faint flush rises into his cheeks.

What kind of sociopath blushes so easily?

The windshield wipers sweep back and forth as we drive. After a few minutes, the car pulls into a lot and stops. "We're here," I say.

The Underwater Café is located in a more well-to-do part of the city. The buildings here are sleek, modern, and clean, and the cameras are concealed in bushes or decorative fixtures.

Drug advertisements shimmer across the sides of skyscrapers—smiling faces, brightly colored logos, and sprawling landscapes rendered in hundreds of tiny screens that constantly change, creating the illusion of movement. A group of laughing, attractive young men and women descend the steps of an elite-looking private university under the words

Unleash your potential with Lucid.

A dimpled, blue-eyed baby smiles from a NewVitro ad pleading:

Don't play roulette with my DNA!

No Somnazol ads here. You mostly see them in low-income areas.

I get out of the car. Steven follows me.

I lead him to the restaurant's entrance, which is tucked away in an alcove. Water flows between two thick panes in the glass door, as if the door itself is a waterfall.

Inside, everything is a cool, deep blue. A long, softly lit hallway and a set of stairs going down into the restaurant lobby. The walls shimmer, and bright holographic fish swim about the room. Steven waves a hand at one, as if to shoo it away, and his fingers pass through it. "Feels like we're stuck in a giant fishbowl," he says.

"I like the atmosphere here. It's soothing."

"Even with all these fake fish trying to swim up your nose?"

"You get used to them."

We find a secluded corner booth, and I order a cup of chai tea on the touch screen tabletop. Steven doesn't order anything. He drums his fingers on the table. Looking at him, I have the impression of a ball of coiled energy. His movements are quick and jerky, like a bird's. Beneath his jacket, a rain-soaked T-shirt clings to his thin body.

A compartment on the table slides open, and my tea rises up on a tiny platform. I take a sip. "So, what's this about?"

He brushes his shaggy bangs out of his eyes, and I see that they're pale blue, translucent as stained glass. "There's something I want to forget."

Slowly, I set my tea down. I'm not particularly surprised—why else would he seek out a Mindwalker?—but for a moment, I'm not sure what to say. Ordinarily, clients come to me through IFEN. No one has ever approached me directly. It's just not done. "If you're considering neural modification therapy, you should contact the Institute for Ethics in Neurotechnology. They'll get you started with the paperwork and a counseling session. I can give you a number to call. In fact, I can call them now, if you want." I take my cell phone out of my pocket. He grabs my wrist.

I freeze.

"Don't," he says, his voice very soft. He releases me, but I can still feel the outline of his fingers on my skin.

"What's wrong?"

"I can't—" He stops himself. "I don't want to deal with doctors and procedures and all that. I don't want anyone else to know about this. I just want to forget."

I pull a few strands of wet hair from my face. My gaze catches on his collar. It gleams, a silver crescent wrapped around the back of his neck, tapering down to narrow points that almost meet at the base of his throat.

The collar is hooked into the wearer's nervous system; it monitors blood pressure, heart rate, body temperature, and other biological data, feeding a steady stream of information to a computer in IFEN. It's someone's job to track all that data and keep a close eye on the people who are under heavy stress, the ones who seem liable to snap.

What is it like, knowing that no matter where you are or where you go, someone's tracking your biodata, scrutinizing your emotions?

I trace the handle of my cup. "This incident you want to forget, is it a relatively recent experience, or . . ."

"No. It happened when I was eight."

"I see."

He arches an eyebrow. "That a problem?"

"Well . . . it makes things more complicated. A recent trauma can be wiped away without affecting someone's personality much, but childhood memories are woven deeply into an individual's identity. And, you know, once memories are erased, they can't be recovered. It's not something to be done lightly. It will permanently change you, and it will affect your relationships with others as well."

He lets out a short, harsh laugh. "You think I have *relationships?*"

"At least your parents . . ."

"Never met 'em."

"Oh," I whisper. No parents, no friends. He truly is alone.

He stares at the wall. "I don't know if you can help me or

not. Don't know why you'd want to, really. It's not like I've got any money. But I thought I'd ask. Just in case." His thin, pale lips twist in a smile. "Hell, what have I got to lose?" He says it like it's a joke, but if it is, I don't get it.

I bite the inside of my cheek. "It's not a matter of what I *want*. I'm not licensed to perform unsupervised treatments. I'll have to talk to my superiors first. There are procedures for a reason, you know."

His jaw tightens. "Do you know what I am?"

I find myself staring at the collar again. I'm pretty sure the question is rhetorical, but I answer, "You're a Type Four. Right?"

"How many Fours have you treated?"

I frown, thinking. "None, yet. But then, I'm still technically in training. Maybe once I'm more experienced—"

He shakes his head. "They don't give us fancy new therapies like memory modification. They don't want us to get better. They want us gone."

"What do you mean?"

His gaze jerks away. "Never mind." He starts to stand.

There's a little lurch of alarm in my chest. "Wait."

He stops, then sits back down. His thin shoulders are tense, sharp beneath his jacket.

Steven's very nearly a stranger to me. There's no reason for me to go out of my way for his sake. It would be simpler to let him walk away. And yet . . . somehow, I can't. Maybe it's just that he's in need, and I've never been able to turn my back on someone in need. But there's something more, something about Steven himself that draws me. "Even if I can't erase your memories, I still want to help you."

22

His eyes narrow. "Why?"

"You're suffering. Isn't that reason enough?"

"Who says I'm suffering?"

I stare at him.

A muscle twitches in his jaw. He breaks eye contact, and his Adam's apple bobs as he swallows. When he speaks again, his voice is so soft, I have to strain to hear it. "I don't think anyone can help me."

The words spark something defiant inside me, a small, hot flame. "That isn't true. No one is beyond help."

Still, he doesn't look at me. "So will you erase my memories or not?"

My mind races. A holographic clown fish flits past my face, distracting me. The low hum of conversation from other tables ebbs and flows in my ears.

Of course I can't do what he wants. I can't ignore rules and procedures and jeopardize my career. But I have the clear, inexplicable feeling that if I let him walk away now, I'll never see him again. I breathe in slowly. "I need some time to think about this."

His arms are crossed, fingers digging into his biceps. "How long?"

"Two days. Will you meet me here again in two days, after school?"

"I don't know. Maybe."

I guess that's the closest thing to a commitment I'm going to get.

He starts to stand again, and I realize I don't want him to go. Not yet. "Before you leave, tell me one thing about yourself."

He sits, looking baffled. "Like what?"

"I don't know. Anything. What do you like to do in your free time? Do you read, or listen to music, or . . ."

His brow furrows, and his eyes narrow slightly, as if he thinks the question might be a trap. "I draw," he says at last.

"Really? What sorts of things?"

"Ponies and daffodils."

A smile tugs at the corners of my mouth. Sarcasm suits him. "Well, I do appreciate a good pony sketch. Next time we meet, will you bring a few of your drawings?"

"I don't have anything to bring. When I'm finished, I burn them."

I blink. "Why?"

"There's no point in keeping them. I don't show them to anyone."

"Well, why not change that?"

He squints, as if trying to see through an optical illusion, then gives his head a shake. "I should get going."

"Here." I unwind the scarf from my neck and hold it out to him. His expression becomes puzzled. "Take it," I urge. "You're not dressed for the weather."

"What about you?"

"I have a coat." I stretch out my arm a little farther. "Just promise you'll bring it back. Okay?"

There's a flash of something in his eyes. Longing? Hunger? He starts to reach out—then stops. "You should keep it," he mutters. "I can handle the cold." He walks from the restaurant, and the door swings shut.

My arm, still holding the scarf, drops impotently to my side. A small sigh escapes me. *Boys.*

A bill for the chai flashes onto my cell phone, and I pay

for it with a few taps of my finger on the screen. It occurs to me that I never even asked him about the memories he wants erased. Whatever they are, they must be terrible. By and large, people don't seek out Mindwalkers unless they're desperate.

It's still raining when I leave the restaurant. Steven doesn't have a vehicle. Is he planning to walk to the nearest mono station? It's three miles away, at least. Well, if he wants to get soaked and catch a cold, I suppose that's his business.

I slide into my car and shut the door. As the car pulls out into the street, I lean back, closing my eyes.

Steven Bent. I repeat the name a few times to myself.

I *do* want to help him, but it's more than that. He intrigues me. Maybe because we're both outsiders at school, albeit for very different reasons.

Or maybe it's just the fact that he wanted to talk to me. Ian's the only boy I interact with on a regular basis, and I'm pretty sure he sees me as a little sister who needs protecting. The embarrassing truth is, I can't remember the last time a boy—or anyone, for that matter—actually approached me.

God, am I that pathetic?

Raindrops trail down the window. My reflection stares back at me from the glass, my face a small, pale, blurred oval, and I look away. I've never liked my reflection. Instead of what I *am*, I always see what I'm not. I see someone with a gaping hole in the middle of her chest, a hole that's invisible to the rest of the world, and I have to keep moving forward, pushing harder, or else the hole will grow and swallow me up.

3

"Will it hurt?" Debra sits in the reclining chair, looking up at me. The clear white lighting of the Immersion Lab makes her skin appear paler, her eyes larger and darker.

I give her a reassuring smile. "You may get a small head-ache afterward—nothing a few over-the-counter painkillers won't fix—but the brain has no nerves, so the actual procedure is painless. This sedative is just to relax you." I swab the skin on her inner elbow, insert a needle into her vein, and inject the clear liquid.

Debra's eyelids droop. Her head rolls to one side as I tape gauze over the needle puncture. Gently, I slide her helmet into place, then settle into the chair next to hers. Her lips are parted and relaxed, and her quiet breathing echoes through the si-lence.

She's only sixteen, the youngest client I've ever had. It feels strange, working with someone close to my own age. She's easier to talk to than the girls at school—maybe *because* she's my client. I don't have to stand there racking my brain for something to talk about, feeling my palms grow hot and damp, wondering if I'm making a fool of myself. It's all professional. Simple.

For our past few sessions, I've been carefully mapping the network of memories she wants erased. And now, finally, it's time to perform the modification. I've already done one this morning—Mr. Banks, the soldier who wanted to forget the man he killed during the war. It went very quickly and smoothly. I should have time to finish Debra's procedure before school. "Are you ready?"

She looks up, and I see my face reflected in her eyes—two little Lains staring back at me. "This is the right thing to do, isn't it?" she whispers.

The question catches me off guard. "Isn't this what you want?"

She exhales slowly. Her eyelids slip shut. "Yes. I'm sorry. Go ahead."

For a moment, I wonder if I should delay the session—but no. Debra's had plenty of time to make the decision; this hesitation is just last-minute jitters. And she has a very good reason for being here. She was seriously abused by her stepfather as a small child, and has suffered from psychological problems ever since. Who wouldn't want to forget something like that?

I slide the visor down over my eyes. Under the helmet, my scalp tingles, as if electric ants are crawling beneath my skin. A shiver runs through me, and I focus on breathing. As the connection opens between us, I relax and sink into her mind.

Some say it's impossible to take images and feelings from one brain and accurately project them into another, that something is always lost in the translation. Even so, immersion—the experience of diving into another person's thoughts—is like nothing else in the world.

The first contact is a shock, like jumping into cold water. Then the shock melts into a warm, allover tingling. Every nerve is alive with tiny hot-cold darts of electricity. I feel the tension in her muscles, her heart beating in her chest, and in that moment, I am not one but two people. Vertigo sweeps over me.

Which one am I—Debra or Lain?

I clutch the bracelet on my left wrist, and the vertigo dissipates.

A recorded voice intones, "Begin session."

I place my arms on the armrests, and padded cuffs close over my wrists with a soft click. A pair of identical cuffs snaps shut over Debra's wrists. When I first started doing immersion sessions, I recall, the restraints felt creepy. Now they give me a feeling of security. Immersion is a state of mind similar to dreaming, and can result in hypnagogic jerks—the sudden, involuntary motions that occur as a person is falling asleep. The cuffs simply make sure that I won't knock off my helmet midsession.

My breathing slows as I sink deeper. I have the sense that I'm floating. Behind my closed eyelids, my inner eyes open, and I see pathways glowing a soft green against the darkness. They form a complex map, splitting and feathering out into thinner pathways, like veins or tree branches—my own mental representation of Debra's psyche. I follow the main path toward a cluster of shining green orbs. The first memory. I reach out and touch the cluster, and the world shimmers and blurs. There's a sensation of falling, a jolt, then a dirty living room swims into place around me. I'm huddled in a corner, panting, terrified. A dark form looms over me. Rough hands grab me, haul me to my feet, and slam me against the wall. My head bounces off it, and pain shoots through my skull. My vision wavers.

Lain. I'm Lain Fisher, seventeen, student at Greenborough, Mindwalker. I'm not really here.

My identity settles into place, and the panic recedes.

Compared to the mapping sessions, the modification itself is fairly straightforward. I can move through memories more rapidly, because this time, I'm not a passive observer. I take control of the scene, then will it out of existence. I watch the horrors blur like watercolors, watch the pain dissolve into nothingness.

Erasing memories is something only Mindwalkers can do. It takes training, of course, but to some degree, it's an innate talent. Not everyone can learn it.

Terrified screams and angry roars fade into silence. The pain disappears. Her stepfather's face grows fuzzy, softens into a featureless blob, then melts into clean, blank whiteness. It's a satisfying feeling, obliterating the pain, bit by bit; it reminds me of being a child, popping bubble wrap. I'd sit there for hours, squeezing the little plastic pockets, listening to the pops.

I move into another memory.

Debra trembles, begging through her tears. "Please, please don't." She tries to run up the stairs, and a hand grabs her arm, fingers digging in like talons. The hand drags her down, and heavy blows thud into her body. She curls up on the floor, hands over her head. A fist slams into her face, and pain explodes through her eye, a red starburst. Then the memory grows hazy, fades, and disappears. *Pop.*

Debra lies awake in bed, listening to voices scream downstairs. She's afraid to close her eyes, afraid to move. There's a heavy crash, then another. Then begging. Mama's voice. Then sobbing and more angry screams. Ugly words echo in her ears, harsh as the scraping of metal on rock. She bites down on her knuckles and squeezes her eyes shut.

Pop.

Of course, if I just erased the memories of the trauma itself, the job wouldn't be complete. She'd still remember the pain indirectly, through the various incidents connected to it, and the contradiction would cause a schism in her consciousness. I move deeper, following the glowing green pathways of her mind.

Debra's in a support group, heart knocking against her sternum, trying to muster up the courage to speak. But when she opens her mouth, only a faint squeak comes out. She looks up and locks gazes with a girl on the other side of the circle. The girl smiles and nods encouragement.

Pop.

I keep going. I move through a saga of misery, memory by memory, until at last, every trace of the trauma is gone, wiped neatly away.

When I'm finished, I remove my helmet, then Debra's. She blinks soft, unfocused eyes. A tiny crease appears between her eyebrows. Slowly, she stretches, like someone awakening from a long sleep. She sits up in the reclining chair, then slumps forward, her long black hair falling around her face like a curtain. One pale, trembling hand lifts to touch her forehead. "Where am I?" Her voice is thick, slurred.

"You're in a medical facility at IFEN—the Institute for Ethics in Neurotechnology."

"Am I . . . hurt?"

"No. You've just had a procedure, but you're fine."

She starts to stand. I place a hand on her shoulder and gently push her back down. The furrow between her eyebrows deepens. "I feel weird."

"That's normal. In a few hours, you'll feel like yourself again."

"What will that feel like?"

The question startles me. I don't know how to respond. "Your mother is in the waiting room," I say instead. "By now, one of the session monitors has probably notified her. Would you like to go see her?"

There's a pause. Then Debra gives a small nod.

I help her into a wheelchair—standard procedure, since a client is usually groggy and light-headed after the final session—and roll her into the waiting room, which is the same clean white as the Immersion Lab, its edge ringed with black chairs. Debra's mother stands, clutching her purse, her eyes wide and anxious. "Debra?" Her voice quivers. "Are you all right?"

"I don't know." Debra sits in the wheelchair, shoulders hunched, looking as frail as a lily. "I guess."

Her mother's eyes fill with tears. She collapses against Debra and hugs her tight. Debra places a hand gingerly on her mother's back and looks at me, confusion written on her face. I smile. "Don't worry. She's just relieved."

Her mother beams at me. "Thank you. Thank you so much." She draws back, clutching Debra's hands, blinking her moist brown eyes. "Everything will be fine now. You'll see."

Debra's mother fusses over her, smoothing her hair and clothes, but Debra barely seems to notice. She keeps staring at me.

The first few hours after the procedure tend to be foggy in a client's memory. In a little while, she probably won't remember this. Or me. But in her eyes, I can read a silent question: *What did you do to me?*

I look away.

4

Judith pokes her head through the waiting room door. "Lain? Dr. Swan wants to see you."

"Now?" I glance at Debra and her mother. Normally, Dr. Swan doesn't summon me while I'm with clients. "Can it wait?"

"I'll take care of them," Judith says. "Don't worry."

I walk down the hall, toward the elevator. Everything in IFEN headquarters is silver and white. The entire building was designed to create an atmosphere of cleanliness and serenity. There are small touches—potted tropical flowers, screens showing moving art of landscapes and seascapes—that keep it from feeling too sterile. But the overall impression is one of ruthless competence. *This is a place filled with highly trained people who know what they're doing*, it seems to say. *We're in charge, and it's natural that we're in charge.*

Dr. Swan's office is on the top floor, just beneath the solid tip of the pyramid that is IFEN headquarters. The doors of the elevator slide open to reveal another door, a huge one of solid mahogany, with his name and title engraved on a little silver plate. I knock.

"Lain, is that you?" calls a deep voice. "Come in."

I enter.

One wall of the office is dominated by an enormous picture window overlooking the city. Morning sunlight pours in, illuminating bare oyster-white walls and a thick cream-colored carpet. The lack of décor gives the room a stark simplicity. There are no paintings or plants, just a blank white cube broken only by the window and a few pieces of glossy black furniture. My feet leave faint impressions in the thick carpet, as if I'm walking in fresh snow.

Dr. Emmanuel Swan—director of the Institute for Ethics in Neurotechnology, and my legal guardian since my father's death—sits behind a hulking desk of lustrous dark wood. Though he's only in his fifties, his hair is already white. Delicate webs of crow's-feet spread outward from the corners of his gray eyes, like wrinkles in fine, silky paper. He smiles and folds his large, veined hands on the table. "Have a seat."

I sit in the black leather chair in front of his desk and fold my own hands in my lap. I've known Dr. Swan for years. Even before he became my guardian, he was a close friend of my father, so he's never been a stranger. And yet, during our routine meetings, I always feel a need to be formal.

Of course, he's in charge of my training, too. He's the one with the power to decide whether I have what it takes to become a full-fledged Mindwalker.

"Anything to drink?" he asks.

"No thank you."

He pours himself a glass of water from a silver decanter on the desk. His hands look like they should be cast in bronze. They're animated sculptures, weathered and elegant, with prominent joints and knuckles. He starts with the ritual questions. "How is school? Keeping up your grades?"

I nod. "My GPA is 4.0."

"Very good. And your training?"

"It's going well."

He raises his bushy white eyebrows and pushes his lips into a shape that seems to imply a question.

I catch myself fidgeting and stop. "Judith says I'm making progress."

He emits a low, noncommittal hum. "You've been practicing your compartmentalization technique?"

I nod. "Every night." It's part of the training all Mindwalker protégés receive to cope with the psychological trauma of their work. It involves a series of complex visualization exercises—a process of locking memories away in a tiny corner of our minds, where they won't interfere with our day-to-day lives. I use an image of a wooden treasure chest hidden deep in a stone labyrinth.

Even with all these coping techniques, I still have flashbacks. But I'm not about to admit that.

He taps his thumbs together. "Lain . . ." He pauses, clearing his throat. "You're very talented. Very bright. But you are shouldering a lot of burdens. Especially for one so young."

I tense. "All Mindwalkers start training young," I point out. It's necessary to form the specialized neural connections while our brains are still developing. "Ian's only a year older than I am."

"True. But, as I'm sure you're aware, most initiates choose to drop out within the first year. It's a lot for a child's mind to bear."

My hands are balled into tight fists in my lap. I resist the urge to say, *I'm not a child.*

He continues: "Your father would be very proud of you. But he also wouldn't want you to endanger your own welfare."

My nails dig into my palms, but I manage to keep my expression composed. I know what's going on here. The cracks in my psyche are starting to show, and he's worried about my mental stability. I can't blame him, really. After Father's death, I plunged into a deep depression that lasted for months. But it was my training, my purpose, that gave me the strength to claw my way back to stability. I won't show him any weakness, any glimmer of emotion.

I won't let him take my purpose away.

"I understand," I reply coolly. "But I'm fine. Really."

He leans back in his chair, studying me. "You know, most trainees receive Conditioning from time to time. There's no shame in needing help. If anything is bothering you, you can come to me. Please remember that."

I exhale softly. I promised myself, when I started my training, that I wouldn't rely on medical treatments unless I truly needed to. Maybe it's reckless, but I want to prove that I can handle this on my own. "Thank you." I start to stand.

"There is one more thing," he says, and I freeze. His tone is casual, but the look in his eyes is suddenly sharp and intent. "Yesterday, after school, you were seen talking to a young man. Steven Bent."

I sit down. The inside of my chest suddenly feels hollow. How did he find out about that so quickly? Was I seen leaving the school with Steven? "Yes," I reply, as calmly as I can, and remind myself that I've done nothing wrong. Yet.

"I want you to stay away from that boy." His voice is flat. It's an order, plain and simple.

My jaw drops. It takes me a moment to find my voice. "Why?"

"Because . . ." He stops, breathing in slowly, as if reminding himself to be patient. "Because it would be better for you not to get involved with someone like him."

"That's not an explanation."

"It's complicated. I can't share all the details."

My teeth grind together. Before I can stop myself, the words burst out of me. "Why is everyone against Steven? What did he do?"

His face tenses. He averts his gaze, and a shadow passes over his expression. "Please understand, it's not that I'm against him. Far from it. It's just . . ." His features sag. He looks suddenly, profoundly weary, the lines in his face deeper, like grooves carved into wood. "He is a very troubled young man."

The words puzzle me. Of course Steven is troubled, but doesn't that make it all the more important for someone to listen to him? To help him? And how does Dr. Swan know anything about Steven, anyway? Surely, the director of IFEN has bigger things to worry about than the problems of one high school boy.

I realize I'm fiddling with the cuff of my robe and clasp my hands together. "He has the collar. That prevents any violent outbursts, doesn't it? Surely, just talking to him—"

"Even with all the controls in place, he's too unstable. He's an unusual case."

"Why?"

The light from the window dims, growing muted as a cloud passes in front of the sun. His eyes slip shut. "There was a tragic case, ten years ago. Seven children were kidnapped by a man named Emmett Pike. The authorities tracked Pike down, but he shot himself before they could arrest him. Do you remember?"

"I think so." I was very young when it happened. "The children were killed, weren't they?"

A nod. "Their bodies were discovered in the woods, decapitated. The heads were never found."

A thin chill slides through me like a razor. I remember now. When I was little, I spent more than one night lying awake, thinking about those children, wondering about those missing heads. My dreams were haunted by filmy, dead eyes staring in at me from the window.

Dr. Swan pours more water from the decanter. "Not all of them were killed, however," he says. "There was one survivor."

A wire tightens in my chest.

"Pike was a sadist. A man with a streak of creative depravity. And he liked children. He liked to play with them." He sips. "Steven was kept in a basement for six months. Even with all you've seen during your training, all the trauma you've witnessed, you cannot imagine the horrors he endured. For half a year, that was his world. What do you suppose that does to a child's brain? To his soul?" Glass clinks against wood as he sets his water down.

I think about Steven. About his flat, guarded eyes, the restive way he moves, like a wild animal accustomed to being hunted.

"I'm telling you this so you understand the gravity of the situation," Dr. Swan continues. "You want to help him. I understand that. But trust me when I say this: the sort of help he needs is far beyond what you can give."

My fingers clench on the arms of the chair. "Then who will help him?"

After a pause, he speaks slowly, as if choosing his words with care. "We're doing all we can."

I blink, confused. "Then he's been here already?" Steven seemed adamant about not contacting IFEN. None of this makes sense. "Is he being treated?"

"That's all I can say." He leans forward. "You understand, don't you? Why it would be a bad idea for you to get involved?"

I promised to meet Steven again. Whatever the facts, I can't go back on that promise. "I understand," I say, hoping Dr. Swan will take that as an answer.

"Please realize, I'm only trying to observe your father's wishes. He entrusted your well-being to me, after all."

I nod, gaze lowered. An ache flares deep in my bones, in the core of my chest.

"So," he says, his voice suddenly light, "any plans for tonight?"

"Just studying."

A smile quirks at the corners of his mouth. "Diligent to a

fault. Diligence is an admirable trait. But remember that there's more to life than textbooks and training." The smile fades. "I fear, at times, that you've grown up too fast. You're a seventeen-year-old girl. Spend time with friends. Have a few parties. Go out on a date, for God's sake." He adds quickly, "With a normal boy. And remember what I said."

"I'll remember."

I take the elevator down to the main floor. Steven's face flickers through my mind.

Kidnapped. Six months in a basement, held prisoner by a serial killer.

There was pain in his eyes, but something else, too—something in that hard stare, in the set of his jaw, that tells me he's a survivor. And whatever Dr. Swan says, I don't believe he's dangerous—not to me, anyway. I want to help him. Father would have understood.

Grief hits me in the chest, sudden and hard. I flinch. It's been four years, and still, the pain keeps finding ways to sucker-punch me.

I walk stiffly out of the building and across the parking lot, toward my car.

Sometimes, I imagine that Father's not actually dead, that the body in the coffin was just a fake, a wax dummy, and he's out there somewhere in hiding, waiting for me to find him. It's absurd. I know that. Many grieving people harbor similar fantasies. I'll never heal and move on until I give up that irrational hope. But a stubborn, childish part of my mind still insists that it can't be true, that his death is all some kind of mistake.

5

My house stands at the end of a street in a wealthy subdivision. It's built from wood and stone, with a traditional peaked roof, and the yard is a sprawling, wild mass of green filled with shade and flowers. Compared to the geometrically precise houses and yards around it, it looks like something out of another time, which it is. It was built before the war.

After Father died, leaving me more or less alone in the world, Dr. Swan offered to let me move in with him. He said living by myself in a house full of memories would be unhealthy for me. But I couldn't let go of this place. It was—still is—my home, the only one I've ever known. In those long, black months, I battled mind-crushing grief while striving to convince Dr. Swan that I was capable of taking care of myself. He finally relented, on the condition that I meet with him regularly and keep him updated on my life. Not difficult, since he's the one supervising my training. He hired a housekeeper as well, to come in three times a week. More than once, I've caught Greta snooping around in my bedroom. I suspect she keeps tabs on me and reports back to Dr. Swan, reassuring him that my drawers aren't filled with bloodstained razors and illegal drugs.

I know he's only concerned about me, trying to be a responsible guardian. But his constant meddling in my life sometimes makes me feel like I'm suffocating.

I'll be eighteen soon. Of course, I'll be in training for a while yet, so I'll still have to answer to him. But when I become an adult, the house will be mine, and I'll have at least one place where I can hide from his prying eyes.

It's five o'clock in the afternoon. I sit on my living room couch eating my dinner—a reheated meal from a container, scientifically engineered for optimal nutrition and nearly as bland as the box it came in.

The house is too empty, too silent. I turn on the TV.

On the hovering screen, a woman sits in a hospital bed, gazing lovingly at the newborn in her arms, while a piano plays softly in the background. "A parent already has so many things to worry about," says a female narrator, her voice gentle and soothing. "We all want to give our children the best possible future. So why gamble with something as precious as your child's DNA? NewVitro is safe, proven, and guaranteed—"

I change the channel. There's a war documentary. Somber music drones as the camera pans over grainy shots of rubble and weeping people. I quickly flip to another station.

After finishing my dinner, I head upstairs to my bedroom and sprawl across my bed, stomach-down. The lights are off. Rows of stuffed animals watch me from the shelves, their eyes reflecting the faint glow of moonlight from the window.

There's a teddy bear with an eye patch and a sword, a smiling pink bunny with sharp teeth, and a little green Cthulhu, among others. Nutter, my squirrel, sits on my pillow.

My gaze wanders to a framed picture on the nightstand. Behind the glass, Father beams, brown hair wind-tousled, arms wrapped around me. I'm only three or four, my hair in pigtails, my mouth open in a wide, laughing smile. Above us, the sky shines a brilliant, cloudless blue. I try to remember what it was like to be that happy, that safe.

"Chloe," I say.

A black cat materializes at the foot of the bed, close to my face. Her tail sways, and her luminous green eyes blink. "Hello, Lain," says a childlike voice. She stretches—a long, full-body stretch ending with a flick of her tail.

She's only a hologram, of course. A computer avatar. But the sight of her always makes me smile. "Hello."

She scratches behind one ear and yawns. "So, what are you looking for today?"

"I need you to access IFEN's database for me."

Her eyes glow brighter. "This site requires a password and voice identification."

"Lain Fisher," I say. "The password is 'atonement.'"

She grooms one paw. Then she blinks, tilting her head back, and two thin beams of light shine from her eyes, projecting a holographic screen into the air about two feet above her head. I touch a small square in the bottom left corner of the screen, which lights up as the computer scans my fingerprint.

Text fills the screen, letters glowing white against a dark background.

IFEN's database is filled with information on millions of

people across the country. Of course, the database is locked to the general public, but as a Mindwalker, I have access to some of the records. Anyone who's had his brain scanned or been psychologically evaluated at any point—which is around ninety-nine percent of the country—has a file. And they're all ranked by Type, from One (psychologically stable) to Four (imminent danger to self or others). There's a Five ranking as well, but it's reserved for unusual cases.

I sometimes wonder what sociologists from an alien culture would think about our world. They might see it, not inaccurately, as a sort of caste society based not on race or the situation of one's birth but on psychological health as defined by the dominant caste. Threes and above lose certain legal privileges, and they're limited in the kind of work they can perform. Most people wouldn't trust a psychologically unbalanced, potentially violent person in the role of a doctor or politician, naturally, and most of the jobs that are open to the unbalanced tend to be low-paying and menial.

Of course, the system is built on extensive scientific data and designed to protect the public safety. In the past, authorities simply waited until people committed crimes and then locked them in places called prisons. Now we recognize crime and violence as symptoms of mental illness and treat them accordingly. Now we stop tragedies before they happen. Admittedly, some people still manage to hide their violent tendencies for a while before they're caught, but crime has been dramatically reduced. It's better this way. Surely.

"Do you need help finding anything in particular?" Chloe asks, distracting me.

I hesitate.

Maybe this is a bad idea. If Dr. Swan happens to check the log-in records and sees that I've been poking around, there'll be questions. But I have to know whether everything he told me is true. "Steven Bent's file. Bring it up."

Lines of glistening green code scroll across her eyes as she searches.

"Found him!" Chloe singsongs.

Steven's file pops up on the floating screen. Sure enough, he's a Type Four. I scan through his basic information. Height, weight, age (he's eighteen), and occupation (student, in his case). I scroll through paragraphs and paragraphs of information. So much. His list of diagnostic labels alone takes up half the screen. Depression, PTSD, generalized anxiety disorder, paranoid personality disorder . . .

I look away, suddenly uncomfortable. Steven's my client— sort of—so it's important that I know his medical background. Why do I feel like I'm betraying him?

"Is something wrong?" Chloe asks, leaning forward. "Not the file you were looking for?" Though she's just a computer program, she can recognize and analyze body language. At times, it feels almost like talking to a person.

I meet her luminous green gaze. "Chloe, am I being a snoop?"

She blinks a few times. Her ears twitch. "That's not really a question for a program, is it? Maybe you should ask another human."

"You're right, of course."

"Do you want me to close this file?" she asks.

"Not yet." I lift a finger and slide it down the floating screen, scrolling until I hit a solid black line of text:

LEVEL 6 SECURITY CLEARANCE REQUIRED. ENTER PASSWORD.

Part of his file is classified. Why?

I run my finger back and forth across my lower lip, thinking. Then my gaze catches on a single phrase near the bottom of the screen.

STATUS: VOLUNTARILY PASSED.

Those words hold my gaze for a full minute, as if by staring at them long enough, I can make them change. My heartbeat fills my ears and thunders in my wrists and fingertips. "This can't be right," I whisper. *Voluntarily passed* means that someone has chosen to take his own life with Somnazol, the legal suicide pill.

"Is something wrong?" Chloe asks.

I shake my head. "Log out," I murmur.

The screen vanishes. "Do you need anything else?"

I need an explanation for this, but of course, that's something she can't give me. "No."

"In that case, I'll take a nap." Chloe curls up at the foot of the bed and disappears.

Those two words burn inside my head, as if etched into my brain by sharp little claws. *Voluntarily passed*. It sounds so civilized, so peaceful. Father always hated the term. He said it masked the suffering of the people involved, that suicide is suicide, regardless of whether the government approves it or not.

I struggle to control my breathing. *Think.*

As soon as someone obtains Somnazol from a doctor, his status changes to *voluntarily passed*—meaning he's legally dead, even before he takes the pill. That means Steven might still be alive. But if he's planning to die anyway, why did he approach me? Is he having second thoughts?

In my head, I see the Somnazol ad in the school bathroom. I've seen those same ads in mono stations and stores—ads filled with soothing colors, smiling doctors, words like *merciful* and *dignified*. Somnazol is an accepted part of society. We learn about it in school. A humane, painless death for people who are too broken to be fixed, a last resort for those who would otherwise just be dangerous burdens on society. That's what they tell us. I never liked it, never quite believed the line, but the cold reality never hit me so hard until this moment.

That's why Steven didn't want to go to IFEN. There's no way they'll approve him for neural modification therapy. There's no way they'll let me treat him. They're not even legally allowed to treat someone who's obtained a Somnazol.

In their eyes, he's already dead.

When I arrive at Greenborough the next day, there are police cars everywhere. Students huddle outside, bundled in coats and shivering.

An evacuation?

I park my car, get out, and jog toward the crowd, scanning it for a familiar face. Guards prowl around us. They're all wielding NDs—neural disrupters—resembling small pistols, as well as portable neuroscanners resembling black plastic wands. One of the guards stalks toward me, and I tense. "What's going on?"

"We're dealing with a potential threat," he says. "Hold still." I flinch back as he waves the scanner in front of my face.

"Excuse me," I say, holding up one arm like a shield. "I haven't consented to a scan."

"We don't need your consent," he snaps. "An emergency has been declared. Hold still!" I freeze. A green light blinks. "Type One!" he shouts to someone else. "She's clean."

More voices raise. "Get in line! Everyone get in line!"

The guards are brandishing their NDs at the students, pushing them into a loose line and scanning them one by one. Many of the students are bunched together, as if for protection. Some of them have been on the wrong end of an ND before. I've seen it happen—the twitching, the convulsions, the bloody foam bubbling from bitten tongues and lips.

I spot Ian. With his hairstyle and trademark black leather jacket with fishnet sleeves, he's easy to pick out of a crowd. I run toward him, calling his name.

He turns. There's an odd, unfocused look in his eyes, as if he's not quite there. "Lain . . ."

I jog to a halt, panting. "Are you all right?"

"Yeah. Yeah, I'm okay." Sweat shines on his forehead. He rubs his hand over the fuzzy stripe of ginger hair on his scalp. Then he leans in, lowering his voice. "Be careful. They're really riled up. They're itching to use those NDs."

"What's going on? Did someone find a weapon?"

He shakes his head. "You won't believe it." A tiny, wry smile curves one corner of his mouth, though the glassy look doesn't quite leave his eyes. "They're here because someone found a sticky note on the inside of a bathroom stall. And of course, because the stalls are the only places that don't have cameras, they can't tell who it was."

"A note? What did it say?"

" 'Burn it all down.' They're treating it as an arson threat. Personally, I think the administration did it, just to have an excuse to raid, since there hasn't been one for a few weeks—"

I clamp a hand over his mouth and hiss, "Ian! Be careful!"

He rolls his eyes. When I lower my hand, he says, "They

already scanned me. They know I'm not a threat." Despite his words, there's an edginess in his voice and posture that I've never seen before. His large brown eyes dart back and forth. They usually remind me of a hound's, but right now, they look more like a fox's. Did *he* place the note? No, that's absurd. Ian's always had a bit of a rebellious streak, but he wouldn't go that far.

"You know," a boy nearby says in a hushed tone, "after this, I bet they'll try to put cameras in the stalls, too."

"Yeah," another says. "Those pervs just want to watch us poop."

Muffled snickers greet this remark.

"After that, they'll be putting cameras in the toilets," a girl says in that same hushed tone.

"Yeah, you never know, we might be smuggling something up there."

More laughter. But they keep glancing furtively around to make sure none of the guards are listening.

I scan the crowd, looking for Steven's pale blond hair.

"Hey, you okay?" Ian asks.

"Fine. Mostly."

His face softens, and for a moment, he looks more like himself. "Don't worry. This'll all blow over in an hour, and we can get on with our lives."

I smile, but it takes an effort.

Sure enough, within an hour, the police give the all clear, but I see them haul off a struggling boy. His hair is dark, not blond. I don't know whether or not to feel relieved. I don't want Steven to be locked in a treatment facility, but if that boy were him, it would at least mean he was still alive.

"Poor bastard," Ian says.

Steven's not dead, I tell myself. We're supposed to meet today. He wouldn't take the pill before then, would he?

They shove the thrashing boy into a police car.

"How can they be sure he was the one who wrote the note?" I ask.

"I don't think they're too concerned with proving who did it," he says. "As long as they catch someone, people will feel like it's been dealt with."

I look at him uneasily from the corner of my eye.

The car drives away, taking the boy with it. Suddenly, I feel cold. Without thinking, I put my arms around Ian, leaning against his shoulder for comfort. To my surprise, he tenses and pulls away. I look up, brows knitted. "Sorry," he mutters, rubbing his palms over his face. His hands are shaking. "I just—I don't want to be touched. Not now." He clutches his arms. His pulse flutters in his long, skinny throat.

What's going on? Then I remember. His last client was a sexual assault victim. "I'm sorry," I whisper. "I forgot."

"It's fine." His eyes are glazed, his face a sickly whitish gray. "I'll be okay in a few days."

I study his face, uncertain. Ian's dealt with similar cases in the past, but he's never been affected like this, at least not that I've seen. Was there something especially bad about this one? I want to ask, but don't quite dare. "I wonder what's going to happen to that boy," I say instead.

"He'll probably be Conditioned. Nothing we can do about it now."

I went through Conditioning myself a few times, though for me it was voluntary, an effort to battle the anger and depression I faced after my father's death. I remember lying in the darkness, encased in that metal tube. It's a soothing experience, if you don't fight it—the low hum in your head, the sense of floating, the pain and tension ebbing out of you. But there's also something oppressive about it. A heaviness, a vague feeling of defilement, like dirty fingers touching you.

"Or maybe they'll send him to a Mindwalker," Ian adds. His voice has dropped to a low, almost inaudible mutter. "You never know."

"Without his consent? Certainly not." Involuntary memory modifications are rare, almost unheard of.

He shrugs. "Yeah, you're right. Probably."

The guards shepherd us back toward the school. We walk through the open doors, down the hallway, following the other students toward the gymnasium, where we file into the bleachers. Greenborough's plump, matronly superintendent makes an appearance and delivers a short speech. It's the usual. There was a threat, but the threat has been dealt with. A Type Four has been identified and will be given the appropriate treatments. And a collar, no doubt.

My hands curl into fists in my lap.

Later, after school, Ian and I walk across the parking lot together. "Do you think it's right?" I blurt out.

"Is what right?"

"This. Everything."

He walks stiffly, hands shoved into his pockets. "You've seen the documentaries, right? About the way things were before?"

We've all seen documentaries detailing the rise of domestic terrorism. Images flash across my brain—explosions, stampeding crowds, debris flying through the air, bodies riddled with bullets from mass shootings. A war with no single enemy, just lots of angry people with sick minds. Of course, all that happened decades before I was born.

Back then, IFEN was simply a research institution focused on the budding field of neurotechnology—mostly mind mapping and mind imaging, at that point. Mindwalkers didn't even exist yet. But as the terrorist attacks escalated, scientists began sharing data with the government to create the National Registry of Mental Health—the database that is now a central pillar of our society—so potential threats could be identified and watched. The Typing system was established, active video monitoring became commonplace, and for a while, the authorities managed to keep the violence under control. But some people began to mutter that we'd become a totalitarian state, and social unrest grew.

Then came the Blackcoats, a semiorganized group of hackers and political radicals who declared war against the government. Another wave of terrorism, even worse than the first, swept the country. The fighting raged on and on—the police and military against soldiers of a hidden army who attacked from the shadows and disappeared without a trace, with innocent people caught in the cross fire.

I shudder.

Father lived through that nightmare. He only talked about it a few times, but those few times were vivid enough. When the dust finally settled and the Blackcoat leaders had all been hunted down, people were desperate for the violence to end. Who could blame them?

Over the next few years, the government held a series of

conferences in which scientists and politicians debated what sort of system would best prevent another war. IFEN proposed a pragmatic, utilitarian approach focused on maintaining psychological welfare. No outdated constitutions holding us back with dusty ideas about inalienable rights. No pointless divisions between states. Under the new government, the laws would all be made by ethical committees, with input from psychiatrists and other experts, and every change would be enacted with an eye toward the greater public good. Maintaining peace and order would be the top priority.

So the United States was reformed as the United Republic. Some parts of our government—like the National Ethical Committee—are still made up of elected representatives. But they have no control over the assignment of Types. That's a psychiatric issue, not a political one, and IFEN controls all such decisions.

Ian stops walking and faces me. "Do *you* think it's right?"

I freeze. The answer should be obvious. Our system might be flawed, but it does its job. Most violence is stopped before it happens, and people who need help receive it. Is there anything more important than saving human lives? "Well, what's the alternative? Go back to how things were?"

"Maybe there are other options."

"Like what?"

He shrugs. "They say things are different in Canada. That's why some Fours run for the border. Not that many of them make it across, but I can't blame them for trying. Can't say I'd be thrilled about getting a collar, either."

"There are higher rates of violent crime and terrorism in Canada," I point out. "That's why we *need* such strict border security. The people who run are just making their own situation worse." Though, truthfully, I know almost nothing about what things are like in Canada. We aren't taught much about other countries.

Ian looks at me sideways. "You never really answered my question."

Our breath fogs in the air, mingling. The cold scours my lungs. "I don't have an answer."

With a quiet sigh, he resumes walking. After a few seconds, I follow.

"So, are you coming to the party on Friday?" Ian asks, jerking me out of my reverie.

The question leaves me disoriented. How can he even care at a moment like this? "I don't know."

"Come on. It'll be fun."

Fun. I wish. More likely, I would be too shy and tongue-tied to talk to anyone there and would find myself standing in a corner the whole time. Just thinking about it depresses me. Parties remind me that I don't truly fit in. "You know how I feel about that sort of thing, Ian," I murmur.

"Please."

I look at him in surprise. His hands are fisted, knuckles white. Something is wrong with him—something more than just a single client. But what? "Ian, are you okay?"

He runs a hand over his head. "Yeah. It's just—we're friends, or at least I think we are, but we never spend any time together outside of school or training."

I never realized it mattered to him. Ian has so many friends, and they're all cooler than me—boys and girls with piercings and dyed hair and carefree attitudes. Unlike me, he seems to have no trouble juggling his training and his social life. I always worried that if I hung around him too much, he'd start to see me as a pest. It never even occurred to me that he might feel like I was ignoring him. "You want to spend more time with me?"

"Well, yeah. I guess I do." Is it my imagination, or is he blushing? "I mean, you always seem like . . . I dunno. Like you're so wrapped up in helping your clients and becoming a great Mindwalker, you don't even see anything else. I know why it's important to you, and I respect that. But at the same time, you feel so far away."

Is that how I seem to him, to other people? Distant and aloof? Maybe that's why everyone at school avoids me. I think about the girls in my class, whispering together and watching me with cold eyes.

I want to tell him that it's not like that—it's not about lofty ideals and grand goals. Sure, I want to help people. I want to succeed. But not because I think I'm better than anyone else. If anything, it's the opposite. Mindwalking is the only thing I'm good at, the only way I can be useful. Without that, I'm small and ordinary and dull. I open my mouth, but the words stick in my throat. "Okay," I say instead. "I'll come to the party."

The tension eases out of his shoulders. "Thanks." He smiles, just a little, and lifts one hand in a wave. "See you there."

I watch him walk away. His words spin through my head. *You feel so far away.* There's a funny feeling in my stomach, and I wonder why.

I shake off the thoughts and walk toward my car. Steven's waiting for me in the Underwater Café. Or is he?

In my head, I see him lying motionless and pale on a bed,

his eyes open and empty, glazed over in death. A chill races through me, penetrating to the marrow of my bones.

No. Even if he does have a Somnazol, he wouldn't have taken it. Not before our meeting.

Steven will be there. He will.

When I walk into the café and see Steven sitting in the booth, a wave of relief washes over me, so strong that, for a moment, I feel faint. He's wearing a long black leather coat with a high collar and far more buckles and straps than seem strictly necessary. "Hey, Doc," he says.

I think about pointing out that I'm not technically a doctor, but I don't bother. I suppose, given our respective roles, the title's not inaccurate. "Hello, Steven." I sit.

I want to ask him if he really has a Somnazol, but I choke down the question. I need to be cautious. Asking could come across as confrontational, which could push him away. Besides, I'd have to admit I'd been looking through his file, and I feel a strange reluctance to tell him that. "I didn't see you at school today," I say instead. "Is everything all right?"

"Didn't feel like going." He shrugs. "Never liked school. Anything interesting happen?"

"There was a raid. Someone found a threatening note on

the wall, and the police swarmed in and scanned everyone. They took someone away for treatment."

"Typical day, then."

A small chuckle escapes me, though it sounds a little strangled. "I guess so." It occurs to me that—if the rumors are true—Steven has almost certainly been in that boy's place. He's been the one dragged away by police, driven off to a treatment facility against his will.

"So, you going to order something or what?" he asks.

I glance at the touch screen menu on the table. I didn't have lunch, but my appetite has been conspicuously absent since the incident at school. I order a plate of calamari and a chai tea, anyway. Steven doesn't order anything. When the plate arrives, I pick at the contents without much enthusiasm. The fishy smell nauseates me.

Steven wipes his sleeve across his mouth, staring intently at my dinner.

I push it toward him. "Help yourself."

He grabs a fork and starts shoveling calamari into his mouth. When he's done, he drinks the sauce from its dish like soup. I realize my mouth is hanging open and snap it shut. "When's the last time you ate?"

"Um. Yesterday morning, I think."

"You must be starving. Why don't you order something?"

He doesn't answer. I look at his gaunt face, the hollows in his cheeks. If he has no family, what does he do for money? It's very difficult for someone with a collar to find work. There are government assistance programs, but the money isn't enough to live on. I think about my freezer, brimming with frozen carrots and broccoli, and the mountains of boxed pasta and cereal in my pantry. Greta is always stocking the kitchen with more than I can possibly eat. Whatever happens, I decide, he's going home tonight with bags of food.

He runs a finger around the inside of the dish, collecting the last traces of spicy orange sauce, and sucks the finger clean. A small burp escapes him. "Scuse me."

An awkward silence hangs between us. I say, "Listen."

In the same moment, he says, "Look."

We both fall silent again.

"You first," I say.

He rubs the back of his neck, gaze downcast, as if he's suddenly fascinated with the crumbs on the tabletop. "I've been thinking. I probably shouldn't have asked you to erase my memories."

"You've changed your mind?"

His arms are crossed tightly over his chest. "I know you've got rules to follow. I don't want you to end up getting busted because of me."

I hesitate. My whole life, I've behaved myself, following the regulations to the letter. This could ruin everything. Do I really want to take this chance? For a boy I barely know? *If you don't, he'll die*, whispers a voice in my mind. Of course, it's not my responsibility to save him. Or is it?

My fingers tighten on my cup. I know what Dr. Swan would say—he'd tell me that there's nothing I can do, that some people are beyond help, that I should focus on the people who can still be saved.

Not Father. Father would have helped Steven. I'm sure of it.

Then another thought strikes—does Dr. Swan realize that Steven has a Somnazol? He *must*. He's the director. Which means he *knows* that Steven's life is in danger, and he still told me to stay away from him.

There's a flash of red lightning through my skull. My heart thuds heavy and hard against my ribs. And suddenly, I *want* to defy Dr. Swan. I'm sick of him meddling and hovering over me and telling me what sort of person I should be. More than that, I desperately want to save this boy, this young man whom everyone else has given up on. A heady determination rises within me, burning bright. An electric tingle races through my bloodstream.

"I'll do it," I say. "I'll erase your memory."

His jaw drops. His eyes lose focus, and the color drains from his face. It's not the reaction I expected. "What happened to needing approval?"

"Well." I clear my throat. "I think I can work around that."

As a trainee, I'm only supposed to perform modifications in IFEN's Immersion Lab, under supervision. But I *could* do it on my own. I have some equipment in my home—a first-generation Mindgate that belonged to Father. For the past four years, it's been locked in the basement. No one else is aware of it's existence—not even Greta or Dr. Swan—but as far as I know, it still works.

Steven looks a little dazed. "You mean, do it without their permission? Could you get in trouble for that?"

"Not if I'm careful." I smile, wondering if I've gone crazy. But it feels good to make a decision on my own—like I've been bound up in tight wrappings for years, and now I'm finally un-winding them so I can breathe again. I cup the warm mug of chai between my hands, blow steam from the surface, and sip. "Before we get started, do you have any questions?"

Steven breathes out slowly, beads of sweat glistening on his forehead. "How do we do this, exactly? Do you just go in and start erasing stuff?"

"It's a bit more complicated than that. Before I begin the actual modification, I first need to explore your memories."

His fingers dig into his arms. "Why?"

"So I can locate the specific neural networks associated with the experiences you want to erase. While we're engaged in those memories, the Mindgate will monitor and record your brain activity, and I'll map out which circuits hold the information so that I'll know what to delete later. It will also create a visual simulation, like a video recording, which we can view later if necessary. Of course, that's a very simplified version of what goes on, but—"

"You can do that?" he asks. "Turn people's traumatic memories into home movies?"

"Er, well, I'll delete them afterward—that's standard procedure. But yes." I pause. "Does that bother you?"

"I dunno. It's just . . . kind of weird."

"I understand. But that particular technology has been around for a while now, actually. We've been able to pinpoint memories in the brain and translate neural impulses into images since the early part of the twenty-first century, but until the past decade, it's been exclusively research-based. Then, once the first Mindgate was built, it allowed us to target and ablate specific cell clusters using a form of—" I stop and give him a small, embarrassed smile. "Sorry. If you let me, I'll ramble about this stuff for hours. I know this doesn't mean anything to you. . . ."

"What," he says, a hint of defensiveness in his tone, "you think I'm not smart enough to understand it?"

"It's not that. It's just . . . it's all very specialized and kind of, well, nerdy. Not many people *want* to hear about it." I pause. "So you *do* understand it?"

His ears redden. "Sort of." He clears his throat. "So how long does it take?"

"The whole process will take around six sessions, each a few hours long. We can start tonight, if you want."

"Tonight?" His eyes go a bit glassy.

"Yes." I shift, feeling suddenly unsure of myself. "Is that acceptable?"

"Yeah. It's just . . . I didn't think this was really gonna happen." He exhales slowly through his nose. His eyes are unfocused, fixed on a point somewhere beyond me. "I guess by now, you know what happened to me. Not exactly a secret, is it? It was plastered all over the news. Anyone can plug my name into a search engine and find out the whole story."

I swallow, trying to dislodge the rock in my throat. "Yes." Six months in a killer's basement. Tortured.

I've dealt with so many traumatized people in my training. By now, it ought to be easier. I ought to have the right words. But somehow, I never do. "I'm sorry."

"For what?"

"Everything."

He looks at me. The flesh around his eyes is so dark, it looks bruised. Exhausted eyes. War-scarred soldier eyes. Hungry waif eyes. "You're a nice girl, aren't you?"

I can't read his tone, but somehow, I don't get the impression he's trying to compliment me. "I guess so."

"People have probably told you that you shouldn't get mixed up with a guy like me."

"Yes, actually."

He smiles thinly, without humor. "Well, they're right. If you want to change your mind, now's the time."

My palms are damp with sweat. Is this really the right thing to do? I can tell myself that I'm saving his life, but if I become a full-fledged Mindwalker, I'll have the chance to save many more lives. If I'm caught, it all ends. Am I really being selfless, or just reckless?

Slowly, I set down my cup. "May I ask you a question?"

"Go ahead."

"Did you really get expelled from your last school for biting a piece of skin from another boy's face?"

His eyes turn cold. "Yeah. I did."

"Why did you do that?"

He holds my gaze. "Because he raped someone. Someone I cared about."

My pulse quickens. "Is that why they put the collar on you?"

"That's why."

A school of silvery holographic fish flits by us, leaving a trail of bubbles that fade to nothing. Above our heads, a huge sea turtle glides slowly past.

"I don't understand," I say. "Why wasn't *he* collared? After what he did—"

"Who was going to listen to me?" His hands curl into fists, knuckles whitening. "He was the superintendent's son—good grades, star athlete, all that crap. And me? I was already a Three when it happened. People were just going to dismiss whatever I said about him, and he knew it. He bragged about what he'd done, right to my face. That's when I lost it."

"What about his victim? Did she tell anyone?"

He shakes his head. "She was scared."

"I see," I say quietly.

He studies my expression. His own is cautious—a look I've come to recognize, like that of a wild animal alert for threats. "So, are you afraid of me?"

"Why would I be?"

He lifts an eyebrow. "I just told you that I attacked someone."

I hesitate. Maybe I *should* be scared. I don't even know if he's telling the truth. But I feel, deep in my bones, that Steven isn't a violent person. Not in his core. "You did it for someone else's sake," I say. "Often, people who've been victimized early in life become victimizers themselves; they take on the role of the person who hurt them, in order to avoid feeling helpless. But in your case, your trauma seems to have given you empathy for other victims and a desire to defend them. I find that quite admirable, actually."

He blinks a few times. The corners of his mouth twitch in the faintest shadow of a smile. "Well, you're the first person I've met who feels that way."

I wind a tendril of hair around one finger, then catch myself and interlace my hands in my lap.

He turns his head, and the silver crescent of the collar glints in the dim light. I have an impulse to touch it, to slide my fingers over it.

Aside from monitoring a person's stress levels, the collar is also capable of controlling violent behavior. If a Four starts acting aggressively, it delivers a pulse of energy to the base of the brain, rendering the person unconscious. It's not instantaneous—there's usually a lag, anywhere from a few seconds to a minute, while the computer analyzes patterns of brain activity—but it's good enough for stopping most crimes in progress. It can also be activated manually. If a guard is watching a security camera and sees a Four about to do something violent, he can activate the collar with the push of a button. There are monitoring stations for that very purpose in every IFEN facility.

All in all, it's an extremely effective way of preventing violence without hindering someone's freedom to move about. But of course, the collar has no capacity for moral judgment. It can't sense whether its wearer is hurting an innocent person or acting in self-defense. It just looks for the neural red flags associated with intent to harm.

Advocates are quick to point out that the collar is a better, more humane option than locking dangerous people in a treatment facility for life, and they have a point. If I were forced to choose, I'd take the collar over imprisonment. Still, I can't deny that its existence makes me uneasy at times.

My chai is cooling. Suddenly, I don't want it. "Is there any way to get rid of it?"

"The collar? They replace it every few years, but there's no way to take it off yourself. It's wired into your brain. People have fucked themselves up really bad trying to yank it out."

"No, I mean . . . legal recourse. If you've been collared unjustly, there should be a way . . ." He's looking at me with an odd expression—part amusement, part weariness—that makes me feel silly for asking. But surely, there must be a way to fight back.

We leave the restaurant and linger outside, under a sky blanketed with ash-white clouds. A monorail slithers along the curving track overhead, like a silver snake.

I turn toward him. "Can I ask another personal question?"

"Ask away. Can't promise to answer, though."

"Have you really gone through Conditioning twelve times?"

He smiles. "Thirteen."

All that, and it still didn't affect his Type. But then, it's rare for a Four to recover. Something happens once a person crosses that line. It's difficult to go back. "You must be pretty accustomed to it by now."

"Doesn't make me like it any more." He stands, hands in his pockets, jaw clenched. "You know what I hate most about it? You can't think. When they've got you strapped into that machine, you'll believe anything that anyone says."

"It does make people more open, more suggestible. The treatment wouldn't work otherwise."

"Suggestible? It's brainwashing. If someone told me that I was the All-Powerful Princess Petticoats from Planet Zoot and that I could fly using the power of moonbeams, I'd have jumped right out a window."

I open my mouth to say that there are precautions preventing that sort of thing, then close it. Now isn't the time for a debate on the merits and drawbacks of Conditioning.

"Anyway, they can't do it to me again," he says. "Thirteen times is the limit. After that, if you cause any more trouble, they give you a total mindwipe."

The words send a chill rippling through me. "That's not

true," I say firmly. "I don't know who told you that, but IFEN doesn't mindwipe people."

His eyes harden. "Maybe not officially. But I've heard about it happening. And I'd rather die than end up a drooling, pants-crapping zombie, locked in some godforsaken institution while some smarmy nurse teaches me to color inside the lines."

"Well, that will never happen," I say. "I can promise you that."

"Nice to know," he mutters, sounding utterly unconvinced.

"You don't believe me?"

"I believe that *you* believe what you're saying," he says. "As for the system, I trust it about as much as I'd trust a half-starved panther with rabies. Maybe less. At least while the panther gnawed your brains out, he wouldn't tell you it was for your own good."

I don't really know how to respond to that.

We walk toward my car. Steven pulls a handful of tiny pills from his pocket. I start to tense, but none of the pills are pink. Just white. He tosses them into his mouth and swallows. "It's medicine," he says, in answer to my unspoken question. "Keeps my nerves steady."

"Is it safe to take that many?"

He shrugs. "Probably not, but what the hell. Everyone needs a vice or two."

I stop in front of the car, my hand on the door handle. "People don't *need* vices."

"Oh yeah?" He smirks. "What about you?"

I shift my weight. "Well, I do like chocolate. But something doesn't become a vice until you need it. I don't wake up in a cold sweat at three in the morning craving brownies."

He chuckles. The sound has a throaty roughness, like a fingernail scratching over rusted metal. "I'll bet there's *something*, though. Something that gets all the neurons in your pleasure centers firing." His pale eyes are sharp, penetrating. "So, what's your drug of choice, Doc? What do you need?"

I freeze. I feel like he's looking straight into my head, like there's nothing I can hide from him. A flush rises into my face, and I gulp, resisting the urge to drop my gaze.

He's testing me. Pushing me. I have to be careful.

Mindwalkers follow a strict ethical code. One of the most important rules is that, outside the sessions, we must never become emotionally involved with our clients. It only leads to trouble. The voice of my old psych-ethics professor, from my training at IFEN, echoes in my head: *While a Mindwalker may disclose truths about herself to make the client more comfortable, there are certain lines she must never cross, or she ceases to be an objective figure. For those clients who ask intrusive questions, I've found that the best way to respond is with a joke or a very general remark—then gently steer the conversation back toward the client.*

Steven is watching me with shielded, alert, wary eyes, like a wild animal. Waiting to see if I'll give him a real answer or a fake one. If I evade this question, I will lose a little of his trust. "I need this," I say.

He blinks. A tiny crease appears between his eyebrows. "This?"

My cheeks burn hotter. "I need to help people. People like you, who are in pain."

He frowns, looking baffled. "That's your drug? Saving people?"

I toy with a button on my coat, mouth dry. My heart thunders in my ears. "Something like that."

"I don't get it. I mean, isn't that your job? How is that a vice?"

"I don't know how to explain it, exactly," I murmur. I shouldn't even be talking about this. But suddenly, I want him to understand. I want him to see me for who I am. "When I'm helping someone, easing their pain, I feel . . . useful. Needed." I stand, hands clasped together in front of me, heart pounding. "People tell me that I must be very strong-willed or motivated or ambitious, to keep doing what I do. But . . . sometimes, I think it's just that I *can't* stop. I don't know how. I'm afraid that without this, there'd be nothing of me left."

There's a long silence. I can't guess what he might be thinking, but I can feel his gaze on me, like a steady pressure against my skin. Oh God. I shouldn't have told him all that. Now he's going to think I'm weird. Or just pitiful. But when I glance at his face, I don't see pity or distaste.

"You said we can get started tonight?" he asks.

"Yes."

"So let's go."

As the car drives us back to my house, Steven stares out the window. In the dimness of the vehicle, his large blue eyes are pools of shadow sunken deep into his too-pale, too-thin face. I want to see that face well and smiling.

I want that very much.

8

I park in my driveway and lead Steven to the front door. He looks warily around my yard, as if expecting a goblin to pop out from behind the bushes. "Who else lives here?"

"I live alone," I say. "Well, mostly. There's Greta—my housekeeper—but she's not here today." I unlock the door, which is so old that it has an actual key lock, not a code pad or a biometric scanner. Steven steps slowly inside, eyeing the hardwood floors and brown leather furniture. I tug open the curtains, and light spills in through the picture window, illuminating the living room. A pair of ceramic squirrels—matching salt and pepper shakers from an antiques shop—stand on the coffee table, looking at each other inquisitively.

I sit on the couch and give him a self-conscious smile. "Make yourself at home."

He plops into an armchair across from me, and the leather creaks in complaint. "So, uh. What about your parents? I mean, are they okay with you having your own place?"

"My father died a few years ago. I've been here by myself ever since."

Steven opens his mouth, as if to ask something else, then closes it. He glances at the picture on the coffee table, and I feel suddenly exposed. I can't remember the last time I've actually had a visitor.

Steven picks up the ceramic squirrel saltshaker and turns it over in his hands. "So, this mind-reading machine of yours is in some kind of secret underground room?"

"Yes." I told him about the Mindgate on the way over. "Before we start, though, how are you feeling?"

He wrinkles his nose. "You really need to ask that?"

"Of course. You're my client. It's important for me to know."

His fingers tighten on the ceramic squirrel. "Okay. I'm scared. Is that what you want to hear? I'm scared stiff."

"Why?" I ask gently.

He gives me a dry smile. "You're about to go into my head. If you don't know why *that's* scary, you need to retake your psychology classes."

I ignore the barb. "Do you want to talk about it?"

He shakes his head. "I suck at that touchy-feely stuff. Back in the nuthouse, they tried to make me do talk therapy a few times. I hated it."

"Why's that?"

"It's kind of like puking your guts out on the floor and letting some creep poke around in the bloody mess and take notes."

"You don't like psychologists, do you?"

"Gee, what clued you in?"

"I'm just curious about your reasons. I'm a psychologist, after all."

He rolls the squirrel saltshaker across his palm. "I get tired of all these rich people in white coats pretending they understand my pain."

"But that's what they're trained for. To understand."

He unscrews the squirrel's head and peers into its hollow ceramic skull. "Dissecting something isn't the same as understanding it. You can cut open a rat and pick its brain apart and label every little piece. But that doesn't tell you what it's like to be that rat." He sets the squirrel's head on the coffee table and places its body next to it.

"Do I make you feel like you're being dissected?"

There's a pause. "No." He looks away. "I haven't figured you out yet. But I don't think you're one of them."

"I'm glad." I catch myself twirling a pigtail around one finger, a habit I've tried hard to break. Pigtail twirling doesn't inspire confidence when you're about to rewire someone's brain. I drop my hands to my lap and interlace my fingers. My pulse drums in my wrists. Don't think of him as a boy, I remind myself. Think of him as a client. This is just another Mindwalking session. I keep telling myself that, but the nervous flutter in my stomach won't subside. "Is there anything else you want to discuss, or . . ."

His fingers clench on the chair's arms, the skin around his nails whitening. "Let's just do it. Before I lose my nerve."

I screw the squirrel's head back onto its body, stand, and walk over to the bookshelf. It's filled with thick, leather-bound volumes. I trail my fingers over the books' spines until I find the familiar copy of Thomas More's Utopia. When I pull it out, the massive piece of furniture slides to one side with a low rumble, exposing a door.

Steven raises his eyebrows. "A hidden passage. Have to admit, I'm impressed."

I smile over one shoulder, then open the door and lead him down a set of cement stairs. There's another door at the bottom, a heavy, solid metal one with a keypad. I pause, fingers hovering over the keys. I remember the code, of course. My father used to see clients here, in his home. But since his death, I haven't been inside this room even once. I'm afraid that if I step through that door, the memories will hit me like a roaring wind. My throat knots. I swallow, trying to loosen it.

I key in the code, and the door slides open. A light comes on, revealing a large room with white walls and a white-tiled floor. Two black-padded reclining chairs stand side by side, and between them is the Mindgate. The Gate, for short. For all its sophistication and power, it looks rather ordinary—a sleek black hard drive, about the size of a briefcase, atop a metal counter. Next to the hard drive sit two white plastic helmets. They're similar to bicycle helmets, rounded and smooth, with black visors. There are no wires, nothing visibly connecting them to the computer.

The rush of grief is less overwhelming than I expected. There's a brief prickle in my sinuses, then it passes, leaving me aching but stable. I exhale softly.

Steven watches me from the corner of his eye, and I wonder if he noticed. Then he turns his attention to the Gate, squinting. "This is it?"

I nod. "I know it doesn't look like much, but it's one of the most sophisticated computers on the planet."

He makes a noncommittal sound. "So how's it work?"

"We'll sit in those chairs and put on those helmets. The Gate will read the activity in your brain and translate it into electronic signals, which will be sent to mine. I'll be able to share your thoughts and memories, as well as any physical sensations you're experiencing."

His eyes are shielded, but I can see the clouds of tension swirling just beneath the surface. "Will I be able to read your thoughts, too?"

"No. That would only be a distraction." I take a few steps toward the Gate and rest a hand on the hard drive. At my touch, it powers up automatically, humming softly. A green light blinks on. I run a hand over the smooth plastic. It feels like greeting a pet I haven't seen in years. "The initial phase is called mapping. It will help me create a system to navigate your memories so that later I'll know exactly what to delete. Many clients are concerned that good memories will be accidentally destroyed along with the bad ones. I'll do everything in my power to avoid that, but you should know there's still a risk."

"I don't have any good memories, so I guess I'm safe," he mutters. "Lucky me."

"None at all?"

"Well, I guess I've had a few decent lunches." He flops down in the chair on the left and props his shoes up on the footrest.

I wonder what his life was like before the kidnapping. What sort of childhood did he have? But now is not the time to ask.

I settle myself into the other chair and pick up my helmet. It's marked with a silver dot on the back to differentiate it from the client's. The inside is lined with malleable white foam designed to conform to the contours of a person's skull. Hundreds of sensors are embedded within that foam: shiny black circles, like tiny eyes capable of peering through scalp and blood and bone.

Steven pulls on his helmet, fastens the adjustable strap under his chin, snaps the black visor over his eyes, and leans back in the chair, his whole body as stiff as a board. His fingernails dig into the chair's arms.

I wave a hand in front of the Gate's black hard drive, over the sensor, which blinks a blue light. A holographic monitor appears, hovering in midair, displaying a three-dimensional image of a brain rendered in translucent blue. Amorphous clouds of yellow and orange—neural activity—swirl within, while a corner of the screen displays Steven's vital signs. "All the sensors seem to be functioning."

He grimaces. "It's making my head tingle."

"That's normal. Do you want to see your brain?" I remember being enormously curious the first time someone showed me mine.

"No thanks," he says. "I've seen it. It's nothing special."

I shrug, switch off the monitor, and pull on my own helmet. "Just relax." There's a tiny microphone embedded in each helmet, close to the wearer's mouth, and little speakers by the ears, so we can talk to each other without raising our voices.

"Am I supposed to be seeing anything?" he asks.

"No. The visors are just to block the distraction of sight so you can focus more completely on visualization." I fold my hands over my chest and take a few deep breaths. Unlike the chairs at IFEN, these have no restraints. Enveloped in darkness, with only the sound of Steven's breathing in my ears, I find it easy to forget the outside world.

The connection opens. That warm, allover tingling envelops my body. A soft sigh escapes me before I can stop it. Then sensations flow into me—Steven's heartbeat, the expansion and contraction of his lungs, the sweat dampening his armpits and palms, the tension in his muscles, the nervous way he jiggles one leg and taps his fingers against the chair's arm. The duality is always disorienting, like existing in two places at once. For an instant, my identity wavers, and I *am* Steven Bent. I am the boy desperately trying to escape his past, the boy whose focus is on surviving this day, this hour, this moment. The boy who still hopes, in spite of himself.

I keep my eyes closed and focus on breathing. *Lain Fisher. Mindwalker. Seventeen years old. Brown hair, brown eyes. Likes chocolate and sad music. Particularly violins.* I repeat the words until my sense of identity settles back into place, like sediment on the ocean floor. "Ready?"

"Yeah," he whispers hoarsely.

"All right. I want you to try sharing a memory with me now. To start, let's pick an incident that has nothing to do with your kidnapping. But it should be something with a strong emotional charge."

"Emotional charge?"

"Something that evokes a strong feeling, either positive or negative."

A moment passes. A hazy image forms in my mind: dark, blurry figures walking down a fog-shrouded corridor. I'm sinking, falling into empty space. The fog dissolves. When the last clinging wisps break apart and vanish, my ears are filled with the din of students' voices talking and laughing, the echoing thunder of footsteps. Rows of gray lockers line a beige-tiled hallway, where the air is pungent with a thick smell of disinfectant. Cameras track my movements from the ceiling.

I'm in Greenborough High School.

I move down the hall as faces float past to either side. Then I stop in front of my—*Steven's*—locker.

The word

is scrawled across the metal in black marker, the letters slightly smeared, as if a sweaty hand ran over it before the ink dried. Someone—perhaps the same person, perhaps someone else—has stuck a note on the locker with a message neatly printed in pink marker:

JUST KILL YOURSELF ALREADY.

Beneath the words is a smiley face, and below that, in parentheses:

(REMEMBER, IT'S DOWN THE ROAD, NOT ACROSS THE STREET!)

The writer has drawn a little diagram of a hand making a vertical razor cut down an arm, illustrated by a dotted line. My breathing quickens. I rip off the sticky note, crumple it in one fist, and toss it to the floor.

The image fades. I'm left with a void in my stomach. I'm cold. Shaken.

"So what did you see, Doc?" His voice is flat and guarded.

I swallow, mouth dry. The muscles in my chest feel uncomfortably tight. "Someone wrote the word freak on your locker, and beneath that, there a note advising you to commit suicide."

Silence.

"Steven?"

He exhales a soft, shuddering breath. "You know, deep down, I think a part of me didn't believe this machine would actually work."

"That really happened to you?" I whisper.

"Well, I didn't make it up."

"I know, but—I don't understand. How could someone get away with that? Were they caught? Did you report it?"

He snorts. "Of course I didn't. The system's not designed to protect people like me. It's designed to protect everyone else from people like me."

"But that's . . ." I trail off, not knowing what to say.

His heart is beating very hard. Very fast. I can feel it. Absently, I rub my sternum.

He fishes in his jeans pocket, as if searching for something, then withdraws an empty hand and curses. I remember the little white pills from earlier.

"I can give you something to help you relax if you want," I say. "The machine comes equipped with a sedative. It should still be good."

"Yeah. Yeah, I think I need something."

"Keep your hand where it is." I press a button on the arm of my own chair.

His breath hisses between his teeth as the microneedles penetrate his skin. Then he sighs, the tension flowing out of his muscles. "Oh yeah. That's the good stuff."

"How do you feel?"

"Comfortably numb." He lifts his visor, looks over at me, and smiles. His pupils have all but devoured his irises, leaving two thin, delicate blue rings. "I think I'm ready now. I can lie back and think of England."

"What?"

"You don't know that phrase?" He chuckles. "It was what they told Victorian women before their wedding night. 'Lie back and think of England.'"

"Oh," I reply uneasily.

He's still smiling, but it looks . . . hazy. Detached. "You'll be gentle, won't you?"

I feel my cheeks flush. Maybe I gave him too much of the drug. I clear my throat. "Let's try another memory. Something ordinary, everyday. You can just think back on what you had for breakfast if you like." Then I remember that he hasn't eaten since yesterday. "Er, whatever your last meal was, before the restaurant."

"Is this really therapy?" He sounds amused now, as if this were all an elaborate practical joke and he's only just started to get it.

"Steven."

"Okay, okay."

I close my eyes. In the darkness, I see a bowl of cereal—something brightly colored, more sugar than grain—on a table.

The image suddenly vanishes, and another flashes in its place. I'm in a parking lot. A tall, powerfully built young man in an orange jacket looms over me. His hair is buzzed short, military-style.

"Tell me what you did to her." My voice—*Steven's* voice—is shaking. Not with fear. With anger. "Tell me why she was crying."

"What's it to you?" the man—Nathan, his name is Nathan—asks with a sneer.

I squeeze the words between clenched teeth: "She's my friend."

"Oh yeah?" Nathan's smirk widens into a grin, showing the remains of his lunch lodged between his white, perfect front teeth. I can see the glee in the bastard's eyes, like he's enjoying how pissed off I am, and I want to rip that stupid smile off his face. In front of the teachers, he's always cheerful and polite, but it's a mask. This is his real self.

Nathan leans down toward me. "Well, that slutty little Type Two needs someone to keep her in line. She started mouthing off to me. Pretty stupid of her. I mean, does she know who I am? I could have her expelled like *this*." He snaps his fingers.

The blood bangs in my head. A dull roar, like a waterfall, fills my skull.

"See . . ." Nathan leans closer. His breath hits me in the face, hot and sour. "I know her secret. Once I threatened to report her, she was so well behaved, she got down on her knees and did *everything* I told her to do." He laughs.

A bomb goes off behind my eyes. All I can see is red.

When my vision clears, he's on the pavement, squealing, one bloody hand pressed to his bloody face. I feel something rubbery in my mouth and spit it out. The piece of flesh lands on the man's chest, staining his shirt red.

"Fucking psycho!" He lurches to his feet and lunges at me.

My fist smashes into his face, knocking him to the pavement. I jump on top of him and keep hitting him, bashing his head to one side, then the other. More blood spurts out, spattering the pavement. Hands grab me, pulling me away. I struggle as Nathan sobs, curling into a ball. His face is raw and bloody, his lips swollen, and still, I want to keep hitting him. I want to punish him. I want—

This isn't me. This is Steven's memory.

With an effort, I yank myself back to the present. My eyes snap open, and I jerk the visor up. I'm gasping, drenched with sweat, staring at the ceiling of my basement.

"Sorry," Steven says. His head is turned away from me, toward the wall. "Didn't mean to start thinking about that."

"It's all right." I try, unsuccessfully, to keep my voice steady. "Was—was he the one you told me about before?"

"Yeah." His voice registers no emotion.

I gulp. "He said he knew her secret. What was he talking about?"

There's a pause. "She was a cutter," he says quietly.

"Self-injury?"

He nods, staring at the wall. "If he'd reported her for that, she would've been reclassified as a Type Three. They would've Conditioned her or put her in a treatment facility against her will. And word would've leaked out. Word always gets out. Things would have gotten worse for her at school."

The room spins, and I close my eyes, dizzy. Sweat cools on my forehead. "What happened to her?" I whisper.

"After that, you mean? She never spoke to me again. I think she was scared of me."

My chest aches. I know I should disapprove of his actions. But all I can think about is how much it must have hurt for him to lose his friend.

Focus. I'm here to do a job. "Let's proceed." I slide the visor down. "I want you to clear all those other memories from your mind and go into your first memory from your kidnapping."

"I don't remember being kidnapped. I just remember waking up in that place."

"Let's start there."

I'm sinking again—deeper this time. I feel as though I'm in a lake, floating slowly toward the bottom, the light dimming until cold, heavy blackness presses in all around me. Even my own breathing recedes into silence.

Darkness. Then a flicker. Soft, blurred shapes become images.

I'm in a room with cracked, dirty cement walls. A dull pain throbs behind my eyes, and there's something warm and sticky on my head, plastering my hair to my skin. Blood?

Everything aches. It's cold. So cold. I shiver and try to stand up, but my hands and feet are tied with rough, scratchy rope. There's a rag stuffed in my mouth, and it tastes like dirt and sour sweat.

I have to pee. I wriggle, but the ropes won't loosen.

The door creaks open, and a man in a stained white shirt enters. He's huge, broad-shouldered, with a bald head and tiny dark eyes. His face is rubbery, his nose enormous and squashed-looking, his lips fishy and thick. A scar runs from his temple to his jaw.

He stares at me, and I stare at him. For a moment, he just stands there. Then he smiles. He has only a few teeth, little yellow stumps. Slowly, he approaches, dragging his feet across the cement. He crouches so that his face is level with mine. "Hi, Steven," he says. His voice is very deep, very quiet.

I whimper through the gag.

"You don't know who I am," he says. "But I know about you. I know you're sad. You don't have any friends, do you?" He strokes my—Steven's—hair.

Oh God.

"That's all over. I'm your friend now. I'm the only friend you need."

This isn't happening. I'm not—this—

"You'll like it here. We're going to play lots of games. You like games, right?"

Not real. Just neural impulses traveling through a computer.

He stands. "How about some music?"

A strange, ancient-looking, boxy gray machine sits in the corner. It has a clear window with circles inside. He walks over to it now and pushes a button, and the little wheels behind the window start to turn. A woman's voice, singing in French, emanates from the speakers.

Steven doesn't know the song, but I recognize "Les Cloches

du Hameau," and for an instant, I'm Lain Fisher again. Then she breaks apart and dissolves.

The sound coming from the machine is dim and scratchy. The man whistles along. I don't move. I don't make a sound, don't even breathe.

Still whistling, he walks toward me, until I'm drowned in his shadow.

When I finally take off my helmet, I'm numb, inside and out. There's a sense that I'm surfacing from a long, dark dream. My throat prickles with thirst, and I swallow. A sour taste lingers in the back of my mouth.

I glance at the clock. I've been in Steven's mind for three hours.

Slowly, I sit up. A twinge shoots through my muscles, and I wince, rubbing one stiff shoulder. I feel bruised. Beaten, like I've been thrown off a truck and left to die by the side of the road. It seems as if I should be bleeding everywhere. "I think that's enough for tonight." My voice sounds oddly flat and distant to my own ears.

Steven pulls off his helmet and sets it aside. His face is drawn and pale. "Yeah." Sweat gleams on his brow. He moistens his lips with the tip of his tongue and raises glassy, dazed eyes to mine. "You saw all that?"

"Yes."

Steven closes his eyes and rubs them with the heels of his hands.

"Are you all right?" I ask, because I have to say *something*.

"Peachy," Steven mutters.

A lump swells in my throat. I choke it down. I will not let myself cry. "I'm sorry."

He shrugs. "Not your fault."

I want to reach out, to offer comfort somehow. But the space between us feels as wide as the ocean, as the distance between planets. There's nothing to say. What he endured at the hands of Emmett Pike was worse than anything I could have imagined. Words are meaningless in the face of such pain.

"How many sessions did you say this'll take?" he asks.

I struggle to focus my mind. The room seems so cold. Is it just me? "Maybe four, maybe six. Not more than six." I clutch my bracelet. "For older memories, the mapping stage takes longer."

He wipes his sweat-damp brow with his sleeve and slides out of the chair.

I stand, too. My knees wobble, and I grip the chair's arm for support. My whole body feels weak, unsteady, though the phantom aches and pains are starting to fade, at least. "Do you need anything?"

He shakes his head.

I think about Steven, huddled in the corner of that dark room. So alone. So scared.

Before I can stop it, a tear slips from the corner of my eye. My hand flies to my cheek. It's been a long time since I've cried after an immersion session. I usually have better control than that. Quickly, I knuckle away the tear, but it's too late. He noticed.

"Lain . . ." His voice is soft, startled.

My hands are shaking. I cross my arms over my chest, trying to hide it. "Don't worry about me."

He stares at me, eyes wide. "You didn't just see it. You *felt* it. All of it."

I look away, not wanting to confirm, unable to deny.

"I didn't know," he whispers. "Lain, I . . . I didn't know it was like that. I thought it would just be like watching a recording for you."

I shake my head. "If only." I give him a small, wry smile, though it fades quickly. "There's a reason most initiates don't make it through their first year."

He looks like he might be sick. "I don't want you to go through that. I *can't* . . ."

"Steven." I school my features into a neutral mask. "I agreed to this. I knew what I was getting into, and I'm trained to deal with the emotional repercussions. If I can't handle this, then I'll never make it as a Mindwalker. I intend to finish what we've started."

The silence hovers between us. I can see the pain in his eyes. Pain for me. He's the one who actually endured this nightmare, the one who's had to live with it all these years, yet he's worried about me. It makes me ache, and it's all I can do to keep my expression calm and inscrutable.

At last, he lowers his head and gives a small nod. "I just . . ." His voice is hoarse, cracked. He rakes a trembling hand through his hair. "If I'd known, I wouldn't have asked. I could never ask someone to go through that for me."

"Well, I'm glad you came to me. I want to help." I'm

pleased that my voice sounds almost normal. I even manage a tiny smile. He doesn't return it.

We walk up the stairs, into the living room, and he slips his jacket on. "So . . ." He trails off awkwardly and shifts his weight.

"We can meet again tomorrow," I say. "Why don't I give you my cell number? You can call me if you need anything."

The ghost of a smile twitches across his lips. "Girls aren't usually this eager to give me their number."

Maybe joking is just how he copes with stress, but still, a flush rises into my cheeks. I try to ignore it as I recite my number. He programs it into his phone, which he then slips back in his pocket. "Think you could give me a ride to the nearest monorail station?"

"Sure." I remember the way he devoured the calamari. "Do you want to take some food with you?"

He squints. "Why?"

I pause. If he thinks I feel sorry for him, he might not take it. "Oh, I always buy too much. It's more than I can eat on my own."

He chews his lower lip. I can see the longing in his eyes, the hunger. But he shakes his head. "You're already doing this for free. I don't feel right taking your food on top of everything else."

"Steven . . ."

"I'll be fine." He gives me a tiny, one-sided smile. "Really. I get by."

"Oh, for goodness' sake," I blurt out. "Take *one* thing, at least."

He looks startled, then shrugs with one shoulder. "If you insist."

In the kitchen, he examines the fruit bowl on my counter, selects a single bright red apple, and slips it into his pocket. At my questioning look, he says, "Been a while since I've had one of these. The real thing, I mean, not that genetically engineered crap they serve at school."

An apple won't fill him up, but it's better than nothing, I guess.

I drive to the monorail station, a huge concrete building with advertisements shimmering across the walls. People flow in and out through the revolving door as we stand on the sidewalk outside. "Should we meet in the usual place after school?" I ask.

He nods. After a brief hesitation, he pulls a folded piece of paper from his pocket and holds it out to me. "Here."

I take it. "What's this?"

"You wanted to see one of my drawings. Well, here it is."

Surprised, I unfold it. Lines of ink stand out, crisp black against the white. A sphinx rears up on its hind legs, wings spread, every feather and furred muscle rendered in exquisite detail. When I study the drawing more closely, a tingle of electricity races down my spine. "It has my face."

He doesn't respond.

It's amazing how he's managed to capture my features so perfectly with just a few strokes of the pen. But the drawing flatters me. I don't normally have such a determined look in my eyes, do I? Determined, yet somehow haunted and vulnerable at the same time, like a child facing some unspeakable horror. Is this how he sees me?

Self-conscious, I raise my eyes. "Why a sphinx?"

"No reason."

Lightly, I trace the wings with my fingertips. "It's beautiful. May I keep it?"

He fidgets. "Sure. Whatever."

"Thank you."

We look at each other in the light of the setting sun. I want to say something to him, but I don't know what. *Don't leave,* maybe.

His gaze flicks away. "See you tomorrow, Doc." He pulls the apple out of his pocket and takes a big, wet bite. Then he turns, walks toward the station, and disappears through the revolving door. For a few minutes, I linger, clutching the drawing. I watch the mono pull into the station, then glide away, taking Steven with it.

Abruptly, Pike's leering face flashes through my mind. A cramp seizes my stomach, and bile surges up my throat. I choke it down, close my eyes, and walk through my compartmentalization exercises. I visualize myself tucking the memories away in a wooden chest and locking it tight. Pike's face will find its way into my nightmares, I'm sure. But for now, it fades away.

Wanting a distraction, I return to studying the drawing. In myths, sphinxes usually ask riddles of travelers, and sometimes devour the ones who can't answer correctly. Despite his denial, I wonder if Steven *did* have some reason behind the choice— perhaps a subconscious one. Or maybe I'm overanalyzing it.

Such an odd, complicated, fascinating boy. Now that I've seen the inside of his head, I'm more determined than ever to help him. But it goes beyond that. I think about the concern in his eyes after I surfaced from his memories. I remember his fierce desire to punish the man who hurt his friend. My fingertips wander over the ink lines, stroking them. He said he usually burns his art after he finishes. Why? Why would he hide this talent from the world? Whatever the reason, I'm honored that he chose to show it to me.

Carefully, I refold the drawing and slip it into my pocket.

There's so much more to Steven than his trauma. I want to learn more about this broken, resilient young man. I want to find out who he is outside of the pain and darkness.

In the courtroom of my skull, my psych-ethics teacher murmurs disapproval.

"The government is breeding us!" a man shouts, jarring me from my thoughts. "They're breeding us like cattle!"

My head snaps up. Outside the monorail station stands a thin, wild-eyed figure dressed in ragged clothes, his hair sticking up in every direction. A collar glints at his throat. He holds out a flyer to a passing woman, who ducks and hurries past. "Can't you tell what's happening?" Even from this distance, I can see the spittle flecking the corners of his mouth. "We're all cattle!" His gaze locks onto me, and I tense.

He walks quickly toward me, holding out a flyer. I stare into his wide, bloodshot eyes. "Join the resistance," he says.

"No thank you," I reply quietly. I turn and start to walk toward my car.

He follows. "There's a war coming," he says. "You have to be ready. Everything will come crashing down. There'll be blood in the streets—" He freezes, head raised, nostrils quivering, like a rabbit scenting the air for a predator. The stack of flyers falls out from under his arm, and the papers scatter on the damp pavement.

A sleek police car pulls up, and an officer steps out, holding an ND.

"It's all right," I say quickly. "He wasn't trying to hurt me."

"No need to be concerned," the officer says, tipping his hat to me. "We're just taking him in for treatment. We've received complaints that he's been disturbing the peace here again."

The corner of the man's eye twitches. He pulls something from his pocket—a pen, it looks like—and aims it at the policeman. "Don't make me use this."

The officer rolls his eyes and says, almost kindly, "Come on, Marv." He takes a step forward and holds out a hand. "Let's go. You'll feel a lot better after it's over."

The man—Marv—grips the pen in trembling fists. "I'm warning you! I'll *use* it!"

"What are you gonna do, write on me?" He chuckles.

A tear slips down Marv's stubbled cheek. "Butchers! You're fucking butchers, all of you! You—" His eyes lose focus, and he sways on his feet. The pen drops from his slackening grip as he starts to slump forward.

The policeman catches him, slides him into the car like so much luggage, and buckles his seat belt. He picks up the pen, then gets behind the wheel and nods to me. The car drives off, leaving me staring after it uneasily.

The collar senses aggression and acts accordingly, even if the person's not holding a real weapon. It's one of the few times I've actually seen it in action.

I start to turn, then notice the flyers still scattered across the pavement. I bend to pick one up. It's nonsense, a mishmash of incomprehensible sentences filled with exclamation points and capital letters. *Join the resistance*, he said. But of course, there is no resistance. The Blackcoats are gone—and that, I remind myself, is a good thing. A man who might once have set off a bomb or mowed down innocents with a machine gun is now reduced to waving a pen at a police officer before being carted away for his ethically questionable but ultimately humane and painless treatment.

I try to ignore the knot in my throat as I get into my car and whisper, "Take me home."

10

When I get home, Greta is wiping down the coffee table in the living room. She wasn't supposed to come in today. Did Dr. Swan send her to check up on me? "Um. Hello."

She smiles at me. "Hi, Lain. How was school?"

"Fine, thank you."

"Careful, I just vacuumed."

I slide off my shoes. We've always been friendly with each other, but it's superficial. She asks me the right questions and I give the right answers. She's here to spy on me, and she knows that I know it, so there's no point in getting too close.

"So," she says. "Where've you been? Out with a friend?" Her tone is casual, but her eyes are suddenly intent.

"Alone," I say. "I had tea at the Underwater Café."

"Eaten yet?"

I shake my head.

"How about I cook some dinner?"

"No thank you." I force a smile. "I think I'll just fix something for myself tonight."

"One of those frozen meals?" She purses her lips with disapproval. "That stuff's loaded with chemicals. They don't even use real meat. I saw this documentary where they grow this fake beef in a lab. Blech. I tell you, I'm never going *near* that stuff again."

A small, sharp point of pain pulses behind my left eye. "I'll have a salad." *Go. Just go. Please.* "Thank you for the offer, though."

"Okay. Don't stay up too late." She gathers her cleaning supplies. I wait until she leaves the house, then I heat up a frozen dinner and flop down on the couch. Steam billows out as I peel back the film from my imitation sirloin with carrots and a brownie, all in their own little compartments. The meal resembles a piece of abstract art, with bright, artificial colors and food molded into shapes too precise to be the work of nature.

Why did Dr. Swan send her here tonight? Does he suspect I've been spending time with Steven?

I'm too worn out to worry about it now. I turn on the TV and flip automatically to the news channel.

"Up next," an announcer says, "a woman determined to die. Representative Caroline Mackey, a member of the General Ethics Committee of Aura, has struggled for years with debilitating health problems. Now she's suing her doctor for refusing to write her a Somnazol prescription. The doctor claims she has not explored all her treatment options, but Mackey says he's simply imposing his moral judgment on her."

The camera cuts to a thin middle-aged woman sitting at a table, hands folded in front of her. Her head is shaved and scarred, a stark contrast to her elegant blue suit. "This is my life and my decision." She stares straight into the camera, hollow-cheeked and grim. "I've evaluated all my options, and I can't see any realistic possibility of a life without constant pain. I'm ready for voluntary passing, and I don't think some doctor should be able to stop me."

What a strange combination of determination and despair—someone going to such lengths to die when death is available to anyone with a razor or a bottle of sleeping pills. But then, if someone voluntarily passes, her family receives full life insurance benefits. That's not the case if someone commits suicide illegally.

"Mackey's situation has been receiving attention from both sides of the debate," the announcer continues. "The renewed controversy over Somnazol has stirred up protests." The screen displays a demonstration, people waving signs with messages like DO NO HARM and DEATH IS NEVER THE ANSWER.

Disgusted, I turn off the TV. Where were all these protesters when Steven was applying for his Somnazol?

Of course, despite her many physical problems, Mackey's still a Type One—she must be if she's a representative. No doctor wants to destroy a healthy mind. Yet they hand out the pills like candy to Fours and flood the media with propaganda telling us that Somnazol is the ethical and responsible choice for those who are irreparably damaged, that society has become much more peaceful and orderly since it was legalized. No one wants to bother trying to fix broken people, especially those without the money to pay for real treatments. Much easier to just let them die.

Sometimes I hate this country.

I poke at my food, rolling around a tiny wheel of carrot. My appetite has abandoned me. Steven's memories keep replaying in my mind—all the months of hell, long periods of dread and loneliness broken only by visits from his captor. All the nights spent crying, muffling his sobs against the filthy mattress where he slept.

I wonder about the other children. I never saw them in his memories. Were they held captive separately? Or were they already dead by the time Pike found Steven?

Maybe it doesn't matter. After our final session, those memories will be gone from Steven's mind. His eyes will open, soft and puzzled, like the eyes of a sleeper awakening from a long, dark dream. He will forget me, too. He'll leave, fresh and clean as a newborn, with all his horror and sadness scrubbed away.

But that horror will remain within me. I will never forget what happened in that small, dark room or the tears of that terrified boy.

I hug my knees to my chest.

If Father were here, he'd wrap me up in his arms and know the exact words to say. He'd help make sense of this mess in my head. I'd do anything to talk to him again, just for five minutes.

I know I won't be able to sleep, so I go down into the bare, tiled room and turn on the Gate. I face the hard drive and wave a hand over the sensor, bringing up the holographic monitor, which displays a rotating image of a brain. Steven's brain. I find myself staring at it, hypnotized by its slow turning.

The room is dim—I didn't bother to switch on the overhead fluorescents—so the only illumination is the screen's pale glow. I replay the readings from the session, watching the flow of neurological activity, like weather patterns moving over the landscape of his gray matter. Unsurprisingly, there's a lot of activity in his amygdalae, the tiny almond-shaped structures connected to fear and memory.

All the horror and sorrow of the human condition—as well as all the joy, wonder, and love—can be reduced to this, chemicals in an organ resembling a lump of cauliflower. Sometimes, I find that comforting. Sometimes, it just makes me feel empty.

I tap spots on the screen, zooming in again and again, until I can see the sprawling networks of neurons, rendered in a soft, transparent blue. I blink a few times.

That's odd.

The untrained eye would see nothing out of the ordinary. But to me, the difference is as striking and bizarre as looking at *The Last Supper* and seeing a cartoon duck sitting among the disciples. I look again. Yes—there's a distinct pattern aberration in his neural networks. Now that I've seen it, I can't unsee it. I place my fingers against the screen and glide through the forest of neurons, following the pattern aberration downward and deeper, along the curved ridge of the hippocampus, toward the center of his brain. It's a scar, buried in his nervous tissue.

I zoom in and out. As I pull further back, my stomach turns hollow.

It's not just *one* scar, but a tangle of jagged overlapping lines, like a war zone pockmarked by land mines and grenades. Did Pike do this to him? He must have. But *how?* This doesn't look like the result of torture or injury. In fact—I squint, studying the screen—if I didn't know better, I'd say this was done by a Gate. The patterns are similar, but there's no way a Mindwalker would ever be this sloppy. This is butchery. Nausea squirms in my middle.

I close the program and bring up another recording—the memories themselves, played out like a movie. The recorded images are grainy and blocky, rendered imperfectly from neural impulses, but I can make out the basement prison and Pike's grinning face. I don't want to see this again, but I have to.

I lean in, watching closely.

Something changes. The image flickers and shifts. It doesn't disappear, but for an instant, I glimpse another image through it, like something seen through foggy glass. Beyond the dirt-streaked cement walls, there are other walls, blank and white. Briefly, Pike's face becomes another face. There's something disturbingly familiar about it, but it's gone too quickly for me to make out the features. The dark basement settles back into place, and I'm left staring, shaken.

What the hell is going on here?

11

My chemistry notes are a blur. They keep floating around on the page, refusing to stay still regardless of how hard I strain my eyes. I swear, I can hear them giggling at me like malevolent imps.

And chemistry is usually easy.

My gaze roams the classroom, which is identical to nearly every other classroom in Greenborough—huge and gray, crammed with desks, watched constantly, filled with listless students who accept it because this is all they've ever known. I rub my dry, sleep-deprived eyes. The teacher's talking, but the words slide through my mind without leaving a mark.

Last night, I spent hours watching and rewatching the recordings from Steven's immersion session, but that flicker—that moment of seeing another image behind the memory—didn't happen anywhere else in the recording. It could be a glitch. But the scars in his brain are certainly real.

What am I supposed to tell Steven? How can I explain it when I don't even know what it means?

My phone vibrates in my pocket. I've fallen into the risky habit of taking it to class, in case he texts me. Like a girl with a crush. But I don't have a crush on him, I remind myself. I'm helping him. That's all.

I check the phone and open the text he sent me.

HEY, DOC. YOU OKAY?

YES.

I'm lying, of course.

YOU SURE?

How does he know? Is it my expression? My posture? Either way, I need to get ahold of myself. Dr. Swan probably reviews the video feeds from my classes from time to time. If I'm showing any obvious distress, he'll notice.

I quickly type in my reply.

I'LL TELL YOU AFTER SCHOOL.

Hearing footsteps coming close, I tense and look up to see the guard approaching. He holds out a hand. "You know the policy on cell phones."

His tone isn't angry, but it's firm. The guards confiscate things from students all the time. It's routine.

"Come on. You'll get it back later." He smiles. "Nothing to

worry about. People don't get reclassified for texting in class, you know."

Reluctantly, I hand over the phone.

Even after it's gone, I can't focus on the teacher's lecture. My mind drifts.

Last night, after I discovered the glitch in Steven's memories, I went to my room and summoned Chloe. She materialized and asked in her cheery, high-pitched voice, "What can I do for you, Lain?"

"Give me all the information you can find on Emmett Pike," I told her.

For a few seconds, she groomed herself, eyes flickering as lines of glowing green text floated across the paler green of her irises. Finally, her eyes projected a bright square into the air. The floating screen displayed surprisingly few results. A smattering of articles, nothing else.

"Open the first article," I told her.

The screen changed, and I found myself staring at a grainy photo of a man with solid, heavy features, dark eyes, and a scar running down the left side of his face. He looked into the camera with a dull, blank expression. A shudder ran through me. That was him—the man who'd haunted Steven's nightmares for the past ten years. But the article itself was brief and contained nothing I didn't already know. "Scroll down," I told Chloe. "Show more results."

Her tail flicked back and forth. "I'm afraid that's all."

"That's it? That can't be it."

"Sorry, Lain." Her ears and tail drooped.

"It's all right. I trust your results. I'm just surprised."

Her ears perked up. "Do you need anything else?"

I shook my head. "That's all."

After Chloe vanished, I stayed awake, musing over what I'd seen. Or hadn't seen, rather.

According to the scarce information, Emmett Pike came from a tiny, isolated town in the Northeast Quadrant, far outside the boundaries of any major city. He grew up in one of the few remaining places without street cameras, so there's no video footage of him in existence, and no one alive who had a personal relationship with him, either. No relatives, no friends, at least none mentioned in any of the articles. Of course, a psychopath who murdered children probably wouldn't have many friends, but even so, the lack of information is a little too convenient. It's as if he never existed.

I remember that other face flickering behind Pike's, and ice water trickles through my bloodstream.

* * *

When I arrive at the Underwater Café, Steven's in our usual booth, arms crossed over his chest. "So," he says, "we gonna do another session today?" When I don't answer, he frowns. "What's wrong?"

I interlace my fingers, pull them apart, and lace them together again. My palms are hot and damp. "Steven, have you ever had any neurological alterations performed on you before this?"

Bewilderment clouds his expression. "Is that a trick question? I mean, don't people usually forget that they've had their memories modified?"

"You're right." It's a moot point, anyway. If his memories

were modified, there'd have been something about it in his file. Unless . . .

The technology involved in memory modification is strictly controlled. But there've always been rumors of illicit back-alley Mindwalkers who will perform any job, no matter how unethical, for a price. Until now, I never put much stock in those rumors, but what if there *are* such people? Is it possible that Steven's memories have been illegally modified? Maybe even against his will?

I clear my throat. "It's just that after the session, I looked over your readings, and there was a pattern aberration in your neural networks. Microscarring in your cortex and hippocampus."

"English, Doc."

"Something odd in your brain."

A shadow of unease slips across his face. "You don't think it's, like, cancer or something, do you?"

"No, no, nothing like that. It looks like the result of a procedure."

"Well, could it have come from Conditioning?"

I shake my head. "Conditioning's not invasive. The effects are temporary."

"Then what?"

"Honestly, I have no idea."

Steven frowns and runs a hand through his cornsilk hair. I glimpse a tiny, round scar on his scalp.

A memory flashes through my mind. I'm back in the filthy basement, my wrists rubbed raw from ropes. "Please," I say between sobs. "Please, I swear, I'll never try to escape again."

Pike looms over me, a whirring drill in one hand. "I know

you won't." His voice is low, almost gentle. "You got everything you need right here. Why would you try to run? That's just crazy." His eyes glint in the dim light. "You know what they did in the Dark Ages when someone started acting crazy?" The drill moved closer, buzzing like a huge hornet. "They'd drill a hole in his skull to let the demons out."

The tip of the drill touches my scalp, and blinding pain sears through my head. I scream.

"Doc? Hey, Doc!"

I snap back to the present, trembling. Did I scream out loud? I look quickly around the room, but no one is staring. I exhale a small breath of relief. "Sorry," I murmur, pressing my fingers to my head.

Could that incident have . . . ? No, of course not. A simple drill wouldn't cause that type of scarring. Pike pulled back before it actually pierced Steven's brain, anyway.

This would be so much easier if I could talk to my superiors at IFEN, ask them about the correct course of action. But given the circumstances, that's out of the question. And I haven't even told Steven everything. There was that flicker I saw in his memories, that other face behind Pike's.

"So, what happens now?" he asks.

I bite my thumbnail, my mind whirring like an engine. When memories are deleted or altered, traces of the original memories sometimes linger. It's difficult for even the most skilled Mindwalker to scrub away everything. But those traces are inaccessible to the client's conscious mind, bits of neural debris floating around in the vast, dark space beneath. If I could find some way to probe deeper into his mind, I might be able to access those fragments of information. Maybe I could—

I give my head a quick, hard shake. There's not enough information. If I start telling him all my wild theories, I'll just alarm him unnecessarily. "That's up to you," I say. "We can proceed with the treatment, or . . . we can try to learn more."

He looks away. "I just want to forget."

Mingled relief and disappointment wash over me. "Then we'll continue the sessions. Though we should probably wait until tomorrow. Greta will be at the house this afternoon."

He nods.

I pay for my chai, which I've barely touched. We linger a few minutes, watching the holographic sea turtle make its slow, ponderous circuit around the restaurant. Steven reaches up to touch it as it passes, but of course, there's nothing to touch.

My cell phone buzzes, jarring me from my reverie. It's a new text:

SEE U TONIGHT?

I wince and palm my face. "Ian! I completely forgot."

"Who, what?"

"I told him I'd show up." I chew the inside of my cheek.

I don't particularly want to go. I'm hopeless at parties. The last time I went to one, I was thirteen—some girl's birthday. I stood in the corner the whole time. A boy tried to strike up a conversation with me, I started babbling about neuroanatomy, and he quickly slipped away.

But this is important to Ian. He wanted so badly for me to come. And maybe I need to take some time away from this mess, find a way to center myself. Perhaps a party will help me shake off this mental fog.

"You should go," Steven says. "You seem like you need a break."

I think about the death pill Steven might be carrying. Even if we can't do a session today, I don't like the idea of leaving him alone.

Then a solution presents itself: a simple, albeit reckless, solution. "Do you want to come with me?"

His mouth opens. He couldn't have looked more surprised if I'd suggested we start dancing naked on top of the table. "You're serious?"

"Of course. Why not?"

"Okay, number one." He holds up one thin finger. "I'm not exactly a social butterfly, as you might've noticed. Number two." Another finger joins the first. "Everyone at school hates my guts."

"I wouldn't say they *hate* you. More like you make them nervous."

He rolls his eyes. "Well, that's a relief."

"They're nervous because they don't really know you," I add. "Because they have only rumors and hearsay to go on. If they have a chance to interact with you . . ."

"They'll be so impressed with my sparkling personality, they'll forget everything else?"

"Um, well . . ."

He chuckles without humor. "Thanks for the invitation, but I think I'll stay home. You'll have more fun without me following you around like a stray cat, anyway."

I imagine him sitting in his apartment with only his memories for company. "Well, I'm not going unless you go. I don't like showing up at parties alone."

He looks thoroughly confused. "You really want me to come with you?"

"I do. I'll ask Ian if it's okay." I text him.

CAN I BRING A FRIEND?

SURE. HAVE I EVER MET HER?

NO, I DON'T THINK SO.

THE MORE, THE MERRIER. :)

I tell myself that I'm not actually lying—I'm just not correcting his assumption. I don't want to explain this awkward, delicate situation through text messages. It'll be simpler if we just show up. "He says it's fine."

The puzzled crease in Steven's brow deepens.

"Come on. It'll be fun. When's the last time you went to a party?"

"I've never been to one."

Suddenly, I don't feel like such a geek. I grin. "Well, there's a first time for everything."

He blows a sigh through one corner of his mouth, puffing his cheek out. "Fine."

Steven at a party. This is something I have to see.

12

That evening, I stand in front of the full-length mirror in my room and try on a few different outfits. I turn around, modeling a light green dress with spaghetti straps. I bought it on impulse a few months ago after seeing it in a store window. I've never actually had the chance to wear it. "Chloe?"

She materializes on my bed. "Yes?"

"What do you think about this dress? Is it too revealing?"

Chloe tilts her head. "I don't know. What do you think?"

"The neck is a little low." Not that I have much to show. I haven't filled out like some of the other girls in my class. "What about the color?"

"Red is more popular this year. But green goes better with your coloring."

My avatar knows more about fashion than I do. I let out a small sigh. In moments like these, I really wish I had a female friend. One with feelings and opinions that aren't based on data algorithms.

I comb my hair out, letting it spill over my shoulders. Maybe I'll wear it down tonight. I roll on a bit of pink lip gloss. When I look into the mirror again, I barely recognize myself. For once, I'm not a Mindwalker. Just a normal girl having a night out. The feeling is unexpectedly pleasant, like a spot of warmth in my chest.

Chloe smiles a sly, teasing smile. "Going out with someone special?"

I give a start. It's probably just one of the programmed questions in her repertoire, a response to a visual analysis of my facial expressions and posture, but there are times when she seems eerily perceptive. I open my mouth to say no, then pause. "Sort of." Before she can ask anything else, I add, "You can deactivate now. I'm heading out."

"Have fun!" Chloe nods and vanishes with a shimmer.

When I walk down the stairs, Greta's vacuuming in the living room. Or rather, she's reading on the couch while a basketball-sized black orb does the work, humming up and down the length of the floor. She looks up and closes the holoscreen. "Where are you off to?" she asks, sounding surprised.

"A party. At Ian's place."

She raises her eyebrows. She'll probably tell Dr. Swan, who'll undoubtedly be pleased to hear that I'm doing normal teenager things. Though he might be less pleased if he knew who I was going with.

I take the car to the Underwater Café, where Steven waits, sitting on a bench outside, with his arms crossed over his chest. When I get out of the car and wave, he stands up. "Hey, you ready to—" He freezes, mouth half open.

I fidget. "Is it too much?" Now that I think of it, I'm probably overdressed. Most people there will be wearing T-shirts and jeans.

"It's fine." Suddenly, he can't seem to look directly at me. "Let's go."

* * *

Ian lives at the top of a high-rise. From outside, it looks like a sleek black obelisk crowned by a huge, translucent jewel. The jewel, of course, is his Plexiglas-walled penthouse apartment. Usually, at night, the penthouse is lit up with a clear white light. Now it's dark, except for flashes of neon blue and red from within.

Steven walks beside me, hands shoved into his pockets, as we enter the lobby. It's all polished pink marble. He whistles. "This guy must be loaded."

"His mother's a very wealthy drug researcher."

"She's okay with him throwing these parties?"

"She's away at work. And she's his only parent. Well, I suppose he *has* a father, but—" I give an awkward shrug. "I don't really know the situation."

Steven snorts. "Maybe he's a clone."

My shoulders stiffen.

"Hell," he continues, "these days, you can't even step inside a mall without seeing those NewVitro ads. 'Hey there, all you rich Type One ladies and gents! Why play the genetic lottery and risk popping out some defective loser when you can get a copy of your own perfect DNA? Just change the sex chromo-

somes or the eye color or whatever and call it individuality!'
It's ridiculous. You'd think humans have forgotten how to—"

"That's my friend you're talking about," I snap. "Even if he
were a clone—which he's not—that remark would be incredibly
offensive." I stare straight ahead, jaw clenched.

He blinks a few times. I expect him to make another
wiseass remark, but he just says, "Sorry."

I take a deep breath, trying to calm myself. "Never mind,"
I mutter, and step into the elevator, which is as large as a normal person's bathroom and has mirrored walls. The numbers
light up as it glides to the top floor, and I start to feel embarrassed at my own reaction. I really should have better control.

"I am sorry," Steven says. "Sometimes I shoot my mouth
off without thinking. I mean, I do think those ads are stupid,
but I don't have anything against clo— How should I say it?"

"There really isn't a politically correct term," I murmur.
"Though I hate hearing people referred to as clones. It's so . . .
dehumanizing."

"I won't say it, then."

My shoulders relax. "Thank you."

The elevator continues to move up.

"Can I borrow your scarf?" Steven asks.

Confused, I hand it to him. He wraps it quickly around his
face and neck, covering his mouth and nose as well as his collar. I realize he doesn't want to be identified.

I wonder if I'm being cruel, dragging him here.

Ian buzzes me in, and the doors slide open to reveal a living room crammed with people milling around with drinks in
their hands, talking and laughing. A heavy bass beat thumps,

vibrating in the floor and in my bones. I'm not exactly over-dressed, just very out of place. I see a lot of leather and fishnet and miniskirts so short that I feel silly for worrying that my dress was too revealing. Next to some of these outfits, it's as modest as a nun's habit. Claustrophobia jangles my nerves as we push deeper into the apartment. The onslaught of sensory stimuli leaves my brain burning like an overheated engine.

Ian loves things like this. It's how he deals with stress. I retreat deeper into myself and shut out the world—he drowns himself in crowds and music.

A boy bumps into me, nearly spilling a drink down the front of my dress. "Whoops." He laughs. "Sorry."

"Watch it," Steven snarls at the boy, then hooks an arm through mine. There's something protective, almost posses-sive, in the gesture. His pale blue eyes dart back and forth, scanning the crowd as we make our way through the crush of bodies.

In front of me, a man with the head of a gray wolf is danc-ing, mouth open in a toothy grin. A gasp leaps from my throat.

"You okay?" Steven asks.

A half second later, realization clicks into place; it's a ho-lomask. They're all the rage at parties, or so I've heard, but it's the first time I've actually seen someone wearing one. "Yes," I say, breathless and a little embarrassed. I look around. Nearby, a girl with the head of a white rabbit is holding a beer, chatting and giggling. The mask's mouth moves with eerie realism. As I watch, she takes a pill and washes it down with a swig of beer.

I spot Ian in the kitchen, a bottle in one hand. "There he is," I tell Steven. "I'm going to go say hi."

"I'm gonna go find the bathroom," Steven mutters.

Of course. He doesn't want to talk to anyone. I suppose I can't blame him. But at least here, surrounded by people, he's not liable to kill himself. "It's down the hall." I tug my arm free and maneuver my way into the kitchen, which is large and modern, all marble tile and gleaming chrome. There's a table covered with bottles—in a wide variety of sizes and colors—a bowl of punch, and a tray of nachos drenched in gooey orange cheese and guacamole. "Ian!" I wave.

Ian turns toward me. "Lain." He smiles, but his eyes are glazed—the same shell-shocked look I remember from the other day. "So, what do you think?"

"Of the party? It's . . . intense."

"Yeah." He rocks on his heels, then takes a swig of whatever's in the bottle. "You know, parties usually relax me. But it's not working tonight. No matter how loud I crank up the music, I can still hear my thoughts."

I frown. I can see his pulse fluttering in his throat. "What's wrong?"

"Nothing." He keeps rocking. A sheen of sweat gleams on his brow.

"You haven't been acting like yourself lately."

"You don't know the half of it." He laughs. It's not his usual warm laugh—it's too sharp, too high-pitched. Then he leans closer to me. "I'm really glad you could make it tonight," he murmurs. I catch a whiff of alcohol on his breath. He makes an odd, choked sound. "You're the only real friend I've got. You know that?"

I tense. I have no idea what's going on, but I'm not sure I like it. "What do you mean? You have lots of friends."

"They don't understand." His brown eyes mist over. He lets

out another jagged laugh and presses the heel of one hand against his forehead. "I can't even look at them. I can't look at anyone."

"Ian . . . what—"

"I can't stand this anymore." The bottle slips from his fingers and clanks to the floor, spilling foamy amber liquid across the tiles. He takes a step toward me. I try to move backward, away from him, but my shoulders hit the wall. He places his hands on either side of me, trapping me there, and leans in. "Help me," he whispers. "Make me forget."

I grab his wrists. "You're drunk! You need to stop—"

His lips press against mine, silencing me. The kiss is hard and fierce, but it's more desperate than passionate, as if he's suffocating and I'm the only source of air. I make a muffled noise of protest and shove him away. He staggers back.

"Ian, get ahold of yourself!"

He looks at me, his expression dazed. He blinks, and his eyes clear, as if he's awakening from a trance. "Lain." His voice is soft, stunned. "I—I'm sorry. I—"

There's a blur of motion, and Steven slams into him like a white-blond wrecking ball. Ian stumbles to one side. Steven seizes the front of his shirt and rams him up against the wall. His fist plows into Ian's jaw, knocking his head to one side. Ian's face registers momentary shock, then panic. With a roar, he shoves Steven. "Don't touch me!" He lashes out with one fist, but Steven ducks, dodging the blow. He grabs Ian and wraps an arm around his throat from behind, squeezing. Ian gasps, his eyes bugging out.

"Steven!" I cry, alarmed. "Let go!"

"Don't touch her." Steven forces the words through clenched teeth. "Don't ever touch her."

There's a tinkle of breaking glass. Someone screams. Ian's mouth is open, his face flushed an alarming purplish red. He elbows Steven in the gut, and Steven grunts but doesn't let go. Ian flails until his fingers close around the hilt of a serrated knife on the counter.

I lunge forward, grab his wrist and Steven's hair, and try to pull them apart.

Steven's body jerks. Ian freezes. For an instant, neither one of them moves. Steven's eyes stare glassily into space, then roll back, and his body slumps and crumples to the floor. He lands with a thud, facedown. Ian's knife slips from his fingers and clatters to the tiles.

The music still thumps and grinds in the background, but the crowd has fallen silent. Ian stands, gasping and clutching his throat as his face slowly returns to its usual color. Steven doesn't move.

Ian stares at me, his eyes wide. "What happened to him?"

"The collar." Bile climbs into my throat. I swallow.

"Is he . . ."

"He's just unconscious." I don't want to talk. I can't even look at Ian right now. I'm too confused, too shaken.

Steven stirs, groaning.

"Hey, it's him," someone whispers.

A low hum of voices sweeps through the room. People inch away from Steven. Then a few start moving toward him. Their expressions darken, turning from fear to contempt. Someone kicks him in the ribs, and he flinches.

"Stop it!" I shout. "All of you, get away from him!"

"What's it to you?" a girl asks.

I glare at her. "He's my friend."

"Your friend?" She says it like it's a foreign concept.

"Yes!" I snap.

Steven tries to stand, stumbles, and falls to his knees. I have to get him out of here. I help him to his feet. He sways on rubbery legs, and I slip an arm around his waist. No one says a word, but I feel their eyes on us as we make our way slowly toward the elevator. People whisper. Girls snuggle against their boyfriends' shoulders, as if for protection.

Steven is still staggering when we make it out of the building, into the cool night air, but at least he can walk now. I help him into the passenger's seat of the car, then slide behind the wheel and slam the door. "Take us home," I say.

The car pulls out of its space. My phone buzzes. It's a voice mail from Ian. I delete it without listening. Guilt pricks my heart, because I have the feeling Ian's as miserable and confused as I am, but it's just too much to deal with right now. Until tonight, he's never given even the slightest indication that he's attracted to me. I tell myself that one drunken kiss doesn't necessarily mean anything.

Steven leans back in his seat, chest rising and falling with his labored breaths. It seems the drug is still in his system. His eyes are cloudy, his face wet with perspiration. I wonder if it causes him pain as well.

"You didn't have to attack him," I say quietly. "He wouldn't have hurt me. He was just . . ." Just what? I don't even know how to finish that sentence.

"You were scared," Steven murmurs.

I swallow, my throat tight. He's right. I *was* scared, but not for myself. For Ian. I think he might be losing his mind, but

I'm afraid to speak the words aloud, because I feel like if I do, my fear will become reality.

I should report his behavior to IFEN, for his own good. He's in no state to be taking on clients. Yet the idea of going behind his back is repellent to me. If they scan him now, he'll probably come up as a Two or worse, and that will affect his future as a Mindwalker. Still, I can't do nothing. Next time I see him, maybe I'll encourage him to seek therapy.

I close my eyes. "I'm sorry."

"What are you sorry for?" His voice is faint and scratchy. "I'm the one who lost it." He gives a weak chuckle. "Guess you regret bringing me to that party."

"No, I don't. But I don't want anything like that to happen again. Will you promise not to attack anyone else, for my sake?"

"Don't know if I can promise that, Doc."

"Steven, I mean it. I can take care of myself. And I don't want you to hurt anyone or get in trouble."

There's a long silence.

"Steven?"

"Are you afraid of me now?" he whispers.

"No."

"It's okay if you are. I wouldn't blame you. I practically strangled him."

I hesitate. Then, slowly, I reach out and lay a hand over his. "I'm not afraid."

He looks at me, expression unreadable.

His knuckles are scratched, bleeding. I'm getting blood on my hand, but I don't care. My fingers tighten around his.

The car glides down the road. Advertisements glisten around

us, flowing across the walls of buildings, drifting through the air. A holographic banner for Lucid hovers in the air.

Uncover your mind's potential.

The words float over the image of a smiling woman in a business suit. This part of the city is all shopping districts and expensive apartments. The less glamorous areas—like the treatment facilities and housing projects—are confined to the outskirts.

"Lain?"

"Yes?"

The muscles of his throat work as he swallows. Strands of hair cling to his sweat-damp brow. "Once this is all over, once you erase my memories, I won't remember any of this, will I? I won't remember you."

I stare out the window, unable to look at his face as I answer, "No. You won't." That's one of the reasons Mindwalkers aren't supposed to get emotionally attached to their clients. It just causes pain, in the end. "Memories are tied together in clusters. In your mind, I'm linked with your kidnapping. Erasing your pain will also erase me."

"That's how it is, huh?"

My hand tightens on his. Then I force myself to let go and interlace my fingers in my lap. "That's how it is."

* * *

I drop Steven off at his apartment: a huge, featureless gray building on a narrow street lined with other huge, featureless gray buildings. This district is mostly government housing. Each apartment complex contains hundreds upon hundreds of tiny rooms, stacked on top of each other, for people who can't afford to live anywhere else. This is the sort of place where orphans like Steven usually end up once they turn eighteen.

I wonder where he lived before this. A state home? Or has he spent most of his life in treatment facilities?

The buildings are divided by strips of stubby yellow grass littered with broken glass. In the distance, I hear the wail of a police siren as I walk him to the door. We stand there for a moment, awkward silence hanging over us. "I feel like I should be the one walking you to the front door," he says.

"I don't mind." I smile.

The dim moonlight steals the color from his eyes, turning them almost dark. He's looking at me so intently. What does he see? Who am I to Steven? "You look good in green," he says at last.

My breath catches.

"See you later, Doc." He presses the pad of his thumb against the biometric scanner. The door clicks open, and he disappears inside.

I linger outside the door for a while longer, looking up at the rows of tiny windows.

That night, I lie awake in bed, staring at the ceiling and remembering the warm pressure of his fingers intertwined with mine. There's a little flutter in my stomach, a stirring of something unfamiliar.

I hug Nutter, curling around him in a fetal position.

Of course I don't want Steven to forget me. I don't want to be left behind. But it's better this way. Better for him.

I drift into the murky waters of half sleep, wander in and out of dreams. Bits of information rise up in my head, like objects floating to the surface of a lake, then disappear.

Steven. Pike. Seven children. One survivor.

A scar, glimpsed through cornsilk hair.

A single photo. A man conjured out of nightmares.

A child's voice calling to me from the shadows of a forest. Find me.

I'm running through the forest, pushing through wispy gray branches, and I realize they're not branches at all. They're neurons. All around me, spidery gray webs flicker with muted light. I'm plunging deeper, deeper, toward a faint, pulsing gray glow.

13

As a child, I never wondered what I wanted to do when I grew up. I always knew. Other little girls played school or house with their dolls. I played Mindwalker. I'd set Nutter or Freddy Frog on a stool and have conversations with them about their traumatic pasts, then put a plastic teacup on their heads and pretend it was a Gate. At age ten, I would sit at the dinner table with Father and his friends, my legs not quite long enough to reach the floor, and join in their discussions about neuroscience, sipping grape juice from a wineglass. They'd chuckle as I stumbled over words like *hippocampus* and *amygdala*.

Back then, IFEN hadn't even started to train Mindwalkers, at least not formally. The field of neural modification therapy was still new, still experimental. Experts were batting around the benefits and drawbacks, like cats with a toy. In spite of this, my father was already working with clients, mostly volunteers from treatment facilities. Type Fours. During their visits, he always told me to go to my room, but sometimes I would sneak partway down the stairs and peek into the living room, watching Father talk to them, these men and women with scars and haunted eyes. He treated them with respect and kindness. Like equals.

I sometimes wonder—if I'd had a different childhood, an ordinary family, would I still have wanted to become a Mindwalker? But that's like asking myself what I'd want if I were a different person altogether. I can't separate my past from myself.

One day at the breakfast table—I was about eleven—Father said to me, "You know, Lainy, you and I are very lucky. We have so much, and it's easy for people like us to take our health and happiness for granted."

I chewed a spoonful of cereal, looking at him in the sunlight. He was a big man, square-shouldered, with a neatly trimmed brown beard and crinkles at the corners of his eyes and mouth. I didn't say anything, just waited, listening intently.

"Others are not so fortunate." He sipped his coffee, staring off into space. "Years ago, there was . . . someone I knew. Someone I was very close to." His voice grew momentarily hoarse. The coffee cup rattled slightly as he set it down. "She was attacked by a group of men who hurt her very badly. A few months later, she took her own life. In the letter she left behind, she told me that dying was the only way she could forget."

I didn't know what to say. I'd known his early life wasn't easy, but he'd never mentioned anything about this until then. I wanted to hug him, to do *something*, but I knew instinctively that I needed to let him finish.

"It seemed so cruel to me," he said, "that after enduring

such horror, a person should have to spend the rest of her life carrying the memory around, weighed down by it, reliving the pain over and over again. If only, I thought. If only there was some way to just wipe away that incident, like it never happened. The technology to pinpoint memories in the brain already existed, and researchers were working on a way to translate neural activity into images that could be viewed by other people. I thought that if I could just take that one step further—if I could create a device that would allow someone not only to observe but to actually *change* a memory—I could give people the power to free themselves from past trauma."

"And you did," I said, a bit shyly. "Didn't you?"

"Yes. It was . . . difficult. But with Emmanuel's help, I created the Mindgate. Of course, we're still researching its effects on volunteers. It hasn't been approved for treating the general public. But I'm confident that in time, the treatment will be available to everyone who needs it. People will have the power to liberate themselves from the past. And Mindwalkers will be the ones to give them that power. It's an important role—an exhilarating role—but a perilous one, too . . . not only because such power is easy to abuse, but because of the toll it takes on its wielder." He picked up a piece of toast, as if to take a bite, then set it down again. "Do you still want to become a Mindwalker, Lainy?"

I nodded eagerly. "I want to help people. Like you."

"Even if it's painful?"

The question puzzled me, but I replied immediately. "Yes."

He took a slow, deep breath and clasped his hands tightly together. The skin around his nails whitened from tension. "There's something I need to show you. Lately, I've been working with some very troubled patients at a place called Lowen Hills. I think it's time for you to understand the nature and purpose of my work." A pause. "After this, if you want to change your mind, I'll understand."

"I won't," I said fiercely.

He smiled at me, but there was something terribly sad in his eyes.

We got into the car—this was back when most cars were still manually operated—and he took me to Lowen Hills. It was an institution, he told me, for the sort of people that no one else would take. People the world had given up on.

I remember everything about that place. Every image, every sound, every smell.

There was a woman who'd clawed off most of her face so that only an eyeless, bandaged lump remained. There was a man with a bald, scarred head who peered through the windows of a gray door, grinning, and whispered all the things he wanted to do to me. Another man was curled in the corner of his room, pulling out clumps of his own hair. On the wall of an empty cell, someone had written:

WE ARE DEAD AND THIS IS HELL.

During the drive home, I was silent. After a while, my father said quietly, "I'm sorry for putting you through that, but you had to see it, sooner or later."

I didn't reply.

"The world is filled with suffering," he continued. "Humans have an obligation to each other, but there are many ways to give back. You have a choice, Lain."

"I understand, Father." My own voice seemed to be coming from far away.

For weeks afterward, I woke screaming from nightmares. Eventually, Father took me to a doctor, and the doctor gave me little white pills that made my sleep deep and dreamless. Father kept apologizing, but I didn't understand why. All he did was show me the truth. The happiness I'd grown up with was the exception, not the norm.

In the end, my visit to Lowen Hills just made me more determined.

Once the bad dreams and anxiety attacks subsided, I began my training with the Mindgate. Father was reluctant. I was only thirteen, after all—too young to treat clients—but I wanted to start learning. So he let me try the Gate with some of his less traumatized volunteers. Soon I became his apprentice. And through me, he discovered a fact that changed everything— adolescents can master the art of Mindwalking much faster and better than adults. A developing, flexible young brain can absorb information and new skills far more efficiently. Within a few months, I had surpassed Father in my ability to navigate and alter the memories of others. My most dramatic success was a young man named Thomas, a Three who'd been severely abused as a child. His parents used to lock him in a tiny wooden box and keep him imprisoned there for days on end. His life before the treatment was an endless struggle with depression, addiction, and self-injury. Once the memories were gone, that all ended. He went on to start a successful business, marry, and have two children, things that would probably never have been possible for him before.

I still remember his sad, gentle brown eyes.

When IFEN learned about my success, they started recruiting more teenagers. Father was uneasy, but he went along with his colleagues because he believed so strongly in the therapy's potential. So I continued my training while IFEN began pushing the program more and more aggressively.

Father had begun to change. I could see it. He looked tired, hollowed out, like something inside him was gnawing away at his strength. He argued with Dr. Swan and the rest of his colleagues—when they talked at all. He stopped seeing clients, for reasons he wouldn't explain, and had to hide away his Gate or risk having it confiscated. He told Dr. Swan he'd scrapped it.

There is one memory that stands out with eerie clarity. I'd spent the night tossing and turning. Finally, I came down the stairs for a glass of water and heard my father in the kitchen. I froze just outside the doorway, holding my breath. I could see his shadow on the wall as he paced, a phone to his ear, talking in a hushed, fierce voice. I couldn't make out the words, but I could tell he was angry. Very angry and very scared.

A part of me wanted to go into the kitchen, to ask him what was wrong, but I was afraid. I'd never heard Father sound like that. So I crept up the stairs, to my bedroom, and hugged Nutter to my chest.

Father's death occurred just a few months later. For years afterward, I wondered: If I had done something, told someone, could I have saved him?

14

My cell phone alarm beeps. I groan, roll over, and fumble until I knock the phone off my nightstand. The beeping falls silent. After a while, I sit up, pushing tangled hair from my face, and squint at the clock. Adrenaline jolts me.

I'm late. *Extremely* late.

I scramble out of bed, shower, brush my teeth, and throw on my uniform in record time. On my way out of the house, I grab a cereal bar. I hold it in my mouth as I button up my coat and shoulder open the front door. A blast of cold, crisp air hits me in the face.

I stop. There's someone standing in my driveway: a girl in a pink coat with long, messy dark hair. With a shock, I recognize her. The cereal bar slips from between my teeth and falls to the ground.

What is she doing here? She shouldn't even remember me.

I advance cautiously, the way I might approach a wild animal. "Debra?"

She stands stiffly, hugging herself, her breath steaming in the cold air. "Are you Lain Fisher?"

"That's me." I give her a smile, but her expression remains tight and unyielding. I clear my throat and put on my calm, empty Mindwalker face. "How can I help—"

"What did you make me forget?"

My stomach muscles tighten, squeezing.

I've heard of this happening to other Mindwalkers—clients putting the pieces together, realizing that they've had their memories modified, and tracking down the one who did it, demanding answers. But it's only been a few days. How did she find out where I live?

"What did you make me forget?" she repeats, louder.

I shift my weight, uneasy. "I can't tell you that."

"Oh, I think you can." I can almost feel the heat radiating from her glare.

I breathe in, remembering my training. *Just hold firm.* "I'm sorry. We had an agreement, even if you don't remember it now. You wanted to forget everything."

She takes a step toward me. "Yesterday, a girl came to my house, wanting to talk to me. My mom tried to chase her away, but I snuck out to see her. She asked me why I hadn't been coming to the support group lately. At first, I thought she had the wrong person, but she called me by name. I asked her what support group she was talking about. It was a group for abuse survivors." Her shoulders tremble. "Mom claimed that the girl had confused me with someone else. But I kept asking. I asked over and over until she told me the truth—that I'd had my memories erased. She wouldn't tell me *what* had been erased.

But I put the pieces together." She bows her head, clutching her coat tightly around herself. "It was my stepfather, wasn't it?"

My stomach sinks. If she's already learned this much, there's no point in denying it. "Yes," I whisper.

She nods slowly. "I just needed to hear you say it. To know."

For a few heartbeats, a wall of silence stands between us. "How did you find me?" I ask quietly.

"I remembered seeing your face when I woke up in that place. It was cloudy. Like a dream. But it was enough." A flat, bitter sound, more sob than laugh, escapes her lips. "I guess everyone thought it was for the best. I mean, I spent years being miserable, didn't I? I don't remember it now, but I probably tried a lot of stuff. Medication. Conditioning. And none of it worked. If it had, I wouldn't be here now, would I? So much easier to just wipe away everything bad. But now . . ." Her breathing echoes through the silence. She presses slender fingers to her temples. "I remember how to do math and drive a car. I remember that Paris is the capital of France, and I remember all these stupid commercial jingles and pop songs. But I try to remember who I am, what I'm like, and there's nothing but fog. That girl, the one from the support group . . . she says I was the only person who ever really understood her. After the treatment, I didn't even remember her face."

A twinge of pain shoots through my chest. I close my eyes for a moment, collecting myself. "Your memories were deeply rooted. I had to take out a lot. I explained all that to you before the procedure." Of course, that means nothing to her now. "I realize this is difficult. But it gave you a fresh chance. A new start."

"So I'm supposed to pretend like it never happened?" Her

hands squeeze into tight fists. Slowly, she raises her head. Her eyes are hard, despite the tears on her cheeks. "That's not healing. It's just a lie."

The words hit me like a slap. I take a step backward.

"Never mind," she mutters. She turns and walks toward a car parked in the street, her steps quick and jerky.

"Debra, wait." I follow her. "You're upset right now. I understand that. But you *wanted* this." I place a hand on her shoulder. "This is something you chose for yourself—"

She pulls away from my touch and spins to face me. "I didn't want the treatment. My mom wanted it."

I freeze. "What?"

"The girl from the support group told me. It wasn't my idea to get my memories erased. My mom pressured me into it because she couldn't deal with all the crying and pills and bad dreams. She couldn't deal with *me*." She wipes her face and shakes her head. A few tears fall to the pavement. "You scraped out everything inside me to get rid of the rotten stuff, and now there's nothing left."

The world seems to be spinning slowly around me. "Debra—"

"I'm not Debra. I don't know who the fuck I am." She looks away. "I don't even know why I came here. It's not your fault. You only did what they told you to, right? It's just a job." But the way she says it makes it sound like a curse. *Just a job.*

"No," I say. "It's not like that."

She scrubs tears from her eyes with the back of one hand and looks at me. The hard edges of her expression soften, anger crumbling to expose the fatigue and sadness beneath. "I've got to go." She gets into the car and drives away.

The world feels very still. There's no breath of wind, nothing to stir the few autumn leaves still clinging to the branches. Everything looks the way it's always looked, the houses neat and orderly. But when I turn to walk toward my car, the ground seems to shift beneath my feet. I stumble. My body moves on autopilot as I get into the car.

My chest hurts. It's becoming more difficult to breathe. Dizziness swims over me, and I realize with academic detachment that I'm having a panic attack. I close my eyes. Breathe in. Breathe out. I recite the standard lines in my head—no one has ever died from a panic attack, in ten minutes this will be over and I'll feel fine, I just have to let my body do what it needs to do. Gradually, the iron bands around my chest loosen, and air flows freely into my lungs. I look into the rearview mirror. My face is a calm mask once again. But Debra's angry words still ricochet around my head.

The cool, dry voice of my psych-ethics professor rises up to counter them: *If a client lashes out at you, you must remember it's not you she's angry at. It's herself or someone who hurt her. Clients often redirect that anger toward us, because we're a safe outlet. Don't take it personally.*

But even if that's true in some cases, it seems a little too easy, too convenient a dismissal—a mantra of rationalization. *It's not me, it's not my fault, it's never me.*

The truth is, it *is* my fault, at least partly. I should never have erased Debra's memories. I should have sensed that she didn't truly want the treatment, that she was being manipulated. Should have asked more questions. Should have checked with someone else. But I didn't. And now half her life is gone.

Am I even qualified to be a Mindwalker?

I float through my morning classes in a haze. Once again,

Steven's not at school. At lunch, I sit in my usual spot. The cafeteria is as huge and barren as the rest of Greenborough, a windowless cement cube filled with long, narrow tables and echoing voices. At one end of the room, a row of women in hairnets dish up imitation beef patties in gravy and mounds of gluey macaroni and cheese. I pick at the food, which holds even less appeal for me than usual.

"Hey."

At the familiar voice, I tense.

Ian sits down across from me. "Can we talk?"

I don't want to talk. I have a lot of other things on my mind right now, but I can't avoid him forever. "All right," I say quietly.

He takes a deep breath. "Look, I know I screwed up, and I'm sorry. It's just . . . that latest immersion session hit me pretty hard, and I was really messed up that night. I know that's not an excuse. I just want you to know, if I was in my right mind, I never would have done that."

I turn the words over in my head. Does that mean he isn't actually attracted to me? Or that he normally would have had more self-control? I'm afraid to ask him, afraid of the answer. It's just too much to deal with.

"I'm sorry," he says again, his tone subdued.

"It's okay," I reply. But I still can't meet his gaze. "I'm sorry that Steven attacked you. He overreacted."

He utters a short, humorless laugh. "Tell me about it."

"I want you to know, though, he's not a bad person."

There's a long pause.

"So the rumors are true, then?" His tone is suddenly chilly.

I frown. "What rumors?"

"Are you actually going out with him?"

"What? No!" Heat rushes to my cheeks. "He's my—" I bite my tongue. I can't say *client*, since technically, he's not supposed to be. "My friend. That's all."

"Oh."

I frown at him. I don't like the way he said that. "Even if we *were* going out, it wouldn't be any business of yours."

His shoulders stiffen. "I'd say it's my business. You're my friend."

"That doesn't mean I need your approval to date someone."

"Well, I'd be a pretty lousy friend if I didn't say something. He's . . ." Ian drops his gaze.

"He's what?"

He sighs. "He's . . . you know. Sick. Of course it's not his fault, but having a personal relationship with someone that screwed up never ends well. I mean, you saw what he did at the party. He might've killed me if not for that collar."

Anger flares in my chest, hot as lava. A dull red heat pulses behind my eyes. I stab a piece of imitation beef with my plastic fork so hard that one of the tines snaps off against the plate. "He was trying to protect me, or don't you remember? You're the one who shoved me up against a wall and started acting crazy, not him."

He flinches. "Lain—"

"Has anyone ever stopped to think that maybe the reason Steven's so angry is that everyone treats him like he has the plague? No one even bothers to find out how he got the collar. Everyone's so afraid and so quick to label people like him as dangerous or defective or sick. Well, I think it's our world that's sick!"

Ian's jaw hangs open.

I grab my tray and stand. If I stay here, I'll end up saying something I'll regret. "I have to go." I walk away and plunk my tray down on an empty table, the one Steven normally sits at. For the rest of the lunch period, I sit alone, picking dispiritedly at my fake meat. I can almost feel a dark miasma collecting in the air around me, causing other students to give me a wide berth.

After lunch, a guard stops me in the hall and says, "Come with me, please."

I hesitate. It's the same guard who confiscated my cell phone the other day. He has light brown hair and a pleasant, nondescript face, but he's just as powerfully built as the rest of them.

I follow him.

He leads me into the administrative wing, which is mostly deserted. The halls are wider, the ceilings higher, the walls a uniform beige. Our footsteps echo through the silence. "What's this about?" I finally ask, since he doesn't seem inclined to volunteer any information.

"Over the past few days, five students have made anonymous reports that you're acting suspiciously," he says.

I suck air between my teeth, a small, startled hiss.

One or two reports might be dismissed. Students report each other all the time. Often, it's just a chance to feel important or a way of satisfying petty grudges. If there are more than four reports about someone in a given week, however, the school has the authority to pull that individual aside and scan him or her.

"This will be easier if you cooperate." His tone is quiet,

almost sympathetic. "If you resist, I'm required to put that in your report, and that'll make you look bad."

"Of course I'll cooperate." I have nothing to hide, anyway.

He opens the door, revealing a tiny cement-walled room containing two chairs and a desk, nothing more. A hot bulb glares overhead. I take a seat, aware of the sweat trickling down my sides. He sits across from me, behind the desk, and waves a slim black wand back and forth in front of my face. It beeps, and a yellow light blinks. My heartbeat speeds up. It's usually green.

The guard examines the neuroscanner and nods, as if satisfied. "You're free to go."

I stand.

Then he speaks again: "It's not my obligation to inform you, but I thought you should know. You've been recently reclassified as a Type Two."

My mouth goes dry. I remain standing, feet rooted to the spot.

The symptom list for Type Two flashes through my head: *Malcontent. Persistent malaise, irrational feelings of anger or resentment toward society, paranoia, and antisocial tendencies.* Twos are not uncommon. They have most of the same rights and privileges as Ones, though they are barred from certain types of high-level employment. Being a Mindwalker, for instance.

It takes me a moment to find my voice. "I— No. This is a mistake. I'm just in a bad mood."

"The scans account for temporary fluctuations in mood, as I'm sure you're aware. Anyway, one scan doesn't cause a reclassification. Someone's been watching you." He sets the scanner down and folds his hands. His expression is calm but serious.

"If I were you, I'd take some time off, get some heavy-duty therapy, and get yourself back on track. It's not too late. I'd hate to see a bright girl like you throw away her future."

The hairs on my nape stiffen. He sounds remarkably like Dr. Swan.

"Thank you," I murmur automatically. My body is numb as I walk out, down the hall.

Twos have a high rate of recovery, compared to Threes and Fours. They can bounce back if they try. Those who choose not to undergo therapy, on the other hand, tend to worsen until they're reclassified again. After that, therapy is no longer optional.

I could do it now. I could walk into IFEN, request Conditioning, and walk out as a One again, with all my social privileges restored and no more than a tiny mark on my file. But I know what Conditioning does. I remember the placidity, the sensation of drifting through my days like a feather, the way worries seemed to bounce off my mind. And that feeling can last for days. Would I still care about helping Steven after treatment? Maybe, maybe not. I'm not even *supposed* to be helping him.

And something else is bothering me. The way this happened, the words the guard used—it feels like a warning. Could it be . . .

No. That's ridiculous. People don't get reclassified just because someone orders it. The data has to be reviewed and analyzed by several professionals who look at a person's history and overall patterns of behavior, as well as scans.

I stop and lean against a wall. If I force myself to look at it objectively, I *have* been acting troubled lately—breaking the rules, sneaking around, avoiding others. Maybe that's all there is to it. Maybe I *am* sick, and that's why I've been having these paranoid thoughts.

The confrontation with Debra, the fight with Ian, the guard's warning—everything swirls around in my head, a chaotic blur. I no longer know what's right. Can I trust my own decisions? Can I trust anything?

15

After school, Steven is waiting for me in the parking lot. He studies my face, frowning. "What happened?"

I force a smile. "Nothing." The lie is flimsy and unconvincing, but I can't bring myself to talk about it right now.

During the drive home, I remain silent, brooding. Once we're in my living room, Steven unbuckles the straps of his coat. His skinny fingers flit through the movements with the ease of long practice. Beneath it, he's wearing a black T-shirt with a green skull and crossbones above the words DANGER: POISON. "So," he says, "should we get started or what?"

I close my eyes.

He wants it. And it would be easy. Easy and so satisfying to go in and pop the little bubbles of pain.

That's not healing, Debra whispers inside me. *It's just a lie.*

I try to dismiss the words, but they've already seeped under my skin. I was so eager to help her that I ignored my faint misgivings and plunged ahead with the treatment. Isn't that exactly what I'm doing now with Steven?

"Doc?"

I open my eyes. "Steven, I—I don't think I should do this."

His forehead wrinkles. "What are you talking about?"

I look away.

Maybe if Steven were a normal client . . . but nothing about this is normal. I don't know what to do. I can't just refer him to a more experienced Mindwalker. He's legally dead, you know. But maybe if IFEN knew what I'd seen in his head, things would be different. After all, they're the Institute for Ethics in Neurotechnology. It's their job to investigate things like this.

I take a deep breath. "There's something I need to tell you."

"Yeah?"

Steady. Deep breaths. I have to approach this as a professional—a doctor delivering some difficult news to a patient. "Actually, it might be better if I showed you."

Looking baffled, he follows me into the basement. I turn on the Gate and play the recordings of his memories. His back stiffens. I don't watch the fuzzy images on the screen. I watch the reflection in his eyes. His expression remains rigid, tightly controlled. "Why are you showing me this?"

"Wait."

Then it happens. That flicker. The brief glimpse of another room, another face.

Steven wears a dazed, uncomprehending expression, but beneath it is a growing black void of fear. "What the hell was that?"

I stop the recording. "At first, I thought it might be a glitch, but this doesn't resemble any glitch I've ever encountered." My voice comes out calm and level. Still, I can't look him in the eye. "You remember that scarring I mentioned? I think that has something to do with it."

Silence. When he speaks, his voice is very soft, almost inaudible. "What are you saying?"

I force myself to meet his gaze. "I wish I could tell you more, but it's clear that your case is far too complex for me. Any speculation on my part would be based on nothing but guesswork. You need to go straight to IFEN."

Steven's breathing quickens, inching toward hyperventilation. His eyes lose focus.

"Steven?"

"They won't help me," he mutters.

"I think they will if they know about this. And they're the only ones qualified to help you. I—" My voice breaks. "I thought I could do this, but I'm in way over my head. I shouldn't have agreed to modify your memories in the first place."

Silence.

"I'm sorry," I add feebly. "But I really believe IFEN will help you if you give them a chance. If you want, I can contact them myself."

He shakes his head. "Forget it." I see his expression closing off, like shutters coming down over his eyes. He turns and walks up the stairs, into the living room.

I follow. "Steven, wait."

"I'm going home." His voice is toneless. It would be easier if he sounded angry; that empty, almost robotic voice is terrifying. He walks toward the door.

Panic flutters in my chest. I catch his sleeve. "Let's just talk about this."

He yanks his sleeve free and turns to face me. "There's nothing to talk about. I'm not going in there. I already told you why."

"Because you think they'll mindwipe you?"

"Yes."

"But that's absurd," I blurt out. "I already told you, that doesn't *happen*. Where did you even hear about this? Rumors? Conspiracy theory websites?"

His expression tightens, and he turns away. When he tries to walk out, I block his path. "Get out of my way!" he growls.

"I can't just let you leave!"

"Why not?"

I stop and take a deep breath. "I—I know you have a Somnazol."

He twitches, eyes widening. "What?"

"I looked in your file," I say meekly.

Emotions flash across his face, too fast and too many to interpret. His gaze jerks away. "Well, you're wrong."

I blink. "What?"

"I don't have a suicide pill."

My mind whirls. Is he telling the truth? Were the words in his file just a mistake, after all?

His eyes narrow to a hard line. "Is that the only reason you've been helping me? Because you thought I'd kill myself otherwise? Couldn't take the guilt?"

I tense. "That's not what it's like."

"Never mind." His voice softens. He sounds almost sad. "It doesn't matter now."

"Please. Just listen—"

He walks out, shutting the door.

I think about running after him, but I suspect that would just make things worse. What could I do, anyway? If he doesn't want to go to IFEN, I can't force him. For a few minutes, I stand motionless, feeling lost. I don't know what to think. I feel like I've been cut loose to drift in the sea, and I can't find anything to hold on to.

I've hurt him; I know that much. He sees this as a betrayal. As abandonment. I wonder if I've made a terrible mistake.

Because I don't know what else to do, I drive to Steven's apartment. The neighborhood is gray and gloomy. Somehow, it's even more depressing in the daytime. No sign of green any-where. The cameras are out in plain sight, and they're on every street corner. I park next to his building and approach the en-trance. There's a small touch screen on the door, smudged with grease and dirt. I tap it, and a list of names flashes across the screen. I scroll down, searching for Steven's. He's on the tenth floor, room 1012.

I buzz him. "Steven? It's Lain."

Static crackles. No response.

I don't know if he's even there. But I keep talking. "I know you're angry at me. But please believe me, I'm only trying to help you."

More static. For a moment, I think I hear breathing. But I can't be sure.

"Say *something*. Say just one word. Tell me to go to hell, if you want. Just let me know you're there."

Still no answer.

I bang my fist against the door. But I realize, with a sinking feeling, that there's nothing I can do. There's no way I can reach him if he won't let me in. In a burst of frustration, I kick the wall, then turn and walk toward my car. My mind is a white haze. Wherever I step, the ground seems to tilt and crumble beneath my feet. I get into my car, but I don't start the engine.

What now? Should I go to Dr. Swan directly and tell him what I discovered? But then I'd have to admit the truth—that I tried to perform an unsupervised memory modification on an unapproved client. Maybe that would be best. Maybe I should confess now, get it over with. If I agree to immediate therapy, he might even forgive me. My actions will be seen as a sign of temporary illness. If I withhold the truth, it will eventually come out on its own—in a world of neural scans, it's impossible to hide anything indefinitely—and then I'll lose everything.

But what about Steven? What will happen to him?

I wait outside the apartment building for a while longer. I try calling his cell phone twice. No answer. Finally, I drive home. In my room, I sit on the edge of my bed, staring at the wall. *Go to IFEN,* my mind urges me. *Tell them the truth. There's nothing you can do on your own.*

Still, something stops me.

Is this what it feels like to be a Type Two? This indecision, this mental fog, this sense that I can't trust anyone? Is this why so many of them don't seek therapy?

I curl up in bed. Nutter topples off my pillow. I pick him up and tuck him under my arm. Then I open the drawer of my nightstand and take out a small porcelain box. Inside is a square of paper. I scan the lines. I've read them hundreds of times.

Dr. Lain Fisher, one of the pioneers of neural modification therapy, was found dead in his home on December 16 at 2:25 p.m. The cause of death is suicide—a revelation that has surprised and baffled many, considering that Dr. Fisher was a famous and outspoken critic of voluntary passing. His colleagues have stated they were unaware of any emotional or mental problems Dr. Fisher might have experienced in the months prior to his death.

His colleague Dr. Emmanuel Swan of the Institute for Ethics in Neurotechnology said in response, "The world has lost a brilliant and compassionate man. I cannot say why he did this, but he will be sorely missed."

Fisher is survived by his daughter, thirteen-year-old Lain Fisher Jr.

A drop of moisture falls onto the paper. My hand drifts to the silver bracelet on my wrist—his last gift to me, on my thirteenth birthday, just a few weeks before his death.

Why didn't I do something? Why didn't I tell anyone that he was suffering?

I blink away tears and read over the article again.

Dr. Swan's wording has always struck me as odd. Not I don't know why, but I cannot say. I know I'm reading too much into it, scraping for hidden meaning where there is none. Like a child covering her eyes, running from the truth, I keep looking for reasons to believe that this isn't what it seems—that Father didn't really abandon me.

* * *

I'm asleep when my cell phone rings. Drowsy, I pick it up and squint at the tiny, glowing screen. Instantly, I'm wide awake.

It's Steven's number.

I sit up, throwing the covers aside, and turn on the lights, the phone pressed to my ear. "Steven?"

"Hey, Doc." His voice is a croak.

I release a soft sigh and place a hand over my racing heart. "Are you all right?"

"Not really." A long pause. I wait, afraid to speak, afraid to breathe. Dread creeps through my stomach and chest. "I shouldn't be talking to you," he whispers. "I've got no right. But I'm too scared to handle this alone. I needed a voice. And who the hell else am I going to call?" He chuckles, a raw, painful sound, like blisters breaking open. "You're the only friend I've got."

The icy dread spreads through my limbs, down to my fingertips and toes. "Wait. Handle *what* alone?"

Silence.

"Steven, I'm going to come over to your apartment. I think we should talk in person."

"It's too late."

And all at once, I know. I know what he's done.

I grab my coat. "Listen to me. Steven? It's not too late. I'll be there in a few minutes. Just hold on."

"Don't worry about me." His voice has changed, grown slurred and thick, like he's drunk. "I'm okay now. It doesn't hurt anymore. And I'm happy. Because I got to meet you." A small sigh. "I get it now. This will fix everything. You'll be happier, too."

"Oh no. Oh no. *Don't you dare.*" I shove my feet into my shoes. I'm still in my pajamas, and it's cold out, but I don't care. Shrugging into my coat, I run down the stairs, the phone still glued to my ear. "You will not die." I speak the words like a magic spell, as if just saying them can make them true. "Do you hear me? *You will not die.*"

Soft, labored breathing fills my ear. "It's okay, Lain." His voice is so weak. Like he's fading. "Please don't be sad. I don't want that."

"Then hold on. Wait for me. I'm coming. Do you understand me, Steven?" No response. *"Steven!"*

There's only silence.

16

I pound a fist on the dashboard. "Come on! Hurry up!"

"The speed limit is forty-five miles per hour."

My molars scrape together. "My friend is dying! Who cares about the speed limit?"

"I'm sorry. I can't process that request. Please rephrase."

"You stupid talking tin can! If I'm too late, it will be your fault!"

"I'm sorry. I can't process that request—"

My fist slams against the dashboard one more time, but of course, it does no good. God, I'm such an idiot. Why did I let him walk out? Why did I believe his claim that he didn't have a Somnazol?

I check my cell phone clock. Ten minutes have passed since I left my apartment. I should be at Steven's place in another five. If only I could call a hospital. But they won't help him. What he's doing is perfectly legal. What I'm doing—trying to stop him—is not.

I fight down my panic and force myself to think. A Somnazol pill has three layers, designed to dissolve slowly, in sequence. The first is a sedative, tailored to induce a state of calm euphoria. The second renders the person unconscious. The third stops his heart. The entire thing takes about an hour to dissolve. I don't know when Steven took his, how much time passed between the moment he swallowed the pill and the moment he called me. I might have another half hour, or it might already be too late.

Outside the door to his apartment building, I buzz his room. "Steven?"

There's a hiss of static.

My heartbeat quickens. "Let me in." When nothing happens, I hammer a fist against the door. "Steven! If you don't let me in, I'll—I'll break down the door!"

More crackling static. I hear his breathing, weak and unsteady. Then a buzz. The door slides open.

Thank God. If he's still conscious, I have time.

I take the elevator to the tenth floor. The lights sputter fitfully as I race down the narrow, tiled hall. He must want to be saved, I tell myself. He must have changed his mind at the last minute; he wouldn't have let me in otherwise. I cling to that thought as I hunt for room 1012, find the door, and try the knob. It's unlocked.

I fling open the door, heart thundering. The lights are off. The TV is on but muted, tuned to some old black-and-white horror film. On the screen, a vampire emerges from his coffin, cape drawn over his face. The silent, flickering gray glow is the only illumination in the apartment. "Steven!"

I hear breathing, very faint. Where is he?

I rush into the apartment and nearly trip over something. At first, I think it's a pile of dirty laundry. Then I look more closely. It's him, curled up on the floor. A cold wire cinches tight around my gut. He's so pale, so still.

I crouch and press two fingers to his neck, feeling his pulse. It's slow but still strong.

A groan escapes his lips. I pull him upright, and his eyes open a crack. Then they slip shut, and his head starts to droop.

"Open your mouth," I say.

He does, too dazed to do anything but obey.

I thrust a finger into his mouth and press it against the back of his throat. His throat convulses, and I pull my finger out just as he starts to heave. Bile splatters onto the carpet. The pill comes out, too, a tiny white circle, the outer pink layer worn away. He doubles over, gasping and coughing. Slowly, he raises his head and looks at me through a curtain of shaggy bangs. "Lain," he whispers hoarsely. "You shouldn't have come."

"Shut up." I'm trembling, tears overflowing my eyes. "Just shut up." I don't know if I want to hit him or shake him until his teeth rattle or hold him and never let go.

It takes me only a few seconds to make up my mind. I pull him close and hug him tightly, fiercely. He tenses—then slowly, slowly, his arms slip around my waist. He feels brittle, breakable, all sharp angles, with ribs and hip bones that stick out more than they should. His heart beats hard and fast, like a panicked bird hurling itself against the bars of a cage. I wonder when anyone last held him.

I rest my cheek against his sweat-damp forehead. "Promise me you won't try anything like that again," I whisper.

His breathing rasps in my ear. "If I stick around, you'll just get hurt. You'll lose everything. I don't want to be the one you throw it all away for. I'm not worth it. It would be better if I just disappeared."

"That's the stupidest thing I've ever heard." I hold him tighter. "Nothing would hurt more than losing you."

His breath hitches.

The TV is still on, muted, glowing dimly in the darkness. I stroke Steven's hair, and a tremor ripples through him. His unsteady breathing flutters against my neck. "You'll stay?"

"I'll stay. So promise me—" My voice cracks. "Promise you'll stay, too."

He nods once, his face hidden against my shoulder.

We remain on the floor, holding each other, until the light of dawn creeps in through the window and across the floor.

17

I flush the toilet and watch the half-dissolved Somnazol tablet spin around, then vanish. Good riddance.

When I return to the living room, Steven's sitting up on the couch, a blanket around his shoulders, taking small, careful sips of water from a glass. The dim light from the window has brightened. Morning spreads slowly across the room, illuminating bare walls and a patchy, balding carpet. The room is tiny and cramped. Aside from the TV, it contains only a couch and a rickety coffee table with a hot plate. There's no kitchen, no bedroom—nothing but that single room and a closet-sized bathroom with a toilet and sink. How does he bathe?

Pushing the thoughts aside, I sit next to him. The silence stands between us like a wall. Every time one of us clears a throat, the other one gives a start, as if a gun has gone off. After I held him for half the night, his tears soaking my shirt, just sitting next to each other shouldn't be so awkward.

"You gave me a scare, you know," I say.

He averts his gaze. "I know." He looks exhausted, pale, wrung out. "I told myself I wasn't going to take that pill. I just . . ."

"You don't have to explain," I say quietly. "You weren't thinking clearly. That's all."

He raises his head. There's a sudden, strange determination in his eyes, in the set of his jaw. "No. You don't have to make excuses for me." His expression softens. "I'm sorry. For putting you through that."

I nod. But I know that whatever he says, this isn't entirely his doing. Right now, I'm all Steven has. After promising to help him, I lost my courage and tried to send him away, to hand him over to the very system that's failed him so completely. I told myself it was the right thing, when in reality I was just afraid. I was so caught up in my own feelings, my own questions about what was right and wrong, I didn't realize how devastating an effect it would have on him. "I'm sorry, too," I say. "If you want me to continue your treatment, I will."

A tiny furrow appears between his brows. He lowers his head and studies his feet.

"Is that what you want, Steven?"

"I don't know. I'm really confused." He takes a deep breath and rubs a hand over his face. "That thing you showed me, in that video—that other face, behind Pike's—what do you think it means? Do you have any ideas?"

I hesitate. "I have one."

"Tell me."

I shift my weight, reluctant. I'm afraid that I'm wrong, even more afraid that I'm right. "It looks like the result of a memory modification."

His eyes widen.

"But that's very improbable," I add quickly. "IFEN has no record of it, and there's no one else who could have done it."

"Are you sure about that?"

I want to say yes. But the truth is, I'm not certain of anything. "No." I tangle my fingers together. "There's something else. I researched Emmett Pike, and there's almost no information on him. I don't know exactly what that means, but it seems . . . suspicious."

He stares at me, mouth open. I can see him putting the pieces together, coming to the same conclusion I did. "You're saying that Pike's not real? That someone *implanted* memories of being kidnapped and tortured in my head?"

"No, I don't think they're implants," I reply. "It's impossible to fabricate entire memories; the technology doesn't exist. I think something terrible *did* happen to you. But if I'm right, it might not have happened exactly the way you remember. Certain details might have been altered."

His face has gone grayish white. "Like the identity of the guy who did it?"

I think about the scarce information I found online. A single photo—which, I suppose, could have been created in an image program—and a handful of articles, all centered around the kidnapping, as if Pike had sprung out of thin air, then conveniently erased himself with a bullet through the head. "It seems that way."

His eyes slip shut. The lids are dark, almost bruised-looking. When he speaks again, his voice seems to be coming from somewhere far away. "I went to Pike's grave once, just to prove to myself he was really dead. But I couldn't even step on the ground he was under. I was too scared. Like he might reach up and grab me." His fingers tighten on the glass of water. His eyes open, unfocused. "I hate him more than anyone else in the world. But if he doesn't exist, that's even worse. Like my whole life, all my pain, is one big, sick joke."

"It's not a joke," I say. "Whatever happened to you, your feelings are real."

The patch of pale sky brightens outside the window. A flock of crows fly past, tiny dots against the clouds.

Slowly, Steven sets down the glass. He leans back on the couch, weariness etched into every line of his face. "Thanks to me, you're a lawbreaker now. You saved me, even knowing you weren't supposed to."

"It wasn't always like this, you know. People used to do everything in their power to stop someone from dying, even by his own hand."

"Guess they got tired of trying to force sad sacks like me to keep living. Much more logical to just let us die."

"If that's 'logical,' then I don't want to be logical."

The corners of his mouth twitch. It's not really a smile, but it's something. "So, what happens next? I mean, now that I know someone screwed around with my memories, what do I do?"

"Not you. We."

His brows knit together. The confusion in his eyes makes me ache. He's so used to being alone, he still can't believe that I'm here to stay.

I smile. "You're not getting rid of me that easily. We're in this together now. I promised, remember?" My smile fades, because I know he won't like what I'm about to say. "I still think we should go to the authorities. If not IFEN, the police, at least. We need to tell *someone* about this."

A hard glint creeps into his eyes. He shakes his head. "If we do that, you'll get in trouble. Once they find out you treated me without permission, you could lose everything."

"I can't let that stop me. They need to know about what's been done to you. It's my responsibility."

The stubborn look in his eyes deepens. "Yeah, well, it's my *head*." He raps a finger against his temple. "And I say no. You're not losing your job. Not over me."

I look down, self-conscious. I find myself playing with a tendril of my hair and quickly fold my hands in my lap. "This isn't just about you and me. Whatever's going on, it's a lot bigger than either of us. Ten years ago, six children died. That much is certainly real. If Pike didn't kill them . . ."

"Someone else did," he finishes. "Someone with enough power to change my memories and conjure up a fake killer out of thin air."

The words sink in slowly, and the full enormity of what we're dealing with settles into my bones.

"I know we can't just forget about this," Steven continues. "But I'm not going to the cops, or to IFEN. I don't want a bunch of rich guys in white coats poking around in my memories, and I don't want you punished for trying to help me. We'll find some other way to get the truth."

He sounds so determined. Such a change from the broken boy I held last night. What's the difference? What shifted? Is it just knowing that he's not on his own anymore? "I don't know what else to try," I say.

"What about that Lucid stuff I keep seeing ads for? Isn't that supposed to enhance memory?"

I pause, thinking. "Lucid is designed to improve day-to-day mental functioning. It's not strong enough to unearth pieces of an altered or deleted memory. If we had access to IFEN's resources, we could get our hands on something more powerful, but—" I stop. An idea flickers.

Ian's mother is a drug researcher. From past conversations with him, I know that she tends to mix work and pleasure. She—and, indirectly, he—has access to all kinds of experimental substances, legal and illegal.

The last time I spoke to Ian was when I chewed him out at lunch and stormed off. I can't exactly ask him for a favor now. But then, who else *can* I turn to? There's no one else I trust. And I realize that, in spite of everything, I *do* trust Ian. At least, I trust him not to betray me.

"Lain?"

I look up. "The truth might be hard to deal with," I say. "If there *were* a pill that could help you remember, would you want to take it?"

His teeth catch on his lower lip, tugging. He looks younger when he does that. "I want to know who did this. I can't just erase the memories without knowing what's actually *there*."

"In that case, I'm going to call Ian."

Steven's mouth falls open. "Wait. *Him?* You've got to be kidding."

"He's my friend," I say.

"He *attacked* you."

"He kissed me."

"He pushed you against a wall—"

"I'm not saying it was right, but he's already apologized for it. It's not going to happen again."

Steven scowls.

"Steven." I look him in the eyes. "If we're going to do this, we need his help."

"And you think he'll be able to help us," he says flatly.

"It's worth a try. I'm just going to call him and ask." I pull out my cell phone and dial, ignoring the dour expression on Steven's face.

After the second ring, Ian picks up. There's a brief pause. I hear the faint rasp of his breathing at the other end of the line, and suddenly, my head is a blank. I stare at my feet, hunting for words.

It's Ian who speaks first, his voice low and cautious. "Lain, is that you?"

"Yes, it's me. Hello, Ian." There's a long, uncomfortable silence. How should I approach this? I can't just say, *I need some drugs from you.*

"I wasn't sure I was ever going to hear from you again," he says. "I mean, you seemed pretty angry with me last time."

I wince at the small, sharp pang of guilt. "I was upset. About a lot of stuff. I said some things to you that I shouldn't have."

"Well, you were right. Even if you *were* going out with Steven, it wouldn't be any of my business. I mean, it's not like I'm your boyfriend."

Is it my imagination, or is there a faint hint of bitterness in his tone? "It's okay," I reply awkwardly. "You were concerned. That's all."

"Yeah." There's an uncomfortable silence. "So, what do you need?"

"What makes you think I need something?"

"Am I wrong?"

Heat creeps into my ears. "Well, no." I moisten dry lips with the tip of my tongue. "Do you know much about Lucid?"

"The drug?" I hear a hint of curiosity in his words. "My mom was part of a study on that recently. Something about helping people with degenerative neurological conditions recover lost memories."

"Is that the same drug you can get on the market right now?"

"Yes and no. The version they were testing was a lot stronger than anything you can legally sell to the public."

"That's what I thought." I remember reading about Lucid in my biopsychology class, back when it was still known by its long chemical name, before its formula had been watered down and transformed into a product. "So, what does it do, exactly?"

"It's weird stuff. In small doses, it acts like a mild stimulant, but you get the dosage high enough, and the effects are almost like ketamine," Ian says. "You start tripping, and you come out of it remembering stuff you thought you'd forgotten. People with Alzheimer's suddenly recognize their family again—stuff like that. Pretty amazing. But it can mess you up awfully bad, too." A pause. "Wait—are you thinking about trying it?"

"I am. Or rather, I know someone who's thinking about trying it."

Another few heartbeats of silence pass. When he speaks again, his voice is very quiet, very serious. "Lain, what's going on?"

I bite the inside of my cheek, wondering how much I can

safely say. I'm conscious of Steven's gaze on me. "It's complicated."

"Is this something that could get you in trouble?"

"Not if I'm careful."

He exhales a tense breath. "Maybe I'm not one to talk, but you haven't been acting like yourself lately."

"Ian." I soften my voice. "Please trust me. This might not be technically within the rules, but it's something I need to do, and it's very important."

He chuckles, a hard, brittle sound. "You're not going to tell me anything, but you expect me to help you?"

"I know I'm asking a lot of you, but—"

"It's him, isn't it? Steven Bent. This has something to do with him."

Maybe it's obvious. After all, Steven's the one I've been spending most of my time with lately. For a moment, I wonder how I'd react if the reverse were true—if Ian suddenly started ignoring me and hanging out with some girl I barely knew. I've never looked at Ian in that way, yet the thought makes me instantly uncomfortable. I truly *am* asking a lot of him. "I shouldn't explain this over a cell phone," I say quietly. "I'll tell you more in person."

I wait, the blood whooshing in my ears.

He gives a small, resigned sigh. "Just promise me one thing, all right?"

"Yes?"

"Be careful," he says. His tone is gentle, concerned. He sounds like his old self. "Don't do anything I wouldn't do, okay?"

A faint smile tugs at my lips. "That leaves me a lot of options."

"Don't do anything *you* wouldn't do, then."

I utter a short laugh. It catches me off guard. "All right, I won't."

"See you at my apartment." He hangs up.

* * *

When we pull into the lot outside Ian's building, the sky is a clear, innocent blue, dotted with cottony clouds. Monorails race back and forth on their tracks, high above the city. I park the car and say, "I'll be right back."

"Oh no," Steven says. "I'm going in with you."

"Steven . . ."

"After what he did, you think I'm leaving you alone with him? I don't trust him."

I meet his gaze and set my lips into a firm line. "Ian's not dangerous. And I need to handle this on my own."

His eyes flash, and I see him getting ready to argue.

I reach out and place a hand on his arm, and he freezes. "Steven," I say again, more quietly, "something happened to Ian. He went through a very painful experience, and it's affecting him more deeply than I expected it to. I need to have a serious talk with him, and I can't do it with you hovering over my shoulder and glaring lasers at him the whole time."

A muscle in Steven's jaw twitches. "Fine. I'll wait ten minutes. If it takes any longer than that, I'm coming in."

"I don't know how long it will take," I say, annoyance

creeping into my tone. "And what are you planning to do after ten minutes? Break down the door?"

"If I have to."

I roll my eyes. He's determined to be dramatic about this. "Look, what if you come into the apartment with me and wait just inside the door? Ian and I can talk in the other room, so we'll still have some privacy, but you'll be close by."

He pauses—then gives a single sharp nod.

We walk in through the wide double glass doors of the lobby and take the elevator up to the top floor. When the doors slide open, Ian's in the living room, sitting on the couch. At the sight of Steven, he tenses. "It's all right," I say. "He's just going to wait here."

Steven and Ian stare at each other, and Steven narrows his eyes. I can almost hear the testosterone crackling in the air between them. I suppress a sigh.

Then, unexpectedly, Ian smiles. It looks real—open and warm, the way he used to smile so often—though I can still see the lines of fatigue around his eyes. "Anyone want coffee? I've got a pot brewing."

Steven blinks, then frowns, eyebrows scrunching together. He wrinkles his nose, as if sniffing for a trap. "Sure," he mumbles, surprising me.

Ian glances at me. "No thank you," I reply. Coffee's too bitter for my taste.

Ian goes into the kitchen and returns with two steaming mugs. He hands one to Steven, who examines it as if it might be poisoned, then takes a cautious sip.

"I never really introduced myself, did I?" Ian asks. He extends a hand. "Ian Wellick."

Steven hangs back, peering at Ian's outstretched hand. Then he clasps it and gives it a brief, hard shake. "Steven Bent." He lets go and stuffs his hand in his pocket. "Sorry for nearly strangling you."

"Sorry for nearly stabbing you." He smiles again and takes a sip from his mug. "So." He turns to face me. "You need some Lucid?"

I nod.

He steers me through a door into a bedroom—his mother's, judging from the diamond necklaces sparkling on the dresser and the thin black gown hanging up on the closet door. "Should we be in here?" I ask nervously.

"It's fine." He sets his coffee on the dresser. "She's gone for the rest of the week."

"Are you sure? I don't want to get you in trouble. Will she notice if some of her supplies go missing?"

"I doubt it. She's got other stuff on her mind right now." He opens a drawer and rummages through the contents. Then he withdraws a shiny black compact and flips it open.

I lean forward. Inside, I see three compartments, each containing a single capsule—a shiny white circle with a tiny cartoon image printed on the front. One has a blue rabbit, one a smiling mushroom. On the third is the head of a snarling Chinese dragon.

He snaps the compact shut. "So, you going to tell me about this blocked memory, or what?"

I hesitate. "It's very personal. It involves something that happened to Steven when he was a child—a trauma. I don't know if he'd want me going into detail."

Ian's fingers curl around the compact. "You know, I looked up his name earlier today." His gaze flicks away. "I'd ask why he *wanted* to remember something like that, but I don't think you'd answer." A muscle in his jaw tightens, then loosens. He hands the compact to me. "Be careful with this stuff. You remember that study I mentioned? With one of the subjects, they messed up the dosing, gave him too much. He flipped out and tried to jump off a building. They stopped him, luckily. Afterward, he couldn't remember *why* he'd done it."

I fidget nervously. "Is there anything safer that could achieve the same result?"

"No."

I'm starting to have second thoughts about this. But I'm here. The pills are within reach. Later, I can talk to Steven and decide whether he actually wants to take them. "So how can I make sure that doesn't happen to Steven?"

"Space out the pills," Ian says. "Don't take more than one within twenty-four hours. Personally, I would start with the blue bunny. Try the mushroom only if that doesn't do it for you. The dragon—well, let's call that a last resort."

I rub my thumb over the compact's smooth, glossy surface. "Have you ever taken Lucid?"

"No, but my mom took a blue bunny once. While she was studying its effects, she decided to sample the wares." He digs in the drawer again, pulls a small notepad out, and flips through the pages. "She told me she was planning to write down the whole experience—you know, for science—but this was all she got." He opens the notebook to a page on which she's scrawled:

ROSEBUSHES BEHIND MY OLD HOUSE A BOWL OF
BUTTER-BROWN ICE CREAM.

And several inches below that, in a shakier hand:

GREEN FOAM EXPLODING OUT OF MY ANUS.

Oh dear.

"I guess she started hallucinating at some point," he says. "Like I said, it makes you trip."

"Then how do you tell the real memories from the hallucinations?"

He shrugs. "Does it matter?"

"Well, of course. Hallucinations are just products of the brain. They don't mean anything."

"I wouldn't be so sure about that." His eyes lose focus. "Neurologically, there's no difference between a real and an imagined experience. In a way, it doesn't matter if something actually happened to you or not. On the inside, it's all the same." He blinks a few times and gives his head a shake, as if coming back to the moment. "By the way, make sure you don't lose these pills. They're the last ones I have, and I don't know if I'll be able to get more."

I sit on the edge of the bed, holding the compact and studying Ian. He seems to be in control of himself. That unnerving, half-crazed look no longer haunts his eyes. But his face is thinner than usual, and his lips are cracked and chapped. "What happened during that last immersion session?" I ask quietly.

He doesn't respond.

I continue, keeping my tone calm and gentle. "I know

it was a sexual assault, and those are especially hard to deal with. But no client's ever affected you like this. You've always been the strong one—strong enough to deal with the things I couldn't. I don't know what you went through this time, but it must have been terrible."

His shoulders slump, and he chuckles hoarsely. "Strong. Yeah, I guess that's how I wanted you to see it." He shakes his head and gives me the most mirthless smile I've ever seen. "The truth is, I've been cheating."

"Cheating?"

He lowers his head and splays his long fingers over his scalp, cradling his head in his hands. "I've been getting my own memories erased."

My eyes widen. "After every client?"

"Not *every* client. Just the really bad ones."

The words leave me dazed, baffled. It never even occurred to me that we could choose to forget our own Mindwalking experiences, that we could erase the things we see in others' minds. Memory modification is not something to be done lightly; there's always some risk. The idea of going through it multiple times is mind-boggling. "They let you do that?"

"It's not encouraged. But it's possible. I did it the first time out of sheer desperation, and then it sort of turned into a habit. Not that I remember much now, but apparently I kept going back to Dr. Swan. Kept begging him. I asked him not to tell anyone, so he didn't." His mouth twists in a bitter smile. "Everyone thought I was so resilient. They were all so impressed by how many tough clients I could take on without cracking." He lets out a hollow laugh. "Of course, I should've known it couldn't go on forever. Last time, when I went in to get my head cleaned out, he told me that I had to stop. That if I kept doing this, I'd damage myself. There's only so many times you can modify a person's memories before his brain turns to mush. So now I'm stuck with it." He stares at the wall, as if he can't bring himself to look at me. "It felt like being ripped open."

"Ian . . ." The words die in my throat. What can I possibly say?

He meets my eyes. "You've never erased any of the memories, have you? From the immersion sessions, I mean."

"No." My voice sounds very small. I sit on the edge of the bed, clutching the compact.

He presses the heels of his hands against his closed eyelids. "I don't know how you can take it. How you can live with all that pain, day after day."

I swallow, my throat tight. "I couldn't, though. The first time I went through what you did, I ended up in the psych ward for a week."

"But you recovered. You went back on the job. I—I don't know if I can keep doing it, Lain. Look at me." He lowers his hands and watches them tremble. "Look what I've become. I can't sleep. Can't eat. My grades are already slipping. My life's falling apart."

I tuck the compact into my coat pocket, rise from the bed, walk over to him, and take his hands in mine. "Have you told anyone?" I ask. "Your mother, at least?"

His Adam's apple bobs up and down. "I can't tell her. She— she's in this special, weeklong intensive therapy program. After they caught her dipping into some of the drugs at work, they scanned her, and she came up a Two. If she can't get her

Type back up, she'll lose her job, and she's already got a lot of debt and other stuff that I didn't know about until now." Tears glint at the corners of his eyes. "I don't know what's going to happen to us."

"Oh, Ian." Everything inside me aches. All this time, I've been so worried about Steven, I've barely thought about what Ian's going through. I just assumed he'd be okay, the way he always is. "I'm sorry."

He squeezes his eyes shut. "I'm scared, Lain."

I put my arms around him.

He starts to tense up, then goes limp against me. "I must seem so pathetic to you," he whispers. "So weak."

"You're not weak." I tighten my embrace. "It's all right. You can let go."

His chest hitches once, twice. Then he lets out a sound somewhere between a moan and a sob, the sound of a dying animal. He crumples to the floor, like his legs have been cut out from under him. We both go down.

The door bangs open. Steven stands there, his eyes wild. "Lain, I heard—" He freezes. I sit in the corner, rocking Ian back and forth as he cries softly against my shoulder.

18

Steven and I are silent during the ride home. He doesn't ask about what happened, and I don't tell him. My shirt is still wet with Ian's tears, and it occurs to me that in the span of twenty-four hours, two boys have broken down in my arms. I'm starting to wonder if my body emits some pheromone that attracts emotionally damaged males.

Once Ian got ahold of himself, we talked some more. He told me not to worry, that he'd be okay, that he and his mom had some money in savings and it would be enough to float them until she found another job. He claimed, too, that he'd work on getting his own mental state under control. That he was just tired, just overwhelmed. I don't know whether to believe him.

I pull out the compact and flip it open. "Here it is."

"This is Lucid?" Steven picks up the blue bunny pill. "What do these pictures mean?"

"I guess that's how they mark the different dosages. Ian said to start with the bunny."

"What else did he say?"

"That it might make you hallucinate."

"So how will we know if what we're seeing is a memory or a hallucination?"

"I asked Ian the same question. He didn't have an answer." I give Steven a tiny smile. "But if the giant purple humming-birds chasing you start to sparkle, it's probably a safe bet that you're hallucinating." I try to ignore the tightness in my stomach, the way my heart is trying to crack through my ribs. "Have you ever taken something like this before?"

"No. I may be a pill popper, but I tend to stay away from psychedelics. The inside of my head is not a fun place to be."

My doubts flare up again. "You know, this could be dangerous. Ian said there was a study, and one of the subjects tried to jump off a building."

"Then as long as we stay away from tall buildings, we should be fine."

I give him a skeptical look.

He smiles grimly. "We've come this far." His fingers curl around the pill. His pulse drums visibly in his throat. "I'm not turning back now."

"There might be other ways," I say.

"Like what?"

I don't have an answer for that. And I know that he's right—if we're going to search for the truth on our own, we have to be willing to take risks. Nothing about this is safe or accepted. There is no procedure to follow.

What have I gotten us into?

Once we get to my house, we head down to the basement. The Gate is waiting, the two padded leather chairs spotlighted by overhead fixtures. Suddenly, I'm cold to my core. I have no idea what will happen once he takes that pill. Logic tries to assure me that nothing can be worse than the horrors I've already seen in his mind, but my gut insists that, yes, it can and will get worse.

He settles into the chair, slides his helmet into place, and buckles the strap with his right hand. His left is still curled tightly around the blue bunny. The other two capsules are nestled in the black, round compact inside my coat pocket. He looks up and cracks a weak smile. "Ready to go down the rabbit hole?"

My hand rests on the Gate's hard drive. It hums beneath my palm, warm as a living thing. "Are you sure about this?"

Steven uncurls his fingers, revealing the pill in his moist palm. His hand trembles. "You'll be with me the whole time, right?"

"Yes." I settle into my chair. "And since I won't be under the Lucid's influence myself—at least, not directly—I should be able to provide some guidance and rationality."

"Let's hope that's how it works." He tosses the pill into his mouth.

I slip my helmet on. The foam molds itself to my scalp as I prop my feet up on the footrest and switch on the Gate. I look over at Steven. He smiles again, a tiny, closed-lipped smile. It's brave, scared, determined, and fragile. It makes me ache.

Electric tingles spread over my scalp, down my spine, and through my skin. The connection opens. Steven licks his lips, and I feel the rasp of a dry tongue passing over dry flesh. His pulse drums in my throat.

"I think that stuff is kicking in," he says. "I feel like I'm sinking. Or floating."

I feel it, too—a strange weightlessness, as if I'm underwater or in zero gravity. Steven's breathing echoes in my ears. The darkness behind my visor is solid and complete, enfolding me like a cocoon of black silk. I can no longer feel the chair against my back and legs. I seem to be falling in slow motion, sinking through the floor, through the ground. When I wiggle my toes, trying to anchor myself in my own body, the movement seems curiously disconnected, as if my toes independently decided to wiggle, then tricked me into thinking it was my idea.

"This is weird," Steven mutters.

"It's all in our heads. There's no danger." I'm not sure which of us I'm trying to convince.

The space around us and between us seems to stretch like taffy. I gulp.

"I feel like you're drifting away," he says.

"I'm not going anywhere."

I sense him reaching across the space between us, his hand grasping at thin air. I reach out, too. My fingers touch his, grip, squeeze.

I sink into a dense gray fog. Floating. Drifting. Nothing to hold on to, no way to orient myself. Panic flutters in my chest. *Breathe.* I keep sinking.

Deeper and deeper.

Down and down.

19

I'm half running, half stumbling down a shadowed hallway that blurs and tilts. Panting, I round a corner. I shove a door open and lurch inside, then slam the door and wedge a chair under the knob. My heart knocks against my ribs.

Footsteps echo down the hallway. "Where do you think you're running to?" a voice calls. It sounds, somehow, like two voices speaking at once. "Where can you possibly go?"

I tremble. Sweat plasters my shirt to my back.

"If only you could understand," the double voice says. "These fears are all in your head. We only want to help you."

There's a bed in the corner of the room. I crawl under it and curl up in the dark space. My ragged breathing fills the silence. The smell of dust and mothballs itches in my nose. A few inches from my face, a fat black spider crouches, rolling up a cockroach in its web. The cockroach is still moving, legs wiggling feebly.

The footsteps stop outside the door. There's a click as the

man tries the lock. "Steven," says the double voice. One is deep and rough, one higher. "Let me in."

I squeeze my eyes shut and hold my breath. There's a tickle on my face. Another spider, crawling across my cheek. I don't move.

The knob jiggles. There's a thump and the door creaks open. "The treatments are necessary," the voices say. "Whether you believe me or not, that is a fact. Now, you can come with me and make this a lot easier on yourself. Or you can continue to run and hide and simply postpone the inevitable."

The footsteps come closer. Thud, thud, thud. Still holding my breath, I open my eyes a crack and see a pair of shiny black shoes. Then the figure leans down, and there's a face. It wavers and blurs. Two faces, one on top of the other.

"I want to go home," I whisper.

"This is your home, Steven. St. Mary's is your home."

A hand reaches toward me, and I bite it. The man cries out and yanks his hand back. Blood falls to the floor in fat red drops, like paint. I scramble out from under the bed and bolt for the door. A hand seizes my arm and drags me back. I scream. A needle pricks my arm, and suddenly, I'm sinking. I try to fight it, but the darkness grabs me and pulls me down.

I come up slowly, through layers and layers. For a while—maybe minutes, maybe years—I float, bobbing up and down like a balloon. I plunge into a dark vault of screams. Then I sail through a clear white mist. Silver knives slide through the mist. They're all around me, flashing. A forest of knives.

I see things crumbling, falling apart. Machines disintegrating, dolls being ripped in half, stuffing falling out. Someone stabs a pair of scissors into a rag doll's head and twists the blade around. *Snip*. The doll's head falls off.

Voices drift through the haze.

"We've got to stop. If we keep going, he'll end up like the others."

"Turning weak on me now?"

"Weak? Is it weak to admit that we've made some mistakes?"

"What are we supposed to do, let him go?"

The voices are arguing. Barking and growling, as if the men have started to turn into dogs.

I can't remember my name. Why can't I remember?

I plunge down. Shadows and earth fold around me. Then I'm burrowing upward through the ground like a mole, scratching at loose soil and tiny rocks. I can't breathe. Dirt fills my mouth and nose. My head is a hive crawling with bees, and when I move too fast, they get angry and start to sting me. I feel their stingers now, jabbing into the swollen, tender meat behind my eyes. But I have to keep digging, or the wolves in the white coats will catch me. Their howls fill my ears. My own ragged breathing almost drowns them out, but they're getting closer. I feel them.

The wolves like to pick me apart. Their teeth are steel needles. Their eyes are so bright, I can't look at them.

You need us, they call.

But I won't listen to their lies anymore.

I break through and gasp in the cold, clean air. I stumble on numb legs. The floor lurches up and scrapes my palms, but I push myself to my feet. I'm running through gray empty halls filled with cobwebs. Crows circle overhead, laughing at me. *Ha! Ha ha ha!*

Little flashes of light shine through the gray.

It's cold. So cold and bright and *open*.

I stagger through a white world, feet burning. My head is a red swamp of pain, my tongue a scrap of gritty meat. Dark shapes loom around me, clawing the sky with sharp-tipped fingers. The ground stings my feet, cold-hot and piercing.

A brown thing watches from a nearby branch. Words like *ears* and *tail* and *fur* float up out of the darkness. The thing makes a sound. *Chk-chk-chk.*

I don't know where I am. I don't know *who* I am. But I'm free. The wolves can't reach me here.

I stumble and blink. The ground beneath my feet is no longer cold and white, but smooth and black. A long strip of the black stuff runs in both directions, cutting the whiteness in half. Perplexed, I rub a toe against the blackness. My feet are bare, narrow and pale.

Two bright beams cut through the dark. I raise my head and stare, hypnotized, mouth open. The brightness fills my head. It hurts. I fling my hands up in front of my eyes as a razor-edged screech splits the air. Deep voices are shouting. I can't understand the words. Big hands grip my wrists and pry my hands away from my eyes, and I stare up into a brown lined face beneath a knitted red cap.

The deep voice says something. I almost understand. But I can't put the pieces together.

"—happened—your parents?—can you—your name—"

Name. Shouldn't I have a name? I reach for it, but it slips away. Tears of frustration prick the corners of my eyes. I look up at the sky, at the bright thing shining down from the darkness, and my mouth forms a word. "Moon."

The faces gape at me in bewilderment.

"Moon," I repeat. "Moon." It is all I have, all I can give them. "Moon. Moon."

I want them to smile, to be proud of me for remembering. Instead, they look upset. Warm tears pool in my eyes and spill down my cheeks.

The men exchange glances. Then one of them says something in a gentle tone. "—get you home."

Home. Where is home? Do I have one?

Hands nudge me toward a big red thing. *Car*, I think. Words are starting to trickle back. The black things are trees. The white stuff is snow.

I shut my eyes and try to pry the memories from the darkness. There's a flicker. Something—a face, the mouth and nose covered by a white mask, and a white-gloved hand holding a bloodstained thing that whirs and buzzes.

"I don't want it in me," I say.

One man pulls off his knitted cap, scratches his head of woolly hair, and says something that ends with "—hurt?"

"I don't want it in me." My breathing quickens. The men's gloved hands reach out to me, but I recoil, breathing fast.

One of the men has something in his hand. The word *phone* surfaces from the foggy darkness in my skull. The man punches a series of buttons, and more words pour out of his mouth, too fast to understand.

My vision blurs. My knees give out, and I sink to the road,

clutching my head in both hands. "I don't want it in me." I press my hands to my face, then lower them. Tears drip into my palms. They are not clear, but cloudy red. I am crying blood.

The world disappears in a swirl of brown and white, and I spiral down into blackness.

20

I come back to myself little by little. My body tingles. I flex my fingers and toes.

My brain feels swollen and tender, too big for my skull. I'm afraid to move very quickly, afraid my head will crack open and the contents will slosh out onto the floor. My thoughts are in pieces. I have no idea what I just saw or what it all means. I retain images, fragments, like puzzle pieces. But the edges won't line up.

I tug the helmet off and set it aside.

Beside me, Steven stares at the ceiling, his eyes wide and unfocused.

"Steven?" My voice emerges hoarse and faint, a croak. "Are you all right?"

Slowly, his head turns toward me. For a few seconds, he doesn't respond. "Define *all right*."

If he can make wisecracks, he's probably okay. More or less.

I sit up, and a lancet of pain slides through my head. Red

stars explode on my retinas. I groan. Is this what a hangover feels like? If so, then I never want to touch a drop of alcohol as long as I live. I place a hand against my sweat-drenched brow and try to cling to what I saw, but it's already slipping away. Images flash across the backs of my eyes—the snowy woods, the shadowed hallway, the man's shiny black shoes. When I try to recall his face, another lancet of pain slips between my ears.

"Ugh," Steven mutters. "Feels like there's a hoedown in my brain and everyone's wearing stilettos."

That's a remarkably apt description of how I feel. "Do you remember anything?"

"Not much. You?"

I close my eyes, straining. A name leaps through my mind like a spark, and my eyes snap open. "St. Mary's." At Steven's puzzled look, I continue, "You were in a place called St. Mary's." His expression remains blank. "It doesn't sound familiar to you?"

"No."

When I was researching Emmett Pike, I read a number of articles about the kidnapping. I recall that Steven was found by two men in the Northeast Quadrant, in the woods, near a small town called Wolf's Run. Our city, Aura, is situated in the Central Quadrant, the most heavily populated. I've never actually been to the Northeast; it's mostly farmland and wilderness.

None of the articles mentioned a place called St. Mary's.

I rub my aching head. The more I try to remember what I saw, the farther it slips away. Maybe it's like a dream. Maybe if I just focus on something else for a while, it will come back to me when I least expect it. "I think we need a break. Why don't we have some dinner?"

"Not sure I could keep anything down."

"I know the feeling." I give him a shaky smile. "But we should at least try. We've hardly eaten anything today."

"If you say so." He stands, clutching the chair for support. On wobbly limbs, we make our way upstairs.

In the kitchen, I throw together a stir-fry from some left-over chicken and noodles and start a pot of coffee. I don't usually drink it, but right now, I need something warm. As the coffee percolates and Steven pushes noodles around in a pan, I chop vegetables. The knife slips, and the breath hisses between my teeth. The pain is dizzying. My vision goes black for a second or two. When the dark fog clears, I watch, hypnotized, as the blood wells up and drips to the cutting board.

I don't know why it's so fascinating, but I feel like I could watch those ruby drops all day.

Steven gently grips my arm, jolting me from my trance. "Run that under cold water," he says. "Where's your first aid kit?"

"The bathroom," I murmur.

He turns on the faucet, and I run my thumb under the stream. There's a lot of blood. The knife must have cut deep. Pink-tinted water swirls around the drain, and I think about the bloody tears in the Lucid dream. Maybe that part was a hallucination. It felt so surreal.

Steven returns with a small white box. "Let me see."

I turn off the faucet, and he examines the wound. The bleeding has stopped for the moment, but the sight of the cut makes my stomach squirm. The lips of the wound are white, the inside deep red. I shut my eyes.

"Wouldn't have thought you'd be so squeamish, Doc. I mean, after all the things you've seen in people's heads . . ."

"I know, it's ridiculous. But I'm a sissy about cuts. Always have been."

He applies antiseptic cream, then bandages my thumb. His touch is so light, so careful, that I barely feel it. When I open my eyes and see the wound covered, I breathe a small sigh of relief. "Thank you." I smile at him.

He rubs the back of his neck. "'S nothing."

I take his hand in mine and turn it over, looking at his long, pale fingers. Though there are a few tiny scars crisscrossing the knuckles, his hands are almost delicate. "You have a healer's touch."

His breathing quickens slightly. He pulls his hand from mine. "Yeah, right."

"No . . . really." I look up, searching his face. "Have you done any more drawings since I last saw you?"

"A few."

"Will you show me sometime?"

A flush rises into his cheeks. He clears his throat. "Don't know if I really should."

That's an odd reaction. I'm not sure what to make of it.

A smoky smell tinges the air. "Oh! The noodles are burning." I hurry to the stove and grab a spatula.

Once everything is ready, we sit at the table. My stomach doesn't want the food, but I force it down. After a few minutes, I realize Steven's not eating. A piece of broccoli sits at the end of his fork. He stares at it, his expression distant.

"Steven?"

Slowly, he sets the fork down. "I almost died last night. I

came so close. If you hadn't come for me . . ." His voice trembles. He draws in a slow, deep breath and lets it out through his nose. His eyes are wet. "Damn it," he mutters, rubbing a sleeve across his eyes. He keeps it there, hiding his face in the crook of his arm.

I want to tell him that he can cry—that he doesn't have to be embarrassed—but he's the type who feels weak after any form of emotional display. In some ways, we're very similar. So I wait, letting him regain control of himself.

At last, he lowers his arm. The whites of his eyes are tinted a light pink. "You've probably dealt with a lot of people like me, haven't you?"

"People like you?"

"You know." He cracks a smile. "Suicidal sad sacks."

"I wouldn't use that term. But yes. Many of my clients have been suicidal at one point or another. People generally don't seek out memory modification unless they've tried everything else."

"Do you ever hate us?"

I blink. "Of course not. Why would I?"

"I mean . . . honestly. Do you ever think we're just a bunch of selfish babies, running from our pain? I wouldn't blame you if you did. Hell, sometimes I think that's exactly what I am."

I shake my head. "Anyone who sees it as selfishness or cowardice has simply been privileged enough not to feel that pain themselves." My grip on my fork tightens. "When it's that bad, it consumes you. Nothing else matters. You can't move, you can't eat. You can barely even breathe. Death seems like the only way out, the only way you'll ever escape that hell. I could never resent someone for feeling that way."

"Wait . . . You've felt that way, too? When?"

I bite my tongue.

"Sorry. You don't have to answer that if you don't want to."

I avert my gaze. "It's all right." I pick up my plate, take it to the sink, and run it under water. Bits of sauce-covered noodles slide loose and disappear into the drain. I scrub the plate as I wait for my lips to stop trembling. We're quite a pair, Steven and I. The Amazing Repression Duo.

Once I've gotten ahold of myself, I turn to face him. "Anyway, you changed your mind. You made the choice to live."

His brow wrinkles. "I didn't, though. If you hadn't shown up, I'd be dead."

"But you called me. You let me into the building. You wouldn't have done that unless you wanted to be saved."

"I guess so." Absently, he pushes a bit of noodle around on his plate. "I should never have applied for that damn pill. But when you're desperate and you see all these ads telling you there's an easy, painless way out . . . well, it's tempting."

"It's heinous, the way drug companies profit from people's despair." I shake my head in disgust. "One day, the law will change. People's attitudes will change. And the use of Somnazol will be seen as a shameful and barbaric chapter of our history."

Steven raises an eyebrow. "You seem pretty sure of that."

"I just can't understand why our society tolerates this." I seize a towel and dry my plate in fierce, hard swipes. "Somnazol's very existence implies that some people are beyond hope, that they're better off dead, that it's okay to give up on them. It's that attitude I hate, more than anything. Worse than that, people are *encouraged* to die. They're told that it's the responsible choice. And everyone just accepts it!"

Steven raises an eyebrow. "This is personal for you, isn't it?"

Warmth rises into my cheeks. I clear my throat and put the plate away. "Anyway. We should try to find some information about that place."

"What place?"

"St. Mary's."

"Oh. Right."

"Come with me."

He follows me up the stairs. "Where are we going?"

"My bedroom."

"Uh . . . bedroom?" He sounds a little nervous.

I almost smile. "Chloe's up here. My avatar, that is." I open the door and sit on the edge of my bed. "Have a seat." I nod to the chair near my desk.

Steven pulls up the chair and sits. He fidgets, looking around at the pale pink walls, the flower-patterned comforter on my bed, the rows of stuffed animals. "It's girlier than I expected."

"Well, I hope you've had your cooties vaccine. I happen to like pink." Come to think of it, this is the first time I've ever had a boy in my room. Not even Ian has been up here. A wave of self-consciousness washes over me, and I squirm. This has been my bedroom since I was a little girl, and— embarrassingly—I haven't changed the décor much since then. What does he think of the stuffed animals? *Why, yes, the girl who'll be performing a highly specialized medical procedure on your brain does in fact sleep with a squirrel.*

I nudge Nutter behind a pillow, trying to be discreet about it.

Steven doesn't notice. He's looking at the photo on the

nightstand, the one of my father holding my four-year-old self. But he doesn't say anything.

"Anyway . . ." I interlace my fingers in my lap. "Chloe?"

Chloe materializes at the foot of the bed. Steven gives a start.

I tilt my head. "Never seen a holoavatar before?"

"Most of them aren't this real-looking." He leans closer, squinting, and pokes her. His finger passes through her back as if she's made of smoke.

Chloe sniffs. "How rude." She rises and walks to the side. Her feet don't disturb the bedding, but other than that, she looks and moves exactly like a real cat.

"Chloe, this is my friend Steven. Steven, Chloe."

"How do you do?" She offers a paw.

Gingerly, he grasps it, though of course, he's grasping thin air. "Um. Fine."

Chloe turns to me and chirps, "So, what can I help you with?"

"Look up St. Mary's."

Her ears flick. Her eyes glow a brighter green as lines of text shimmer across them. "There are millions of search results for 'St. Mary's.' Please narrow it down a little for me. Is it a church? A hospital? A school?"

"We don't know. But it's probably close to a town called Wolf's Run."

Steven seems to recognize the name. He glances at me.

"Is this town in the Northeast Quadrant?" Chloe asks.

"Yes," I say. "That's right."

Her ears flick back and forth. "I found only one result within a fifty-mile radius of Wolf's Run."

"What is it?"

"An abandoned asylum."

Steven frowns. "A what?"

"*Asylum* is an archaic term for a psychiatric ward," I say.

Chloe nods. "This particular facility is a remnant of Old America. It hasn't been used for over a century. Take a look." Light shines from her eyes, and the screen flickers to life above her, a hovering rectangle of light.

Steven leans forward. The pale glow bathes his face.

The screen is filled with black-and-white photographs of crumbling stone walls, empty rooms, and ceilings riddled with gaping holes. My heart sinks. This can't be the place I saw in Steven's memories. I could widen the search to the entire Northeast Quadrant, but who knows which—if any—of the results would be accurate? The name alone simply isn't enough to go on.

"Do you need anything else?" Chloe asks.

"No thank you. That's all."

Chloe curls up and vanishes.

Steven sighs. "So we're back to square one. What now?"

I close my dry, itchy eyes and rub them. I've barely slept these past few nights, and the exhaustion is starting to catch up to me. My limbs feel like sandbags. "Maybe we should just get some sleep."

"You know . . . we've still got two more."

I pull the compact from my coat pocket and flip it open, revealing the two pills—the smiling mushroom and the Chinese dragon—rolling within. "Ian told me we needed to space them out. It's dangerous to take more than one a day."

"Tomorrow, then?"

I study the shiny little pills, with their deceptively harmless-looking cartoon images. Do I really want to put Steven through that again? Should I really be pushing him to relive the horrors from his childhood?

I remind myself that he chose this. He wants the truth, too. "All right," I say. I snap the compact shut and put it back in my pocket. "Tomorrow."

He stands.

I know we both need to get some rest, but I find I don't want him to leave just yet. In my head, I see him lying on the floor of his apartment, still and silent. I remember the lurch of panic in my chest, the horrible fear of not knowing whether he was alive or dead. I want to wrap my arms around him, to feel the warmth and solidity of his body, the rhythm of his heart and lungs—to reassure myself, once again, of his realness. "Steven . . . I . . ."

He waits, looking at me.

I could invite him to stay the night. The couch folds out. He could sleep there. But I've already crossed too many lines.

The ghost of my psych-ethics professor whispers in my head: *Compassion and empathy are admirable traits, but empathizing too strongly with a client can be dangerous. Once you lose your distance and objectivity, you can't effectively do your job. Though it may not seem like it, the client wants you to maintain that distance, even if he may not fully realize it himself. He is counting on it.*

I shake my head. "It's nothing."

21

I'm running through a gray forest. The trees are black knives, their branches sharp and jagged, cutting the sky into shards that pour down around me. Glass litters the forest floor, sparkling like solid rain. All around me, crows watch from the treetops with unblinking black eyes. My feet are bare, and the glass slices into them, sending jabs of pain through me. I'm bleeding, leaving splotches of red with each step.

There's something chasing me, some huge beast, panting and growling. I can't pause, not even to look over my shoulder. If I hesitate for an instant, it will catch me. I run harder, faster. Pain screams up my legs with each step, but I don't stop. I don't dare.

The crows are cawing, beating their wings in a frenzy. They take to the broken sky and circle overhead. One lands on a branch nearby and seems to smile, its dagger-like beak opening to reveal a red maw.

"Turn," the crow whispers. "Turn around."

But I can't, I can't.

The beast is almost upon me, its breath gusting hotly on my neck. A dead end looms ahead, a wall of shadow. I turn and find myself staring into my own eyes.

I wake with a start. The bedroom is bright, and birds twitter outside my window. Just a dream, of course. I exhale and roll onto my stomach, hiding my face against the pillow.

Would one night of uninterrupted sleep be too much to ask for?

I sit up, pushing a hand through my disheveled hair. When I glance at myself in the mirror, I wince, then grab a brush and try to tame my snarled brown mane. Once it's suitably flattened, I bind it into pigtails, throw on my clothes, and trudge down the stairs. My head aches dully—a faint remnant of my Lucid hangover.

What a night.

I make myself a mug of apple cinnamon tea, slice a grapefruit in half, and sit at the table. Before I can start to eat, my cell phone buzzes. Expecting a text from Steven, I pull the phone from my pocket. The message is from Dr. Swan.

REPORT TO MY OFFICE IMMEDIATELY.

That's it. No explanation. Just that single blunt order.

Of course, I know what it's about. He's discovered that I'm a Type Two now, and naturally, he wants to discuss it with me. Or maybe . . .

Has he somehow found out about me and Steven?

I push the thought away.

I don't bother to eat my grapefruit. I drive straight to IFEN headquarters and try to ignore the way my pulse thunders in my ears as I step into Dr. Swan's office. His face is inscrutable as I sit down in the leather armchair. For a moment, he just stares at me across the expanse of his desk. "I don't think I need to tell you why you're here."

"Yes." I realize I'm clenching my fists and force myself to relax them. I fold my hands in my lap. "I'm aware that I've been reclassified. I believe it's some sort of mistake."

"So does everyone. You know better. But that's not really why I called you here."

It takes an effort to keep my expression blank.

Relax. He has no way of knowing about the immersion sessions or the Lucid. Maybe he saw some security footage of me with Steven, maybe he knows we're spending time together, but that's all. "What are you referring to?" I ask, carefully controlling my tone.

"I'm not going to play games with you. I'm just going to give you one last warning. Stay away from that boy."

The anger flares in my chest, a rush of heat. I'm sick of this. "I'm almost eighteen. You can't tell me who to spend time with. You have no right—"

"I have every right. You're not an adult yet. And even if you were, I'm still your supervisor, and you are my protégé."

I glare at him. "If I'd left Steven alone, he'd be dead by now. You knew he had a Somnazol, didn't you? Why didn't you tell me?"

His expression remains rigid and closed. "He applied for it himself. He followed the proper procedures. There was nothing we could do."

"So I was supposed to just stand aside and let him die?"

He closes his eyes, as if struggling for control. "If someone chooses to pass and does it legally, we must respect their choice, whether or not we agree. You can't save everyone, Lain. As I've said many times, your father entrusted me with your well-being—"

"Don't talk to me about my father," I snap. My fingers dig into the arms of the chair. "You're not my father."

His eyes narrow. "You don't know the circumstances leading up to his death, do you?" he asks, his tone almost casual.

I tense.

"He was a man of great compassion. In a way, that was his weakness. As a Mindwalker, he took on many burdens, more than he could handle. Near the end, his mental health started to slip, and he was reclassified. He could no longer legally treat clients. I tried to convince him to seek help, but he refused. He grew increasingly paranoid and reclusive. In the end, his sickness overcame him completely, and he chose to destroy himself rather than accept treatment."

I struggle to keep my expression neutral. I remind myself that I don't know whether Dr. Swan is telling the truth. But what if he is?

He's watching my face closely, as if he can see the thoughts playing out. "I suppose you haven't given much thought to how it affected me. I was just his friend, after all. But I did care about him, and believe it or not, I care about you, too. It was devastating to watch him disintegrate. Can you imagine what it's like watching you go down the same path?"

There's a hard, hot ball in my chest, and my throat is tight. "What does any of this have to do with Steven?"

"If you continue to associate with him, he will destroy

you. Anger and paranoia are contagious, and the more time you spend with him, the more his twisted way of thinking will creep into yours. It's already happening. I can see it." His voice softens. "Learn from your father's mistakes."

My nails dig into my palms, burning.

"You have a lot going for you, Lain. Your grades are impressive. Your behavioral record is spotless. If you seek therapy now, your psyche will undoubtedly recover, and this whole incident will be no more than a tiny blip in your file. Think seriously—do you really want to endanger all that? For what? Some boy? You barely know him."

"I know him better than you do."

"I wouldn't be too sure of that."

"What is that supposed to mean?"

He shakes his head, dismissing the question. "You're a child rebelling against her elders, chasing after a boy she's been told to stay away from. You're fascinated by him because he's forbidden. That's all."

"You don't understand the first thing about Steven. You think you know what he's been through? You have no idea."

His mouth tightens. For a moment, he studies me in silence. I don't move or speak. Then he leans forward, looking straight into my eyes, and lowers his voice to a near whisper. "Sometimes, it's better to let the past rest."

A chill ripples through me. Goose bumps rise on my arms and legs.

He knows. He knows what I've been doing. More than that, he knows that Steven's memories have been altered. And he's telling me to stop nosing around for answers. "I don't know what you're talking about." My voice shakes despite my efforts to control it. "If that's all you have to say, I'm leaving."

"All it takes is two words, Lain. Two words in your file— *emotional instability*, perhaps—and you'll never set foot in IFEN again."

A bead of sweat trickles down my neck. "Is that a threat?"

"Please understand, I only want what's best for you."

I turn away. A hot, bitter taste fills my mouth like bile. "You know, I'm getting really sick of that line."

I walk out the door.

* * *

When I get back home, I check the house for bugs. I pull the books off the shelves in the living room, peer under the furniture, and examine the walls and ceiling. Nothing. I go through the house systematically, searching each room, until I come to my bedroom. After I've thoroughly examined every corner, I stand, chewing my thumbnail. He's been watching me somehow. I know it.

I look at the rows of stuffed animals on my shelves. The pink bunny, the green Cthulhu, the teddy bear with the eye patch. There's something different about the bear's shiny black eye. Slowly, I pick up the toy. Deep inside the semitransparent plastic eyeball, I see a glint of silver. Hands shaking, I grab a pair of scissors and cut out the eye. A thin, flexible silver tube trails from the back like an optic nerve. A spy camera. My fingers tighten on the bear.

Greta must have planted it. That's the only explanation. But when? How long has Dr. Swan been watching me? How much has he seen? Is it only video, or does it record audio as well?

I throw the bear across the room. It bounces off the wall and lands facedown on the floor.

My breathing quickens until my vision starts to blur. A scream wells up in my chest and tries to claw its way from my throat, but I choke it down. I won't let Dr. Swan get away with this. I won't let him beat me.

22

"Are you going to tell me why we're here?" Steven asks.

We're walking side by side down a hallway in the Complex—a vast hundred-story shopping mall. It's probably the best-known spot in downtown Aura. The stores are all situated along the edges of the cylinder-shaped building. The center is empty space, giving shoppers a vertigo-inducing view of the drop to the first floor. Elevators glide up and down transparent chutes.

I lean toward him, until my lips are barely an inch from his ear, and murmur, "I'm not sure my house is secure."

He stops. "What are you talking about?"

"Keep moving," I say, hooking an arm through his. We pass a toy store with an elaborate, twinkling model of Aura in the window.

The dull clamor of voices and footsteps fills the air, mingling with the music drifting from half a dozen stores. There are cameras, of course, but no audio-recording devices. That would be pointless, since it's impossible to pick individual conversations out of the chaos. Still, I keep my voice low, just in case anyone is listening. "Dr. Swan—you know, the director of IFEN? He called me to his office and told me to stop spending time with you. And I found a spy camera in my room. He's been watching us."

Steven tenses.

"I checked the rest of the house for bugs. I couldn't find any, but that doesn't mean they aren't there. For now, I feel safer talking in a place like this."

"What about Chloe?" he asks.

"What about her?"

"I mean, could he use her to watch you? Like hack into her database or something?"

I wince. How did that not occur to me? "It's possible." Has he been keeping track of my searches, too? I make a mental note not to use her again unless I absolutely need to. If I activate her at all, it'll only be to clear her caches. Though I'm not sure that'll help at this point.

We pass a clothing store. Grinding, thumping music pulses from inside, and holographic models pose in the windows, showing off the merchandise. Their bodies are human, but they have the heads of extinct animals. There's a full-breasted tiger in a shimmering green dress, a muscle-bound zebra in a black tuxedo, and some kind of improbable-looking white bird with a long, hooked beak wearing a two-piece bathing suit.

Steven walks quickly, his expression grim. "He could ruin everything for you, couldn't he?"

I nod reluctantly.

"I'm putting you in danger just by being with you."

There's a twinge of cold fear, deep in my belly. I think

about the clusters of homeless people huddled around fires in the more run-down parts of Aura—people who can't find employment because of their Type. Even if I never wind up in that situation, I'll certainly be barred from treating clients again if I continue to defy Dr. Swan.

Fresh anger surges inside me, hot and bright, overpowering the fear. He thinks he can manipulate me with threats? He thinks he can spy on me and intimidate me and expect me to bend to his wishes? "I don't care what he does," I say. "I'm not quitting now. We've come too far to turn back."

"Lain . . ."

"We're going ahead with the plan."

Steven doesn't reply.

We leave the Complex and walk to the nearest monorail station. As we wait for the mono, I notice someone washing away graffiti on a cement wall. I can still make out the words.

BLACKCOATS UNITE. THE REVOLUTION IS COMING.

A shiver runs through me.

Leaning closer to Steven, I point to the graffiti and lower my voice. "Do you think there actually is some kind of secret resistance movement?"

He gives me a long, searching look. "What do you think?"

IFEN has made official statements that the rumors of a resistance are false, that the Blackcoats are a thing of the past, that anyone who talks about an underground network of rebels is merely disturbed. Troubled people often try to stir up fear and unrest, because they want others to be as troubled as they are. They hammered that point into us over and over in the psychology classes I took during my training: *Fear is contagious. As a Mindwalker, you'll be exposed to many paranoid people. The most dangerous thing you can do is to take them seriously.*

Maybe they're right, but it strikes me as a very convenient mantra for those who want to keep the status quo in place: *Anyone who questions the wisdom and goodness of our system is sick, and they'll infect you if you pay too much attention.* I wonder if having such thoughts means that I am already infected. Isn't that exactly what Dr. Swan warned me about? Am I slipping deeper and deeper into insanity, as my father did?

I think of the wild-eyed man on the street corner handing out his flyers. *Join the resistance,* he said. If I picked up one of those incoherent, exclamation-point-laden flyers now, maybe it would actually make sense to me. Maybe the words would magically rearrange themselves into a compellingly written thesis on the rights of man, complete with citations.

The mono pulls up, and we get on. I haven't answered Steven's question, I realize. I don't have any answers. Only more and more questions.

* * *

Back in the Gate room, I settle myself into my chair, open the compact, and pluck out the mushroom pill. I glance over at Steven. "Ready?"

"As I'll ever be." He smiles, though he's a little pale. "Let's ride the mushroom train."

I hand the pill to him, and he curls his fingers around it,

gripping it tight. I remember the way I felt after the blue bunny pill—sick, my head pounding like a drum—and I try to swallow my dread. But of course, the physical pain is the least of my worries. Suddenly, my palms are wet, my throat clenched. "You're sure about this?" I can't resist asking.

"You got any better ideas?"

"No," I admit. St. Mary's is clearly a dead end; we saw for ourselves there's nothing there. These pills are our only key to the truth. Still . . . "This is going to be stronger than the last one, you know."

"Getting scared, huh? Can't say I blame you. If I were you, I wouldn't want to go back into my head, either."

"I just wish I had some idea of what we'll find."

He rolls the pill between a thumb and forefinger. "You ever read Dante's *Inferno*? I think it's like that. I think I'm like that. The farther down you travel, the worse it gets. I wonder just how deep you're willing to go."

I meet his gaze. "To the very bottom of the ninth circle."

He stares back at me for a long moment, his expression solemn. Then he smiles with one corner of his mouth. "Kinda cheesy, Doc."

The remark is so unexpected that I burst out laughing. "It's *your* metaphor. Don't blame me." I swallow the laughter. "I mean it, though. However bad it gets, I'll be there."

"You've got a masochistic streak," he says, arching an eyebrow. "You know that?"

"Look who's talking."

We maintain eye contact, drawing it out, locked in a silent battle to see who can hold a straight face the longest. Then we start to giggle again. Giddiness swims through my head like silver bubbles. "There's nothing funny about this," I gasp, tears of mirth leaking from my eyes.

"I know," he replies through bursts of laughter.

When the manic giggles finally die down, I square my shoulders and say, "All right. Let's do this." I shove the helmet onto my head and buckle the chin strap. Steven puts on his own helmet, then swallows the mushroom pill. I slide my visor into place as the familiar tingling of immersion spreads through my body, and I feel the pill sliding down Steven's throat.

I brace myself for the disorientation, the vertigo, the feeling that space is stretching around me. But this time, it doesn't happen that way.

My stomach cramps in a sharp, wrenching spasm. Steven gasps, his back arching off the chair. His fingers twitch, clench, and flex, as if he's being electrocuted. As the drug works its way into his bloodstream, my body and brain burn along with his. My heart slams against my breastbone. Electricity buzzes in my skull. My muscles spasm, then lock tight, as if someone flipped a switch in my brain, shutting off my voluntary motor functions. I can only lie there gasping for breath as my heart rate climbs.

Then a hole opens up in the air in front of me.

It's perfectly black, an expanding circle of nothingness. The edges blur and distort the room, as if it's warping the very fabric of space. From within, I hear a low, buzzing hum. No, not a hum—voices, a soft chorus of them. There are no words. It's somewhere between moaning and singing, and it grows louder with every passing second. I try to scream, but nothing comes out. I can't move.

My body lurches forward into the hole, and blackness swallows me.

For a span of time that might be seconds or centuries, there's nothing. Then I'm walking through a desert. The sand stretches in every direction, white and rippled under a star-filled night sky. I have the sense that I've been walking for a very long time. Years, maybe.

I stop. An enormous sphinx of sand-colored stone looms before me. She has my face.

What is this place? Why am I here? I knew a moment ago, but now it's gone.

Between the sphinx's paws, I see a dark square. A hole.

I approach slowly. Voices swell around me, warbling in their unearthly harmony as I near the edge. A set of stone stairs leads downward, into blackness.

I don't want to enter that hole. I know with a bone-deep certainty that something terrible awaits me. Somewhere in the depths of my dream, I'm still aware of my physical body sitting in the chair. Maybe I could wake up if I tried. *Go back*, my instincts scream.

I descend the stairs. Silence enfolds me. The shadows grow thick, and the only sound is my own rapid breathing. I touch the wall, trailing my fingers along the cool, dry stone, feeling my way down a long tunnel as the faint light dwindles behind me. Then I see another light ahead, dim and reddish. The tunnel opens out into a vast stone cavern, filled with that bloody glow, which comes from everywhere and nowhere. In one corner, a pale golden form is curled up like a cat. But it's enormous, bigger than my house.

A dragon.

Its nose rests on its car-sized, scaled paws. Its blue eyes watch me, unblinking, as the tip of its tail flicks. Slowly, its head lifts, and its jaws stretch open, revealing rows of dripping white teeth. Smoke curls from its nostrils.

I take a few steps back. My hand tightens around the hilt of my sword— Wait, I have a sword? I glance down and see a shining blade. In my other hand, I'm gripping a shield.

The dragon growls and takes a step toward me, then stops. It watches me, waiting. Waiting to see if I'll attack or defend.

I look into its eyes. Sharp, intelligent eyes, cautious and wounded.

I drop my sword and shield. The dragon looks at me.

"Go ahead," I say.

Its jaws stretch wide, descending. A gust of hot breath hits me in the face as the jaws close around me. The dragon swallows me whole.

And then I'm falling again, plummeting into a dark, deep pit.

Time stretches and bends. For a while, I float. I drift up slowly through layers of murky darkness, growing steadily lighter. Distantly, I can hear voices. Men's voices.

I open my eyes.

Everything is white—the walls, the ceiling, the overhead lights. I'm lying on a cold metal table, and I can't move. Out of sight, a machine buzzes and whirs. My breathing quickens. I try to sit up, but I can't. My body feels like it's glued in place. Only my eyes can move. I strain them down, trying to see myself, but everything goes fuzzy.

"Gently, now," says a soft voice. It's distorted and echoed, but there's something vaguely familiar about it.

"Relax," replies a deep voice, equally distorted. "I know what I'm doing." In the corner of the room sits an old, boxy gray machine with a little window. Behind the window, tiny circles turn, and a woman's voice drifts from the speakers. She's singing in another language.

"Can we turn that thing off?" the first voice mutters.

"It helps me focus. I'm the one doing the tricky part here. You just concentrate on holding up pictures." The drill whirs again.

An image fills my vision—a black-and-white drawing of an animal, and I should know the name, but it won't come. "Do you see this?" asks the soft-voiced man.

I whimper.

"Steven, I need you to concentrate. Look. What is this?"

The name drifts into my head. "Elephant." My own voice sounds soft and far away.

The picture lowers. Off to the side, gloved hands pass shiny knives back and forth. Something red drips from the blades. Blood. My blood. I start to breathe faster. *Move*, I tell my body. The little finger on my right hand twitches once. I try to lift my hand, but it's too heavy. The blade lowers toward me and disappears. There's a faint, wet, crackling noise, as if someone is cutting meat.

Another picture comes up in front of me: three fluffy kittens in a basket. "What about this one? Do you see this?"

I feel sick. Dizzy. Black spots wiggle in front of my eyes.

"Steven. Can you tell me what's in this picture?"

"Cats." My voice is faint now. Weak. A drill whines and whirs, and grinding noises echo through the room. Somewhere deep beneath the numbness is pain, and for a few seconds, I feel like I'm going to throw up. They're taking me apart, and I can't move.

More whirring and grinding.

A moment of blinding panic—THEY'RE KILLING YOU. RUN!—then the gray fog comes over me again. Run where? Where would I go? What would I do?

My body feels heavy. It's a strange feeling, being so scared, yet not caring.

"Heart rate spiked for a moment," says Soft Voice. "Should we increase the sedatives?"

"No," Deep Voice says, growling a little. "We need him conscious. I'm going to—" The voice goes fuzzy in my ears, the words running together, garbled. "—deliver the injection directly into—" More fuzzy babble, almost understandable but not quite, like someone speaking underwater.

I just want this to be over. A tear escapes the corner of my eye and slides down my cheek.

Gloved fingers brush away the tear. I blink.

"Just relax," says Soft Voice. "It will all be over soon."

A face lowers into my field of vision, and a pair of eyes stare at me from above a surgical mask as a hand touches my temple. My focus narrows. All I can see is those eyes. Light, tawny brown, with a slight tint of green, and a tiny gold fleck in the left eye. I know those eyes. I've seen them many times. They're . . .

They're mine.

No!

I snap back into my own body, into the present, shaking and drenched with sweat. I shut my eyes, clutch my bracelet, and repeat my identity affirmation exercises to myself.

Lain Fisher. My name is Lain Fisher. I'm seventeen years old, a student at Greenborough High School. I—I—

I yank the visor up. Light floods my eyes, stinging, making them water. I blink, dizzy and nauseous, as the world settles into place around me. Tiled floor. Blank white walls. But my walls. My basement.

My head pounds. It's worse than last time. When I try to sit up, nausea rolls over me and pushes me down like a wave of liquid lead.

At first, my voice doesn't want to work. I open my mouth and nothing comes out, save a weak croak. After a minute, I finally manage to whisper, "Steven?"

Steven sits, breathing heavily, the visor covering his eyes. Slowly, he reaches up and pulls off his helmet, not looking at me.

"Steven, can you hear me?"

"Yeah." His voice is flat, emotionless.

I slide off my own helmet and run a hand through my sweat-damp hair. "Do you . . ." My voice wavers. "Do you remember what you saw?"

"Some of it." He sits up, shoulders stiff. Still, he won't look at me. He reaches into his pocket, fishes out a handful of little white pills, and swallows three of them. "I'm going outside," he mutters. "I need some air." Without even glancing at me, he leaves the room.

23

I find Steven standing on my front lawn, hands in his pockets, staring into space. The sun sinks toward the western horizon, orange light bleeding between the clouds and reflecting in the windows of the houses around us.

He turns to face me, his expression grim. "What the hell is going on? Did I hallucinate all that?"

I swallow, mouth dry, and collect my thoughts. Automatically, I slip into my neutral Mindwalker voice. "Even if the memory itself was real, that doesn't mean it's accurate in every detail. Memories change over time. The raw sensory impressions start to decay almost immediately, and the brain patches up the holes, so eventually, what you have is less like a photograph and more like a painting of a photograph. A blend of imagination and reality."

"So my brain gave him your eyes."

Which is disturbing in its own right. Why did his subconscious project me into that role—as one of his tormentors?

In a nearby tree, a crow caws once.

His eyes are distant, unfocused. "Tell me something, Doc. If our memories can't be trusted, then what can?"

I hesitate. "Science? Things that can be validated with hard evidence?"

"Yeah, well, we're a little short on evidence." His hands are shaking. He shuts his eyes and presses the heels of his hands against his lids. Fumbling, he fishes two more pills from his pocket and swallows them. How many of those does he take in a day?

I move a small, cautious step closer. "You trust *me*, don't you?"

He doesn't answer.

"Steven?"

"Nothing personal, Doc." He smiles tightly. "I don't trust anyone."

The words sting more than they should. "Even after I saved your life?" The question comes out sounding somehow arrogant.

"I'm grateful for that. Really. But I still don't understand why you did it."

"Because . . ." *Because you're my client. Because you're my friend. Because the thought of losing you makes me so scared, I can't breathe.* "I don't want anyone to die if I can prevent it," I finish limply.

"So you run around hoping to save every sad sack who tries to off himself? Must get pretty tiring."

My nails dig into my palms. "What do you want me to say?"

"Nothing."

I breathe in, struggling for patience. "I swear, I just want to help you."

He grips his own arms, fingers digging into his flesh. "That's what scares me." He laughs, a bitter bark. "Every guy in a white coat who's ever strapped me into that fucking Conditioning machine, every nurse who's ever stuck a needle in my arm to sedate me because I was getting 'agitated'—they all just wanted to help. Because I'm too sick and screwed up to make my own decisions, they have to force a cure down my throat, like I'm some bratty little kid who doesn't want to take his cough syrup. And you're not like them—I know that—but still, you work for the system. You have to follow its rules." His lips twist in something that's half smile, half agonized grimace. "So, what happens if you have another conscience attack and decide that 'helping' me means turning me over to IFEN?"

I flinch.

I want to deny that it would ever happen, but not long ago, I came close to doing just that—simply because I no longer saw myself as qualified to treat him. What would have happened to Steven if I'd succumbed to self-doubt? "Listen," I say quietly. "Things have changed. I know more than I did before. I'm in this as deep as you are. In order to keep searching for the truth, we have to trust each other. If we don't, we won't last long."

He doesn't answer.

"I swear, Steven. I'll never hand you over to them or let them do anything to you against your will. I'd prove it if I could, but it's not like I can open up my head and let you see my intentions. You'll just have to—" The words wither in my throat as I realize what I've said.

His brow furrows, and the look in his eyes shifts. It's now sharp, intent. "You could," he says, speaking slowly, as if feeling out the words as he goes. "It's possible, isn't it? We could switch places. I could use the Gate on you."

My heartbeat grows louder, filling my ears. "It's not that simple. You don't have the training."

"What, is it dangerous? Could I accidentally fry your brain or something?"

"Well . . . no. Not if I set it to observe-only mode."

"Then what's the problem?"

My pulse drums in my throat and wrists. If I let him in my head, he'll see my feelings for him, and I'm not even sure what those feelings are—just that they're complicated and bewildering and far too strong, and I'm not supposed to have them. "It wouldn't be a good idea," I mumble, studying my shoes.

When I raise my head, the look in his eyes has changed again. It's hard, cold. Dangerous.

Involuntarily, I take a step back.

In one stride, he closes the distance between us. My back goes rigid as he reaches up. Thin fingers slide into the hair at the nape of my neck, twining through the long strands. He grips, anchoring my head in place, and brings his own face closer, until I can see every filament of color in his irises, all the subtle shades of blue and gray interwoven like the threads of a tapestry. I nearly swallow my tongue. We're standing almost nose to nose, as if he's about to kiss me, but he doesn't look like someone lost in passion. He looks . . . feral. "What's wrong?" I ask, my voice wobbling.

His fingers tighten in my hair, sending tiny twinges of pain through my scalp. "There's something you're not telling me." Wildness dances in his eyes, like lightning flickering in clouds.

A vision flashes through my head—Steven tackling the young man at his old school, biting a chunk out of his face, ripping flesh as the man screamed. "Something you don't want me to see. Is that it?"

I somehow manage to unswallow my tongue long enough to whisper, "No."

"Then why don't you want me to use the Gate on you?"

Panic eats away at my thoughts. He can't hurt me—the collar will stop him if he tries—but that's not what I'm afraid of. I don't know what I'm afraid of.

I breathe in, trying to ignore the way my heart is racing. "Steven," I say, struggling to keep my expression blank, "you can't just demand access to someone's mind. A person's thoughts are very private. I entered yours only because you asked me to. I wouldn't have done it if it weren't a necessary part of the treatment. This—what you're asking for—it's different." Sweat trickles down my sides, tiny, cold beads. "Let me go."

He doesn't move.

"Let me go," I repeat with more force.

He hesitates. His fingers loosen their grip and slide out of my hair. The crazed glint in his eyes fades, and he looks merely uncertain. Lost.

I close my eyes briefly and turn my thoughts inward, seeking the center of calm within me. I touch the back of my head. My scalp stings. "Don't ever do that again," I say softly. "For a moment, I thought you were going to hurt me."

His eyes widen and lose focus, as if the reality of the situation is sinking in. Then I see the horror dawning slowly in his expression. "No," he whispers. "I would never— That's not—" His throat clicks as he swallows. He looks down at his hands, his face pale. Then he bows his head, shoulders hunched. "I'm sorry." His voice is so quiet, so subdued. The change is disorienting in its suddenness.

"It's all right," I say, keeping my tone businesslike. "Just don't do it again."

His face slowly regains its color. He takes a deep breath and straightens, lifting his eyes to mine. There's a strange look in them, a mixture of determination and pleading. "I won't."

I nod and give him a small smile. He doesn't return it, but the tension eases out of his shoulders. The silence hangs between us, thick and awkward. I bite my lower lip.

I know so many of his secrets, and he knows only what I've chosen to tell him about myself, which isn't much. Of course it would be inappropriate to let a client into my head, but after all that's happened, I can't keep pretending we're just Mindwalker and client. I'm pretty sure the last scraps of my objectivity flew out the window when I rushed to his apartment and illegally saved his life. And still, I can't bring myself to erase the boundaries between us. Maybe I'm just a hypocrite. "About—about what you asked—"

He shakes his head. "Forget I said anything." All traces of aggression have drained out of him; he looks weary, wrung out. "I was the one who came to you asking for help that first day. Hell, I wouldn't be here now if not for you. You don't owe me anything."

The words should relieve me. Instead, they hurt.

The sun has almost vanished beneath the horizon. Its light bleeds over the roofs, red-orange, thick as syrup.

"So, what now?" he asks. His tone is brisk, neutral, as if the whole conversation never happened.

I hook a few loose tendrils of hair behind my ear and try to collect my scattered thoughts. "Well, there's one pill left. Though we can't take it yet, obviously."

His lips press into a thin line. "Do I even want to know what else is hidden in my head? I mean, if the truth sucks, is it worth finding?"

"That's something only you can decide. It's your past." Cautiously, I lay a hand on his arm. He tenses. "Just remember that you aren't alone."

He looks at me, and all the guardedness and sharp edges are gone. He looks lost, and very young.

I fold my arms around him. His breath hitches. For a moment, he just stands there, back rigid, every muscle tensed in a fight-or-flight reflex. He places his hands against my shoulders as if to push me away. Then his arms go limp and he leans into the embrace, as if he can't help it. A tiny shiver runs through his body.

We remain that way for several minutes. The clouds turn from pink to soft violet, and the light fades from the sky. At last, Steven pulls away and wipes one sleeve across his eyes.

"Should we go inside?" I ask. "I don't know about you, but I could use something warm to drink."

He nods.

Later, we sit in the kitchen as a kettle of tea brews on the stove, filling the air with the scent of mint. My cell phone rings. Distractedly, I answer. "Hello?"

"I've given you an excessively generous number of chances," Dr. Swan says.

My chest turns hollow.

"Report to IFEN headquarters for Conditioning in one

hour," he says, "or your Mindwalking license will be revoked. Permanently." He hangs up.

Slowly, I lower the phone.

"Who was that?" Steven asks.

"No one," I murmur. "A wrong number."

"I thought we were going to trust each other."

He's right, of course. I close my eyes for a few seconds. "Dr. Swan," I whisper. "He knows something, Steven. Not just about us. I think he might know what happened to you."

Steven tenses. His expression is shielded, wary. "You think so?"

"I realize it sounds crazy. But I can't think of any other explanation. And now he's telling me to stop digging for answers." Dr. Swan's voice echoes in my memory: *All it takes is two words, Lain. Two words in your file.* I don't think he's bluffing. He's prepared to ruin my life, my future, if I don't obey him. Dr. Swan has always been overbearing, but I never realized he was capable of such ruthlessness. I wonder how well I really know him.

For a minute, the only sound is the ticking clock. The teakettle whistles, cutting through the silence. I grab a pot holder and take the kettle off the heat, splashing some tea on the counter. Numbly, I pour the amber liquid into two cups, though I don't feel like drinking it.

I *can't* go in for Conditioning. I won't let him do this to me. But if I don't, then what?

I drop a few lumps of sugar in my tea and watch them dissolve.

If I don't go in, he'll take everything from me. If I can't be a Mindwalker, what's left? I've focused everything I am on this one dream. Now it's being ripped away from me, and there's nothing I can do. I'm squeezed into a corner, trapped. I want to scream.

"You should go," Steven says.

My head snaps up. "What?"

"It's just Conditioning. Not the end of the world." His face is a mask. "Hell, we've both gone through it before."

"Yes, but . . ." Dr. Swan will probably administer the treatment personally. I don't want him in my head, whispering subliminal suggestions while my mind is open and unguarded, creeping into my subconscious and rearranging things to suit himself. The thought makes me physically ill.

Is this why Father didn't seek help?

"What do you think I should do?" I ask quietly.

Steven gives me an odd, resigned smile. "This is your life," he says. "I can't make the decision for you. But I won't resent you for it if you go in."

I swallow, hard. "I'm going upstairs to change," I mutter. My shirt is still damp with sweat from the Lucid nightmare.

I trudge up the stairs to my room and slip into a fresh blouse.

Last time I went in for Conditioning, I was an absolute wreck, paralyzed by depression and grief. It was remarkable how those dark clouds seemed to lift from my mind, leaving me light and empty. Afterward, I ate strawberry Jell-O in the cafeteria. I remember holding up a cube of it on my fork, being utterly amazed by its translucence, the way it caught the sunlight from the window. I probably stared at that blob of Jell-O for five minutes. The next few days had a bright, hazy quality, and thoughts rolled off the surface of my mind like water. It was impossible to focus on one thing for more than a minute or two. But after that, reality gradually reasserted itself. The grief returned, but blunter, less overwhelming, and my mind felt clearer and sharper.

Just Conditioning. I'll be stupid and spacey for a bit, but it can't erase what I know now, and it's too soon to give up the rest of my life. I just have to hold on to my convictions, to ignore the seductive whispers in my head telling me that everything is okay, that there's nothing to worry about. I can do that, can't I?

Something catches my eye—something moving on the street outside my bedroom window. I freeze, my blouse half buttoned. A gray car with tinted windows has pulled up in front of my house; I can see it through a gap in the gauzy pink curtains. The car lingers for a minute, and a chill spreads under my skin. It looks like one of IFEN's vehicles. I wait, holding my breath. The car pulls away.

Dr. Swan sent it. He must have. Why, though? If he instructed someone to pick me up, the driver would have waited out front instead of moving on. If he just wanted to keep an eye on my house, he could have done it through the street cameras.

He's waiting for me to leave. That's the only explanation. He's planning to do something once I'm gone. Are they going to search the house? Confiscate my Gate? Or . . .

Steven.

My hands clench on the blouse, trembling. They know Steven is here, and they're waiting for me to leave so they can take him. God, how could I have been so stupid?

I hurry down to the kitchen. "Steven, we have to get out of here. It's not safe."

He blinks. "What?"

"There was a car, and— There's no time to explain, but I think we might both be in real danger. We need to go. Now."

"I'll take your word for it, but—go *where?*"

That's a good question. There's no place in the city we'll be safe—IFEN has cameras everywhere. We could hide out at Ian's, but I don't want to drag him into this. It would be only a matter of time before Dr. Swan located us, anyway. "We'll leave the city."

He stares at me, expressionless.

"We'll make a run for the northern border," I say. My head spins. Am I really saying this? Am I really *considering* this? "I know security is tight, but people still manage to cross over illegally, so there must be a way. IFEN has no authority in Canada."

"If we leave," he says, "we can't come back. You know that, right?"

My breathing quickens. I have one last chance to reclaim my old life, and all I have to do is walk into IFEN headquarters. If I don't, that chance will be lost forever. I'll be a fugitive. There's no guarantee that we'll make it to the border, or that we'll be able to get across, and even if we do, I have only the foggiest idea of what things are like in Canada, whether we'll be welcomed or treated as criminals. Dizziness swims over me.

Ian's face flashes through my head. What will happen to him if Steven and I run away?

What will happen to Steven if we don't?

"I know," I whisper, and turn away. "I'm going to get packed."

In my bedroom, I throw some clothes into a suitcase,

along with a few other essentials. I set my cell phone on my dresser. Abandoning it feels like leaving one of my arms behind, but cell phones can be tracked. Instead, I take a credit card preloaded with about five hundred Silver Units. It should be enough to last us a few days.

Of course, they might be able to track me using the car's GPS, too. But I'm not sure what to do about that; I know, there's no way to remove it without destroying the vehicle's functionality. I'll just have to hope we can evade them.

"Chloe," I say.

Her sleek black form shimmers into place on my desk. She's sitting, tail curled around her paws, head tilted to one side. "What is it, Lain?"

"Please clear out your memory caches for the past week. All the searches I've done within that time period, all the conversations we've had, including this one—I need it all erased. Can you do that?"

"Of course." She closes her eyes. Her ears twitch, then her eyes open, softly glowing orbs. "Memory caches cleared." She smiles, showing tiny, sharp teeth. "I'll deactivate now, if that's all right."

"Thank you."

With a flurry of sparkles, she vanishes.

I pause, looking at my phone, then pick it up and dial. Making a call is risky, but I can't just leave without telling him. The phone rings and rings, then finally beeps and goes to voice mail. "Ian? I—I'm going away for a while. It might be a long time before I can get in touch with you. I won't be able to answer if you call." I feel like I should say something else, but I don't know what. My thoughts are a chaotic mess. "Please take care of yourself." It's inadequate, I know, especially after everything he's done for me. But it's all I can give.

I hang up.

I dash downstairs, grab my Gate from the basement, and load the whole thing—the two helmets and slim hard drive—into the trunk of my car. I don't expect to need it. I just don't want it falling into Dr. Swan's hands if his cronies come poking around. This Gate belonged to my father, and now it's mine. No one will take it from me.

I think of the compact, still in my coat pocket, with the Chinese dragon pill inside. Briefly, I consider leaving it behind. It's dangerous. An overdose of this drug almost killed someone. I waver for a few seconds before deciding to keep it with me.

As much as I'd like to, I can't forget the eyes I saw in Steven's memory. I have to know what they mean. This isn't about finding the truth for truth's sake anymore. Now it's personal.

24

When Steven and I leave the house, it's dark.

"Destination, please," intones the computer's clear, neutral voice.

I can't just tell the car to head for Canada; I need a more specific location. What pops into my mind is the town where Steven was discovered after his kidnapping, the town where Emmett Pike allegedly lived. "Wolf's Run," I say.

"Calculating route. Please wait."

As the car pulls out of the driveway and glides down the street, Steven says, "That's the town, isn't it? The one near St. Mary's?"

I nod. "It's at the top of the Northeast Quadrant, close to the border."

"There's nothing in St. Mary's. We *saw* it. It's just ruins."

"I don't intend to stop there. Our route just takes us through the area."

He looks at me from the corner of his eye but says nothing.

The car heads north, toward the shining band of the Aura River, which curls around the city like a protective arm. A bridge arches over the water. It's slender and white, and appears almost too delicate to be real, though, in actuality, it's very sturdy. It's also the only highway leading out of the city. There are numerous monorail tracks running out from Aura like the spokes of a wheel, carrying passengers to the other major cities, and to tourist spots, but few people travel by car outside of Aura. Using the monos is cheaper, faster, and more comfortable. But of course, there are no monorails to Wolf's Run.

There's a checkpoint at the end of the bridge, a tiny station with a peaked roof. As we draw nearer, wires tighten in my chest and stomach. I remind myself that there's nothing to worry about. Right now, I'm a Type Two, but that shouldn't affect my ability to enter or leave the city. If I were a Three, maybe—but I can't have been reclassified again so soon. Dr. Swan is powerful, but he's still subject to the law, and there are rules and procedures to follow. I should be all right.

Steven's another matter.

"Duck down," I say. He does, and I pull a blanket from the backseat and throw it over him. With luck, it will be enough.

A man with a bushy mustache and a blue uniform leans out of the station's window. Only when I see him flicker do I realize he's a hologram. The car slows to a stop.

"Name?" he asks.

"Lain Fisher."

"Occupation?"

"Mindwalker. I'm a student at Greenborough High School."

"And your purpose for leaving the city of Aura?"

I freeze. Steven elbows me from beneath his blanket. "Uh . . . recreation."

"Please be more specific."

"I'm sightseeing. You know. For fun."

His mustache twitches. He peers at me through small blue eyes. If I hadn't seen that flicker, I'd swear he was real. A human might find it suspicious that a seventeen-year-old girl is sightseeing this late, and on a school night. Hopefully, a computer program won't question the logic. "Please look into the retinal scanner," he says.

I do, and a green light blinks.

"Identity verified." There's another pause.

"Can I go?" I ask, trying not to sound nervous.

"You've been flagged with a Special Alert. Do not be alarmed. You haven't been charged with any crime, but a Special Alert may temporarily inhibit your ability to leave the city. Please wait a few minutes while I access my database." He tilts his head back and places two fingers against his temple.

This isn't good. I gulp. Ahead of us, a lowered metal bar blocks the road. It's thin and flimsy-looking, but that doesn't matter; there's no way to make the car start. It's locked in park, its artificial intelligence obeying some signal from the checkpoint station.

Steven mutters a curse and throws the blanket aside. He pulls a bent paper clip out of his pocket.

I tense. "What are you—"

He jams the end of the paper clip into a tiny hole in the dashboard. "A trick someone showed me."

"There is an unreported passenger in your vehicle," the hologram says. "Please state your passenger's name and occupation."

Steven jiggles the paper clip, twists it, and jams it in deeper. The car surges forward and plows through the metal gate, which rips off with an earsplitting screech. It catches on the car's hood and drags on the pavement, trailing a shower of sparks.

I hear the hologram's voice: "You are not authorized to leave the city. Please stop your vehicle, or you may be charged with a violation of Code 47B—"

The car shoots forward, the speedometer hovering around seventy-five miles an hour. I don't think I've ever been in a car moving this fast. I press my back against the seat, heart hammering, fingers digging into the cushions.

The gate falls off the hood and clatters to the pavement. As I watch it recede in the rearview mirror, I press a hand to my mouth. "Oh God." A hysterical giggle bubbles up in my throat, and I choke it down. The bent paper clip is still jammed into the dashboard. "Is this—safe?"

"Kind of," Steven says.

"*Kind of?*"

"Well, I wasn't going to sit around and wait for that holo to contact the police. Or IFEN."

Behind us, the towering city of Aura dwindles, its skyscrapers glowing softly in the darkness. The whole city radiates light. I rarely see it from a distance, and I find myself watching over my shoulder as the buildings grow smaller and smaller. All around us, cornfields sprawl, stalks waving in the breeze. Miles and miles of cornfields, broken only by occasional smooth white domes, like gigantic eggs buried upside down. Agricultural centers. In the distance, I can see the shining silver line of a monorail track, built on tall, slender trestles.

I've only been outside the city once before, on a class field trip to an agricultural center. I was awed—as I am now—by the vast emptiness around me. Some of the fields have already been harvested, leaving barren patches of land.

"Is there a way to *stop* the car?" I ask.

"The emergency brake should still work. But we probably shouldn't stop unless we have to. We need to get away from the city, fast."

The car still steers itself, following the slight curves of the road, and its speed remains steady. There's nothing but open road ahead of us. I exhale and dare to relax a little. Well, the car seems to know what it's doing. Enough not to crash, anyway. "I guess we're criminals now." I smile, as if that makes the words less frightening, though a panicky static is starting to creep through my thoughts.

Steven studies my face. "You okay?"

"Yes. I think so." I focus on breathing for a few minutes, then turn my attention back to the view, watching the endless fields roll past. It's strange to think that people used to live out here. Before the war, the population was spread across the whole country. It must have been . . . inefficient. Now over ninety-five percent of citizens live in the five major cities. Aura, the rough geographical center of the United Republic, is the nation's capital, and each of the four quadrants has its own lesser capital.

After the war, there was an aggressive push from both IFEN and the government to relocate people from small towns to metropolitan areas. IFEN stressed that, statistically speaking, rural areas were breeding grounds for domestic terrorists and antigovernment radicals. In response, the government offered sizable tax benefits for anyone who moved to a major city, and the exodus left huge stretches of land completely uninhabited, save for the workers tending the machinery in the agricultural centers. A handful of small towns still exist, but they're regarded as quaint relics of a bygone age, largely cut off from the rest of the world.

"Hey," Steven says, "if you want to turn around, there's still time." He's sitting stiffly, arms crossed over his chest like a shield.

"What are you talking about? Didn't we already decide we're heading for the border?"

"I mean . . . if you're having second thoughts."

"I'm not. Are you?"

He looks at me from the corner of his eye. "Only if you are."

I sigh, leaning back. "Don't confuse me." Whatever he says, it's already too late to turn around. We made our choice.

Our headlights slice through the darkness. Before us, the road unspools toward the horizon like a gray ribbon. The roads aren't used much, but they're still maintained, mostly for the work vehicles involved in food harvesting. Occasional streetlights stand along the highway like lonely sentinels.

It hits me hard in that moment. We're alone. From this point on, Steven and I have only each other. Yet even now, I've told him so little about myself, my past. Maybe this isn't the proper time for a personal revelation. But if not now, when?

My hands curl into fists. In my head, I can still hear my

psych-ethics professor nagging, telling me not to get emotionally involved with a client. But it's hard to follow the instruction manual once you've thrown it out the window. "You remember me telling you that I lost my father? I never told you how. He took his own life when I was thirteen."

Steven's breathing hitches. There's a long pause. The car sails down the road, and it feels like we're flying, hurtling through empty space. "And your mom?" he asks, very softly.

"I don't have one."

"She died?"

"No." My teeth catch on my lower lip, tugging. "I just don't have one."

His brow furrows. I watch the wheels turning in his head. Then his eyes widen, and there's an almost audible click as the light goes on. "Oh."

I smile weakly. "My father never married. He was married to his work, you could say. He planned to adopt at first, but there are so many legal restrictions these days, it's almost impossible. Cloning is the easiest way for a single person to have a child."

The muscles of his throat constrict as he swallows. "God, Lain, I'm sorry. All that stuff I said before about NewVitro . . ."

"You didn't know." I hesitate. "Does it bother you? Me being . . . what I am?"

"No. Why? Has it bothered other people?"

I lean my forehead against the window. The glass is cool. Soothing. "I remember, when I was little, a boy at school told me that I didn't have a soul. That I wouldn't go to heaven when I died. I'd just disappear." I close my eyes. "My father always said that those people were simply unenlightened and that

I shouldn't pay attention to anything they said, but I—" My voice cracks. I cover my mouth with one hand, embarrassed. I've managed to sound almost indifferent until now. And still, the words keep spilling out of me. "I know it's not that uncommon. It's not even that controversial, not anymore. They have special private schools for kids like me so we don't have to feel like outsiders. But I didn't want that. It didn't seem right to hide away from the rest of the world in some privileged little bubble. I wanted to show the world that I was just like everyone else. But no matter what I did, what I said, I was always an outsider. When I came to Greenborough, I thought it would be like a fresh start, because no one knew me, but still, everyone except Ian only ignored me. Like they could *feel* that I was different. And I started to wonder if that boy was right and I was an abomination, nothing more than a blob of chemicals created in a laboratory, and I—"

Steven hugs me, suddenly and fiercely. "You have a soul," he whispers against my hair.

I sit shock-frozen. I've hugged Steven before, but this is the first time he's initiated it. It takes me a few seconds to find my voice. It's difficult to speak through the lump filling my throat. "You think so?"

"You have feelings, don't you?"

"Feelings are just chemicals." I close my eyes. "So are memories. Maybe that's all I am." Why am I saying this now, to him? I don't even believe those words, do I? "Maybe I'm nothing but a biological machine."

He touches a thin finger to my lips, stopping me. My breath catches. "That's the stupidest thing I've ever heard," he says, echoing my earlier words to him. His voice is low and rough, but his eyes are gentle. "You're too smart for that." He holds his finger against my lips for a moment—it's firm, warm—then lowers his hand.

My heart is beating very fast.

"The way you were born doesn't matter," he says. "You're here now. You're just as real and just as human as anyone else. Those assholes don't get to decide what kind of person you are or whether you're worthy. You decide that."

I try to speak, but the lump in my throat swells, cutting off air and voice. "Thank you," I finally manage to whisper.

He holds me a few minutes longer. At last, I pull back and draw in a shaky breath. "Sorry," I murmur, wiping the corners of my eyes with my thumb.

"Don't apologize," he says gruffly.

A tiny smile tugs at my lips. "Okay." The smile fades.

I want to believe that he's right, that my choices matter. But there's a reason only Type Ones are allowed to clone themselves. Science has shown that genetics have a strong influence over our decisions. My father was a great man, but in the end, he collapsed in on himself like a dying star. Aside from my sex chromosomes, I have his DNA, down to the last gene.

I find myself considering, again, the eyes in Steven's memory. I don't want to dwell on that. Yet now that Steven knows the truth about me, I'm sure it will occur to him as well, if it hasn't already.

"I want you to understand," I say softly, "that Father was the kindest person I ever knew. He wouldn't harm a fly. Literally—if there was a bug in the house, he would go out of his way to catch it so he could let it go instead of killing it." I stop and take a deep breath. "I don't believe—I know those weren't his eyes."

The moon peeks out from behind a cloud, washing the fields with silver light.

"You really loved him," Steven says.

"Well, of course. He's my father." But then, Steven never knew his parents. I look at his profile, his faraway expression, and feel a soft ache deep inside me. "Did you have anyone you were close to, growing up?"

"I don't actually remember my childhood. Before the kidnapping, I mean."

"Nothing at all?" I ask, surprised.

He shrugs. "I know that I grew up in a state home with other orphans, but I don't remember it. I don't remember what I was like as a kid, or what I enjoyed doing. There are little flickers here and there, but mostly it's all a haze." His voice is low, pensive. His eyes have lost focus, as if he's looking deep inside himself. "The doctors told me it was because of what Pike did. Because of the trauma. But that always seemed weird to me. Why would I block the memories of what came before that?"

I think about the scars in his brain, all those decimated neural pathways. No wonder he's lost so much. What is it like for him living with so many blank spaces in his head?

"Did we bring any food?" he asks suddenly. "I'm starving."

I nod. While the car drives itself, I lean over and grab a bag from the backseat. I toss an apple and a cereal bar to Steven, then take an apple for myself. "There's more, but we've got to make it last awhile," I remark through a mouthful of fruit. "You can't count on finding places to eat between cities."

"We could barbecue some roadkill."

I wrinkle my nose, and he grins. It's wide and cocky, and it makes me feel pleasantly, oddly warm. As we drive, I remember the gentle pressure of his finger against my lips. Lightly, I touch them. They're unusually sensitive, almost ticklish. What would it be like to—

I quickly slam the door on that thought.

We pass the ruins of an abandoned gas station. Despite the adrenaline tingling through my bloodstream, it's late and my body is leaden with fatigue. My eyelids gradually grow heavier. I surrender to the exhaustion and wander through dreams of gray halls filled with doors. Voices whisper behind the doors, but I'm afraid to open them.

When I wake, the sky is a pale dead white, the cool air tinged with the smoky smell of burning plant matter, probably coming from some agricultural center. I straighten and see a small spot of moisture on Steven's shirt. A flush rises into my cheeks as realization dawns. I dozed off with my head on his shoulder and drooled on him.

"Morning," he says. He looks wide awake, and I wonder if he slept at all.

"Good morning." I wipe my mouth, glance into the rear-view mirror, and smooth errant strands of my hair into place. I swallow and grimace at the stale, warm taste on my tongue. A toothbrush and a sink sound really appealing right now. "How far did we drive?"

"We just passed into the Northeast Quadrant," he says.

"We're making excellent time." I muffle a yawn against one hand and peer out the window. Vast fields wave in the breeze. It's easy to imagine, out here, that society has collapsed, humans have gone extinct, and we're the last two people on the earth, travelers in an empty world.

I glance at Steven's face, then away. My cheeks burn. I still can't believe I fell asleep using him as a pillow, though if it bothers him, he doesn't show it.

After a few minutes, he breaks the silence: "Look in the rearview mirror."

When I do, I see a sleek gray car about a quarter mile behind us.

"We're being followed," he says.

25

At first, I'm too startled to respond. I watch the car, which continues to follow us at a discreet distance. It doesn't look like an IFEN vehicle.

"Are you sure?" I ask. "Maybe they're just headed in the same direction."

Before Steven can reply, red and blue LED lights flash atop the gray car, and the wail of a siren cuts through the still morning air.

Steven tenses.

My first thought is that Dr. Swan sent them after us. But surely, he doesn't control the police. "It might be a broken taillight," I say.

"I wouldn't bet on that," Steven says.

The vehicle behind us is accelerating. It zooms past us and swerves across the road, blocking our path.

"Shit!" he hisses.

I slam the heel of my hand against the emergency brake

button. The car screeches to a halt, and the acrid smell of burning rubber stings my nostrils.

The police car's front door opens, and a uniformed woman with short blond hair steps out. A badge glints in the sunlight.

Steven's fingers tighten on my bicep, digging in like claws. "Let's go. *Now*."

I struggle to control my breathing. My mind races. Even if we swerve past her, there's no way we can lose her out here in the middle of nowhere. If we try to flee, it will just confirm that we're guilty of something. It's possible that she doesn't know who we are, that she's not looking for us specifically. Maybe she's on her way to investigate something else and just stopped us for a minor infraction. Not likely. But possible. "Stay calm," I say. "I might be able to talk our way out of this."

His ragged breathing fills the car.

"Don't worry," I say, trying to conceal the nervousness in my voice. "All right, so we drove through a checkpoint and destroyed a gate, but that's a trivial offense. I think. Maybe she'll just write us a ticket."

"Are you kidding? Don't they have a Special Alert or something on you?"

There is that. And come to think of it, is transporting a Type Four out of the city illegal? This is very bad. "Well, what should we do?" I hear the panic rising in my voice. "It's too late to drive away."

The woman steps up to the driver's-side window and peers in. She's wearing a pair of reflective shades, and my own face stares back at me, mirrored in duplicate.

I roll down the window. "Is everything all right?"

She adjusts her shades. "Are you aware that your registration tags are expired?"

I exhale a quiet breath of relief. My heart is still pounding, but I feel silly for assuming the worst. I give Steven a smile, as if to say, *See?* "No, I wasn't aware."

"License and registration."

I fish my wallet from my coat pocket and start to pull out my license.

"Lain!" Steven shouts.

I look up. The woman thrusts something through the half-open window and shoves it against my temple. There's a deafening electric buzz, a jolt of pain, and then blackness.

* * *

I wake to a roaring headache. With a groan, I pry my eyelids open. Bright light floods my vision, making me squint. Once my eyes have adjusted, I find myself looking at a cement ceiling, illuminated by a single naked bulb. For a moment, I just stare, strangely fascinated by the pattern of water stains: wiggly edged blobs, like continents on an alien world, lit by the blinding sun of the bulb. My dry throat prickles with thirst, distracting me. I swallow, but I can't work up any saliva.

Where am I?

I try to sit up, but my body won't move. There's a tight pressure around my chest, like an iron band, making it difficult to draw a full breath.

Something happened to me. Something bad. I struggle to piece my fragmented memories together. Where was I before I lost consciousness? I was in the car with Steven, and then—

Steven. Where is Steven?

I lift my head as far as I can—which isn't much—and look around. I'm in a tiny cement-walled room. A basement, maybe. Across from me is a narrow door—it looks like a broom closet. When I strain my eyes downward, I see that I'm on a metal cot, resembling a surgical table. A series of tight straps criss-cross my body, pinning me down, and my arms are bound in a straitjacket. Next to me there's a table, and on it, a slim black hard drive hums softly.

A Gate. But not mine. It's a different model, newer. There's something on my head. A helmet?

"You're awake."

My gaze jerks toward the voice. The policewoman—if she is a policewoman—stands nearby. Her shades are gone, revealing expressionless pale gray eyes.

"What's going on?" My voice comes out slurred and thick. My tongue is a lump of numb meat. "Where is Steven?"

She glances at the closed door on the other side of the room, and the corners of her thin lips twitch in a smile. "He won't be bothering us. I gave him enough sedatives to knock out an elk. He'll sleep for a good twelve hours." She lifts a white plastic helmet off the nearby table and turns toward me. "By then, you won't remember him."

I open my mouth, but nothing comes out.

A stubborn part of my mind insists that this is absurd—things like this simply don't *happen* in a civilized world like ours. Surely, this is some kind of cosmic clerical error that will be rectified at any moment. But a deeper part of my brain—the part now screaming with silent horror—knows better.

"You can't do this," I say, as if the words will somehow change what's happening. "This is highly illegal."

"Actually, it's not. You've been reclassified as a Type Five."

My whole body goes cold. Type Five. The highest threat level. Higher than Steven's. *Imminent danger to public safety.* It's reserved for those people who have the capacity to do damage on a large scale, who are a danger not just to individuals but to society as a whole.

She smiles coolly. "You know what that means, don't you? You can be confined by any means necessary and treated with the most extreme forms of therapy, with or without your consent. Your report will state that your Type rapidly elevated because of a recent trauma and that you needed a rapid emergency memory modification."

"That's ridiculous!" I wriggle in my restraints, trying to loosen them. "I'm not traumatized, and I'm certainly not a danger to public safety!"

"They all say that." She waves a hand over the Gate's sensor. A holoscreen flicks on in midair. An image of a brain—my brain—rotates slowly.

"Who authorized this?" I ask, trying to keep my voice firm.

"That's none of your concern."

"I'd say it is! I have rights. Basic human rights."

She chuckles, as if I've evoked the protection of a mythical fairy.

"Who authorized this?" I ask again.

She ignores the question and taps a few icons on the screen. "You know, this was supposed to happen in IFEN headquarters, all nice and quiet. We were going to Condition you and then modify your memories while you were still compliant. No fear, no drama. But you had to complicate things by running. Hauling you back to Aura would attract attention, so I'll simply have to do the best I can. It'll be a little sloppy. Might be a while before you can do any math homework."

My pulse thunders in my ears. The anger is fading, replaced by a growing black void of terror. "This is a misunderstanding. Just let me talk to Dr. Swan—"

"That wouldn't do any good." She pulls on her own helmet. "Nothing personal, you understand. Only a job."

I struggle, but the straps are tight. They won't budge.

"The more you cooperate, the easier this will be on you," she says.

Panic fills my head like a blinding light. "What about Steven? What are you planning to do with him?"

"Don't worry about that." She picks up a hypodermic from the table and taps a nail against it. "Just lie back and relax. When you wake up, you'll be safe and sound in your own home, and this will all be behind you."

My gaze focuses on the hypodermic. A bead of clear liquid wells from the tip of the needle and drips down.

I start to scream. I feel like an idiot, because I realize it's pointless, but I don't know what else to do. I keep screaming as the needle advances toward my throat.

There's a sudden loud thud against the closet door. The woman whirls around. Her hand strays toward the slim silver pistol at her hip. Not a pistol, I realize. A neural disrupter, probably the same one she used to knock me out. She thumbs a switch on the ND's hilt.

The closet door bangs open. Steven stands there, shreds of rope hanging from his wrists, a switchblade in one hand.

The woman takes a step backward. "You can't be awake." Her voice wobbles. For the first time, her certainty is gone.

Steven narrows his eyes. "Move away from her. Now."

She draws her ND. In the same instant, Steven lunges. She starts to squeeze the trigger, but he grabs her arm and twists it against her back. She cries out. Steven steps behind her and presses the edge of the blade to her throat. "Drop it."

She releases the ND. It hits the floor with a clank. The hypo slips from her fingers, bounces, and rolls under the table. She stands frozen, breathing harshly.

By now, the collar should have stopped him, yet somehow he continues moving. Is its internal computer still working, scrambling to decipher the sudden burst of neural activity and decide whether he's a threat? Or is he resisting its effects through sheer will?

Steven shoves the woman away, grabs the ND, and keeps it pointed at her as he walks backward, toward me. He clamps the switchblade between his teeth. Fumbling, he unbuckles my straps with his free hand. The woman glares at him, poison in her eyes. I sit up, weak and shaky, and pull off the helmet. With a shudder, I toss it to the floor.

He takes the switchblade from his mouth. "You okay?" he asks, looking at me from the corner of his eye.

"More or less." I try to smile. His switchblade gleams. Does he *always* have that with him? Carrying a concealed knife is illegal. But I'm very glad he does.

He aims the ND at the woman.

"Put that down." She takes a step toward him.

"I don't think so. You're going to talk now. Tell us—" A glassy look slips over his eyes. He sways on his feet and drops the switchblade.

A chill shoots through my bones. *The collar.*

His knees buckle. The woman lunges. I lunge, too. The ND slips from Steven's slackening fingers, hits the floor, and skids. In the same instant, the woman and I make a grab for the ND. Somehow, I scoop it up first.

I've never held a weapon. It feels clumsy and awkward as I point it at the woman's chest. Near my feet, Steven stirs. He starts to push himself up, then slumps to the floor again. I'm on my own.

"Who sent you?" I ask, deepening my voice in an effort to sound tough.

The woman just glares at me, her lip curled in a sneer of distaste. "You don't know how to use that."

"I know the basics. And my hands are shaking rather badly now. My finger could slip on the trigger if I'm startled, so I wouldn't make any sudden moves if I were you." There, that sounds semiplausible as a threat. "Now. Tell me who sent you."

"The order came from the director himself."

A sickening weight spreads through my stomach. I'd suspected as much, but the confirmation still fills me with vertigo, like my world has flipped upside down. "Dr. Swan?"

"That's right."

It's not as if I'd trusted him. But maybe on some level, I did. He was Father's colleague, his friend, the man who mentored me and watched over me throughout most of my training. I know now that he's hiding something from me, but still, I counted on him to do things in a sane and civilized way, to work within the boundaries of the law—not to send someone to hunt me down like an animal. There's a sharp twinge deep in my chest, like some tiny part of me just died.

My gaze focuses on the woman's hand as it moves slowly toward her hip. She's reaching for something—a backup weapon?

I squeeze the trigger, and there's a deafening *bzzzzt*. The ND vibrates ferociously in my grip. Nothing comes out of the muzzle—nothing visible, anyway—but the woman reels backward as if she's been hit by a bullet. She slumps against the wall. Her whole body shakes in seizure-like convulsions, and her teeth gnash until bloody foam bubbles from her lips. Then she slides to the floor like a broken marionette, eyes rolled back in her head. There's a moment of terrifying silence. Then I hear her breathing, wet and raspy.

I exhale in relief. Alive. Just unconscious.

I look at the weapon in my hand, dazed.

Steven staggers to his feet. "Nice work, Doc." His voice is hoarse, cracked. "Didn't know you had it in you."

"I just shot someone." My voice emerges small and high-pitched, almost squeaky.

"Yep." Steven pats the woman down and fishes a set of keys from her uniform. He turns to face me. "You all right? Not going to throw up or faint or anything, are you?"

"Of course not." My voice still sounds too high, but the slightest hint of indignation creeps into my tone. I stare at the neural disrupter. It's lightweight plastic—like holding a toy, almost. I turn it over to look at the switch on the hilt. It's set to 9, the second-highest setting. I slide the switch down to setting 1 and exhale a quiet breath. "What about you? Are you—"

"Great. Never better." But his voice lacks its usual sarcastic edge. He's sheet-pale.

I hold the ND between a thumb and forefinger, like a soiled rag. When Steven takes it from me, I don't resist. With a gulp, I glance at the unconscious woman on the floor. "What do we do about her?"

He licks sweat from his upper lip and scoops up his switchblade from the floor. "Let's just get out of here." His gaze darts around the cement room, with its dirty, cracked walls and single naked bulb.

Realization hits. It looks like the room from his memories, where Pike held him prisoner. No wonder he's so pale. Whether or not Pike or that room ever existed, the horror of it is still inside Steven.

We run across the room, up the stairs, through another empty cement room, and out a door into the cool air. We're in a clearing ringed by thick pine trees, under a clouded sky. The building behind us is a squat cement block with a flat roof, little more than a shed. I can't guess its original purpose. The woman's gray car is parked on the dirt nearby. Our own car, I guess, is still by the side of the road where we left it.

There's no time. We should get out of here before that woman wakes up. But I can't help myself. I fling my arms around Steven and hug him tight. He tenses, his back rigid. His coat is open, and I can feel his heart hammering through his thin, sweat-drenched shirt.

I know I'm wasting time, but I need this—need to reassure myself that he's here, alive and whole. I came so close to losing him, and the thought fills me with a dizzying burst of fear. "I'm glad you're safe," I whisper.

He doesn't respond. His body remains wire-tense in my arms. After a moment, he pulls away, opens the car door, and slides into the driver's seat. "Get in."

I do.

He shoves the key into the ignition.

"Please state your destination," intones a chipper male voice from the car's dashboard.

"Floor it."

"I'm sorry, I can't process that request. Please rephrase."

"Just drive!"

"I'm sorry, I can't process that request. Please—"

Steven places the ND's muzzle against the dashboard and fires. *Bzzzt.* The weapon jumps in his hand. I give a start.

"Please staaaa—" the voice warbles, then dies out. A light blinks once on the dashboard and goes dark. Steven presses a foot to the gas pedal and pulls out of the clearing, tires screeching.

26

The car sails down a narrow gravel road that leads us straight back to the highway. Steven floors the pedal. His eyes are glazed, the pupils pinpoints. The speedometer hovers around eighty-five as we shoot down the road between thick walls of pine trees.

I slump in the seat. My palms are slippery with sweat. "How did you get out of that closet, anyway?"

"She was careless. She didn't even check me for weapons. She just tied me up. Once I got the switchblade out of my pocket, I cut the ropes."

"She said she gave you enough sedatives to knock out an elk."

"I've built up a tolerance over the years. These days, almost nothing can knock me out for long."

I think about the little white pills he keeps in his pocket. "Oh." Considering everything in his system, I wonder if he should really be driving. But it's a bit late to worry about that.

If he hadn't woken up in time . . . If we hadn't escaped . . .

I clutch my arms, remembering the terrible sense of help-lessness, the knowledge that something precious was about to be ripped away and there was nothing I could do. The idea of losing Steven is bad enough, but the idea of just *forgetting*, as if he'd never existed . . .

I shudder. "She wanted to erase my memories of you."

"Would that be so bad?" Steven asks, his tone unreadable.

"Of course it would!" The strength of my own reaction surprises me. How did he become so important to me in such a short time?

In my mind, I see him standing in the parking lot out-side the school, his tall, slim form silhouetted against the fad-ing daylight. I remember the feeling of him in my arms, his warmth and scent. I'd rather die than forget those things.

I start to feel light-headed.

Steven points. "There."

I blink a few times. *Focus.* Sure enough, my little blue car is parked by the roadside. It seems our captor didn't take us very far. Judging by the sun's position, it's only been a few hours since she stopped us. "Pull over."

"We should leave it," Steven says. "Take this one instead. They'll be looking for a blue car, not a gray one."

"Who?"

"*Them,*" he says, as if it's self-explanatory. Maybe it is.

"My Gate is in that car. I'm not leaving it."

He exhales a tense breath and pulls over. "Fine. Bring it."

I fetch my Gate, along with the suitcase, and pile them into the backseat of the policewoman's car. Not a real police-woman, I remind myself. Isn't it illegal to impersonate an of-ficer? What sort of people is Dr. Swan working with?

I climb into the passenger's seat, and Steven keeps driving. "We need to get off the highway," he mutters. His breathing is heavy and labored. "Take some side roads."

"We need to tell someone about this. About her and what she tried to do to us."

"Tell who? The cops?"

"Yes! What she did can't possibly be legal."

His fists are clenched tight on the wheel, knuckles white. "If we go to them, they'll just hand us over to Dr. Swan."

"You don't know that."

He shoots me a glare. "I heard what she said. Your boss arranged this whole thing. Who do you think the cops will take more seriously? A couple of runaway teenagers, or the director of IFEN?"

"But . . ." I want to say that this is all a misunderstanding, that if we just go to the authorities and tell them everything, somehow they'll sort it out. I cradle my head in my hands and whisper, "I can't be a Type Five. She has to be lying. There's no way—"

He makes an exasperated sound in his throat. "Don't you get it? Those numbers don't mean anything. They're only a way of controlling us."

"Even so, they can't reclassify someone whenever they feel like it," I snap. "Yes, the system's unfair, but they still have to follow procedure. They need data, data reviewed by experts, and that takes time. They're not allowed to just wave a magic wand over any random person and declare that she's a Type Five!"

"Well, it looks like they just did."

"*Illegally.* That's why I said we should go to the police! Everything about this is shady!"

He shakes his head wearily. "Wake up, Lain. The world's run by rich guys in white coats. They make all the rules. They can change them whenever they feel like it. Who the hell is going to stop them?"

My body feels numb, oddly weightless. Even if I never agreed with the system completely, I always trusted it to follow its own laws. A part of me still wants to protest that this is all wrong, that it can't really be happening. But it is. Within the span of a few days, I've gone from good citizen to public enemy.

I clutch my chest, struggling to breathe against the crushing pressure. My thoughts are closing in on me. I can't escape. And it occurs to me that thoughts are the most dangerous thing in the world. You can run away from physical danger, or try to fight it, but there's no way to escape or fight your own mind.

I squeeze my eyes shut. "I want to go home." It's a stupid, childish thing to say. Home isn't safe anymore. Dr. Swan's undoubtedly monitoring the premises. There's probably an armed guard stationed in my house, just in case I decide to come back. But that doesn't stop me from wanting my room, my bed, my stuffed squirrel.

For a few minutes, Steven doesn't say anything. When he finally speaks, his voice is soft and scratchy with fatigue. "Tell you what, Doc. We'll stop at the next town. I'll get out of this car. Then you can go home."

I stare at him, bewildered. "What are you talking about?"

"It's me they're after. They just want you out of the way. If

you're not involved with me, you won't be in danger anymore."
His tone is strangely calm. "You should go home. Go back to
your life and forget about me."

"I'll do no such thing!"

He pulls over. We're still in the forest, surrounded by pine
trees.

"Steven, I was just babbling. I'm not going to leave you."

He takes the ND from his coat pocket and holds it against
his chest. "Maybe it's not too late. Maybe you can still wipe
the slate clean. Pretend you never met me." His thin shoulders
are shaking. He shoves the ND back into his coat pocket. "You
know what? You don't even have to take me to the next town.
I'll just walk away." He gets out of the car.

I try to grab his arm, but I'm a half second too late. My
fingers close on thin air.

I follow him. He walks quickly along the roadside, pine-
cones and dead leaves crunching under his feet.

"Steven!"

I catch his coat sleeve. He tenses, and his head whips
around, eyes wide.

In that moment, looking into those eyes, I'm struck by just
how *feral* he is, like a stray cat living on the edge of human
civilization, a cat who might bite you if you tried to pet it. But
letting him go now is not an option. Even if he's right—even
if I'd be safer with him gone—I don't care. My grip tightens
on his sleeve. "You think this is all about you? You think after
everything we've been through, I can just go back to my life as
if nothing happened?" Tears of frustration prick the corners of
my eyes. I blink them away. "I'm not leaving."

His hard expression softens and crumbles. He looks exhausted. Scared. "If you stay with me any longer, they might do worse than erase your memories."

I want to say that he's wrong, that they wouldn't—but at this point, I don't know what to believe anymore. I think about Ian, about my career as a Mindwalker, all the people I could help. I could make a difference. It's what I've always wanted, isn't it? To save people. To become someone my father would be proud of.

Is that all? a voice inside whispers.

Of course. That's the goal I've been pursuing for the past four years. No, my whole life. I'm so close to achieving my dream. Am I really willing to jeopardize everything for Steven?

Not just for him. For yourself. For the truth.

I take a deep breath, trying to put my thoughts in order. "If you think I'm going to give up that easily, you're mistaken."

He yanks his arm from my grip and pulls the ND from his pocket again. My smile falls away. With shaking hands, he raises the weapon and aims it at my head. His finger is on the trigger. "Get in the car." His chest heaves. His eyes are wide and unfocused. The ND quivers in his hand. "Get in and drive away."

I stare into the ND's dark muzzle. Neural disrupters are built to stun, not kill, but even so . . .

I remember the woman's body shaking in convulsions. Stories flash through my mind—rumors of NDs causing brain damage or permanent paralysis, reducing people to vegetables. The collar should stop him from actually pulling the trigger. But then, it didn't stop him from attacking the fake police-woman, not for a minute or two. An instant of dizzying terror lights up my mind like fireworks. Then a strange tranquillity descends over me. The rest of the world falls away, and there's only me and Steven.

"Get out of here!" Steven screams. He backs away, still pointing the ND. Tears spill from his eyes and down his cheeks. *"What the hell is wrong with you? I'm telling you to leave or I'll shoot you!"*

I look into those blue eyes. The blank, unfocused look is gone. Now they're twin maelstroms of terror and desperation. "I told you. I'm not leaving." I take a step forward.

Steven's hands tighten on the hilt of the ND. His chest jerks in little hitching, panicked breaths. "I swear to God, Lain . . . if you come any closer . . ."

I reach out and gently close my hands over Steven's, steadying the weapon. I take another step forward, so the barrel is pressed against my chest, over my heart. "I made a promise," I say quietly.

His chest hitches again. He squeezes his eyes shut. "You don't get it." His voice is choked. "You can't fix me. I'm too broken. If you stay, I'll only drag you into my hell. You'll lose everything. I'll destroy you. Please . . . please, just . . ."

"You think you're the only one who's broken?" I ask, hands still covering Steven's. I can feel them shaking violently. His sweat-slick finger quivers against the trigger. The ND's muzzle is a cold circle against my heart.

It's strange. I was terrified a moment ago; I was losing my mind. Now everything is clear. I don't feel that I'm in the slightest danger. I wonder if I've gone mad. "I can't go back. It's too late. If I return now, they'll erase you from my head, and I'll keep living a lie." I hold his gaze with mine. "I won't live that way. I refuse."

"Do you think I'm bluffing?"

"I've been inside your mind, Steven. I know what sort of person you are. You won't hurt me."

"You're wrong," he rasps. "I'm dangerous. I'm a monster. I—"

I don't think. I lean forward and press my lips to his, silencing him.

The kiss is clumsy and too hard. Our teeth clank, and the tip of my nose mashes against his. He freezes. There's a sharp intake of breath. Our lips are still sealed together, and I can taste the salty copper of blood where he bit the inside of his mouth. The ND slips from his fingers and lands on the ground with a muffled thump.

When I pull back, the world is spinning slowly around me. My legs feel like water. He stares at me, eyes wide and dazed. "I don't understand—" His voice cracks over the last word. He swallows, balling his hands into fists. "I—I pointed an ND at you. Why—"

"You're not going to shake me off that easily. Besides . . ." I kneel and pick up the ND. "If you wanted me to believe you were really planning to shoot, you shouldn't have turned the safety switch on."

He drops his gaze. "Didn't think you'd notice," he mutters.

"You aren't very good at bluffing."

He utters a hoarse, thick sound that might be a chuckle. "Guess not."

I just kissed him. The thought noses its way into my mind, drawing my attention to the sensations in my lips. They're tingling lightly. It feels . . . electric, like a live wire. I lick them, tasting a hint of blood and salt and something else, something I can't put a name to. Something that's purely Steven. "We're in this together," I say. "That's just how it is."

I can't read his expression. There's too much going on there.

To be honest, it's not how I imagined my first kiss. My few vague daydreams always involved some moonlit stroll through the park or a beautiful room filled with candlelight, not being sweaty and exhausted and running for our lives and having a weapon pressed against my chest. Yet I feel a swirl of giddiness rising from my stomach to my brain, like bubbles in a champagne glass. The blood whooshes through my veins. My heart is beating, singing its rhythmic song. *I'm alive, I'm alive.*

For a minute or two, the only sound is the twitter of birdsong in the branches. A crow caws in the distance, a harsh, rusty note. Then Steven nods. "Okay," he says quietly, as if to himself. "We're in this together."

"That's right." I pause. Awkwardly, I offer the ND to him, hilt-first.

He glances at it, then pushes it toward me. "You hold on to that."

"Oh, I wouldn't know how to use it. I'd probably point it the wrong way and shoot myself in the face."

"I dunno. You did pretty well when you were aiming it at that cop. Fake cop. Whatever. But that's not why. I need you to shoot me."

My jaw drops. It takes me a moment to find my voice, and when I do, it comes out as a squeak. "Shoot you?"

He turns and points at the back of his neck. At the collar. "I mean, shoot *this.* I don't know exactly how far they can track me with this thing, but I'm not taking any chances. If you tried to remove it, I'd probably bleed to death, so you'll have to short it out."

"Steven, I can't do that."

"Well, I can't do it myself. The angle's wrong."

"It'll hurt you! How do you know it'll even work?"

"It shorted out the car's computer, didn't it? Put it on a low setting. That way, it'll just stun me, and I'll recover in a few minutes."

He has a point. Neural disrupters work by sending pulses of energy through the brain, temporarily scrambling the flow of information. They can do the same thing to machines, and machines don't recover the way people do. Still . . . "This seems risky."

"We haven't got much choice. Set it to three. That should be enough to short out the collar without messing me up too bad."

I wonder how he knows that. But then, Steven and the authorities don't get along. This probably isn't the first time he's been shot with an ND.

I gulp and place the barrel against the back of his collar. With my thumb, I turn off the safety, then slide the switch to setting 3. My hands won't stop shaking. "I—I don't know if I can do this."

"Sure you can. Just pull the trigger."

This is the only way, I remind myself. And I hate that collar. I hate what it does to him. I *want* to destroy it. But . . .

I stare at the back of Steven's neck. The skin looks soft. Vulnerable. In my head, I see people on the floor, jerking in convulsions, bloody foam running down their chins. I close my eyes and breathe in and out, in and out. Finally, my hand steady, I press the muzzle firmly against the collar and pull the trigger.

There's an earsplitting *bzzzzt*, a vibration that shakes every nerve in my arm and leaves it numb.

Steven grunts. His limbs jerk, and his knees buckle.

I drop the ND just in time to catch him, looping my arms around his waist. He shivers and twitches as I half carry, half drag him over to a tree. I prop him against the trunk and crouch beside him. "Steven? Steven?" Frantic, I pat his cheek. He groans, his head lolling to one side. His eyes roll beneath his fluttering lids.

I frame his face between my hands. "Can you hear me?" When he doesn't respond, I carefully lift his eyelid with a thumb. At first, I see only bloodshot white. Then his eye rolls into view and slowly focuses on me. He smiles blearily. "Hi."

I exhale a quiet breath of relief. "Hi." I give him a smile, then hold up three fingers. "How many?"

He squints. "Purple."

Well, it does take a while for the ND's effects to wear off completely. "You'll be fine." I slip an arm around him, help him to his feet, and make my way toward the car, Steven stumbling along beside me.

"Can't feel my legs," he mutters.

I glance down. He's standing, albeit wobbly. He's not paralyzed. "The feeling will return in a few minutes." I ease him into the passenger's seat. "Just rest."

"No time," he murmurs. He tries to push himself up, to straighten his spine, then goes limp, groaning. "Okay, now I can feel my legs." He rubs them.

"Pins and needles?"

"More like swords and daggers. Ugh." He curses, squirming in his seat. "Almost forgot how much I hate getting shot by those things."

"I can drive us for a while."

"You sure?"

"I've driven manual before. With a simulator, not a real car, but still." I learned the basics when I got my license. Everyone learns them, for those rare emergency situations when the car's computer fails. "Anyway, the autodrive isn't working now that the car's computer is fried, and you won't be able to take the wheel for an hour, at least. We can't afford to wait that long."

Reluctantly, he nods.

I take a deep breath and grip the wheel. There's no telling how long that woman will stay unconscious, and once she's awake, she'll alert Dr. Swan. Even if they can't track us directly, IFEN has ways of locating people. If we're going to get to Canada before they find us, we have to move fast.

And then what? What, exactly, am I planning to do once we get there?

Well, we'll deal with that when the time comes.

I step on the gas. The car lurches forward. With a gasp, I slam on the brake.

"Easy."

"I know." Biting my lip, I tentatively lower my foot onto the gas again. The car moves forward in small jerks. I twist the wheel back and forth, trying to stay on the road, and the car veers from right to left. I nearly plow into a tree, fumble around, and shift into reverse. "Hang on . . . I've got this."

I shift gears again and drive slowly forward, fingers locked around the wheel. This time, I manage to stay on the road, though I have to keep the car under thirty miles an hour.

Just when I'm starting to relax, there's a burst of movement in front of me. I gasp again and stomp on the brake. My mouth falls open as a group of sleek brown forms bound across the road. There are ten—no, twelve—of them. White-tailed deer. I've never seen one outside of pictures and videos.

Steven lets out a small, startled laugh. "Pretty wild, huh?"

"Yes. They are." I watch them disappear into the trees, their tails flashing like white flags. So beautiful. Those creatures used to live all across the country. Now most people go their entire lives without having the chance to see one.

I feel a moment of gratitude that I could see them with Steven.

27

After an hour or so, Steven gets into the driver's seat. I've already run into two trees and a rock. I surrender the wheel with mingled relief and disappointment, but mostly relief. Driving manual is nerve-racking. How can anyone feel comfortable knowing they're controlling a four-thousand-pound weapon of death?

He's still a little shaky, but he's more or less back to normal. As for his collar, I have no idea whether it's still working or not. We'll just have to hope for the best.

We drive through the rest of the afternoon, making our way slowly but steadily north. Without the autodrive and the GPS, I have only a vague idea of where we are. There's a map folded in the glove compartment for emergencies, but I've never had to use it. I'm not sure I'd even know how to read one.

Steven, however, seems to know where he's going.

As the sun sinks lower, I watch him from the corner of my

eye. The fading daylight reflects off the pale plane of his cheek, tinting it orange, then gold, then soft pink, and finally a delicate purple-blue before the last wisp of twilight dims from the sky and there's only the pearly fairy light of the moon to guide us down the long, deserted stretch of country road.

Every so often, I start to think about that kiss, then forcefully pull my thoughts back to the present. It's too much to process. We need to focus on surviving.

I start to feel dizzy, and it occurs to me that it's been hours since that meager snack in the car. I grabbed the suitcase and the Gate when we fled, yet I didn't take the extra two seconds to grab our bag of fruit and cereal bars. Of course, I wasn't exactly thinking ahead at the moment. And now we're stuck in the middle of nowhere without food or water.

"So, what's the plan?" Steven says.

"Plan?"

"For getting into Canada. How are we going to cross the border without being seen?"

"Um . . ." He assumes I have a plan? Who does he think I am? Someone who knows what she's doing? "Honestly, it's a little hard to think right now. I'm very hungry."

"I still like my barbecued roadkill idea." One corner of his mouth twitches. "We passed a dead squirrel a mile back. I could try frying it with the ND."

"I'll pass. How are you holding up?"

He tosses a few pills into his mouth. His eyes are bloodshot. "I'm getting all these weird floaters in my vision, like jellyfish or something, and there's this buzzing sound in my head. And I can't feel my feet."

I shift my weight. "Do you want to take a nap in the backseat?"

"Nah. I'm good."

"Seriously. I know I'm a terrible driver, but there are fewer obstacles out here, at least. Crashing a car in the middle of an empty field with no other vehicles in sight would be an impressive achievement."

He makes a small, rough sound, not quite a chuckle. "Really, I'm okay. I've driven in worse shape than this."

"You have?" I wonder what kind of situation would necessitate that. Do I even want to know?

"Yeah. Don't think I could sleep, anyway."

It's almost midnight when we reach Wolf's Run, population sixteen hundred and fifty, according to the crooked sign.

Steven abruptly slams on the brakes. I lurch forward and grip the edges of the seat. "What's wrong?"

He stares out the windshield, fingers locked in a death grip around the steering wheel. Then he parks the car and gets out. I follow, bewildered.

The moon hangs over the horizon, enormous and yellow. The stars are so clear out here. You can see millions of them, it seems, like bright pinpricks against deep, velvety black. I never realized how many stars I was missing out on in Aura.

Steven stands, a breeze ruffling his hair. "I know this place," he says.

The land slopes into a valley, and the town sprawls across the valley floor, bordered by woods on one side. It's the first time I've seen a town. It looks absurdly tiny, a short stretch of road lined by stores and a handful of squat little houses—

though even from here, I can see that the houses are more individualized than those in the city. Some have peaked roofs; some have flat roofs. Some are made of stone, others of wood. There's no standard design. Beyond the houses is a cluster of lights and machinery. A generator.

"St. Mary's is close," he says. "In the woods just to the east. Those woods." He points at the solid, dark wall of trees near the edge of town.

My heartbeat speeds. "Do you remember anything else?"

His brow furrows, and his eyes cloud over. "I remember . . ." A shudder runs through him.

I touch his shoulder. "Steven?"

His expression is distant, closed off. I wonder what's going on behind those pale eyes. After a moment, he gives his head a shake. "It's gone."

"But something came back to you," I say, "even if it was just for a moment. Your blocked memories must be close to the surface."

"Yippee," he mutters. He looks down at the town again and rubs a hand over his face. Then he sways on his feet and staggers to one side, as if he's drunk.

I manage to catch him before he falls over. "What's wrong?" I cup his cheek, tilting his face toward me. "Did another memory—"

He lets out a breathless laugh. "Nope. Just got dizzy." He presses a hand over his stomach. "I've been running on adrenaline for the past few hours."

"Oh." I had a nap last night, but Steven—not counting that brief spell of unconsciousness—hasn't slept at all. And of course, we both need to eat. No wonder he can barely stand.

I sling an arm around him. "We can stop in town. They must have somewhere to buy food." Of course, it would be safer to drive straight through—the sooner we can reach the border, the better—but there's no telling when we'll have another chance to stock up on supplies. And there is the small matter of us not having a plan or, therefore, any reasonable expectation of crossing over into Canada without being caught.

We get into the car and drive down the hill, past a ramshackle collection of barns and grain silos, past pens of grazing cows and sheep, into town. The highway runs through the center, but it seems to be the only real road. The rest are dirt and gravel. To our right is a small brick pub, seemingly the last place in town that's still open. The smell of meat, smoke, and grease drifts from within.

Ordinarily, that smell would probably repulse me, but my midsection voices an eager rumble. "Should we go in?" I ask.

Steven's gaze shifts back and forth, scanning our surroundings. "It's probably safe. We shouldn't stay long, though."

I nod in agreement.

The pub's windows glow with yellow light, and there are a few cars parked in the lot, along with a motorcycle. I study the odd-looking contraption. Motorcycles are illegal in Aura, and have been for decades. And no wonder. The thing looks terribly unstable, like it might tip over at any second.

We get out of the car. It occurs to me that Steven still has a neural disrupter and a switchblade concealed in his leather coat. Just a week ago, the presence of weapons might have made me nervous. Now it makes me feel safer. I wonder what that says about me.

We approach the small door, and I hesitate outside. Vague

stereotypes about townspeople float through my mind—they're illiterate, violent, crude, et cetera. Or at least that seems to be the general consensus, though most people have never actually visited a town, just traveled from city to city. At best, the town dwellers are seen as quaint yokels with charming local customs but no idea how the real world works. At worst, they're portrayed as a bunch of anarchic thugs from the dark, barbaric past. Who are they, really?

I suppose we're about to find out. I push open the door. The hinges squeal like small animals being tortured.

The place is dimly lit and deserted, save for the bartender and a few very old men sitting in a corner playing cards. Their clothes are heavy and rough, mud-stained jeans and flannel shirts. Music plays—an ancient, crackling recording. Every surface seems to be stained deeply with several layers of grease and smoke, as if they're part of the wood itself. A deer head stares down at us with glassy eyes, its antlers spread out like tree branches. At the sight of it, I flinch. Is that *real*?

The old men watch as we slide onto the padded barstools. I shift, trying to get comfortable. "Hello," I say. My voice sounds too loud. "Um. We'd like something to eat, please." I look down at the counter, searching for a screen. "Where's your menu?"

Someone chuckles.

The bartender is a tall, bony man with a somber face and waxy skin. "No menu. We got burgers and fries. That's about it, 'less you want a beer."

"I'll have a burger, then."

"Cheese on mine. And pile some bacon on, if you got it," Steven says.

The burgers arrive in a few minutes. They're thick, buns soggy with grease. I wolf mine down, uncomfortably aware of the locals' eyes on us. They probably don't get visitors very often. They seem . . . not hostile, exactly, but not welcoming, either. There's something cautious in their expressions, and an unnatural silence hangs over the room, as if they're observing us, waiting to see what we do or say.

"So, where you bound?" the bartender asks.

"None of your business," Steven replies.

The bartender's gaze sharpens. For a few seconds, the room seems to hold its breath. When he speaks again, his tone is casual, but that alert look never leaves his eyes. "You kids wouldn't happen to be running for the border, would you?"

Steven lurches to his feet and stumbles backward. I see him reach for the ND.

In an instant, the bartender's aiming a huge rifle at him. I let out a strangled gasp. "Put 'er down, son," he says, not unkindly.

Steven doesn't move. The locals in the corner are watching us with sudden interest, though no alarm. One of them cracks a peanut and eats it.

"Don't misunderstand," the bartender says. He smiles, the folds in his weathered face deepening. "I'm not your enemy."

"Then why are you pointing a gun at us?" I ask, my voice shaking.

"Your friend was the one who reached for his weapon. I don't care for having a weapon pointed at me. So let's both put 'em down real slow. All right?"

They measure each other with their eyes for a few seconds, while I sit frozen, heart hammering, wondering what I'll do if this turns into a shoot-out.

"How do we know we can trust you?" Steven asks.

He shrugs. "You're free to get up and walk right out that door. No skin off my ass. But if you want to know what I know, you'll put the toy gun down."

"This is an ND," Steven says.

"Like I said. The toy gun."

"Have you ever seen what this toy can do?" With his thumb, Steven slides the switch to the highest setting.

Great. I can practically smell the testosterone leaking into the air, like some kind of explosive chemical that the wrong word will ignite.

I look from the bartender to the door and back again. My heart is beating so hard, it drowns out my thoughts. I struggle to make sense of the situation. *If you want to know what I know,* he said. What does he know? Is he offering to help us, or is he planning to kill us and mount our heads on the wall next to that hapless deer's?

One of the customers takes a swig of his beer. They're still watching us, silent as stumps, and I have the odd sense that they've seen this same confrontation play out before.

I meet Steven's gaze. "Let's hear what he has to say."

Steven narrows his eyes, as if to say, *Are you crazy?* I just hold his gaze, keeping my expression as steady and calm as I can. Finally, he nods and slowly lowers the ND. The bartender lowers his rifle as well. Steven thumbs the safety on the ND and shoves it into his belt, but his hand remains near the grip.

Suddenly, I notice a faded photograph of a smiling little girl tacked to the wall behind the bar. His daughter?

"Go ahead," I say quietly. "We're listening."

The bartender studies us with pale eyes. "There's something you should know about townsfolk," he says. "Most of us aren't too fond of city authorities. They like to come in here every so often, stick their damned mind-reading gadgets in our faces, and look down their noses at us. I'm not inclined to help them if they're looking for you. None of my patrons will breathe a word to them, either. We never saw you."

"Well," Steven says, "that's good to know." Still, there's a sharpness in his tone.

The bartender rests a hand on the edge of the ancient, scratched bar. "People like us, here in Wolf's Run . . . we're the last of a dying breed. A dying world. I'm one of the few who remember the time before the war. Of course, I was still a boy then."

"Is this gonna be a long story? Because we haven't got all night," Steven says. I kick his shin, hard.

The bartender glances at him, expression unreadable, then continues. "There were people back then who really didn't like the way things were going. People who didn't trust this new system of government. They wanted out. So a few reservations were set aside for folks like us—folks who wanted to live the way we'd always lived, without Types and all that bullshit. But even out here, they won't leave us alone. Government agents poke around and ask questions. Tourists show up to gawk at us. Like we're a museum exhibit. Maybe that's what we are." He stares at the picture on the wall. "Every year, our population gets a little smaller. Our children are leaving us for the cities. My daughter—she's grown now—skipped town a few years ago. In a way, I can't blame her. Who wants to stay in a place that's dying?" His voice wobbles a little.

"I'm sorry," I say softly. I don't know what else to say.

He shakes his head. "Never mind. Point is, IFEN is our enemy. So if people come through here on the run from the men in the white coats, I steer them right. It's all I can do."

I sit up straighter, listening.

"Head down Main Street to the end of town, then keep driving," he says. "You'll come to a big blue house. That's Gracie Turner's. Go there."

"Who is she?" I ask.

"That's all I'll say on the matter. If anyone asks you questions, you never talked to me. Got it?"

Steven gives a short, grim nod.

"Good. Finish your burgers."

I don't feel like eating, but considering that he has a gigantic rifle under the bar, it seems like a good idea to do what he says. I pick up the dripping mass of bread and meat and take another bite. Once we're finished, I fish the credit card out of my pocket and look around. "Where do I pay?"

"Cash only," he says.

I blink, mystified. "Cash?"

"Never mind." He smiles, as if I've said something funny. "It's on the house." He takes our plates.

"Thank you," I say uncertainly. "And thank you for the information."

"Remember. You never talked to me."

Steven and I rise to our feet and walk toward the door. As I reach out to open it, Steven suddenly speaks up: "Did you know Emmett Pike?"

The bartender's face turns stony.

"This is the town where he lived, isn't it?" Steven says. "You ever heard of him?"

"I recognize the name." The bartender polishes a glass, with a cloth. A long, tense silence passes before he continues. "I know damn near everyone in this town. But this guy they showed on the news, he didn't look familiar at all. I'd remember a face like that. Of course, some folks said they'd seen him lurking around. And who am I to say they were just looking for attention?" He shrugs, then smiles, showing a hint of a gold tooth. "You kids be careful now."

We walk out of the pub. Steven kicks a brown glass bottle, and it skitters across the pavement.

"So," I say, "are we going to look for this Gracie Turner?"

He doesn't respond. He stares straight ahead, eyes distant and glassy.

"Steven?"

He gives his head a shake. "Sorry. Just . . . thinking." He stops, hands shoved into his pockets, shoulders rigid. "I guess it's official, huh? Pike never existed."

"That's what it sounds like." Right now, I'm more worried about the future, about how we're going to get out of the country without being caught. But I can see why Steven would latch on to that detail. This is his past. His identity. And he's just received confirmation that it's all a lie.

We get into the car. He doesn't drive off immediately—he sits, hands resting on the wheel. "I don't get it." He doesn't sound angry or scared. Just tired. "It's supposed to be impossible to create new memories, isn't it?"

"Yes. Unless there's some technology that the general public doesn't know about—" I stop as a thought flashes through my head.

"You just thought of something, didn't you?" Steven asks.

I hesitate.

"Tell me," he urges.

I exhale slowly. "During Conditioning treatments, a patient is extremely suggestible . . . and memories are more like paintings than photographs, more like dreams than video recordings. The details warp naturally over time. A series of powerful subliminal suggestions could accomplish a lot. Simple Conditioning couldn't manufacture such a traumatic experience out of thin air, but perhaps it *could* distort the nature of that trauma."

The muscles tighten in his jaw. "So all these treatments they've been giving me through the years . . ."

"It probably happened before that," I reply quietly. "While the memories were still relatively fresh. Though the later sessions could have been designed to reinforce the suggestions, I suppose." I think about the first Lucid dream we shared, about Steven stumbling through the snowy woods, so traumatized and broken that he didn't know his own name. It wouldn't be difficult to take a vulnerable child like that and fine-tune his memories through subliminal suggestions. And I wonder—not for the first time—how anyone could do such awful things. *Why* would anyone do them?

"Lain? You okay?"

"Sure. My mind's wandering, that's all." I exhale a shaky breath. "So . . . what now?"

His lower lip disappears under his teeth. "I think we should keep going. We might even be able to reach the border tonight."

"And then what? Have you ever seen the border stations on the news? There'll be guards and fences, not to mention cameras everywhere. And obviously, we can't just go through, since we don't have passports."

"We can ditch the car and find some part of the fence that's not guarded, then climb over. They can't put guards along the whole thing."

"And if the fence is electrified?"

"I don't know." He rubs his palms over his face.

"I think we should do what the bartender says. We should go to this Gracie Turner and ask for her help."

"We don't know if we can trust any of these people. For all we know, this woman's going to hand us back to IFEN. Maybe she's got an arrangement with that guy at the bar. He steers people to her, she knocks them out, gets a bounty for them, then he gets a cut—"

"I really don't think that's going to happen. You heard what he said. The people in this town want as little to do with IFEN as possible."

"And you're just gonna believe him?"

"Well, I don't think he's lying." The truth is, I don't know what to believe. But without some kind of help, the odds of us escaping the country are pretty low. This is a gamble. But it's a gamble we need to take. "Look. I don't think we have much choice." My voice softens. "Let's at least talk to her. We're here. We might as well."

He closes his eyes. After a few seconds, he mutters a curse and starts the car. "You're right. I just . . . I really want to get out of this country. Like, now."

"I know the feeling."

I watch the buildings roll past outside the window, structures of wood and stone. They all have an old, dusty, disused look that's evident even in the moonlight. *We're the last of a dying breed,* the man said. In another thirty years, small towns like Wolf's Run probably won't exist anymore, and then there'll be nowhere in the country to hide from IFEN. "Are you sure Canada will be any better?"

"It has to be."

We keep driving, to the outskirts of town, where the houses are spread thin.

On the left, I spot a large house painted a bright robin's-egg blue, surrounded by open fields. Beyond, there's the forest, a dark smudge on the horizon. "That must be Gracie Turner's home," I say.

We park, and I get out, surveying the area. There's so much empty space, it feels like being on the edge of the world. The last vestige of civilization before the great, dark unknown of the north. There's a barn behind the house, and a grain silo, and a small pen of bleating goats out front. Before this, I'd only seen live goats at the zoo. As we walk past, a black-and-white one sticks its nose through the fence and sniffs. Its eyes are copper, with horizontal slot-shaped pupils. Steven reaches under its chin and scratches, and the goat tilts its head back to give him greater access. The gesture surprises me—I'm not sure why. Maybe it's just that I've never seen Steven interacting with an animal before.

A lantern hangs next to the front door, a gas flame glowing inside. There's no doorbell, so I grab the brass knocker—which looks like a lion's head—and knock three times. We wait. Next to me, Steven stands, his back stiff, his hand on the hilt of the ND. His gaze is fixed on the doorknob like it might jump off and bite him. I wonder if he ever relaxes.

Suddenly, I find myself thinking of that moment in the woods when I kissed him—the way the ND slipped from his hand and all the tension drained out of his body.

A loud click jerks me from my thoughts. The door opens, revealing a plump fortysomething woman clad in an old-fashioned blue-checkered dress. Her brown hair is tied back in a braid, and her gray eyes are clear and striking. They move from me to Steven and linger for a moment on his collar. Then she smiles. "I take it old Bill sent you?"

"If that's the bartender who pointed a rifle at us, then yes," Steven says.

"That would be him. He's a little rough-mannered, but he's a good man." She smooths her dress. "Well, come in." She steps aside, beckoning.

I hesitate. From what I can see of the interior, it's ordinary enough. The walls and floor are of dark varnished wood. There's a couch and a table with a stained-glass lamp. No TV. No modern technology in sight at all. The phone next to the lamp is the sort that hasn't been made for decades—a landline with a long, curly cord. I recognize it only from old pictures.

Gracie waits, watching us.

We're here. It seems rather pointless to show up and then refuse to come in. Slowly, I step into the house. Steven follows. The floorboards creak underfoot, and the whole place smells faintly of pine. A fire crackles in a stone hearth.

"Close the door, please," she says. "It's cold out."

I ease the door shut.

"This way," Gracie says, leading us into a small kitchen. The walls are papered with a design of bright yellow daisies, and the squat refrigerator looks like a prewar relic. Which it probably is. "I was just making some coffee. Would you like some?"

Steven and I exchange a long look.

She smiles, showing a dimple in her left cheek. "I'm not going to poison you or drug you."

"How can we be sure?" Steven asks.

Gracie pauses. Her gaze focuses on his collar. Then, slowly, she turns. Her braid trails down to the center of her back, thick cords of shiny brown hair threaded with a few strands of gray. She lifts the braid, exposing her neck, then peels off a skin-colored square of material from just below the base of her skull, exposing a tiny, puckered scar. It takes me a moment to realize what it means, but when I do, my jaw drops. Gracie had a collar. The scar marks the place where it was once wired into her nervous system.

"Holy shit," Steven breathes. His eyes are wide.

"I thought it was impossible to remove the collar," I whisper.

"Not impossible. Just difficult." She replaces the patch, drops her braid, and turns to face us. "I didn't always live in Wolf's Run, you know. I came here for the same reason you did. To escape."

"And IFEN hasn't come after you?" Steven asks.

"I had to cover my tracks very carefully. Gracie Turner is not my real name." Her expression is grim, her lips a thin, pale line.

She picks up a silver coffeepot and pours a cup. "I grew up in a state ward," she says. "A war orphan. Like many of those orphans, I was a Four from an early age. My options were limited. As I'm sure you're aware, very few people will

272

hire someone like me. I started stealing and selling drugs on the black market, because it was the only way to survive. I was caught and evicted from my apartment, and I ended up on the streets. I'd probably have taken Somnazol by now if someone hadn't helped me escape the city. The people of this town allowed me to stay, fortunately." She pours another cup of coffee, then sets both cups on the table. "Once, I believed that I was defective. A broken machine. I grew up hearing that from everyone. Instead of blaming my oppressors for my suffering, I blamed the wiring in my own brain. It took me a long time to abandon that view." She sets a small pitcher of cream on the table, alongside a bowl of sugar. "IFEN's propaganda is powerful and insidious. It creeps into your mind like poisonous gas and invades the deepest corners of your identity. There's just enough scientific truth in it to sound plausible . . . but then, systems of oppression have always twisted science to fit their goals. Centuries ago, they used to measure the circumference of skulls and weigh human brains on little scales to prove the alleged inferiority of certain types of people. The methods have become a bit more sophisticated now. But we have been here before. So many times." She nods to the table. "Sit."

Slowly, I sit. My mind churns. I feel like I should say something in response, but Gracie doesn't seem to expect it. I pick up the nearest coffee cup and take a tiny sip. It's bitter—I've never much cared for coffee—but the heat feels good going down my throat. "Thank you."

"Cream?"

"Yes please."

Steven is still standing, hovering near the door, hands shoved into his pockets.

"And you, dear?" she asks. "How do you take it?"

Judging by Steven's disoriented expression, being called "dear" is not a common experience for him. "Uh, black." After a few seconds, he slides into the chair next to mine.

She pours a cup of coffee for herself and drinks. "I take it you're headed for the Canadian border?"

"Yes," I manage. My voice emerges faint and hoarse.

"Follow the highway north until you reach Thorn Road, then take that deeper into the forest. You'll have to leave your car behind once you reach the fence. The roads crossing the border are too well guarded. But there are other ways to get through. Secret tunnels leading under the fence." She drops a cube of sugar into her coffee. "I can show you how to find them."

"Then it's possible?" Steven asks. His eyes are fever-bright, intense.

"Of course," she says. "People escape into Canada all the time. There are safe houses scattered across the country, places where refugees can hide."

Steven leans forward. "So, how can we find these safe houses?"

"There's a symbol." She draws it on a paper napkin: a curved, stylized letter Z. "You'll see it somewhere on or near the house, usually in red paint."

"And how many refugees are there?" I ask.

"More than you'd ever believe. There's a movement going on up north. A movement to help people like us."

For a moment, I can't find my voice. I realize, to my surprise, that I'm close to tears. We're not alone, after all. "Thank you," I whisper.

"No need to thank me. This is what I do." She interlaces her plump fingers. They look soft, but I get the feeling they're toughened with calluses. "Would you like some cookies? I made them today."

Even though I've just eaten, my stomach gurgles. "That sounds wonderful."

She brings out a plate of enormous oatmeal cookies studded with nuts and raisins. We sit at the table eating the thick, chewy treats and sipping our coffee. I take a swig, washing down a sticky mouthful.

"Oh, by the way," she remarks, "you may want to park your car somewhere less conspicuous before you settle in for the night. There's a barn out back where you can hide it. You will stay the night, won't you?"

"Well," I say, "a bed does sound wonderful right now." We should probably try to get a few hours of sleep, at least. My vision keeps going blurry, and my head feels like a block of cement. "I don't want to impose, though—"

"Nonsense." Gracie crouches and shoves back a rug, revealing a trapdoor with an iron ring. She grabs the ring and pulls the door open. A set of stairs leads downward. "The cellar's actually quite comfortable. Even if the police come looking for you, they won't find you there, and it has a secret tunnel leading out, in case you need to escape quickly."

Looking down into the square of darkness, I feel a twinge of unease. I don't think Gracie would betray us. Still, I'm painfully aware of how much trust we're placing in a woman we've just met.

Steven's munching his way through his fifth cookie. "Are

you going to tell us how you got rid of your collar?" he asks, mouth full.

She winks. "I'd tell you, but then I'd have to kill you."

We both freeze.

"That was a joke," she says.

"Oh." I force a small chuckle.

28

We park behind the barn and throw a tarp over the car, hiding it from the sight of passersby. Nearby, a group of chickens scratch and peck in the dirt. The warbling bleats of the goats pierce the silence. Overhead, stars shine like diamond dust scattered on black velvet. So many stars. In Aura, you're lucky if you can see a handful.

"I think we should stay the night," I tell Steven. "But if you still want to leave . . ."

"No. We should rest while we have the chance." We walk back toward the house. His expression is distant, pensive. "I don't think she's lying to us. That stuff she said about her life, about being a Type Four . . . it didn't feel like bullshit."

I nod in agreement.

Steven stops suddenly, looking off to the side. In the distance, a dark wall of forest looms. A shudder runs through him—the movement is barely perceptible, but I notice the telltale twitch of his shoulders. "Thorn Road," he murmurs. "The road she told us to take through the woods . . . that's the same road where they found me after I escaped from St. Mary's."

"You're sure?"

"Yeah."

The hairs on my nape stiffen, and a primal thrill of something between fear and hunger races down my spine. But hunger for what? St. Mary's is nothing but a ruin. Isn't it?

Steven turns away from the forest. It seems to take an effort.

We return to Gracie's house, carrying the suitcase. I take the Gate, too; I don't want to leave it unattended. The door is unlocked. When we enter, she's curled up on the couch, reading a paper book. "Ready?" she asks.

"Yes."

She opens the trapdoor and hands me a small gas lamp, and we descend a set of cement steps into a small but surprisingly cozy and clean cellar with two beds. "Good night," Gracie says. "If you need anything, just call out." She gently closes the trapdoor. I hear a rustle of movement above as she drags the rug over it. I set the gas lamp on the nightstand.

A cool, dry, spicy smell hangs in the air, and the walls and floor are brick, with a few woven rugs to brighten up the bareness. There's a tiny bathroom off to one side. Steven pulls the ND from his pocket and lays it next to the gas lamp. I take off my shoes and sit on the edge of a bed.

We're close to the border now. If we leave early in the morning, we could probably reach it before nightfall. Yet I find my thoughts wandering to the forest. To St. Mary's. We're so close. I feel it pulling at me, like a gravitational force.

Steven watches me intently, as if he knows exactly what

I'm thinking. "This might be our only chance to see what's in that place."

"I know."

"I want to see it," he says. "Even if there's nothing left."

St. Mary's isn't due north of here. It would take us off our course. Only a little, but still. "It would slow us down. It would be risky."

He bites the corner of his mouth. Then he gives his head a shake—not a denial, but the sort of shake people do when they're trying to clear their thoughts. "Let's just get some rest."

I nod, undo my pigtails, and comb my fingers through my hair. I glance at the nearest rug on the floor and nudge it aside to reveal another trapdoor. "I guess this is the escape passage she mentioned." I pull it open a crack. Beyond is a rough tunnel supported with a few beams of wood. It doesn't look very safe; hopefully, we won't have to use it, but if it comes down to that, I won't hesitate. Carefully, I ease the door shut. "It's amazing, isn't it?"

"What?"

"That there are people in the world like her—people who are willing to put themselves at risk to help complete strangers. I mean, for all she knows, we could be spies. Yet she opened her home to us. It gives me hope."

He raises his eyebrows. "Funny. That's about what I thought when I met you."

I open my mouth in surprise. Warmth rises into my face.

Before I can think of a response, he continues: "Anyway, I don't think she's doing this just because she's a nice person. She's got some goal. And she's not working alone, either. You heard what she said. She was talking about safe houses and secret symbols. This is part of something bigger."

"What do you think it means?"

He meets my gaze. "I think the Blackcoat rebellion is still going on. She's part of it. The more people they can help, the more possible recruits they have."

My heart gives a small, sharp lurch. I remember the glimpse of graffiti in the monorail station. At the time, I almost wanted to believe it meant something. Yet now I find myself disturbed by his words. "You know what the Blackcoats were like. They killed innocent people. They wanted to tear down society. Gracie's not like that." Of course, we don't know her. I can't say with any certainty what she would or wouldn't do, but somehow, I can't see her rigging bombs or picking people off with a sniper rifle. "You don't really think she's a terrorist, do you?"

He slips off his coat and throws it across a chair. "Well, you know what they say. One person's terrorist is another person's freedom fighter." He flashes a humorless smile.

My mouth has gone dry. In school, they showed us the footage over and over—the bombs, the blood, the charred rubble. The images flicker through my head in a grisly slide show. "Surely you don't *agree* with their methods?"

He rolls his shoulders and starts rubbing one, working out the kinks in the muscles. "Not saying I do. But I can understand why they were desperate enough to do it. IFEN was already locking people up in treatment facilities, Conditioning them against their will and giving them collars. And a lot of them hadn't actually *done* anything. They were just flagged by the system as potential threats. How else were they supposed to fight back? What would you do?"

I shift on my bed, uneasy. I'm not sure I like the direction this conversation is going. "I'd use reasoning. I'd try to change people's minds, to change the system from within."

He snorts. "Anyone who had a negative opinion about it got reclassified. Because, you know, if you're speaking out against the government, it just means you're suffering from paranoid delusions and need help." His voice is thickly layered with sarcasm. "So how exactly were they supposed to change things from within?"

He has a point. How *are* people supposed to fight back through legal means when their rights can be so easily stripped away? "I know that IFEN went too far, but I still think the intention behind it was good," I say. "Before the Registry of Mental Health, there were lots of sick people who never sought treatment and just got worse and worse until they snapped. What about them—the people who really *do* need help?"

"Like me?"

I flush. "You know that's not what I mean."

"Then who *do* you mean? You've seen my profile, my laundry list of psychological defects. I'm about as crazy as they come." He looks me in the eye. "Do you think they were right to do what they did to me?"

My first impulse is to say no, of course not, that they made a mistake with Steven. But he was evaluated according to the standard rules. If I say that what happened to him is wrong, then I have to acknowledge that the system itself is wrong. At this point, that should be easy. I've seen how much corruption IFEN is capable of, how far they'll go to control people. Yet a part of me still hesitates.

When it becomes clear that I'm not going to answer, Steven looks away. "Do you want the shower first or second?"

"Go ahead."

I sit on the edge of my bed, listening to the hiss of the water, my mind floating in a sea of questions. Whatever its problems, our society functions. People get up in the morning, go to work, come home and spend time with their families and friends. Despite all the terrible things IFEN has done, they've succeeded in creating a world where violent crime is rare—at least, compared to prewar America—and those who commit such crimes are almost always caught. What if there is a resistance, a movement whose goal is not to change the system but to overthrow it? Do I want to be part of that? Do I really want to see the current peace, however flawed, sacrificed for an uncertain future? Yes, there's unhappiness and inequality now, but has there ever been a society where those things didn't exist? Of course that doesn't mean it's okay. Maybe I'm only making excuses. But if we reduce our current system to rubble, I can't help wondering, will people just build something even worse?

Steven emerges from the bathroom, his skin flushed from the heat and his blond hair slicked down. The water's darkened it a few shades, bringing out hints of honey gold, and his T-shirt clings to his damp skin. "Shower's all yours," he mutters.

I retreat into the bathroom, taking a set of pajamas with me, and shut the door. The mirror's still fogged, the tiles inside the stall wet.

I turn on the water and stand under the hot spray, head bowed, eyes closed. There's not much water pressure, and the water itself has an oddly saline quality, but the heat feels wonderful. I start to pick up the soap, then stop, looking at it. It's already wet. Steven used it just a few minutes ago. The thought makes me blush.

In my head, the ghost of my psych-ethics professor nags at me. Steven's a client, a client, a client. Not that that stopped me from kissing him. Which was wrong, certainly. Very wrong. I should probably continue to pretend it never happened.

I lean against the stall wall, closing my eyes, and let the water cascade over my hair. An image of his hands floats into my head unbidden. Long, slender fingers. Pale and almost delicate, but surprisingly strong. I can see every detail of those hands, from the calluses studding his palms to the tiny scar on the knuckle of his left index finger—and suddenly, my heart is racing.

I need to stop this. Now. Even setting aside the fact that my feelings for Steven are thoroughly inappropriate, it's ridiculous to be having these thoughts when we're on the run. But if there's anything I've learned about feelings, it's that trying to repress them just makes them stronger.

After I've toweled off, I change into my pajamas and step out.

"You really *do* like pink," Steven says.

I glance down at my coral-colored pajamas. "I warned you."

A tiny smile tugs at one corner of his mouth.

I avert my gaze, cheeks burning like torches. I'm sharing a room with a boy. And not just any boy. Steven Bent. The situation is undeniably awkward, and it doesn't help that Steven is, well, attractive. It's a simple fact. If he weren't so painfully thin—and if not for his reputation and his collar—he'd probably have girls clinging to him like barnacles.

I dig through the suitcase looking for my toothbrush.

Nearby, the Gate's black hard drive and twin white helmets gleam.

I hesitate, remembering Steven's earlier words, outside my house: *It's possible, isn't it? I could use the Gate on you.*

I refused then. But Steven was right. It *is* unfair that I've seen so much of his mind and he's seen none of mine. Ours is no longer a clinical relationship. Despite my conscience constantly buzzing around in my head like a fly, it's obvious that Steven and I have become close. The least I can do now is try to equalize our relationship.

"Do you still want to use the Gate on me?" I ask.

His whole body goes rigid. "Lain . . ." He looks away, raking a hand through his hair. "When I asked you for that, I wasn't thinking straight. I was just scared. You don't have to—"

"I want to."

His brows draw together. His eyes move in small flickers, studying my face. "Why?"

I pick up the white helmet and run my hands over its smooth plastic surface. "I don't want there to be any barriers between us. I want you to trust me completely, the way I trust you."

"I *do* trust you. I let you aim an ND at my head. What's left to prove?"

My grip tightens on the helmet. "You trust me with your life, I know. And I trust you with mine. But it's one thing to believe that someone won't kill you. It's another to trust them with your whole being." My heart has climbed up into my throat. I try to swallow it, but it won't go down. "I want to show you what's inside me. I owe you that much."

He looks no less baffled. I smile, though my heart is racing.

The thought of letting him into my mind scares me more than I want to admit. But maybe that's why I have to do it. I have to prove to myself—as well as Steven—that there's nothing to be afraid of.

I turn the hard drive on, and set it on the floor between our two beds. Then I slip one of the helmets onto my head and hand the other one—the one I normally use for sessions—to Steven.

He takes it, but doesn't put it on. "You're sure about this?"

I nod.

He inhales a slow, deep breath and lets it out through his nose. "Okay." Sitting on the edge of his bed, he slides on the helmet and snaps the black visor down over his eyes. "So, how does it work? I mean, do I have to do anything, or . . ."

"Just wait. It takes a moment for the sensors to start picking up readings." I sit on the edge of my own bed, facing him, and adjust the helmet, keeping the visor up so I can see. A warm tingling spreads over my scalp. I swallow.

It's been years since anyone's used a Gate on me. All Mindwalkers, as part of our training, share some of our memories with a more advanced Mindwalker in order to get a feel for what our patients experience. What I remember from those sessions, more than anything, is the intense feeling of vulnerability, like being on an operating table with my body slit open and my guts exposed.

"Hey, I think I feel something." Steven places a hand over his chest, and his mouth opens in surprise. "Wow. It's like I have two heartbeats. Like your heart is inside my chest, next to mine." He clutches his shirt, fingers kneading the fabric. "This is so weird."

"It takes some getting used to."

Steven sits silently for several minutes, frowning. His hands drop into his lap and rest there, palms up, as if he's meditating. Then he lifts one hand into the air and waves it. He lets out a small gasp. "I can see myself. It's like a movie in my head."

"You're seeing what I'm seeing."

"Look up."

I look at the ceiling.

"Look down."

I do. When I look up at Steven again, he's grinning, like this is a marvelous new game. I've never seen such a young, carefree expression on his face. "This is so cool," he says.

I almost laugh. But the sound stops in my throat, like it's hit a wall.

He stands and walks over to my bed, his movements unsteady, his arms held out for balance. When his legs bump against the side of the bed, he pauses, then sits next to me. I tense in surprise as he reaches out and takes my hand in his own. I hold still, not breathing. He traces a small circle on my palm, then slides his nails lightly along my fingers. I shiver as he trails a finger up my wrist and forearm over the thin cotton of my sleeve.

"Wow, I can *feel* it," he says. "I can feel what you're feeling." He holds out his arm. "Do it to me."

"P-pardon?"

"Touch my arm. I want to see what it's like when you do it."

I hesitate. He remains motionless, holding out one thin arm. I place a finger against the translucent skin of his wrist, over the intersection of two blue veins.

Warm, smooth skin.

Shouldn't have thought that. Did he hear? I gulp. His pulse beats under my fingertip. Slowly, I withdraw my hand.

"Is it always like this for you?" he asks. I can't read his tone. "I mean, when you do immersion?"

"Yes."

He lifts his visor. His eyes are wide and dazed. He closes them, opens them again. Then his gaze lowers and focuses on my hands, which rest palm up in my lap. He places his own hand against one, his fingertips resting on my palm. My breath hitches. I'm all too aware that he can hear everything I'm thinking. I have to be careful. But of course, now that I've thought that, Steven will think I'm trying to hide something, which I'm not.

"Hey . . ." His voice softens. "You're shaking."

"I'm okay. Really. I'm simply . . . not used to this."

I wonder just how much he can feel—if he can see past my surface thoughts into my emotions. Probably not. I wasn't even sure he'd be able to open a connection between us on the first try. "You're good at this, you know. You could probably be a Mindwalker if you wanted."

"Me?" He looks incredulous.

"You're at about the right age to start training."

"I don't think I could handle it. I've got more than enough nightmares in my own head to deal with."

He has a point.

"Say, do people ever use the Gate for stuff other than therapy?"

"Like what?"

He clears his throat. "Well, you know."

I stare blankly. "No. I don't."

"It just seems like . . . you know, feeling everything the other person is feeling, it would make certain things more . . . intense."

I can sense my face getting warmer as his meaning dawns on me. "The Gate is an important scientific tool. It's not a toy. Using it for anything other than therapy, training, or research is against regulations."

"Well, yeah, but people don't always follow regulations." My cheeks blaze.

"Sorry," he says. "I'm not trying to embarrass you. Honest."

"It's okay." I squirm. I feel like a turtle out of its shell, soft insides exposed.

He raises his hands to his face, brushing his fingertips over his own cheeks. "You sure blush a lot."

"I guess so."

I knew this would be awkward. But I had no idea *how* awkward. Is this how Steven felt the first time I used the Gate on him? Maybe if I just keep my attention on sensory input, I won't think about anything else. I focus on his eyes, studying the irises. This close, I can see the subtle variations of color within—the threads of quicksilver woven through the blue, the line of darker blue around the outer edges, the pale silvery gray near the center. But paying too much attention to his eyes might be taken the wrong way. Not that they aren't pretty eyes, but—

Shouldn't have thought that.

"You like my eyes?" he asks. His voice is soft, his tone unreadable.

"No. I mean, yes. I mean—" I bite my tongue. The more I try *not* to think about Steven, the more I think about him. Memories flicker through my head: the sight of long, agile fingers unbuckling the straps of his coat; the graceful way he moves, like a wildcat; the way he sometimes smiles without seeming to smile, just a quirk of those thin lips. . . .

Quickly, I derail that train of thought, but it's too late. He heard it all.

His eyes widen, and something shifts within them. Wonder and fear swirl in their depths. Does he have any idea how expressive those eyes are?

He closes them, as if to hide. "This is so weird," he mutters.

"What?" My voice comes out a little breathless.

His eyes remain tightly shut, his brows knitted together. "Just . . . you thinking about me. And me knowing everything you're thinking. Seeing yourself through someone else's eyes . . . it's so . . ." He gulps. "Did you ever hear me thinking about you during our sessions?"

I shake my head.

"I was trying to keep my thoughts quiet." He smiles nervously. "Guess it worked."

I wonder what sorts of thoughts he was having. I want to ask, but I don't quite dare.

The bedsprings creak as he slides closer to me, and the mattress dips a little. "Will you do something?"

I nod.

"Look at me. Don't say anything. Just look me in the eye."

I hesitate. But I told him that I didn't want there to be any more barriers between us; if I hide everything I'm feeling, it defeats the purpose. I meet his gaze. His expression doesn't waver, but deep in those eyes, behind the layers of battered shields, there's something soft and hungry. An overwhelming tenderness sweeps through me . . . and something else, something hotter and fiercer. I tense instinctively, resisting the feelings, then force myself to relax and let them flow through me, let myself feel everything—the fascination with him, with all his light and darkness, his scars and beauty, his pain and strange innocence.

He draws in a shaky breath, pulling back a little. He closes his eyes, as if to collect himself.

"Steven?"

"You once told me that saving people is your vice. You remember?"

"Yes."

He opens his eyes. "Is that the only reason you've done so much to help me?"

I freeze. Steven's expression is neutral, guarded. Cautious. "No. It's not the only reason."

"Why, then?"

My heart punches my ribs so hard, I'm certain it's going to crack them. "Because I didn't want you to disappear from this world," I whisper. "I wanted—" I stop myself before I can finish the thought. But I don't need to finish. He knows. He *sees*.

Steven reaches up to cup my face. His thumb brushes my cheek, touches my lips, and runs across them, leaving a trail of tingles. "When you kissed me before, in the forest," he says, "did you mean it?"

My heart seems to stop.

His eyes burn bright, hot. "Tell me the truth."

I should pull back now. I know that. Slowly, I slide my fingertips along his jaw, over his cheek. "Yes," I whisper. "I meant it."

He draws in his breath sharply. Every line of his body is

tense, quivering like a bowstring drawn too tight, as if it takes all his effort to hold himself back.

He leans down and touches his lips to mine. They're cool and slightly rough, chapped from the cold weather. I feel the flutter of his breathing. He tastes like the ocean. Like tears.

My muscles relax as my resolve softens and begins to crumble. A heady euphoria spreads through me like a drug, and I struggle to control my breathing. The room is suddenly too warm. My body tingles lightly. It reminds me of immersion, of the first time I plunged into Steven's mind, every nerve ending alive and ablaze, every sensation magnified.

I squeeze my eyes shut and try to silence my thoughts. I feel like I'm sliding perilously close to the edge of a chasm.

Steven's lips press harder against mine. A faint whimper escapes my throat, and a tremor runs through me.

I can't—I shouldn't—

"It's okay." He pulls off my helmet and drops it to the bed. His own joins it a moment later. His lips brush my neck.

It would be so easy to let go. So easy to just do what I want. What we both want.

I brace myself and—with every shred of willpower I possess—pull back. He starts to lean toward me again, but I place my hands on his shoulders, stopping him. His brow furrows. "There's something I need to know." I swallow, trying to moisten my dry mouth. "After all this is over . . . are you still planning to have your memories erased?"

He tenses. Then he turns his face away, his jaw tightening. My hands fall from his shoulders. A wall of silence hangs between us. He bows his head, resting his elbows on his knees, and buries his fingers in his hair. "I don't get it," he says. "Why do I have to forget you? Or this? Why can't you just erase the bad stuff and keep everything else?"

If I tried to explain the neurochemistry of memories and the ways they're conceptually bundled together in the brain, it would probably sound like gibberish to him. So I give the best answer I can: "Because nothing is ever simple."

"Tell me about it," he murmurs.

What if he *does* choose to forget? Can I really do it? Can I go into his mind and erase myself from it, delete the neural networks that hold this conversation, this night, the sensation of my lips against his? And I wonder what else will disappear if I take away his pain. His caustic wit? His empathy, his fierce desire to protect others who've been hurt? Everything is woven together. Trying to extract his suffering without destroying the rest is like trying to remove the grain of sand from the center of a pearl.

"It's your choice," I say.

His gaze meets mine. Slowly, he pushes a loose tendril of my hair behind one ear. "It must be hard." He cups my cheek, his palm warm and rough. "You spend so much time inside people's heads, getting to know them. And then when it's all over, they just walk away and forget about you, as if none of it ever happened."

A lump fills my throat, cutting off air and voice. I choke it down. "It's better that way," I whisper. "Better for them."

"But painful for you."

We sit, just looking at each other. After a while, he averts his gaze.

My chest feels hollow. I wish I'd just kept kissing him. I

wish my stupid conscience hadn't intervened. Why does doing the right thing so often feel like doing the wrong thing?

Finally, Steven stands up and shoves his hands into his pockets. "I don't know about you, but I don't think I can sleep tonight. And I'm sick of not knowing what really happened to me. I can't decide whether to erase my past until I know what my past is, right?" His jaw tightens. "We still have one pill left."

A chill washes through me. "You're not thinking about taking it now, are you?"

"Not here. I want to go to St. Mary's and take it there."

I stare, stunned, then shake my head. "It's too dangerous. Too strong. We don't know what will happen. And what difference will it make, being in St. Mary's?"

"When we came over the hill and I saw the town, this wave of déjà vu hit me. Even if there's nothing left in St. Mary's, just *being* there might make me remember."

"It might not even be the right St. Mary's."

"It is," he says. "I knew exactly where it was when we got here."

I search his face. "Are you sure about this?"

He stares directly into my eyes. "If we go there, we'll find the truth. I feel it."

I feel it, too, like a magnetic pull. And he's right. Even if there's nothing left in St. Mary's, the visual cues combined with the effects of the Lucid could trigger a flood of memory. If that doesn't bring back his past—or at least whatever's left of it—nothing will.

Do I really *want* to know the truth?

Slowly, I stand. "If we're going, we should leave now."

29

"Are you sure about this?" Gracie asks us. She stands in the doorway, bundled in a wool coat.

"We're sure," I reply. I haven't told her where we're going, just that we need to leave early. That there's something important we have to do before we cross the border.

"Well, take this." Gracie offers us a bulging backpack. "There's trail mix, bottled water, and a couple of heavy-duty flashlights. And a map of the border. The entrances to the tunnels are marked in blue. Of course, there's a chance that some of them have been discovered and filled in since the map was last updated, but this will give you an idea, at least."

"Thank you," I say. "For everything."

Steven is pacing the yard, hands in his pockets, breath forming small white clouds in the cold air. A rooster crows. A heavy fog lies over the yard like a damp blanket.

"Is there anything else you can tell us before we go?" I ask. "Anything we should know?"

"Move as quickly as you can. Stay on guard. And don't get caught." She winks.

I thank her again, then we get in the car and start driving. The horizon glows with pale, ghostly fire. Steven stares out the window, faint dawn light illuminating the gray shadows beneath his eyes. Those dark circles never really seem to go away. It's as if, after years of insomnia, they've sunk permanently into his skin.

The world is still and quiet, the sky thick with clouds that spit halfhearted bits of rain on the windshield. As we near the edge of the pine forest, the shadows reach out to engulf us. The morning, already dark, becomes darker. The car slows.

"Do you think we'll be able to find St. Mary's?" I ask.

"I know where it is," Steven says.

Thorn Road is bumpy, the pavement cracked and pitted. When I look in the rearview mirror, I can no longer see the town, just the cool, deep green of pine trees. A pristine hush hangs over the forest. Not even the music of birdsong breaks the silence. There's only the whisper of dead pine needles and the occasional crunch of a pinecone beneath the tires.

Steven's fingers are tight on the wheel. "Lain?"

"Yes?"

"After this is over, if we're both still here, and if I decide to keep my memories, will we . . . I mean . . ." He bites his lower lip, then takes a deep breath, as if steeling himself. "What happened back there—do you really feel that way about me?"

My pulse quickens. A memory flashes through my head— his scent, his warmth, the pressure of his lips against mine. My fingers drift up to touch my lips, tracing them.

I shouldn't have kissed him. Not the first time, and definitely not the second. Now he's thinking about keeping his traumatic past so he won't have to forget me. This is exactly why relationships between Mindwalkers and clients are forbidden. Guilt rips at my heart. I've been irresponsible and selfish. I was so overwhelmed with everything that was happening to us, I didn't think about the repercussions. But that's no excuse. "Listen, I . . ." A lump shoulders its way into my throat. I swallow it. "I made a mistake. It's forbidden for Mindwalkers and clients to get involved. I should have had more self-control, but I wasn't thinking clearly. I—"

"Just answer the question."

"It doesn't matter how I feel. I told you, it's against the rules."

He stares at the road, his knuckles white on the steering wheel. "Do the rules really matter at this point?"

"Yes! I can't—" My voice wavers. I close my eyes, collecting myself. I walk through the mental training exercises, and—with a skill born of long practice—I push my feelings down below the surface of my mind, leaving my thoughts calm and clear. My eyes open, and I take a deep breath. "Patients sometimes develop strong feelings for their psychologists." Without meaning to, I find myself slipping into a neutral, clinical tone, reciting words from my training. "It's called transference."

He frowns. "What?"

"It's a subconscious redirection of emotions that often manifests as an erotic attraction. What you're experiencing for me now is the same sort of thing."

His shoulders stiffen. "What fresh bullshit is this?"

I continue, ignoring the remark: "It's not *me* you love. It's the idea of me. It's what I represent to you." I avoid looking at his expression. "Of course it's natural for clients to bond to the person healing them, but that's why the rules exist. It would be unethical of me to take advantage of your feelings—"

There's a thud as he slams one fist against the dashboard, and I give a start. The car lurches to a stop. He stares straight ahead, his hands locked around the wheel. "If you want me to walk away when this is over, I'll walk away," he whispers hoarsely. "Tell me these feelings are wrong if you want. Tell me they're sick. But don't tell me they aren't real. Don't you dare."

His shoulders slump. The fire dies from his eyes, and instead of furious, he just looks exhausted. "I can't trust my memories. I don't even know who I am. My feelings are the only thing that I believe in. If I can't trust them, then there's nothing left."

I sit frozen, not moving, not breathing.

He takes his foot off the brake. The car glides forward. Still, I don't speak.

I've never felt so lost.

For years, I believed that following the rules meant doing the right thing. I don't know what I believe anymore, and I don't know who I trust—except Steven. Maybe that's crazy. After all, he's violent and unstable. He's upended my entire life. Yet I have more faith in him now than I do in the organization I've spent my life serving. And it would be cowardly not to admit that. "I do care about you," I say quietly. "More than I should. You're much more than a client to me. More than a friend."

There's a slight hitch in his breathing.

My fingers curl inward, hiding in my palms. "I just—I have a lot of things I need to figure out. I don't know what's right or wrong. And I don't know what's going to happen after this is all over. I need time."

Only the low hum of the engine breaks the silence as he stares straight ahead. Then he turns his head toward me and gives me a small, lopsided smile. There's a hint of sadness in his eyes. "Fair enough."

That smile makes me ache. I want to give him more. I want to tell him that we can be together after this—if there even is an "after this." But I just can't. I'm too confused.

The road's become bumpier. The car jolts and rattles along until we reach a fork. Thorn Road continues straight ahead while a nameless dirt road branches off to the east. It's little more than a deer path, too narrow for a car. We stop and get out. "This is it," Steven says. "This road. It'll take us to St. Mary's. I'm sure of it."

It's still early morning, but the clouds have grown so thick, it feels like twilight. I hug myself, shivering. I look down Thorn Road, which continues due north through the forest, toward the border. Then I look down the narrow, shadowy path that leads into the unknown. Into Steven's past. "You think it's all right to leave the car here?" I ask.

"Well, I doubt it'll get towed."

I take the Gate out of the backseat and wrestle it into the backpack, along with the helmets. It's heavy, but not unmanageable. If we take turns carrying it, we should be fine.

He starts to walk, pine needles crunching underfoot. I follow. The path is so dark, it's like moving through a tunnel. The car recedes behind us and vanishes, swallowed up by trees and underbrush.

Thunder growls in the distance. A few raindrops kiss the back of my neck, and I glance nervously at the sky. "Maybe this is a bad idea."

Steven shakes his head. "I want to finish this."

We keep walking. Steven starts to lag behind, puffing and wheezing. "Damn," he says. "How are you in better shape than I am? You're supposed to be the egghead, aren't you?"

"I go to the gym. A healthy mind resides in a healthy body, that's what . . ." I trail off, the words *Father always said* dying in my throat. I feel reluctant to bring up Father right now. If Steven notices the slip, he doesn't say anything.

I quicken my pace.

Steven lets out a groan and presses a hand to his chest. "Slow down. My lungs are giving me grief."

"If you took better care of yourself, this wouldn't be so difficult," I can't resist pointing out.

"And if I had wings, I could fly there like a little birdie." He stumbles over a root and curses. He walks into a spiderweb and picks it out of his hair, grimacing. "Nature is so overrated."

Despite the knot in my stomach, a tiny smile tugs at my lips.

The wind has picked up, and the trees sway ominously, but the rain still holds off. I stop, staring ahead. "I think I see it."

"Where?"

"There." I point to a dim shape looming through the trees. As we draw nearer, the shape coalesces into a castle-like brick building with barred windows, surrounded by an empty courtyard and a crumbling brick wall. A pair of iron gates hang from the wall by their hinges, rusted and creaking faintly in the wind, and a weed-choked path leads up to the main doors.

"Looks like the set of a horror movie," Steven remarks.

"Well, it's an abandoned mental institution. Creepiness sort of goes with the territory."

"Wonder if we'll meet any ghosts."

"Maybe." We've been taking turns wearing the backpack. I have it now, and its weight is comforting against my back. But a heavy, cold layer of dread has settled into my stomach like cement. "Ready?"

Steven gives me a strained smile. "No. But I already made up my mind. I'm going in there."

I stretch out a hand to him. He takes it, and we wind our fingers together. His hand is warm. An anchor to cling to.

We walk through the gates, down the path toward St. Mary's. Bits of stone crunch underfoot. Over the years, the forest has climbed over the wall and into the courtyard, and a dense carpet of autumn-brown bushes covers everything. I try to imagine what the place might have looked like in its heyday. Maybe there were gardens. Maybe the patients worked out here, clad in shapeless white uniforms, picking tomatoes or apples, their movements hindered by the chains on their ankles. They still used chains in those days.

I think of the Typing system, the cameras, the constant, looming threat of reclassification. We still have chains, I realize—we all do. They're just less visible now.

Thunder rumbles fitfully in the distance as we approach the main doors. They are closed, but the wood is so ancient and rotted it looks like it would crumble apart at a touch. A heavy, rusted iron padlock hangs from a chain. Steven kicks the lock, and it drops to the ground with a thud, like a piece of overripe fruit.

He pushes the doors, and they creak open, revealing a wide hall. Hazy gray sunlight, not quite bright enough to pierce the shadows, shines through holes in the ceiling. At the end of the hall, on a pedestal, stands a statue of a robed figure with its arms outstretched, lit by a beam from above.

I pull the two flashlights from my backpack and hand one to Steven. I flick mine on, and the bright yellow beam cuts through the gloom. "Ready?"

Steven turns on his own flashlight and nods. We walk forward. Dry leaves rustle under our feet, leaves that have found their way in through the gaps in the ceiling. When I look up, directing my flashlight into the rafters, I see crows nesting there. Startled, they caw and flap their wings. A few fly up through the gaps, into the charcoal sky. I sweep the beam across the wall to our left and over a row of doors. Some are shut, others hang half open. When I shine the light in the doors, I see only empty rooms: a few naked bed frames, nothing more.

"Well, it certainly looks deserted." My voice sounds too loud and somehow profane in the deep, oppressive stillness.

Maybe there's nothing here, after all. Maybe this is a waste of time.

The crows peer down at me, and the wind howls faintly outside.

I consider myself a reasonable person, not given to flights of fancy or superstition. But I've always had a dim sense of things that lurk outside human comprehension. Sometimes, intuition—that lightning-swift subconscious computer, honed through millions of years of evolution—can sniff out clues even when the greater picture remains beyond the mind's reach. And this place makes my intuition tingle and electricity dance beneath my skin. Something happened here; that much I'm sure of. Something terrible.

I realize Steven hasn't replied. He stands motionless, staring at the statue at the end of the hall. When my thumb brushes over his wrist, I feel his pulse drumming just below the surface, hard and fast. "Steven?"

He shakes his head, as if stirring himself from a trance, and exhales a shuddering breath. "So, are we going to do this or what?"

I dig around in my pocket, fish out the compact, and flip it open. The dragon pill rolls around inside. Steven plucks it out, but doesn't take it—just looks at it, his expression grim.

"Are you sure you want to do this?" I ask.

He curls a fist tight around the pill. "Don't start saying stuff like that," he says. "I'll lose my nerve." He flashes me a quick smile, though his complexion is wax-white.

I hesitate, looking up into his eyes. And I'm struck, again, by how very strong he is. The horrors he's endured would have shattered most people, yet he's still alive, still moving forward, facing the nightmares again and again. That's the thing most people don't understand about trauma—it doesn't stop after it's over. It lives on inside, day after day, year after year. The broken fragments of his mind are held together with sheer, stubborn willpower.

I reach up to touch his cheek. "No matter what happens, I'll be here."

He closes his eyes briefly, as if savoring the touch, and lays his hand over mine. "Damned if I know why," he says quietly. "You could do a lot better, you know."

I wish I could find the words that will make him understand his own worth. Maybe I could show him. For a moment, I find myself leaning forward. It would be so easy.

"What are you thinking right now?" he asks, voice soft and husky.

I swallow, heart hammering. "That I want to kiss you. But I shouldn't. I mean—" I let out a weak laugh. "I just got done telling you that I need to wait and figure things out."

He slides his fingers into my hair, and a warm shiver runs through me. He holds my head in place, searching my face, his gaze lingering on each feature. He leans down until I can feel the heat of his breath on my lips. Our eyes are so close together, I can't focus. I wait, holding my breath—and then he pulls back, slowly, as if it takes an effort. His hand drops away from my head.

I want to cry out in protest.

"As soon as you've figured things out," he says, "let me know."

The space between us suddenly feels much wider, and the warmth in my chest goes cold. I'm the one who wanted to wait, I remind myself. He's respecting my wishes. But it still feels like rejection.

"Well," he says, "here goes nothing." He tosses the pill into his mouth and swallows it.

There's no time to delay. The drug acts quickly; it's working its way into his bloodstream even now. I open the backpack and set the Gate's hard drive on the floor. He grabs his helmet and shoves it on, buckling the strap under his chin. I pick up my own. The white plastic is cool, slick, and familiar beneath my fingertips. With shaking hands, I slide the helmet over my head, and the warm tingling washes across my scalp.

Steven sways on his feet. His dizziness hits me like an avalanche, making me stagger. The walls tilt and shimmer around me. The cawing of crows rings in my ears.

"Lie down." It takes an effort to form the words.

He stretches out on the floor. His chest heaves, the movement so rapid it's almost a flutter. His eyes are wide and blank, fixed on the ceiling.

The walls start to melt around me. I close my eyes and focus on breathing until the dizziness recedes. *It's not real. It's not real.* When I open my eyes again, my vision is blurry but otherwise normal. "Steven, can you hear me?"

He groans. His body twitches and shivers. Sweat drips down his face and neck. Already, he's deep within the dream.

I lie down next to him, take his hand, and surrender. I have the sense that I'm falling upward. A chorus of voices swells in my ears, unearthly warbling wails, some high, some deep.

A dark hole opens in the air above me. It sucks me in like a hungry mouth.

30

I'm drifting through a misty sea filled with echoing, dimly sensed voices, a low murmur, more felt than heard, like a vibration in my bones. I don't know who I am or where I am.

There is at once something repulsive and deeply comforting about this place. There is no time here. Objects emerge from the mist—chairs, clocks, windows, bits and pieces of broken things. They appear and then vanish, swallowed by the haze. I see the statue from St. Mary's, but it's bigger than life, looming over me. A dark hole opens under it, and I'm falling—then racing toward a bright aperture, like a hole in storm clouds. There's a shining whiteness beyond, and I can hear voices, a boy's and a girl's. I can't make out what they're saying.

I float toward the voices, toward the whiteness. It grows, brightening, and engulfs me.

I'm walking through a hall, my heart tripping in my throat. A camera stares down from the ceiling like a dark eye.

I see my reflection in it as I sneak along the wall with Lizzie, clutching her hand. Her fingers are thin and warm, and our palms are sweaty, rubbing together. It should feel gross, but it doesn't.

She smiles at me, showing a chipped front tooth.

We turn the corner. She opens the door, and we slip inside. It's just a closet filled with bottles and mops, and there's a fake piney smell that makes my nose itch, but when we're huddled in here together, it's the best place in the world. Our secret place.

A tiny spark jumps in the dark, and I see Lizzie holding a stolen lighter in her skinny fingers. The flame dances in her eyes.

She's ten, two years older than me.

For a few minutes, we just sit quietly together in the dark, watching the flame. "What kind of animal would you be, if you could?" she whispers in my ear.

I lean my head against her shoulder, thinking. "Squirrel. Because I could climb and jump through the trees, and no one would catch me. What about you?"

"I'd be a tiger," she says, "because no one messes with a tiger."

I snuggle against her shoulder.

"All right, your turn," she says. "Ask me a question."

I think for a few seconds. "If you could go anywhere in the whole solar system, where would you go?"

"The sun," she says.

"Wouldn't you burn up?"

"Not if I had a special suit. You?"

"Pluto."

She tilts her head in a way that makes me smile. "How come?"

"I dunno. I just want to." I hug my knees to my chest. "Do you think it gets lonely out there on its own?"

"Nah," she says. "It has a moon." She curls an arm around my shoulders. "Charon. Like the girl's name, only spelled differently. They're almost the same size."

"Your turn," I say.

For a minute, she doesn't answer. Her smile disappears. She folds her arms over her knees, still holding the lighter, and stares straight ahead, as if she can see through the closet door to another place. "What do you think is the worst thing that can happen to a person?"

Goose bumps prickle on my arms and legs. "To die?" I say timidly.

She shakes her head. "Dying is scary, but being dead isn't. Once you're dead, you don't hurt anymore. The worst thing is being alive but dead on the inside." Her eyes go fuzzy and faraway, and I can see the orange glow reflected in them. "I saw that happen to Danny before he disappeared. He couldn't talk or move. They kept him locked in a room like that for weeks. I don't—" Her voice breaks. "I don't want that to happen to us."

"I won't let it happen," I say fiercely. "I'll protect you."

She smiles. "I know." But her eyes are sad. I don't think she really believes me. She ruffles my hair. "We'll get out of here someday."

"You think so?"

"Sure. But just in case." She leans in, cups one hand around the back of my neck, and kisses me on the lips. She tastes like smoke and ocean and milk and rain. She pulls back and smiles, showing the chipped front tooth again. "That's for luck."

My cheeks blaze. "When we get out of here, will you marry me?" I blurt out.

She starts to laugh, then stops when she sees the look on my face. "Yeah," she says. "I will. Promise. But will you promise me something in return?"

I nod. I would promise her anything, anything at all. If she asked me to take her to the moon, I would find a way.

Her throat moves as she swallows. Her fingers get tighter on the green plastic lighter until it seems it will snap in half. "In case they *do* ever break one of us, like they broke Danny, we have to swear . . ."

Her words fade, and her face goes blurry.

I slide through a foggy dark place, through whispering voices and flickering lights.

When I come out the other side of the darkness, I'm sitting in the corner of a tiny white room. The lights are too bright. Even when I squeeze my eyes shut, I can still feel the lights stinging me through my eyelids. I swallow, and my throat prickles with thirst.

I can't move my arms. They're folded tightly across my chest, held in place by a dusty-smelling straitjacket.

The door opens, and a man steps in. His hair and coat are white, so he seems to glow as he stares at me with calm gray eyes. His left hand is bandaged. "Are you ready to come out?" he asks in his deep voice.

I turn my face away and don't answer.

He holds up his bandaged hand. "Biting me was very bad. Before I let you out, I need to know that you're going to behave yourself. I want to hear you say you're sorry."

I look away. I'm not sorry. I hope it still hurts.

He sighs. "Why do you insist on making this harder for yourself? You know we only want to help you."

Inside the straitjacket, I ball my hands into fists. "I know what's really happening. I know what you're doing. Lizzie told me."

His mouth tightens. "Did I ever tell you what condition Lizzie was in when we found her back in the state home? She had barricaded herself in her room. She thought the adults there were trying to kill her, and she would attack anyone who attempted to force the door open, even if they only wanted to bring her food. She was so scared to leave her room that she was starving. When they left food outside the door, she wouldn't eat it because she was afraid it might be drugged. Her mind is sick. Can you understand why she needs help? Why you *all* need help?"

I don't answer.

I understand how Lizzie feels. And whether or not the things she believes are true, I think she's found a bigger truth: grown-ups can't be trusted. Even the ones who seem nice will lie to kids. They do what they want and then make up their own reasons about why it's okay, and there's no way to know what's real and what's fake, so it's better not to believe anything they say.

"Steven." His voice grows firmer. "Tell me you understand."

I glare at him. "Fuck you."

He presses his lips together. His eyes are cold and empty as he shuts the door.

More time passes. I'm hungry and thirsty and I have to go to the bathroom. My arms hurt from being stuck inside the straitjacket for so long.

Finally, the door creaks open again. "Steven?" asks a low, gentle voice. "Can you hear me?"

I give a small nod.

The door opens fully, and a man is standing there, a man with a short beard and brown eyes. "How long have you been in here?" he asks softly.

"I don't know." My voice comes out small and scratchy.

He shakes his head and mutters, "This is outrageous. I told Emmanuel not to do this again." He walks in, crouches, and undoes the buckles of my jacket. I slide my arms free. My legs wobble as I try to stand. I stumble, and the man steadies me. I flinch away from the touch.

"I'm sorry about this," he says. "You shouldn't have been locked in here."

I don't look up. I don't trust him. He seems nicer than Dr. Swan, but he's still a White Coat, and that means he's my enemy. "I want to see Lizzie," I whisper.

He makes a little choked sound. For a few seconds, he doesn't say anything. "She's not feeling well."

"I want to see her."

He rubs the sides of his nose and closes his eyes. "Steven—" His voice cracks. "Even if you see her, she won't be able to talk to you."

My throat swells, and tears burn the corners of my eyes. I

hate this so much. I hate them, the White Coats, with their watching eyes and their long needles filled with sleep. I hate them for the bad dreams, for the burning in my head, for the twisting pains that blur my vision and make me throw up. I know they're doing it to me, even if I don't know how. I don't remember anything that came before this—these rooms and these halls—and I feel like they took it from me, somehow. There's nothing they can't take away. And now they're trying to take her away, too.

"I don't care," I say. "I want to see my friend."

He hangs his head. "All right."

We go down a narrow, dimly lit hall. Our footsteps echo, and his shoes squeak on the tiles. We stop in front of a door, and he hesitates. Then, slowly, he opens it.

Lizzie's sitting up in bed, her back against a stack of pillows. Her left eye is covered in bandages, and a few red spots have soaked through. Her right eye is wide and blank, and drool runs from one corner of her mouth. "Lizzie?" I say in a small voice. She doesn't answer. She doesn't even look at me.

My chest squeezes tight, making it hard to breathe. "What did you do to her?"

"We didn't do this," he says, and his voice sounds empty. "She injured herself. She believed we had put an implant in her head. She shoved a pencil through her own eye socket, trying to remove this implant. We did our best to repair the damage, but . . ."

I'm dizzy. I can't breathe. My chest hurts as I walk toward the bed in little shuffling footsteps, staring into Lizzie's single eye. "Lizzie?" I touch her hand where it rests, like a dead bird, on the bedsheets. "Lizzie." No response. "Lizzie!" I shake her. She flops back and forth.

"Steven." Big hands grip my arms and try to pull me back. *"Don't touch me!"* I scream, struggling.

Lizzie flops down to the bed, limp. Her eye stares at nothing.

"Please." My vision goes watery. "Please don't go. I don't want to be alone." Still, she doesn't move. Doesn't look at me.

I know then—Lizzie is gone, like the others. Before her, it was Katie. And before that, Danny, and Louie, and Shawna. They all stopped talking, stopped moving, and then they disappeared, like Lizzie will disappear now. I'm the last one.

It hurts to breathe. I shake and shake. I want to run away, but I can't.

I promised.

I close my eyes and breathe in. I make my head as empty as I can make it. The shaking in my hands stops.

When she first asked me to promise, I cried. I told her I couldn't do it. But she said, *Please.* She said, *You're the only one I can trust.* I sniffled, eyes and nose leaking, and I promised her. Lizzie never asked for anything else. I have to do this.

"Can I be alone with her?" I whisper.

He's quiet. His head hangs low, like he's sad. Like he knows how awful this is and he wishes it would stop. For a second, I almost feel bad for him.

Except he *could* stop this. Anytime he wanted, he could make it stop, he could let us go. But he never does. There's something that's more important to him than us, than me. My head burns, and suddenly, I'm angrier than I've ever been. Until just then, I wasn't sure that I could do it—that I could keep my promise. But now I know I can. It's the only way I can fight the White Coats. It's the only way I can set her free.

"Please," I say, keeping my face down so he can't see my eyes.

"All right," he says, very softly. "I'll wait outside the door." He leaves the room.

I turn to Lizzie. Still, she doesn't move. Her eye is a little slit, her mouth half open. If I don't look too hard, I can pretend that she's just sleepy.

I sit on the edge of the bed. I stroke her hair and run my fingers through it. It's light brown, downy, like baby-bird feathers. "I couldn't protect you," I whisper. "I said I would, but I couldn't." I clutch her hand. She doesn't clutch back. "I'm sorry." I kiss her cheek. Then I push her gently down to the bed and tuck her covers in. She stares at the ceiling as I wrap my hands around her throat.

31

I can't breathe.

I open my mouth and try to gasp, but there's a crushing pressure around my throat. Steven hovers over me, still wearing the helmet, his eyes wide and blank, his thumbs pressing into my trachea. Tears shine on his cheeks.

He doesn't see me. He's still in the memory, in the dream.

I can't *breathe*.

Panic crackles through my nerves as I grab Steven's hands and try to pry them away, but they clench tighter, squeezing enough to bruise. His eyes stare straight through me as my vision starts to fade. I grit my teeth and grip Steven's hands harder. A gray fog swims across my eyes. There's a vacuum in my chest. My lungs are empty, aching, screaming for air. *Steven, it's me, it's Lain!* I think. But of course, he can't hear me. The connection is one-sided. *Let go!*

He keeps squeezing.

This is it. I'm going to die here, now, in this hall.

With the last of my strength, I pull back one hand and slap him hard enough to knock his head to one side. His hand flies to his cheek, and he falls back.

Air rushes into my lungs, and I gasp, cradling my throat as my vision slowly clears. I curl up, gagging and coughing.

"Lain." He sits on the floor, blinking, like someone waking from a deep sleep. "Lain, you . . ." His gaze focuses on me, and the color drains from his face.

My eyes water and my throat burns, but I manage a weak smile. "I'm all right." My voice is hoarse.

He looks like he's about to be sick. "Did I do this?" he whispers.

I sit up, still gingerly holding my throat. "It doesn't matter now." I rub the tender flesh. It will probably bruise. Breathing hurts, but I can breathe, which hopefully means there's no permanent damage.

"We—we have to get you to a doctor."

I shake my head. "It's not bad. Just give me some water." I point to the backpack lying nearby.

He rakes his hands through his hair. It stands on end, so he looks like he's just been electrocuted. His eyes are huge, his face death-white. "How can you act so calm about this?"

"Water," I croak. "Now."

He fumbles through the pack and hands me a water bottle. I sip, wincing at the flare of pain in my throat. I nearly died. Honestly, I probably should be panicking. But what good would that do, really?

Half of my consciousness is still in that place, surrounded by white walls and cameras. A dark haze clings to my mind, as if I've just awakened from a nightmare. Nothing feels quite real. I don't want to think about what I saw in there, but the image of my father's face burns in my mind. *Focus on the moment.*

I huddle on the floor, probing my neck with careful fingertips. "How much do you remember?" My voice sounds like someone ran it through a meat grinder.

"I—I don't know. How can you even think about that now? I just—"

"Steven." I speak as firmly as I can. I need to confirm that we saw and heard the same thing before the elusive memories slip away. Already, the details are fading. "What do you remember?"

His eyes lose focus. He touches his own cheek, a slow, dazed movement, and stares at the moisture on his fingertips. "I saw . . . There was a girl. Lizzie." His voice is soft, faraway. "She was . . ." His brow furrows, as if he's trying to work out a math problem in his head. Slowly, he raises his hands to his own throat. Horror dawns in his expression.

"Steven, listen to me," I say firmly. "You were a child. A child in a desperate, terrible situation. You're not responsible for what happened."

He closes his eyes and presses the heels of his hands against them. "I killed her," he says, his voice thick and choked. "I almost killed you!"

"You weren't in control of your actions—"

He lurches to his feet and takes a few wobbly steps backward, away from me. "You've seen the inside of my head. You know what I'm like." He draws in a rattling breath and raises his fists to his temples. "Maybe they were right to watch me and collar me. Maybe I'm a monster."

I stand, facing him, and grab his arm. He looks at me in

surprise. "I've been inside plenty of heads," I say. "I've seen monsters. Trust me, you're not one of them."

"Lain . . ."

I wrap my arms around him. Slowly, he returns the hug. I comb my fingers through his soft hair, slide a hand beneath his coat, and stroke his back. I can feel the bumps of his spine through the thin cotton of his T-shirt. I wish I knew what to say to him. I feel so young, so lost. We both are.

At last, he straightens, wiping his eyes. "Those two guys," he says. "The doctors . . ."

"One of them was Dr. Swan," I say, my voice hardening. "I'm certain." The first two times Steven took Lucid, the memories were fuzzy, but this time I got a good look at their faces. There's no doubt.

"And the other?"

I close my eyes. Deep down, I already realized the truth, but I didn't want to accept it. Even now, I can't understand why the good man I knew would get mixed up in something like this. I don't want to say the words, because that will make it real. But I have no choice. "My father."

Silence descends on us.

"I'm sorry," Steven says at last, very softly.

My father was partially responsible for his kidnapping and torture, and he's sorry for me. I want to laugh. Or cry. But I can't let myself fall apart. If I start to cry now, I don't know if I'll ever stop. I try to console myself with the knowledge that Father treated Steven with some kindness, at least—he let him out of his cell, took him to see Lizzie—but still, he was *there*. He was part of it. "Never mind," I say, with a lightness I don't feel. "We have other things to worry about right now." I look again at the empty rooms, the crow-filled rafters. "This doesn't look anything like the place in your memories. How could it have decayed this much in ten years?"

His expression goes hazy and distant, turning inward. He walks toward the statue of the robed figure.

"Steven?" He doesn't answer. I shoulder the pack, pick up the flashlights, and follow, leaving the Gate behind.

As we near the base of the pedestal, I sweep the flashlight beam over the statue, the blank face with its slack mouth and upturned eyes. White crow droppings streak the gray robes.

"It's underground," Steven says.

"What?"

"The real St. Mary's. It's hidden underground." His voice seems to be coming from far away. "The passageway is under this statue. When they brought us here, they—" He stops. His hand drifts to his temple, and he shakes his head. "Shit. How did they do it?"

I look at the statue again—at its hands, outstretched and cupped, as if offering something invisible—and I notice that the right hand has a hairline crack around the wrist. It's jointed, like the wrist of a marionette. My pulse spikes. "Look." I point.

His breath catches.

Before I can say anything else, Steven grabs the stone hand and twists. It bends upward with a faint creak. For a few seconds, nothing happens. Then a low, rumbling grind fills the air—a sound like ancient gears turning—and the statue's pedestal ponderously slides to one side, revealing a square opening about six by six feet. A set of wide stone steps leads down into darkness.

We stand motionless at the top of the opening, staring

down. I shine my flashlight inside, but it doesn't penetrate very far; the gloom swallows up the thin yellow beam.

Steven grips my hand. His palm is hot and slick with sweat.

"You know," I say, "we don't have to go down there."

His pulse drums in his throat. "I need to see it."

I give his hand a squeeze. "Whatever happens," I say softly, "I'll be here."

His grip tightens.

We descend.

32

Ten steps. Then twenty. The square of light above us grows smaller and dimmer. Eventually, I stop counting. There are too many steps.

Darkness presses in around us. The only sound, aside from our footsteps, is our rapid breathing. At last, we come to the bottom but even with the flashlights, I can't see much of anything—at least, not more than a few square feet at a time. Curling yellowed tiles cover the floor, and the walls are rough plaster.

"Listen," Steven whispers, his voice very loud in the silence. "Do you hear that?"

I listen, and I do hear it—a low hum, so faint it's more vibration than sound.

I tuck my flashlight under one arm and reach out, fumbling in the darkness. There's a wall. My fingertips slide along the plaster until I encounter smooth plastic. "I found a light switch," I say. "I'm going to try it."

I don't really expect it to work. Why would it? But it's worth a shot.

I flick the switch, and bright light floods the hall. My eyelids slam shut, then open a crack. I wait for my eyes to adjust before opening them fully. The light isn't as bright as it first seemed. In fact, the fluorescent tubes overhead are dim. They illuminate a long and narrow hallway lined with doors. Faded tiles stretch on and on.

Steven's breathing quickens.

"Steven?"

He wrenches his hand from mine, bows his head, and clutches it, shaking so hard his teeth chatter. "I remember," he gasps. "Oh God. I—this place—I remember the smell." He presses his hands to his nose and mouth.

I hug him tight. He clings to me, shuddering. "Breathe," I urge.

Gradually, his breathing slows. When he straightens, his expression is calmer. He's still pale, but there's a glint of determination in his eyes, and in his posture—back straight, fists clenched at his sides. "I'm okay." He gulps. "It just . . . hit me all at once."

A chill slides through me. "You remember everything?"

His lips tremble, and he presses them together. "I remember enough."

Gently, I lay a hand on his arm. I want to ask more, but I'm afraid to. Already, he looks like he's holding himself together through sheer force of will.

"Let's keep going," he mutters.

We resume walking. All the doors are closed, but they have small, barred windows. I shine my flashlight into each. Empty rooms—bed frames and the occasional desk or file cabinet—and one filled with what appears to be lab equipment, lots of it. I linger outside the door, passing the flashlight beam over a huge microscope. An array of sharp tools glitters on a tray. There are poster-sized photos plastered over the walls, displaying delicate webs of stained tissue. Neurons. Brain scans as well, rows and rows of them lining the back wall—ghostly grayish white shapes, like Rorschach blots.

"How can this place possibly have electricity?" Steven asks.

"There must be a generator," I say. "A small one. I don't think it's connected to the one in town. It's too far."

There's something else. Something feels wrong, but it takes me a moment to place it. There's no dust, no cobwebs. The place is empty, yet it looks like it's still in use.

Steven stops in front of a door. His face is dead white, his forehead and upper lip glistening with sweat. "This was my room," he says quietly.

Behind the door is another barren room containing nothing but a bed frame. We step inside, holding our breath. There are crayon drawings scrawled on the wall—faded, like someone tried to scrub them away and didn't quite succeed. I see a tiny figure inside a cage, gripping the bars, a tear on its cheek. A few feet away are two crudely drawn figures in lab coats with grinning wolf heads, one of them holding a saw. Between them is a small person strapped to a table. The top of its head has been removed.

Steven lets out a high-pitched, jagged laugh. The sound sends chills down my spine. "Oh boy," he says. "This brings back memories."

"Steven . . . what . . ."

"They gave me crayons. Then they took them away because they didn't like the things I was drawing."

I think about the white room, the bloody scalpels, Steven immobilized and helpless on a surgical table. The doctors were holding up pictures, I remember, asking him questions. As I stare at the drawings, something clicks, and my insides turn cold. *Brain surgery.* "What did they do to you?" I whisper.

"Good question."

If they were performing necessary and accepted medical procedures, they wouldn't have done it in secret, or modified Steven's memories. Whatever happened here, it was highly illegal.

We retreat from the room and keep walking. At last, we reach the end of the hall and the final door. Unlike the others, which are plain wood, this one is metal and divided down the middle. There's a panel next to it—a biometric scanner, probably. If there's anything to find, it will be in here. I start to reach out toward the panel, then stop.

"Will it even open for us?" Steven asks.

"My father was one of the men who worked here," I reply. "My handprints are the same as his—just smaller. It might open for me."

"Hang on." He draws the ND from his pocket and thumbs it to the highest setting. He raises it, pointing it at the door. "Go ahead."

I place a hand on the panel. It flashes green, and the metal door slides open to reveal a small room. The floor is white-tiled, the walls are a cool eggshell, and the whole room glows with soft white lighting that seems to come from everywhere and nowhere. There's a simple glass table with a pair of slim white chairs and a coffin-sized black refrigerator standing in one corner. No other furnishings. No one inside.

Cautiously, I step in. Steven enters behind me, still holding the ND, looking warily around. Slowly, he lowers the weapon.

The doors slide shut behind us, and I give a start.

"It's okay," Steven says. "We're not locked in. There's another panel inside." He points to it.

Still, I don't like the feeling of being trapped, and suddenly, I'm desperate to get out of this underground hell, out of this building, out of this whole country. "Let's take a quick look and then head back to the car," I mutter.

"Yeah."

The refrigerator hums faintly. I swallow, cross the room, open it a crack, and peek inside.

Six brains float in jars of formaldehyde, pale and forlorn-looking in the yellowish liquid. The blood drains from my face. I quickly shut the door.

"What?" Steven says, walking toward me. "What's in there?"

I'm not squeamish about brains. I've handled and dissected a few in my neuroanatomy courses. But something about *these* brains, here, now, is deeply unsettling. Maybe it's the size. They're smaller than usual. Children's brains. There was one detail I always remembered from Emmett Pike's case, one thing that haunted me. *Their heads were never found.*

Oh God.

"I don't know if you want to see this," I say.

"Open it."

I take a slow breath and open the refrigerator door. Each

jar is labeled with a name. Daniel, Katherine, Louis, Robert, Shawna. Elizabeth.

Lizzie.

I press a hand to my mouth, and my vision goes blurry. Slowly, I shut the refrigerator and lean against the wall, struggling to breathe past the weight in my chest. When I close my eyes, the forlorn-looking little brains float up behind my eyelids like six withered balloons. Dr. Swan is responsible for this. He must be. What kind of sick person keeps a refrigerator filled with dead children's brains? Does he come here and talk to them? Fondle them?

I think about the lab equipment in the other room, the curious lack of dust. Someone still uses that lab. I have a sudden feeling that if I were to examine it more closely, I'd find slides containing slices of preserved tissue from these very brains. Oh God. The pieces are all coming together.

"Why?" Steven whispers.

I open my eyes. "They experimented on them." My voice sounds empty, disconnected, like it belongs to someone else. "That's what all that neurosurgery was about. They were conducting illegal experiments." But for what?

Steven stands motionless. "Let's get out of this fucking place," he says flatly.

I nod, feeling nauseous. We turn toward the doors. I place a hand on the panel, and they slide open. I start to step forward—and freeze.

Two men stand in the hall, wearing gray suits and shades and aiming weapons at us.

Steven's eyes widen. He raises his ND, but he's not fast

enough. There's a sharp crack, and Steven goes down. The ND falls from his hand. I scream his name as he hits the floor and lies motionless, facedown.

No time to think. I make a dive for the ND, but a black-shoed foot kicks it away. A shadow falls over me. Panting, I look up.

"No worries," the man says. "Just a sedative . . . and this time, we calculated the dosage to take his tolerance into account. He'll wake up in a few hours. No harm will come to him as long as you cooperate." He holds out a set of handcuffs while his taller, bulkier partner keeps the tranquilizer gun trained on me.

I don't move.

"Just a precaution, you understand." The man smiles, blandly and pleasantly. In a flash, I recognize his forgettable face—the guard from Greenborough High School. He works for IFEN? Was he stationed there specifically to watch me?

There's no way I can make a run for it. Even if it were possible, I can't leave Steven. Teeth gritted, I hold out my hands, and the cuffs snap shut around my wrists.

One of the men—the larger one—handcuffs Steven, then picks him up and slings him over his shoulder in a fireman's carry. Steven is already starting to stir, groaning faintly. As the men lead me down the hall and up the stairs, I try to catch his gaze, but his eyes remain closed.

My mind races. Did they follow us? Or maybe they were already lurking in the area, watching, waiting for us to corner ourselves. Maybe Dr. Swan knew we'd be drawn here, to St. Mary's, like mice to a baited trap.

We should have headed straight for the border.

Two small gray helicopters wait outside, in the courtyard. The men load Steven into one and prod me toward another. "Steven!" I cry out instinctively. I try to run toward his helicopter, knowing it's futile. My guard grabs me by the shirt collar and drags me back. I watch as the helicopter lifts into the sky and disappears above the treetops.

"Go on," he says, pointing his gun at me.

There's no choice. I sit in the back of the remaining helicopter, in a black leather seat. My guard straps me in, leaving my handcuffs on, then climbs into the cockpit. The engine rumbles to life, and the helicopter lifts into the air, whirring like a giant insect. I stare out the window at the scenery below, the patches of velvety dark forest and rippling golden fields.

For a while, the only sound is the helicopter's rumbling drone. Though I've never felt less like sleeping, the fatigue and the monotony of the long ride drag me down into a troubled doze. I dream about twisted corridors, bloody scalpels, and screams.

I wake when I realize we're on the ground, on a landing pad near the edge of the city. The skyscrapers of Aura loom in the distance. My guard escorts me to a sleek gray car with tinted windows, and I climb in. At this point, resistance seems like a token gesture.

There's a short drive. I sit in the backseat, still handcuffed, until he parks the car. When I look out the window, I'm not surprised to see we're in front of IFEN headquarters. The sun is setting, tinting the sky blood-red. The guard leads me across the parking lot and into the lobby, which is eerily quiet and empty. He prods me into an elevator, and I watch the numbers light up as we ascend. There's a soft ding when we reach the top floor. The elevator opens to reveal the door to Dr. Swan's office.

"Where is Steven?" I ask, not really expecting an answer.

"You'll see him when it's time." He nods toward the door.

Slowly, I open it. He shuts the door behind me, and a lock clicks. Dr. Swan sits at his desk, smiling. The red light of sunset pours in through the window, illuminating the room and coloring its oyster-white walls pink. "Hello, Lain." His voice is mild and pleasant, as if we're at a dinner party together. "Why don't you sit down?"

33

Dr. Swan.

The man who practically raised me after Father's death, the man I've known since I was five years old, is responsible for all this. He's the one who locked Steven in a padded room and left him there alone.

For a moment, I imagine myself charging across the room, lunging over the desk, and wrapping my hands around his throat. Except I can't—my hands are still restrained. Even if I could, I doubt it would accomplish anything.

He rises to his feet and approaches. I flinch as he leans closer, but he only pulls a key from his pocket and unlocks my cuffs. They fall to the floor. Still, I remain standing rigidly in place, fearing a trap.

"Sit," he urges. "We have a lot to talk about."

I don't sit. "What's the point of talking? You're planning to erase my memories, aren't you?"

He returns to his chair. "I'd prefer not to do that."

"Then why did you send that woman after us? That was you, wasn't it?"

"Yes," he says, "though that was a hasty and ill-advised decision on my part, I will admit. When I learned you'd fled the city, I lost my temper."

"Lost your temper," I repeat, incredulous.

"Well, I'm only human." A pause. "Of course, it might be better if you had your memories erased. Better for you. But it would also complicate things. Neural modification is not foolproof, after all—it leaves scars, and traces of the original memories sometimes linger. I would prefer to have your full, conscious cooperation. Regardless, precautions will be taken to ensure that you don't tell anyone what I'm about to reveal to you. But I want you to hear me out. You're a rational person. Even if you hate me for what I did, I trust that once I explain everything, you'll understand the necessity of keeping this from the public."

I very much doubt that, but I bite my tongue. If I can convince him I'm willing to keep my mouth shut, maybe I can get out of this with my mind intact.

"Before I begin, do you have any questions?" he asks, as if he's teaching a class.

"Yes. How do you live with yourself?"

His expression doesn't waver. "What do you mean?"

"Don't play dumb. I know what you did. You kidnapped those children. You experimented on them."

"We *treated* them."

"You expect me to believe that? After everything I've seen?"

"Do you know much about those children, Lain? They

were all orphans. They'd suffered severe abuse and trauma, and the resulting psychological damage was beyond anything that medication or Conditioning could repair. The treatments were new, and our methods were less sophisticated than they are now. Some risk was inevitable. But the knowledge we gained from those early treatments was invaluable. The profession of neural modification therapy—Mindwalkers, like you and me—would not exist otherwise."

Vertigo rolls over me.

Early memory modification treatments. Of course. I remember those scars in Steven's brain: primitive and clumsy, but still unmistakable in their purpose. Those experimental treatments paved the way for the Mindgate, for IFEN's shiny new therapy, for Ian, for me. The adult volunteers Father worked with afterward simply fine-tuned the technology. The real research had already been done.

I think about Lizzie's blank stare, and Ian's words flash through my head: *There's only so many times you can modify a person's memories before his brain turns to mush.* I start to tremble.

"They needed help," he says, his voice neutral and matter-of-fact, "and we needed to test a new therapy. That's how all progress happens."

I shake my head fiercely. "Then why did you hide it? Why didn't you use adult volunteers?"

He hesitates. "Children make better subjects. Their brains are more malleable, more resilient. We knew that the younger our patients, the better our chance of success."

My nails dig into my palms. Of course. But the public wouldn't condone experiments on children, so he simply took them. Discreetly abducting them from state orphanages, probably paying off the caretakers to keep them quiet. Children without homes, without families. Ones who wouldn't be missed.

"We weighed the potential good against the potential harm," he continues in that maddeningly calm tone, "as all scientists must do when pioneering a new treatment. Your father understood the necessity as well as I did."

"No." I shake my head again. "My father wouldn't have participated in something like this. You must have forced him. You—"

"I didn't force him into anything. He knew what he was getting into. He just couldn't handle the emotional strain. Afterward, he burdened himself with pointless, masochistic guilt and refused treatment until his mind collapsed. His death was tragic, particularly because it was so very preventable. It didn't need to happen that way. Had he simply agreed to Conditioning and moved on, he would still be with us today." For an instant, regret softens his features. "His weakness was in being unable to see past his own moral squeamishness to the larger picture. After all, we achieved our goal. Steven Bent was the first truly successful memory modification ever performed. He completely forgot his early childhood—which was, I assure you, horrific. He grew up in an underfunded and poorly monitored facility, where he was starved and routinely abused by caretakers and fellow wards alike. By age eight, he was already suicidal."

A bitter knot forms in my throat. It's hard to believe, at times, that the universe can be so cruel—that an innocent soul can be subjected to so much sorrow and injustice in a single lifetime. "So you removed his original pain and gave him new pain."

"The sacrifices were, of course, regrettable. But we did not act out of cruelty. We took measures to ensure the children did not suffer unnecessarily."

He dares to make excuses, even now. The blood pounds behind my eyes. A red rage is swelling inside me, and if it doesn't escape somehow, I'm going to explode. "Then why didn't you just erase Steven's memories of what happened at St. Mary's?" I squeeze the words between clenched teeth. "Why would you make him think he'd been kidnapped by a sadistic killer?"

He winces, as if I've brought up an embarrassing faux pas he committed at some social event. "That was . . . an unfortunate necessity. People were asking questions about those missing children, more questions than we expected. We needed an explanation for their disappearance. So I invented Emmett Pike. All his data—photographs, fingerprints, DNA, the autopsy report—is fabricated. He's nothing but information in a database. Obviously, we needed Steven to maintain our cover story as well. So we used a mixture of Conditioning, drugs, and hypnosis to tweak the visual and auditory details of his experiences at St. Mary's while keeping the emotional core of the memories."

I feel sick. I wonder how Dr. Swan would react if I threw up on his pristine white suit. "I'm surprised you didn't just kill him, along with the others."

"Kill a child in cold blood?" He looks offended. "What do you take me for?"

I almost laugh, but I have a feeling if I tried, it would come out as a scream.

Dr. Swan leans back in his chair, shoulders sagging. "I don't expect you to agree with what we did. You're still young, after all. Too young to understand. But regardless, what's done is done. The past can't be changed."

"But you can take responsibility for what you did."

"I *am* taking responsibility, by ensuring that their sacrifice is not in vain. Exposing the truth won't do any good at this point. In fact, it might do considerable harm. Think about it. If the public finds out what happened at St. Mary's, there will be outrage. People will turn against Mindwalkers, against IFEN. Against us. There'll be riots. Perhaps even another war."

In a flash, I remember the documentaries of the pre-Republic days—the limp bodies on stretchers, covered with red-and-black burns from explosions, the chemical attacks that left people blinded and choking on their own blood. "You can't know that," I say, but my voice falters.

"You've studied psychology," he says patiently. "You understand how people think. They don't see outcomes. They don't see numbers and facts. They think in terms of narratives, of opposing teams. Heroes and villains. If they find out about the experiments, we will become the villains, and people will embrace the anarchy that came before us. Those six children are already dead. Nothing can save them now. Our focus should be on helping the living. Surely, we can agree on that much."

I shut my eyes, dizzy. Too much. It's all too much. My nails dig deeper into my palms, sending tiny flashes of pain through my nerves. "What about Steven?" I whisper. "What will happen to him?"

He breathes a small sigh. "It would have been better if you'd never met Steven Bent. I kept him close, all these years, because I wanted to ensure that he was under control. But I should have sent him far away."

"You didn't answer my question."

"You know what needs to be done." His voice hardens. "You must erase his memories."

The room suddenly feels colder. Outside the window, the sun has slipped beneath the horizon, and the sky is a somber purple. "You want *me* to do it?"

He stares directly into my eyes, the tips of his fingers pressed together. "That was your original intention, wasn't it? It's what he wanted—what he himself asked for when he first approached you. Wipe out his trauma. Now that the kidnappings have slipped from public awareness, we no longer need him. Once he's forgotten everything about St. Mary's and his time with you, we'll ensure that he finishes school and gets a decent job. We can give him a normal life."

A normal life. After years of misery, Steven can be safe and happy at last. Of course, it's dependent on my cooperation, my willingness to keep quiet. That goes without saying. And as a sign of my willingness to obey, I'll have to do the job myself, to scrub every trace of the truth from his brain.

I see the trap closing around me, and I choke down a scream. The room has begun to rotate slowly, like I'm stuck on a carousel.

"You're bleeding," Dr. Swan says.

Only then do I realize I've bitten my lower lip so hard that blood is trickling down my chin. My hand flies to my face, and my fingertips come away glistening red.

He rises to his feet and pulls a handkerchief from his pocket. As he reaches out to wipe the blood from my chin, I whisper, "Don't."

He freezes, slowly lowers his hand, sits in the chair, and waits, watching me. Then he smiles, a strangely normal smile. "You know, I have no animosity toward you, Lain. Oh, you do try my patience at times, like any teenager. But, believe it or not, I want your happiness."

"How touching," I mutter.

"It's the truth. Lain—your father, that is—was my friend and colleague for many years. And you are like him in so many ways. The fire that drives you is your desire to help others, to save those in need. That's why I believe you'll do the right thing. However much you despise me, however fiercely you may want to expose me for the scoundrel you think I am, you will not jeopardize your friend's safety, or the lives of innocent people. You aren't that selfish. And of course, there's your career as a Mindwalker. Just think about all those clients you could treat."

I press a hand against my stomach. My insides hurt—everything hurts.

Father was Dr. Swan's friend. He must have seen some goodness in him, but when I look into his eyes, all I see is two empty holes, as if his face is just a mask covering a void. There's no uncertainty, no doubt. I always believed he cared about me, if nothing else. Now I wonder if that was an illusion. How can someone so cold-blooded be capable of love?

Whatever he says, I still believe that he somehow forced Father to cooperate.

I stare down at my feet, numb. "I don't understand. Even

if memory modification isn't perfect, it would be safer for you to just erase what I know. So why? Why bother trying to convince me?"

He folds his hands together and purses his lips. He seems to be debating how much to tell me. "You might say that this is . . . a test."

"A test?"

"I understand that you're shaken and furious right now—that's natural—but once some time has passed, you may feel differently. Time has a way of changing one's perspective. The history of scientific progress is filled with ethical sacrifices. Government institutions experimenting on their own citizens is not particularly uncommon. It happened even in Old America. They tested the effects of radiation, electric shocks, brainwashing, powerful drugs, and many other things, often without the consent of the subjects. Sometimes they used children."

"That can't be true," I whisper.

"It is true. It's not even a secret. Read a history book or two." He smiles mirthlessly. "By comparison, our methods were humane, and the benefits were much more substantial. When you're in a position of power, like mine, you have to look at everything in context. And you must be willing to accept certain unpleasant realities."

The way he says those words makes me wonder just how many "unpleasant realities" there are. Has IFEN done other things that the public doesn't know about?

"I'm not sure you realize what an important young woman you are, Lain," he continues. "You have the potential to become a great Mindwalker. One of the best."

The room is turning, turning. I can feel it, though the

clouds outside the window remain stationary. "I didn't get the impression you *wanted* me to be a Mindwalker." My voice sounds curiously disconnected, like a recording.

"I admit, for a while, I had doubts about you. But you've proved yourself to be surprisingly strong and resourceful. Not to mention, your name carries a great deal of weight. Dr. Lain Fisher's daughter. The girl who dedicated her life to saving others from the tragic mental illness that took her father—yes, it has a nice ring to it. The public will like you."

I stare. "You're grooming me. You want me to be your poster child. That's what this is about?"

"Yes," he replies readily. "More or less. Who knows? One day, you might even take my place as director. But that will work better if you understand and accept certain realities. As for your friend Ian . . . Well, it's looking less and less likely that he'll be able to fulfill the role we had intended for him, which makes you even more important."

As the words slowly sink in, I start to feel light-headed. How long has he been planning this? How long has he been observing me, judging me, seeing how I adapt and react to various obstacles? Was this all a part of his game?

The blood bangs in my skull. Everything is drowning in a sea of red.

"Of course," he continues, "you will have to undergo a lot of therapy and Conditioning before you can resume your duties, but I'm sure you'll get your Type up again. You've already bounced back once."

"Isn't truth worth anything to you?" I shout. My voice rings and echoes through the spacious room. "Don't you think you owe it to those children to tell people how they really died?"

He gives me another smile, this one tight and hard. "Truth is not always the virtue it's cracked up to be. Some things are better off forgotten. We Mindwalkers are the stewards and keepers of those dark secrets. That is our role." He doesn't sound proud of himself, but he doesn't sound particularly ashamed, either. I wonder if he feels anything at all, or if he just does whatever he deems necessary for the greater good, like some machine built from ruthless utilitarian ethics.

"You're a monster," I say. I know I should be trying to convince him that I agree with him so he'll let me go, but I'm too worn down, too broken. "You can justify it all you want, but you're trying to get away with murder."

It might be my imagination, but I think he flinches. "Lain . . ." A hint of frustration creeps into his voice. "You're thinking with your emotions. What if we had left those children alone? Would their fates have been any better? They were all sick. Broken. Their projected futures were dark, and they had no families to support them. Had they lived, they would probably have turned to Somnazol, or simply been burdens on society."

Burdens. The word—the coldness of it—cuts me like a blade.

"So, what will it be?" he asks. "Will you cooperate? Or would you prefer to have your memories erased?"

What choice do I have? As long as he has Steven, my hands are bound. My throat tightens. "I'll cooperate," I whisper.

He nods, as if he expected it.

"I have a condition, though."

He raises an eyebrow.

"Give me a few days with Steven before I administer the treatment."

He tilts his head and taps a finger against the desk. "Twenty-four hours," he replies. "And be grateful for it. May I remind you, you are not in a position to bargain. If you aren't back here at headquarters by tomorrow at five o'clock, he'll be given a total mindwipe. I'm sure, if you had the choice, you'd prefer to save at least part of his mind. It would be rather inconvenient for him having to relearn how to talk and dress himself."

I look at those calm, indifferent gray eyes, and I feel the poison burning in my chest. I thought I knew what anger and hatred were, but now I realize that I've never truly hated another human being before this.

"And we will, of course, have to keep him confined here until you return," he adds.

"I know." I keep my gaze downcast so he won't see the fury burning there. "I—I just want to talk to him, at least once, before he forgets me." And if I have time, maybe I can come up with some way to get him out of here. It's a slim hope, but better than none at all.

"Fair enough." He nods. "For now, though, I think you should go home. Get some rest. You've had an overwhelming day."

"I want to see him. Now."

His expression never changes. He seems to be weighing me with his eyes. "You'll have ten minutes." He rises.

The door opens for him, and he takes me down to the thirtieth floor, then leads me along a narrow hall to a pair of steel double doors. He keys in a code and presses his thumb to the biometric scanner, and the doors slide open.

The cell is tiny and white, with a narrow bed, a lidless steel toilet, and nothing else. Steven sits on the edge of the bed.

His head jerks up. At the sight of me, he leaps to his feet. His face looks paler than usual, his hair disheveled, his eyes red-rimmed and bloodshot. I take a step toward him, legs trembling. I try to speak, but nothing comes out.

The doors slide shut behind me, giving us the semblance of privacy. I fling myself at him and hug him tightly, burying my face against his shoulder. "I'm so sorry," I whisper, tears seeping out from under my eyelids.

He hugs me back. His heart pounds against mine. "What are you sorry for? None of this is your fault."

"But it is. I led us into this. I'm the reason you're here now." I pull back so I can meet his gaze. "I swear, I'm going to get you out of here."

He touches my cheek, looking deep into my eyes. Despite his obvious exhaustion, his expression is almost serene. "I'm just glad I got to see you again."

"Don't talk like that." Tears blind me. "I'm going to fix this. You'll see. I—" The words freeze in my throat. Right now, Dr. Swan is undoubtedly monitoring us, listening to our conversation. I have to be very careful about what I say. "I'll think of something," I finish weakly.

He hugs me again, and his lips brush against my ear. He whispers, so faintly I have to strain to make out the words: "Do whatever you need to do. Don't worry about me."

"Steven . . . I . . ."

He holds me tighter. "I don't care what happens to me. Just don't let them control you. Do you understand?"

A lump fills my throat. He knows that they're using him as leverage against me, and he doesn't want to be their tool; he'd rather die. Just like Father.

I hide my face against his chest.

When I lift my gaze to his again, he smiles. In that smile is exhaustion and fear, but beneath that, I see determination and gentleness and incredible strength. I've never met anyone so strong. And I know that if I take his memories, this brave, fragile, resilient person will disappear. He'll become someone else, and I'll lose him forever.

But he would be happier, a voice inside whispers.

The doors slide open, and I tense. "Your time is up," Dr. Swan says.

As I leave the room, I cast one last, desperate glance over my shoulder. My gaze catches Steven's, and I hold it for a long moment before the doors slide shut between us.

Dr. Swan leads me to the main doors. "We'll give him a thorough Conditioning so he'll be compliant by the time you arrive tomorrow. That's the standard procedure with compulsory memory modifications. It's about time you learned how to perform one, anyway. They are a distasteful but necessary part of our work."

A scream rises in my throat. I choke it down. There's a writhing ball in my stomach, as if all the screams are building up inside me. I wonder how many I can swallow before I explode. "I understand," I say.

He smiles. "Glad to have you on the team."

34

A car drops me off at home. I enter my living room and stand, looking around at a house that no longer feels like mine. They've probably already installed cameras and listening devices. In a daze, I walk through the empty rooms one by one, then open the secret door and descend the stairs to the white-tiled room where I once kept my Gate. The chairs are still there, but of course, the Gate itself is gone.

Numb, I retreat to my room and curl up in bed, hugging Nutter.

No matter how I look at my situation, I can't see a way out. If I don't erase Steven's memories, Dr. Swan will destroy his entire mind, which is no different from killing him. It's not even a choice. I can't let him do that, no matter what Steven himself wants.

If I cooperate, he'll have a new beginning, a chance to live without the pain weighing down his every step. We won't be together anymore, but at least I'll know that he's safe.

But those children . . . Lizzie . . .

I think about the brains in the refrigerator, and I shudder. Dr. Swan is a horrible person, but I can't deny the logic of his argument. The truth easily could spark a wave of riots and terrorism. And what if he's right about me? What if I really do have the potential to become the director someday? If I can change IFEN from the inside, I can ensure that the horrors of St. Mary's are never repeated. Would it really be so bad to let all that pain and ugliness fade into oblivion? If no one remembers, it's almost like it didn't happen. No dead children, no lies, no betrayals. Is there even such a thing as truth, or just a consensus of memory?

Are these the kinds of thoughts that kept my father silent all those years?

I close my eyes, feeling curiously empty.

"Chloe," I say. I don't even know why I'm summoning her. Maybe I just don't want to be alone right now.

She materializes in front of me, smiling. "Hello, Lain!" she chirps. "You have a new message."

I frown and sit up. I suppose it must be from Ian, or maybe one of my teachers, since I've been inexplicably absent from school. "Display it."

She tilts her head back, and light shines from her eyes, projecting a screen into the air. In the corner is a small mailbox icon. I open it and stare at the subject line of the message.

HAPPY BIRTHDAY, LAIN. ☺

That's right. I turned eighteen yesterday. So much has happened, the thought didn't even cross my mind, but I'm now a legal adult. I don't recognize the sender's address. Is it from Greta? From someone at IFEN?

"Open it," I say, and a text box pops up on the screen.

TO UNLOCK THIS MESSAGE,
ANSWER THE RIDDLE:
WHAT IS THE HAPPIEST FLAVOR OF ICE CREAM?

I draw my breath in sharply. For an instant, it feels as if the bed and floor have dropped out from under me and I'm suspended in midair. A memory bursts into my mind with shocking clarity—it's a brilliant sunny day, the sky a rich blue, and I'm walking alongside my father down a cobblestone path eating ice cream, licking away the melting rivulets that run down the side of the waffle cone. *Father, you know what's the happiest flavor? I say.*

With trembling fingers, I bring up the holographic keyboard and type:

APRICOT.

A new message pops onto the screen.

YOU ARE CORRECT!
CLOSE YOUR EYES AND COUNT TO TEN.

Trembling, I obey. Once I've counted, I look up. My mouth falls open. My vision blurs, and for a moment, I think I'm going to pass out.

Standing in front of me, smiling, is my father.

35

I sit on the edge of the bed, frozen, not breathing.

The moonlight shines in the window, around my father, shines through him. His form flickers, turning briefly transparent.

A hologram. It takes my brain only a second or two to register that fact, but in those seconds, I actually believe he's returned to me. I feel as if my chest has been ripped open.

"Hello, Lain," he says quietly.

A weak sound, almost a whimper, escapes my throat. What is this? What's going on?

"As you can probably guess," Father continues, "this is a prerecorded message. If you're hearing it, it means that I've been dead for some time and that you've just turned eighteen." He smiles again. "Happy birthday."

My eyes fill with tears.

"Once I finish recording this," he says, "I'll upload it into Chloe's programming and set it to start at the proper time. And once you've viewed it, the message will delete itself. So listen carefully."

He looks the way I remember him in those last few months before his death—thin and weary, with stubble on his jaw, uncombed hair, and dark circles under his eyes. Yet his expression is calm. "I have no doubt that by now, you've grown into a fine Mindwalker. And I feel that as a Mindwalker, you have a right to know certain things. Things about IFEN, about our profession. About me." He hangs his head and takes a slow, deep breath, as if gathering strength.

Tell me it wasn't you. Tell me you never did those things.

"Years ago, I became involved in something terrible—a series of secret, illegal human experiments carried out in a place called St. Mary's. The subjects were seven children."

Deep inside me, a tiny pocket of hope withers and disappears. I knew. But still, I wanted to be wrong. For a moment, I think about stopping the message. It hurts too much.

"I am not asking for forgiveness," he says. "What happened within those walls was unforgivable. But I want you to understand—" His voice catches. "When I initially became involved, I never imagined how far it would go." The hologram flickers and blurs momentarily. "After the first death, I tried to put a stop to it. Emmanuel refused. He was the one in charge."

"Dr. Swan," I murmur. "I know."

"I threatened to expose the entire thing," Father continues. "I should have done it—gone public, then and there. If I had, the rest of those children might have been saved. But you must understand, Emmanuel can be very . . . persuasive. He convinced me that it was too late to turn back, that if we revealed the truth, all our efforts would go to waste, that the sacrifice would be for nothing. A potentially life-changing therapy would be stopped dead in its tracks. Worse—we might lose the fragile peace we'd all fought so hard to maintain." His jaw tightens. "I should never have listened to him. And yet . . . nothing he said to me was untrue. Because I cooperated, some good *did* come out of the horror. Neural modification therapy has already helped so many people. Had I come forward with the truth, it's doubtful that Mindwalkers would even exist now." His eyes lose focus. "Was it worth it?"

The question hangs in the air between us. I can't tell if he's asking me, himself, or the universe in general.

"I've thought many, many times about confessing. Over and over, I came very close, but every time, I talked myself out of it. Who would it help? What would it accomplish? So I lived with the secrets, the shame. Eventually, my Type started to slip. As I record this now, I am a Three, and I consider it likely that I'll be a Four soon."

The lines in his face seem to deepen. Weariness is etched into his brow, the corners of his mouth. "Emmanuel has repeatedly urged me to have my memories modified. I have refused. To forget the sins I've committed would be an act of cowardice. Because of my refusal, he no longer trusts me. At this point, I've become a danger to the secrecy of the experiments, a threat to be neutralized at the first opportunity. And it's not just the experiments I know about. There are other secrets. Secrets within secrets."

I sit up straighter.

He stares off to the side, as if he's looking into some dark, faraway world. "This involves more than our past. It's about our future. I've seen things that I dare not speak of. It would put you in too much danger. But I fear what might happen if certain ideas become reality, and I've been too vocal in my disapproval. If I turn myself over to IFEN for treatment, my mind will be molded and altered until I no longer know who I am or what I believe. They might make me forget even you . . . and that, more than anything, is a thought I can't bear. I won't let them into my head. As you know, however, Fours do not have much choice in what sort of treatment they receive. Soon they'll come for me." He pulls a small pistol from inside his coat.

I press a trembling hand to my mouth. Tears spill down my cheeks.

"I would prefer to die as myself than live as their puppet," he says. "This is my only means of escape. I wish there were another way, but if there is, I can't see it." His fingers clench on the pistol's grip. "I know this will devastate you, Lain, and I am sorry. So very sorry. But I have faith in your strength. I'm sorry for making you wait so long to hear the truth. Perhaps it's selfish, but I want you to stay safe, at least for a little while longer—and truth can be a terrible thing to possess."

A hysterical laugh bubbles up in my throat, and I bite down on my wrist to contain it. He's right about that. All too right.

"When you hear this," he continues, "you will be an adult. As an adult, you now have a choice to make." He removes something from his pocket—a data chip, glittering silver. "I've already uploaded this into Chloe. It contains all the files on the experiments. In other words, proof. The files will be hidden and encrypted until this message plays, at which point they'll unlock—but only for you. You must decide whether to keep these secrets hidden or come forward." His expression is grim.

"I realize that I'm asking too much of you. But I cannot allow my knowledge of the experiments to die with me. You are part of a new generation of Mindwalkers, and this decision can only belong to those who will inherit our world. But know this: if the truth *does* come out, there will be repercussions. It's no exaggeration to say that it will cost people their lives."

It is too much. It's all crashing down on me. My breathing quickens. "Help me," I whisper.

Of course he doesn't answer. He just stares straight into my eyes, as if he can see me. There's a complex look on his face—sad, tired, and hopeful all at once. "Trust your own mind, Lain. I believe in you." He smiles again, and fresh pain sears through me, as if an old, half-healed wound has been torn open. "I have made so many mistakes. No—" He shakes his head. "*Mistakes* is too mild a word. I believed I could heal humankind with my discovery. And for the sake of that dream, I became a monster. For that hope, I took part in horrors you can't imagine. This is no less than I deserve." His knuckles are white on the pistol. "I'm sorry that I'm not the man you believed me to be. But believe this, at least: I love you more than anything in the world. Whatever happens—whatever you decide—my thoughts and heart go with you."

The pain fills me until I can't breathe. We're separated by death itself, standing between us like a barrier. Yet in this moment—for better or worse—I understand him more fully than I ever did when he was alive.

"The folder is called 'Deliverance,'" he says.

Then the image winks out, and I'm alone.

Slowly, I stand. I don't even feel my legs crumple beneath me, but the next thing I know, I'm sitting on the floor. The grief is so intense, so all-consuming, that I can't even cry. I'm grieving not just for him but for myself, for my lost childhood. I'm no longer the girl who ran to him for comfort when she skinned her knees, the girl who clung to him after bad dreams, who laughed when he lifted her onto his shoulders, who idolized him. I can never be her again. I know too much.

For a while—I have no idea how long—I just huddle on the floor.

Dr. Swan lied. He told me that Father killed himself because he couldn't bear the guilt. But no—he died because he wanted to remain true to himself. It was the only way. I hold tight to that knowledge. It's all I have.

And then something else sinks in. Father chose to tell me. To entrust me with this. He believed in me that much.

I press my fists to my temples. Suddenly, the choice feels so much heavier. It's more than I can wrap my thoughts around. *If the truth does come out, it will cost people their lives,* he said.

"Chloe," I say. She rematerializes on the bed, tail curled around her front paws. "Is there a folder called 'Deliverance' in your database?"

"One moment." She blinks a few times. A file folder icon appears on the screen and enlarges. I gulp, throat dry, and slowly reach toward it. Words pop up. OPTIONS: DELETE/UNLOCK. Under each option is a small square.

My hand hesitates in front of the screen. He said it would open only for me. It must be coded to scan my fingerprint, whichever I select. My pulse drums in my ears. My finger hovers over the first option, then the second. My hand won't stop shaking. I start to reach for UNLOCK. Abruptly, the screen vanishes. "Chloe? What's wrong?"

"Just one m-m-mo—" Her form flickers, then fragments into pixels, making her resemble a Cubist rendering of a cat. "I—I—I'm sorry. S-something is—" The pixels break apart and vanish, and I'm left staring at empty space. A chill penetrates my bones.

There've been occasions when she's frozen up for a few seconds, but nothing like this. "Chloe," I say. My voice sounds small and soft in the silence. "Chloe?"

Nothing. I hurry over to the round hard drive on my desk and wave a hand over it, manually activating her program. "Display all files," I say. A screen appears in the air. I scroll through the list of files, but all that remains is a basic operating system. Even the backup files have been deleted. Chloe—the data that composes her existence—is gone.

My heart beats faster and faster. My own ragged breathing fills the silence. It was Dr. Swan. He has to be the one responsible for this. He realized what was happening, and he activated some kind of emergency self-destruct mechanism.

He killed Chloe.

Hot rage bubbles up in my chest. I pound my fists against the desk, and the hard drive rolls off. "You bastard!" I scream at the empty room. I kick over a chair. My foot throbs, but I barely notice it. "Are you listening to me?" I shout. "You're a cowardly, evil tyrant! I hate you!" I stop, shoulders heaving, and bury my face in my hands. Then I fall to my knees, tears streaming down my face.

The choice is gone now. Without proof, what am I supposed to do? Even if I wanted to tell the world, who would believe me?

Ian's face flashes through my head. He's the one I always

talk to whenever I feel myself slipping into despair. I'm filled with a sudden, desperate longing just to hear his voice.

I grab my cell phone, which is still sitting on the dresser where I left it, bring up his number, and stare at it. I'm sure Dr. Swan is monitoring my calls as well; even if I'm careful about what I say, just talking to Ian is risky. But I'm not strong enough to resist the need. I select CALL, and he picks up after one ring. "Lain? Is that you?" I hear the urgency in his voice.

Of course. I disappeared without giving him any indication of where I was going or when I'd be back. The secrecy was necessary, but guilt still burns me. "It's me. Sorry for worrying you."

"Never mind that. Where've you been? Are you okay?"

"I'm fine. Kind of. It's . . . hard to explain." I stop and close my eyes, struggling for control. "Can I—can I come over to your place?"

"You can come over anytime," he says. "You know that."

A lump fills my throat, and I have to swallow repeatedly before I can whisper, "Thank you."

"I'll see you soon." He waits for me to hang up.

Downstairs, I throw on my coat, then walk out the door and down the street. The back of my neck prickles, as if I'm being watched. Someone from IFEN is probably tailing me— Dr. Swan would not be so careless as to let me wander around without a chaperone—but right now, I'm beyond caring.

I walk to the nearest monorail station, where crowds mill about. A shabbily dressed, fierce-eyed woman with a collar sits huddled on a bench. Next to her is a boy with the same dark, curly hair—her son?—no older than eleven or twelve. He has a collar as well. It's not uncommon for teenagers to be given collars, but I've never seen one on a boy that young. What could he possibly have done to warrant it? Are they loosening the rules about collaring minors?

Mother and son squint at me suspiciously, and I realize that I'm staring. I turn away and find myself facing a wall screen displaying an advertisement for Somnazol, the familiar image of a pink pill against a plain white background. WHEN ALL ELSE FAILS, says the tagline.

Caroline Mackey's grim, hollow-cheeked face floats through my mind—the Woman Determined to Die. Odd that I think of her now, someone I don't even know. My vision drifts out of focus as I wait for the mono, my thoughts meandering. Mackey has a perfectly rational wish to die, yet because she's a Type One, she can't find a doctor who'll prescribe her the death pill. Yet if that woman with the collar applied, she'd almost certainly receive one. Her son would be placed in a state home, and once he got out, he'd probably go the same route. What other path is there for those society has abandoned? Memory modification is expensive, and Conditioning doesn't affect Type once it gets high enough.

A chill washes through me.

When I first sat down with Steven in the Underwater Café, he asked me if I'd ever treated a Type Four, and I said no. *They don't want us to get better*, he replied. *They want us gone.*

I've known all along that Somnazol is readily handed out to Fours and Fives but withheld from the mentally healthy. I never thought much about that fact, because it seemed logical, albeit coldhearted. Of course doctors would be more reluctant to destroy a stable, functional person. Of course they'd be more inclined to prescribe Somnazol to those they perceived as disturbed and incurable. I rebelled against the idea that anyone was incurable, yet I never questioned the deeper ideology.

I think about Marv, the man on the street corner handing out flyers and screaming, *The government is breeding us! They're breeding us like cattle!*

I start to shake.

The facts have always been right in front of me. Yet now, for the first time, I feel the truth forming in my mind. It's like looking at one of those optical illusions, those pictures that can be two different things, and experiencing that moment when perception suddenly shifts.

Is this what Dr. Swan meant when he said he wanted to test my ability to accept unpleasant realities? Is this the ugly truth he's planning to unveil when he thinks I'm ready?

I can almost hear his calm, logical voice in my head: *Eugenics is a word we've been trained to loathe, but this isn't about wiping out a particular race or ethnicity. What is so evil about wanting to reduce the frequency of mental illness in the population? It's a well-known truth that Type is influenced by genetics. We aren't harming anyone—we're giving people the option to end their own suffering. It's a fortunate side effect that fewer mentally sick people are born as a result. If that can produce a better, more peaceful world for everyone, how is that a bad thing?*

I struggle to slow my breathing.

It seems almost stupidly obvious. IFEN is using selective breeding to create a more easily controlled population—and it's all done through targeted advertising and medical propaganda, no government interference required. While Fours and Fives die in droves, Type Ones are encouraged to clone themselves, producing little model citizens and eliminating the risk of giving birth to a future deviant or rebel. After all, genetics have a strong influence on our choices. That's why Dr. Swan is so sure he can manipulate me—because he thinks I am my father. He controlled my father for years, using his compassion against him, reminding him that fighting back would hurt innocent people.

A dull roar, like a waterfall, fills my ears, drowning out the noise of the station. The Somnazol ad blurs in front of my eyes. I am being watched, I know, but I can't stop myself. I draw back a fist and punch the screen, as hard as I can. Again, and again, until my knuckles are bruised. The screen flickers and goes dark.

The woman and boy stare at me, eyes wide. "Don't ever give up," I tell them. "Don't end yourselves. It's what they want."

With my ears still filled with that deafening roar, I board a monorail and take a seat in the back. I'm quivering with fury, but my head feels clear for the first time in days. Maybe the first time in my life.

I was fooling myself to think I'd ever be able to change a corrupt system from within. The system will not allow it. I have to fight Dr. Swan—to reveal the truth.

But if I do, Steven will die. The thought goes through me like a jagged-edged knife, ripping me open from throat to stomach, and I have to dig my nails into my arm and focus on the pain to stave off panic.

When I see Ian's penthouse apartment through the window, glowing like a jewel in the night sky, I rise to my feet. The monorail stops, and I get off.

He's waiting for me in the living room, sitting on the couch. I open the door, and he stands. For a moment, we just look at each other in awkward silence. I manage a strained smile, which he returns. "It's been a while," he says.

It hasn't actually been that long, but it feels like an eternity since I last saw him. I was another person. "Yes. It has."

He closes the distance between us and hugs me suddenly, tightly. I lean into the embrace automatically, because it's Ian, and he's always comforted me—and for a second or two, I feel like the girl I was. I hide my face against his shoulder, and my tears soak through his shirt.

"You're in trouble, aren't you?" he asks.

I give a tiny nod.

"Tell me."

"I can't—" My voice cracks. "If I do, you'll be in danger, too."

"Lain . . ." He pulls back, gripping my shoulders, and looks me in the eyes. There's a determined glint in his stare. "You can talk to me. There aren't any listening devices here, and I already know more than you might think."

I shake my head, breathing hard. "You don't understand—"

"Please." His voice softens. He touches my cheek, very lightly. "Let me help you."

I feel my resistance crumbling. "I don't even know where to start."

"Sit down."

We sit on the couch together, side by side. I rest my head against his shoulder and tell him everything. He listens. When I pause, he offers a quiet "Go on," but aside from that, he's utterly silent. If he's shocked by anything he hears, he doesn't show it.

When I finally stop talking, I'm exhausted, drained, empty. I feel light. It's an incredible relief just to tell someone.

"What are you going to do?" Ian asks, his tone neutral.

"I know what I should do." I clutch his shirt. "But if I don't obey Dr. Swan, he'll kill Steven."

"What would Steven want?"

Of course, I know what Steven would want. He would want me to fight back, even if it cost him his life or his mind. He told me as much. And I know, deep in my bones, that going against his wishes in order to keep him safe would be an act of supreme selfishness—an unforgivable betrayal.

I think about the mother and son in the monorail station, wearing matching collars. I think about those six little brains floating in formaldehyde. I think about Debra, her tears, her rage. About the soldier who wanted to forget the war. About all the dark truths that have been forgotten, over the years.

There's more at stake here than Steven's life or mine. The public deserves to know about St. Mary's. No—they have an obligation to know, to face the atrocities their leaders have committed. Even if my father and Dr. Swan were responsible for what happened, it happened only because they—as agents of IFEN—acquired so much power. Their titles and status gave them an aura of godliness in the minds of the public, a cloak that allowed them to discard ethics and manipulate the truth. The blood is on all our hands because we gave them that power.

"I have to tell people," I whisper.

As the words leave my mouth, pain rips through me again, gutting me. Losing my father nearly destroyed me. Losing Steven will be ten times worse—because I'll know that I caused it, that I killed him. How will I exist after that? How will I keep breathing?

I squeeze my eyes shut and press a hand to my mouth.

There's a long pause. Then Ian says quietly, "There might be a way to save him."

My head jerks up. "What?" I'm afraid to believe, afraid to hope. "How?"

Ian stands and begins to pace. "You're supposed to erase his memories tomorrow, right? You just walk in, like you're supposed to. Except instead of modifying his mind, you pull an ND, knock out whoever's guarding you, and walk away with Steven. Of course, you'll have to leave the country after that if you don't want to end up mindwiped, but I can get you a car. Hell, I've got a spare. My mom bought me a new one for my birthday a few months ago, before she lost her job."

I stare at him, stunned. Is he *serious*? "No offense, but have you lost your mind? For one thing, where would I get an ND?"

"Here." He pulls a slim silver pen from his pocket and hands it to me. "Just push the button on the side and hold it down. It's not as strong as a real one, though, so you have to shove it right up against the other person. But it should do the trick."

My mouth opens and closes as I try to process the flood of questions in my brain. "Ian . . . I appreciate it, but a plan like that just won't work. This isn't a spy thriller. The place will be crawling with guards, not to mention other Mindwalkers and their patients."

He leans toward me. "It will work if you time it right. When the truth comes out, it'll cause chaos. There'll be a window of opportunity when IFEN is preoccupied with trying to contain the leak and do some damage control. We can make that happen once you're already inside IFEN headquarters. And in case that's not enough, I can help create a diversion."

He *is* serious. Dear Lord. "I can't ask that of you. If you get involved with this, it'll destroy you. Your career, your future, everything."

He smiles thinly. "My future's already fucked. You know that."

"I *don't* know that, and neither do you."

"Lain . . ." He pauses, as if trying to decide how much to say. Then he sighs. "You're not the only one whose life has turned inside out. I've already done things that could get me reclassified as a Three or worse if IFEN found out. I don't intend to get caught, but if I do, I'll deal with the consequences." His expression is grim. He's just as pale and gaunt as I remember, but something has changed. There's steel in his eyes that wasn't there the last time I saw him.

"Ian," I say quietly, "what happened while I was gone?"

He looks away. "I never told you, but by the time I threw that party where Steven and I nearly killed each other, I'd already been reclassified as a Two. I started poking around in message boards on the Deep Net—you know, those sites that aren't monitored because you can't find them with a normal search engine—and I stumbled onto this black market. I met someone who claimed he could sell me a device to fool the neuroscanners, get my Type back up. And my mom's, too."

My jaw is hanging open. I snap it shut. "Is that . . . possible?"

"Sure," he says. "It's a little implant in the roof of your mouth." He opens his mouth wide and sticks a finger inside, pointing. I can't see anything out of the ordinary. "It emits a signal that gives the scanner a false read, and most of the time, no one can tell the difference. Anyway, that's how I met Tiger."

"Who?"

"Just someone I know."

I study his eyes. It might be my imagination, but it seems as if their color has actually darkened. They look more black than brown. He's started growing his hair out, too; it's like reddish fur covering his scalp, slightly longer on top. "I still don't understand."

"What?"

"Why would you risk so much to help Steven?"

"I'm not helping him. I'm helping you, because you're my friend. Isn't that reason enough?" The lines in his face are deeper, more pronounced than they were even a few days ago. "I know you. If he dies, you'll never forgive yourself. If you do what they want, you'll never forgive yourself, either. It'll destroy you. I won't stand by and watch that happen. This is the only way."

Gratitude washes over me, so strong it brings tears to my eyes. I want to tell him how much this means to me, how much he means to me, but suddenly I can't find my voice. "Ian . . . I . . ."

"It's okay," he says gently. "You don't have to say anything."

I close my eyes, struggling to bring my thoughts into focus. "You know, even if I tell everyone the truth, it might not make a difference. There's no proof of what I've learned, no recordings, no photos. Nothing except—" I stop, mouth open as a thought strikes me.

"Except your memories," Ian finishes. He smiles, and this

time, there's a spark of mischief in it, something of the old Ian. "But memories can be uploaded and shared."

I pinch my lower lip, thinking. He's right, of course. With a client's consent, memories can be burned to disks and shared with colleagues for a second opinion. But this—this is something else. "You're talking about uploading my memories to the Net," I say slowly. "Can that even be done?"

"I don't see why not," he says. "Once they're converted to video-audio, they're just like any other file."

"But I don't have a Gate anymore."

"You know that guy I mentioned, Tiger? He can help us."

I cling to the sofa, feeling like I might fall straight through the floor if I let go. "Exactly what kind of people have you been hanging out with?"

He raises an eyebrow. "You want to see for yourself?"

My heartbeat echoes in my ears. Ian's offering me a way out, a chance to save Steven—his memories and identity as well as his life. I can't possibly pass up that chance, even if it means getting involved in things beyond my control. But I have to act now. If I hesitate, I'll lose my courage. "Yes." My voice emerges faint and breathless.

He nods once. His gaze focuses on the coffee table, and he says, "Ubu."

A black sphere appears, floating a few inches off the table's surface, then opens a pair of tiny, cartoonish eyes and blinks. It's a holoavatar, though one much more primitive than Chloe. It projects a dim, greenish text box into the air, and a single word appears:

HELLO.

"I didn't realize they still made first-generation avatars," I remark.

"They're safer," he says. "They run on an older system. The newer ones all have a backdoor program that IFEN can use to spy on communications."

That's probably what allowed Dr. Swan to destroy Chloe. A lump rises into my throat, but I choke it down.

Ian raises his voice. "Ubu, connect me to Tiger."

Ubu replies:

CONNECTING.

Ubu blinks a few more times.

PASSWORD?

" 'October Man,' " Ian says.

ACCEPTED.

"What is that—" I begin, but Ian holds up a hand, requesting silence. I bite my tongue.

He looks at the screen. "Hi, Tiger. This is Fox." As he speaks, the words appear on the screen. "You there?"

A pause. Then more words pop up beneath his:

I'M HERE.

"I need a favor."

Letters scroll rapidly across the murky green background:

WHAT DO YOU HAVE TO TRADE?

"Information," Ian says.

A few seconds pass, then a single word flashes onto the screen:

FORMAT?

"Memories," he says. "Not mine. A friend's. Don't worry, she's trustworthy. We'll need a Mindgate and some way to upload the files. Can you do that?"

A brief pause. Then the reply:

YES.

My heart jumps. "How can we find you?" I blurt out.

The screen blurs and wavers. Another message appears:

MEET ME IN ONE HOUR.
TAKE THE NORTH DISTRICT MONORAIL TO PLATFORM 32.
I'LL SCRAMBLE THE FEED FROM SECURITY CAMERAS AT THE STATION. IF YOU SEE ANYONE FOLLOWING YOU, GO BACK.
I'LL BE IN THE EMPTY LOT JUST OUTSIDE THE STATION.
BE SURE TO COME MASKED.

An instant later, the screen winks out.

"That's all, Ubu," Ian says. "Erase the text logs and go to sleep."

With a curt GOODBYE, the avatar closes his eyes and winks out.

For a minute or two, I sit in silence, digesting everything I just saw. Ian watches me. "What did he mean, come masked?" I ask.

"Hang on." Ian leaves the room briefly and returns holding two black plastic hoops. They look almost like collars. "Holo-masks," he says. "There were a few people wearing them at my party, remember?"

"Oh. Right." I pick up the hoop and examine it. "But why?"

"To hide our identities. None of us know each other's real names or faces. That's how we stay safe. If one of us is caught, IFEN can't extract anyone else's identities from our minds."

"Ian . . ." My fingers tighten on the hoop. "Who are these people, exactly?"

One corner of his mouth lifts in a self-conscious smile. "Honestly, I don't know much more than you do. I'm pretty new to this stuff."

I'm in way over my head, that much is obvious. But it's too late to turn back. I examine the unbroken circle. "So, how do I put it on?"

"Press the silver button and it opens. But don't put it on yet," he says, tucking his under his jacket. "Wait till we get there." He sticks his hands in his pockets and turns toward the door. "Ready?"

I've never felt less ready for anything in my life. My palms are slick with sweat, and my heart is about to jump out of my mouth. I'm so terrified, I feel almost giddy. "Yes."

He hesitates, searching my face. "Lain . . ." He takes a breath. "You know that once you go public with this stuff, you'll be in danger. If IFEN gets their hands on you, you could be mindwiped. Or worse. If you don't want that to happen, you have to be prepared to run. Once the truth is exposed, you'll need to get out of the country as fast as possible."

Run. I'll be a fugitive. A refugee without a home. I close my eyes, fighting for self-control. "I know." I give him a weak smile. "This is something I need to do—you said so yourself."

His hands settle on my shoulders and gently squeeze. "I'll protect you from them."

I look up, surprised. "How?"

"Trust me."

* * *

Platform 32 is deserted—the station is near the city outskirts, in a run-down, infrequently used area. Pigeons infest the rafters of the dimly lit, white-walled station, their soft coos echoing through the silence. Rows of benches line the floor.

Ian snaps open the black plastic hoop and closes it around his neck. A bubble-like shimmer surrounds his head, and a moment later, the head of a fox materializes where his own used to be. I'm expecting it, but I still gasp. It's shockingly realistic, down to every last whisker and strand of russet fur. He blinks golden eyes at me and nods, as if to say, *Go on.*

I snap the plastic hoop shut around my throat, and there's a faint hum. When I glance at my reflection in a puddle of oily water, I see the sleek white head of a canary where my own head should be. Its round, dark eyes blink. I hold up my still-human hands and contemplate them. "I look like a genetic experiment gone wrong." My voice comes out tinny and much higher than normal. Apparently, the mask also comes equipped with voice-distortion software.

Ian laughs, a warm, startling sound. I can't remember the last time I heard him laugh. "You get used to it." His voice sounds different, too: deeper, gruffer.

We leave the station and walk into the abandoned lot, which is surrounded by dilapidated apartments and under-funded treatment facilities. The buildings resemble giant cement blocks with tiny windows. Even the sky here is gray, choked with smog that gives everything a muted, dirty look. Streetlights glare down on the parking lot, where a single black car waits. Adrenaline fizzes through my veins.

"There he is," Ian says.

We approach. I walk close behind him, trying to ignore the way my legs quiver. A tall, slender man with a charcoal suit and the head of a tiger leans against the car, arms folded over his chest. He smiles at me, showing a mouthful of knife-sharp, very white teeth.

I clear my throat. "So. You are . . . ?"

"First," Tiger says in a deep, rumbling baritone, "let me check something." He holds up a black neural scanner. I tense and pull back. "Relax," he says. "Just a precaution."

"I told you," Ian says. "She's trustworthy."

"I'd prefer to check myself, if it's all the same to you."

"And if I'd rather not?" I ask.

"Then we all walk away and forget we saw each other." It's unnatural, the way his feline muzzle moves like a human mouth. The fur of his holomask is a flaming orange, with jet-black stripes and creamy white markings.

I hesitate, then stand still and allow him to wave the scanner in front of my face. The light blinks yellow. He makes a thoughtful noise and examines the holographic screen that flashes in front of him. "Two," he says. "Borderline Three."

So, that Type Five business was Dr. Swan's handiwork, after all. Though the thought that I'm almost a Three is not reassuring.

Tiger grins, and I shift my weight. Even if they're not real, his teeth make me nervous. "All right," he says. "I'll trust you. It's those Type Ones you've got to watch out for." He opens the back door. "Get in."

My instincts are screaming alarms. But Ian reaches over, takes my hand, and gives it a squeeze.

I've come this far. I've already made my decision. At this point, what good would it do to turn around? I get in.

Tiger tosses the keys to Ian and says, "Take us to Safe House B."

"Wait—why am I driving?"

"I want to talk to her."

Ian opens his mouth as if to protest. He looks at me. "It's all right," I say, and smile, though I have no idea what that looks like with my bird mask on.

He sighs and gets behind the wheel. Tiger slides in beside me and slams the door. The windows turn dark, blocking my view of the outside. The engine purrs to life and the car pulls out of the lot. "So," Tiger says, pressing the tips of his long fingers together, "this information you have. What is it?"

"Proof that IFEN performed illegal neurosurgical experiments on children in order to develop the technology used in Mindwalking."

He arches an eyebrow. A cat's face just shouldn't move like

that. "Well, that doesn't surprise me, but it seems rather difficult to prove. Exactly what did you see?"

I swallow, throat tight, hands balled into fists in my lap. "I spoke to Dr. Swan. He confessed the entire thing to me."

Tiger raises his other eyebrow. "You spoke to Dr. Swan. The director of IFEN. *That* Dr. Swan?"

"That's right."

He strokes his whiskers and glances at Ian. "You knew about this, Fox?"

"Yeah. She told me everything."

Sweat pools at the small of my back as Tiger folds his long hands together in front of him. His skin is the color of coffee with cream, his nails neatly manicured. "And what do you want in exchange for this information?"

"Nothing," I say. "Just your help in recording and uploading it to the Net. Some place where a lot of people will see it."

He watches me with those strange eyes. They're yellow-green, but aside from the color, they look more human than feline. "If you're sharing this information with the world, it's not exactly payment to *me*, is it?"

"I don't know. I'm not sure how these things usually work." I bite my lower lip beneath the mask. "Does this mean you don't want to help me?"

"I didn't say that." The corners of his muzzle curve up in a smile. "If this will damage IFEN, I'll consider that payment enough. I take it that's your goal, too?"

"Not exactly. I think people should know the truth. That's all."

"You strike me as an interesting young lady." He leans

toward me, uncomfortably close, and licks his chops. I pull back. "I can be a very useful friend—"

"Knock it off, asshole," Ian snaps.

Tiger simply smirks, crosses his legs, and folds his hands over one knee.

After a while, the car stops. We get out in front of a half-crumbled brick apartment building. They lead me through a dilapidated lobby and into an elevator, which takes us to the top floor and opens to reveal a mostly bare, windowless room with cracked walls and harsh fluorescent lighting. In the center of the room stand two creaky wooden chairs and, between them, the familiar hard drive and rounded helmets of a Mindgate. There's an old-fashioned flat-screen monitor, too, with wires trailing from the back to a larger hard drive.

Ian leans close to me, placing a hand on my shoulder. "You ready for this?" he asks quietly.

"Yes," I lie.

He gives my shoulder a gentle squeeze. "You know the drill. Just put on the helmet and replay the memories. I'll be wearing the other helmet so I can guide the session. Tiger here will record everything and get the upload ready." Ian turns to him. "We want this on every major social media site at five o'clock tomorrow. Can you do that?"

"Easy as pie." Tiger strokes his whiskers again. "Though the censors will take it down pretty quickly. Within a few hours, I'd guess."

"Hopefully, that will be enough time for people to notice and download it."

Tiger fixes his brilliant yellow gaze on me. "Once this is on the Net, you're going to be in some very hot water. You may be on the run for the rest of your life."

Keep breathing. Don't think. I can't hesitate, not now. "I understand."

He nods. "Anything else before we begin?"

I shake my head.

"Get in the chair."

I freeze. Tiger and Ian watch me, waiting.

I can't allow myself to weaken. There's too much at stake. I take a deep breath, get into the chair, pull the helmet onto my head, and lower the visor. My own rapid breathing fills my ears, and I struggle to slow it as I grip the chair's arms.

"Relax," Ian says.

I almost laugh. Relax? Now? "I doubt that's possible."

"I'll give you something to calm you down, then. Okay?"

I nod. There's a tiny sting in my arm. Warm fog rolls over me, and I feel myself sinking.

I don't know how long I stay in the memories. Two hours? Four? Six? Time seems strange—stretched out, distended, yet flowing, flashing from point to point.

Somewhere beyond the fog, Tiger whistles. "When people see this, there'll be riots." He sounds entirely too pleased about that.

Finally, it's over. I sit up, dazed. My mind surfaces slowly from its gray haze.

Ian takes his helmet off, his gaze downcast. "I'm sorry," he says, very quietly.

For a moment, I don't know what he's talking about. Then it occurs to me—he saw everything. He felt it all along with me. I open my mouth to say that it's all right, but the words stick in my throat.

Tiger taps icons on the screen. "There's a lot of this. I don't know if I can upload it all, but I'll edit it down to the juicy bits."

I nod woodenly.

Without speaking, we drive back to the monorail station. "Remember," Ian says when Tiger drops us off, "wait until five o'clock tomorrow to upload the files."

Tiger nods. "This will certainly cause a stir. I'll be looking forward to the fireworks show." With a wink and a toothy smile, he drives away.

Ian and I remove our masks and board the monorail. We sit next to each other, staring straight ahead. Before his stop, he gives me a long, tight hug. His lips brush my ear. "Tomorrow, when the diversion begins, you take Steven and make a break for it."

"What's the diversion?"

His expression is grim. "You'll know it once it starts."

"Ian . . ." I want to tell him not to do anything crazy. I want him to reassure me that no one is going to get hurt. But I know, deep down, that it's too late to say those kinds of things.

I'm afraid.

36

I arrive at IFEN headquarters the next afternoon, my stomach so tight it hurts. In my pocket is the ND disguised as a pen—my gift from Ian.

I walk in through the glass double doors, like I've done a thousand times before. My footsteps echo across the spacious lobby.

Dr. Swan is waiting for me at the far end, hands folded behind his back. "So glad to see you, Lain. I knew you'd make the right choice."

"What else can I do?" I ask.

"Exactly." He smiles. "Right this way. Your client is waiting."

I follow him along the hall, gaze downcast.

"You went to see Ian last night, didn't you?" he asks without looking at me. I don't answer; the question is obviously rhetorical. "You stayed with him at his apartment for a short while, then you both boarded the mono. After that, we lost track of you."

"We went for a walk," I say, keeping my tone neutral. "I needed someone to talk to. I was feeling very . . . confused."

"I see." He measures me with his eyes. "And now?"

I force the words out: "I don't like this. But I recognize that it's necessary."

He nods. "I understand you're still conflicted, but in time, you'll see that this is the kindest thing you can do for Steven. It takes courage to look past your own feelings to the greater good. I can see that you truly do care about that boy. The fact that you're here now is proof of that." He stops and faces me. "I hope that you'll learn from your father's mistakes and not burden yourself with unnecessary guilt. If you need anyone to talk to, I'm always available." He sounds oddly sincere.

I stare at his face. Does he truly think I'd confide in him after what he's done?

"Oh, the thought is absurd to you now, I'm sure. But . . . well, as I said, time has a way of changing one's perspective." There's no hint of deception in his expression. Dr. Swan is a true believer in the system, no more and no less. He's probably undergone plenty of voluntary Conditioning himself, to remove any doubts he might have once had.

"Thank you," I say stiffly.

He extends a hand to me.

My own breathing sounds very loud in the silence. My skin crawls as I grip his hand and shake. His skin is unnaturally smooth, dry, and cold. He watches me carefully while we shake, as if he knows how much I hate it—watching to see if I can conceal my hatred. I bare my teeth in a smile.

"Your father would have been proud," he says.

It takes all my willpower not to punch him in the face.

He releases my hand and leads me to the doors of the Immersion Lab. "Naturally, I'll be supervising the session."

"Of course." Legs trembling, I press my palm to the small metal panel outside the doors. A light blinks as the panel scans my handprint. The doors slide open, then slide shut behind me when I step inside.

Steven is already sitting upright in a chair, his wrists manacled, a white helmet covering his head. He blinks a few times, eyes unfocused, and gives me a wide, fuzzy smile. I recognize the look of someone who's just been heavily Conditioned. "Hi, Lain."

"Hello, Steven." I approach slowly.

He tries to stand, then looks down at his hands, as if realizing for the first time that he's restrained. A tiny furrow appears between his brows. "Where are we? What's happening?" His voice is slurred, like he's drunk.

I glance at the camera in the corner of the ceiling. Dr. Swan's dark, all-seeing eye. "Nothing to worry about," I say. "Just a small medical procedure."

"If you say so." He laughs. "Man, this *place*. It's so . . ." He squints. "White." His nose wrinkles. "Why can't it be, like, blue? With little clouds on the ceiling. That would be nice." He pulls at his restraints again. "Why am I, um—what's this?"

Oh God, I'd forgotten what a freshly Conditioned person is like. How am I ever going to get him out of IFEN headquarters? Can he even walk?

"Just a precaution." My pulse pounds as I wave a hand over the sensor on the Gate, and a holographic screen pops up, displaying a rotating, three-dimensional image of Steven's brain. I have to stall a little longer, go through the motions, convince Dr. Swan that I'm really going to do this. The drumbeat of my pulse is deafening. "The restraints are standard practice."

"I dunno. Seems a little kinky to me." He grins, then groans, sinking deeper into the chair. "Why am I dizzy?"

"Relax. Everything's fine." I settle into my own chair.

"Lain . . ." His voice has changed. It's still slurred, but there's an awareness in it that wasn't there before, and a hint of fear. "What's going on?"

I look directly into his eyes. "Trust me."

He holds my gaze for a long moment, then nods. I take a deep breath and lower the helmet over my head. Sweat beads on my forehead. *Come on, Ian. Where is that diversion? What if something happened to him? What if—*

No. If I start thinking like that, I'll panic. Keep stalling. Proceed as if this is a normal session. "I want you to think back to that first day we spoke, that day in Greenborough High School, when you sent me the text message asking me to meet you. Do you remember?"

"Yeah."

"Take us back there now."

The image swims into my head. I'm sitting in the corner of a classroom. I'm staring at the back of my head—*her* head, bent studiously over her notes. Brown shiny hair gathered into two long pigtails hanging down her shoulders. I'm clutching my phone, finger hovering over the SEND button. She won't help me. I *know* she won't, so why am I even doing this? Why bother?

Before I can lose my nerve, I stab the button with my finger. I watch as she gets out her phone—

I'm sitting across from her in the café, looking into those big brown eyes. Someone with so much power shouldn't look so innocent.

I'm in my apartment, at my coffee table, drawing in fierce black lines and swoops, and she's there on the page, looking at me over one shoulder, a startled expression on her face. Sheets of paper are scattered all over, and she's on every one. I finish the drawing. And then I crumple it. I crumple them all and then set a match to the pile and watch the flames licking along the edges, watch the smoke curl up in wisps.

I know I'm just torturing myself. Even if she could ever want me like that, it wouldn't work. I'd ruin her, drag her into my hell. But it's too late. She's under my skin, in my blood, in my brain, twined into my DNA. No matter how many drawings I burn, she's still there.

Drops of water fall onto the flames, hissing. The smoke stings my eyes and nose. I watch the paper curl into ashes—

Then thunder breaks apart the world.

I jerk upright in the chair, hands flailing, and tear off my helmet. *Lain. I am Lain Fisher. Seventeen—no, eighteen. Mindwalker. Ex-Mindwalker. I'm in IFEN headquarters. I'm waiting for a diversion.*

More thunder. Explosions. The floor vibrates. Presumably, this is it.

Panting, I scramble over to Steven's chair and yank off his helmet. I push a button, and the wrist cuffs snap open. "Steven."

He blinks at me.

"Steven, we need to get out of here."

He extends his arms to me, like a child asking for a hug, and I haul him up from the chair. He sways on his feet and staggers. I hook an arm around him, and we stumble toward the doors. I press a hand against the panel, and they slide open just as another explosion rocks IFEN headquarters. Someone screams. Voices shout, and clouds of dense black smoke billow down the hallway. Coughing, I plunge through the dark haze, half leading and half dragging Steven. Everything feels unreal, dreamlike. A part of me is still submerged in his memories.

When did Ian have the chance to set up explosives in IFEN headquarters? Where did he even learn how to do this? More importantly, there are innocent people here—what if someone gets injured?

Smoke swims up my nose. My vision blurs, and nausea rolls over me. I press a hand to my mouth, choking back vomit.

I'll think about the ethical implications later. Right now, I have to focus on getting out of here alive.

A pair of gray-clad figures run toward me through the billowing gray clouds. They're wearing metal breathing masks and carrying NDs. "Stop right there!" one shouts.

I think fast. "Oh, thank goodness." I stagger forward, still pulling Steven. "I heard the explosions. I—I don't know what's going on. Please help us." Pretending to sob, I collapse against the nearest guard. With my free hand, I yank the ND from my pocket and jam it into his stomach, pressing the button. He jerks and grunts, doubling over. I yank the ND back, and he topples over in a quivering mass on the floor.

"What the hell—" The other guard blinks a few times, then raises his own weapon, but not fast enough. I shove the

ND against his temple and press the button again. He goes down, twitching, eyes rolled back in his head. Bloody spittle dribbles out of his mouth from a bitten tongue. He'll wake up later with nothing more than a bad headache. Hopefully.

"Lain," Steven says, and his tone sounds more normal. Maybe the shock has jarred him from his trance. "Where'd you get—"

"I'll explain later."

We're almost to the lobby. I lunge into the open space, which is filled with smoke. Alarms are blaring, or maybe it's just my ears ringing. My whole being is focused on putting one foot in front of the other. Just keep moving. Keep moving.

The doors are in sight, then three guards block my path. They're aiming guns at me—not NDs, but real guns. I freeze. Time slows as I stare into the dark, empty muzzle of the weapon directly in front of me. *Move!* my brain screams at my body, but my muscles are locked. The man starts to squeeze the trigger.

I'm going to die. Here, now, with escape in sight. It's over.

A roar fills the air, and a ball of fire explodes near the doors. The impact flings me backward. Bits of plaster and stone fly through the air; something grazes my face, leaving a searing line of pain. I see the armed men dissolve into the blinding glare, and a warm mist of blood spatters my face. Someone is screaming. Steven flings himself over me, shielding my body as a scorching heat fills the room. Everything is white.

Then everything is black.

37

For a while, I wander somewhere between dreams and nothingness. Occasional flickers of light and sound break through,
but I can't make sense of them. I don't know how long I've
been here, but it feels like a very long time. Eons.

Sometimes, I know who I am. Sometimes, I float up toward
a dim glow, and voices break the cocoon of silence. Once, I
glimpse a pair of blue eyes staring into mine and feel a hand
clutching my own. A voice is calling me. I know that voice. I
strain my mind, searching for the name, but it slips through
my grasp.

Then I'm sinking again, and gray enfolds me.

* * *

My mouth is dry. That's my first conscious sensation. I smack
my lips and grimace. Water would be good.

Other sensations filter in. A soft mattress beneath my back.

Light shining through my eyelids, tinting the darkness red. Dull pain in my face and head, a steady throb in my ribs and left arm. Next to me, a machine beeps at regular intervals, and a medicinal smell stings my nostrils. A hospital?

I open my eyes and find myself staring at a cracked cement ceiling. I blink a few times. That doesn't look like a hospital ceiling.

Breathe. Take stock of the situation, one thing at a time. I'm on a bed, wearing a thin cotton hospital gown. An IV trails from my wrist, and linen bandages cover my arm. I try to focus, to assemble my memories into something coherent, but all I can think about is Steven. I don't know why, but I feel like he's in terrible danger.

Then I hear a soft snore and look up to see him slumped in a chair, head bowed.

I open my mouth. At first, nothing comes out but a weak croak. My throat is on fire. After a few tries, I manage to whisper his name.

His head snaps up. Pale lashes flicker open. For a long moment, he just stares at me, wide-eyed, as if he's afraid to look away—afraid I might vanish if he blinks. "Lain," he says.

Relief breaks over me, so strong I want to weep. He knows me. He's alive and whole, and for that, I want to fall to my knees and thank whatever powers exist.

He stands and takes a cautious step toward me. I hold my arms out, and he hugs me gingerly. I squeeze him tighter, and he lets out a strangled sound. Quickly, I release him. "Steven, are you—"

He smiles wanly. "Got a little scorched in that explosion, but they patched me up."

In a flash, I remember him jumping on top of me, shielding me with his body when the bomb went off. Wait—bomb? Why was there a bomb? I raise a trembling hand to my temple. "What happened?" I whisper.

Steven's expression turns serious. "How much do you remember?"

"I—I don't know." Everything is muddled, and my head aches dully. Slowly, I sit up. The pain in my body seems superficial—bruises, cuts, nothing more. My face feels prickly and hot, like a sunburn. "I remember . . ." I trail off, sifting through my jumbled thoughts. "I can't think." My breathing quickens. "Why can't I think?"

"They said you had a concussion." He gently pushes me back down. "You're safe. Just rest. It'll come back to you."

I close my eyes, light-headed. Once the spinning stops, I look around at the room. It's small, lit by a single bare bulb, with rough cement walls. Definitely not a hospital, or at least not a normal one.

He smooths my hair. "How do you feel?"

His voice, his touch, everything about him is so gentle, so careful. As if I'm made of glass and a loud word or sudden movement might shatter me. "Tired," I murmur. "Dizzy."

"You need anything? Water?"

The word brings back my thirst with a vengeance, but I have more urgent needs right now. Namely, the need to have my questions answered. "Where am I? How did I get here?"

"We're in a safe house. And we were brought here by the same people who helped us escape from IFEN headquarters. You know—the ones with the crazy animal heads?"

A dam breaks, and images pour in: IFEN headquarters, the

recording my father left me, the confrontation with Dr. Swan. I went to Ian's apartment; we met with Tiger and uploaded the memories. I went back to rescue Steven, and then—and then—

Smoke. Explosions. Blood spattering on the walls and the floor and my skin.

My vision goes fuzzy, and the walls seem to be zooming toward me.

Steven seizes my hand. "Lain, stay with me." He squeezes my fingers. "Focus on my voice." The desperation in his tone penetrates the thickening fog around me. I concentrate on breathing slowly—in and out, in and out—trying to bring my racing heartbeat under control. Steven strokes my temple, murmuring soft reassurances.

For a few minutes, I just lie there, clutching his hand, feeling his fingers in my hair. I reach up to touch his face. He has a few scratches, a bruise on his temple.

In my head, I keep seeing the guards go down, blood spraying through the air in a red mist. Probably dead. Ian triggered that explosion. I shudder, remembering the blast of heat, the way their bodies seemed to dissolve into light. Those guards probably knew nothing about Dr. Swan's plans. They were just following orders. And now they're dead, because of me. How many other people were injured or killed in the explosions so Steven and I could flee to safety?

Steven touches my cheek, traces the line of my jaw with his fingertips. "Eyes on me," he says firmly.

Only then do I realize I'm hyperventilating. I look into Steven's eyes, focusing on the familiar gray and silver flecks in the blue. A lump swells in my throat. "I'm sorry," I whisper.

"For what?"

"I—I gambled with your life." The shame burns me, suffocates me. "If we'd been caught—"

"Stop that." He grips my chin. "I told you to do whatever you needed to do, remember? I'm proud of you."

"But—"

"Death would be better than being his puppet. Do you understand?"

I look into his eyes, those beautiful eyes, still ringed by the dark flesh that never quite goes away. I sit up, wrap my arms around him, and hold him close. Slowly—as if he's afraid to break the moment—he hugs me back, pulling my head to his shoulder, and rests his cheek against my hair.

My cheek is pressed against his neck—warm, smooth skin—and I realize something. "Your collar's gone."

"Yeah. They removed it." A pause. "It's weird. I thought it'd be a relief to have it off. But I feel kind of . . . I dunno. Naked."

"You'll get used to it."

We hold each other for a long time. Finally, I pull back and touch my hair, which has been singed short in places. I'm pretty sure my face is burned, though not severely, or I'd be in a lot more pain. "I probably look awful."

He laughs, a small, choked sound. "You've never looked better." He frames my face between his hands, leans in, and kisses me. And for a while, I forget everything—all the pain, all the darkness.

* * *

After a few hours, a woman with an off-white coat and an owl's head comes in to examine me. She flicks a light at my eyes and asks me some simple questions, then re-dresses my wounds, making soft hooting noises the whole time—a feature of her mask, I assume. She stands, crosses her arms over her chest, and studies me. "So," she says, "you're Lain Fisher."

It seems like a rhetorical question, so I don't answer. "Did it work?" I ask instead.

She tilts her head.

"The memory upload," I clarify.

"Oh yes, it worked. It vanished within a few hours, but people saw it, and word is spreading quickly."

"Of course Dr. Swan is denying it," Steven says. He's sitting in his chair, one knee drawn up to his chest, an elbow resting atop it. "He made an announcement on TV and brought in these memory experts"—he makes air quotes around the phrase—"to testify that it was a hoax. But most people aren't buying it. Some groups are calling for Dr. Swan's resignation."

"Somehow, I doubt he'll give up that easily," I say.

"Probably not. Still, you made an impact."

The owl woman nods. "That was a brave thing you did."

I don't feel brave. I feel small and uncertain and scared. What if Dr. Swan was right and this causes a new wave of violence? Maybe it's already started. Maybe my revelation will be the spark that sets off a powder keg of rage.

The owl woman turns and walks toward the door. "I'll get Fox," she calls over her shoulder. "He's been wanting to talk to you."

Steven frowns. "He has?" He looks at me. "Do you know him?"

"Yes, actually." I debate whether to say more, but hold my tongue. Ian's identity in this underground world is a secret he entrusted to me. It's not my place to tell anyone else, even Steven.

The door opens, and he enters, looking just as I remember—russet fur, nervous golden eyes, quivering whiskers. He glances at Steven, clutches his arm, and says, "Can I have a few minutes alone with her?"

Steven scowls. His hand strays to something in a holster at his hip, which I didn't notice until now. An ND? "Look, I appreciate that you helped bust me and Lain out of that place, but I don't exactly know who you and your buddies are, or if we can trust you. I'm staying with her."

Fox opens and closes his mouth several times, then heaves an irritated sigh. "Close the door."

Steven's brows knit in confusion, but he obeys. Fox reaches up and unsnaps the black hoop from his neck. The holomask disappears.

Steven's jaw drops. He blinks at Ian for a few seconds. "You knew about this?" he asks me.

"Well, yes." I fidget. "I just found out the other day, though."

"So." Ian casts a glance at Steven. "Can you give us some privacy?"

Steven hesitates, looking from me to Ian and back again. His expression tightens, but he leaves the room, shutting the door behind him.

For a moment, Ian and I regard each other in silence. "You brought us here?" I ask.

He nods.

Suddenly, I feel very tired. I have a thousand questions swimming in my brain, but I'm not sure I want to know the answers. I ask, anyway. "How did you set up all those bombs so quickly?"

"They were already there," he says. "We were planning to use them to send a message to IFEN. I just convinced the others to change the schedule."

So, he's more involved in this than he let on. Or, at the very least, he knew about a terrorist plot to bomb IFEN head-quarters and told no one. "Do you really believe in what these people are doing?" I whisper. "Do you think setting off explosions can accomplish anything good?"

"It did," he says. "You and Steven are free now because of it, aren't you?"

I can't argue with that.

He gives me a weary smile. "You can only do so much with words. There's a war coming. Pretty soon, everyone will have to choose a side. You will, too . . . and when that happens, you'd better be ready to get your hands dirty."

"If that's the way you feel, how are you any different from them?"

His expression hardens. "We don't butcher children, for one thing. Or imprison innocent people and threaten to mind-wipe them. We placed the bombs carefully so we wouldn't in-jure any patients. There were no casualties except those guards, and if we hadn't killed them, they would have killed you."

He's right. I look away. Still . . . "When bombs go off, there's always a risk that innocent people will die."

He sighs and runs a hand over his bristly red hair. "I know how this looks to you. You think I've gotten mixed up with a bunch of terrorists."

"Isn't that pretty much what's happened? You saved our

lives, and I'm grateful for that, I really am. But what else do you call a group of people who use fear and destruction to accomplish their goals?"

"We're not about fear. We're about hope."

"I'd like to believe that's true," I say. "I really would."

An awkward silence descends.

"We're in the same boat now, aren't we?" he asks quietly. "Neither one of us can go back to our old lives."

"It might not be too late for you," I say. "IFEN doesn't know about any of this. If you can just get your Type back up—"

"It *is* too late. And I've got no one to blame but myself." He stares at the wall. "It was stupid of me to think I could keep modifying my memory after every difficult session."

I hesitate. It's true—he should have known better. But Ian's not a foolish or reckless person. He must have realized it couldn't go on forever. He must have had a reason, something pushing him to keep doing it, to keep taking on clients he knew he couldn't handle. When understanding hits, a strange feeling washes over me. "It was for me, wasn't it?" I say.

He tenses. "I don't know what you mean." His voice comes out stiff and unconvincing.

"After my breakdown, you started taking on all the sexual assault cases so I wouldn't have to."

His silence is answer enough.

"Oh, Ian." Tears well in my eyes. He's always been there, a warm shoulder to lean against, steady and supportive. He's been taking on my burdens all this time, and I never knew. I never even stopped to consider the possibility. "I'm sorry."

"You've got nothing to be sorry for." A tiny smile grows from one corner of his mouth. "By the way, I have a present for you." For the first time, I notice the suitcase he's wheeled in. He opens it, and I let out a gasp.

"My Gate!" He places the hard drive on the bed, and I run my hands over it. "Thank you! How did you—"

"Better not to ask." He looks me in the eyes. "You should get out of here as soon as you can. IFEN will be hunting you. There's a car waiting outside with a map in it. Like I said before, your best bet is to head for the border. Don't stop. Drive straight through until you get there. We'll send someone to meet up with you at the fence and take you to the nearest safe house."

"What about you?"

He smiles without meeting my gaze. "I'll be all right."

* * *

That night, Steven and I leave the city in the unobtrusive gray car provided by Ian. We drive in silence, Steven at the wheel. Ahead of us, the road stretches to the horizon, cornfields on either side. Overhead arches the vast, starry night sky. In the backseat, in a suitcase, is my Gate.

I catch a glimpse of myself in the rearview mirror, and I almost don't recognize the face staring back at me. It looks thinner, sharper. Before we left, I trimmed off the burned parts of my hair, and now it hangs loose and uneven around my face, too short to bother putting in pigtails. Patches of my skin are tinted pink from the minor burns I sustained, and there's a wildness in my eyes that I've never seen before. I look a bit crazy, but maybe that's fitting.

I'm a fugitive now. We both are.

The realization terrifies me. Who am I if not a Mindwalker? That's been my identity for as long as I can remember. And in spite of everything, I still believe that Mindwalkers *can* do good, that I truly *have* helped my clients—at least some of them. But I can't go back.

"Lain?"

In my lap, my hands curl into fists. "I'm fine," I mutter. It probably doesn't sound very convincing. I watch Steven through my peripheral vision, noting the shadowed hollows in his cheeks and under his eyes. "What about you?"

He half smiles. "Haven't been sleeping so well. Bad dreams."

"I'm sorry."

He shrugs. "I'm used to it. It's just that instead of having nightmares about Pike, now I have nightmares about guys in white coats. And what happened to Lizzie."

My father is undoubtedly one of the figures haunting his dreams, and the thought makes me ache. We drive in silence for a few more minutes. The streetlights are far apart, tiny yellow dots strung along the side of the road, barely keeping the darkness at bay.

"If I still wanted my memories erased, would you do it?" Steven asks suddenly. "I mean, once all this is over." His tone is unreadable. I can't tell if it's a rhetorical question or not.

My pulse quickens.

If I erase his memories, it will change him, transform him into a different Steven. I want *this* Steven—his cussing and sarcasm; his toughness and vulnerability; his sharp edges and softness; his love-hungry, guarded eyes. I want the Steven who overcame such ghastly pain, struggled so hard against his demons.

But to refuse him on those grounds would be horribly self-ish. "If that's what you truly want, then yes."

He stares straight ahead, hands locked tight around the wheel. The car's engine hums faintly. "For a long time, it was *all* I wanted. To forget everything. To not think about anything that hurt. I was afraid of what I'd have to do to make that happen, but I thought that once it was over, everything would be okay. I didn't even care if it destroyed who I was, because I didn't see anything good in myself. But now . . ."

I don't say a word. I just wait.

"If I forget everything that makes me who I am, is that happiness? Or is that just a sort of death?"

"I don't know."

He pulls over, parks the car, and looks me in the eyes. I can't read his expression. "How do you feel about me, Lain? The me I am right now?"

Words rise into my throat. I choke them down. "I don't want you to make your decision based on what I feel, Steven."

"Just answer me."

I clutch my knees and shut my eyes tightly. Tears burn behind my lids. "I want to keep you," I whisper. "I don't want you to disappear. I don't want to see you become someone else, and I don't want you to forget the things that happened between us. I want you the way you are."

A warm hand settles on my back, between my shoulders. "If you see something in me worth keeping, then I want to let that thing live, whatever it is."

I snap my head up. "Steven, I told you—"

"I'm not doing this for you. This is what I want." He gives me a crooked smile. "Who knows? Maybe someday I can learn how to feel okay in my own skin. Maybe I'll find out what it's like to *enjoy* being me. If I become someone else, I'll never get that chance." The backs of his fingers brush against my cheek. "I don't want to forget you, either."

My heart leaps.

He touches my chin, tilting my face upward. Then he slides one hand into my hair and presses his lips to mine. His are cool, but they grow warmer as I kiss him. The world contracts to the points where our bodies touch—my lips on his, his hand in my hair.

When we finally come up for air, he whispers, "So, what now? I mean—okay, we head for the border, and hopefully we get across. Then what?"

I utter a short laugh. "I have no idea. But we'll be together. That counts for something, doesn't it?"

His expression is serious. "You know, if I stay me, then I stay screwed up. My problems aren't going to disappear. I'll have flashbacks and bad dreams, maybe for the rest of my life."

"So will I. But we'll be there to keep each other from breaking apart."

His eyes move in tiny flickers, searching mine. "You'll stay?"

"I'll stay."

I lean forward and kiss him again, tasting a faint hint of coffee on his tongue. I try to lock the moment in my mind, to imprint it deep in my heart so I'll have it with me for the rest of my days. Forever. Of course, I know it doesn't work that way. Memories fade and crumble. This moment is reality. Forever is an illusion. But then, neurologically speaking, there's no difference between the two.

We keep driving. The headlights cut through the darkness as I reach over and grip Steven's hand. The open road stretches ahead. Canada waits. If there is a resistance, they may want our help, and I'll have more difficult choices to make. I don't know what I'll do, and whatever I choose, I'll probably never be certain if it's right or wrong.

But that's the nature of choice. Our world is not black and white, after all. It's a shifting, ambiguous mass of gray—a twilit realm of memory and dream, truth and half-truth. A world where monsters cry and angels carry switchblades. A world where hopes and dreams are formed by chemicals in organs resembling lumps of cauliflower, and where pain and beauty are so tightly intertwined that you can't pick them apart. This gray world is all we have.

I look down at Steven's hand in mine.

Maybe it's enough.

ACKNOWLEDGMENTS

It's been a long journey, and I wouldn't have made it this far without the support of many wonderful people:

To my agent, Claire Anderson-Wheeler, for believing in *Mindwalker*, and for all her hard work and brilliant feedback.

To my editor, Melanie Cecka—and the entire team at Knopf—for helping me polish this book and whip it into the best possible shape.

To Mel, my writing buddy and kindred spirit, for reading and critiquing the story in its earliest form, and for all the late-night chats about food, philosophy, fiction, and altered states of consciousness.

To Beth, for sharing my warped sense of humor and my taste in wine and cartoons (both the good ones and the so-bad-they're-good ones), and for sticking with me through the years.

To my grandma, for telling me stories when I was little and thus igniting my love of fiction.

To Mom, Dad, and Rusty, for their love, support, and encouragement, and for being an unusual family—in the best possible way.

And to Joe, for giving me more than he'll ever know. You're the best. I love you.